LUMINIFEROUS

THE QUESTRISON SAGA: BOOK FOUR

J. DIANNE DOTSON

J. DIANNE DOTSON

CONTENTS

DEDICATION

For my siblings: Todd, Greg, and Brenda
In memory of my father, Cecil Fred Gammon
In honor of my mother, Ethel Janice Gammon
For my children, Daniel and Allen
And for all those who look up to the stars at night and see possibility.

ACKNOWLEDGMENTS

What a journey the last thirty-four years has been, from when I first dreamed up a galactic woman who looked human but wasn't, with crazy fashions and hair to match, in East Tennessee. It is fitting that I should finish this book in the same place these stories began, although my road to return was paved with heartbreak. I lost perhaps my biggest supporter, my dad, Fred Gammon, in May 2020. I've questioned many times what I could possibly say that could capture my gratitude for the many gifts he bestowed on me. A natural storyteller and a traveler, and ever a seeker of knowledge and the superlatives here on Earth, Dad instilled in me the desire to see what was on the other side. And here I am, on the other side of this series, as I bring it to its close. Thank you, Dad, for everything.

My family, James, Daniel, and Allen, as ever have endured my long hours writing in a difficult time. I thank them for putting up with the distraction of having a dreamer in the house. At least I bake yummy treats!

Thank you to my beta reader and friend, Pam Magnus, for all her support and for her friendship.

I also want to thank my writer and editor friends Gareth Powell, Bradley Nordell, Mya Duong, Jonathan Maberry, Rusty Trimble, and Jessica Springer for their words of encouragement.

I thank Liz MacDonald, PhD and space weather scientist, for her insight on atmospheric phenomena.

Thank you to my supporters Carter Allen, Robert Young, and Richard Czernik.

I want to thank my editor, Lisa Wolff. For the fabulous cover, I thank Leon Tukker for the art, and Dash Creative Group, LLC, for book layout and design.

And oh, my stars, thank you to all of my readers! You've lit the way. Ad astra!

1

HUNTREN

I am a destroyed person.

Sometimes Galla could hear herself saying this in a dream, just before waking. And then she would awaken and lie staring at the cracked ceiling of her bedroom, and think again how stagnant the home felt. She would want to run out of the house into the fields, to feel the wind. In the wind she felt as though the pain might blow away.

She knew her first name, but she remembered nothing else.

Every day, she woke from the same sense of devastation, and had for over twenty years. Cuz and Meeya Huntren no longer fretted, or worried, or sighed over it: this was the routine of the Huntren home. Only after Dek had arrived did they accept that this was the way it would always be.

They had found only her, without clothing or hair, amid nothing more than burn marks scattered broadly over the farm. Shrapnel from a ship. It was not that uncommon on Quopeia, for the world did not let everything into its atmosphere intact. In fact, there were few places on the planet where anything could enter at all. Its magnetic field behaved unlike that of any other planet. That was the official excuse.

Galla had endured her new home, but felt no love for it. Meeya had treated her as a thing, and not a person. The woman was suspicious of the mysterious lady, who despite deep bruises had survived the extraordinary impact. At first, she would not even let Galla bathe. And Galla did not remember what it meant *to* bathe. Ultimately Cuz, who normally ceded control of the homestead to his wife, reached a breaking point.

"She is a person, Meeya," he said, face plum-hued and pockmarked from working in the sun. "We need to treat her like one. We don't know where she came from, and it don't matter. Give her a bath and stop dressing her in our cast-off clothes."

Meeya had clenched her teeth and brushed back her cropped grey hair, pursed her wrinkled lips, and fumed in silence. She relented, to a point, and kept Galla clothed and clean. She kept Galla in a constant state of flux: of feeling that she did not belong, or that she should not be allowed to intermingle with anyone outside the farm. Cuz and Meeya fought over this for years. But Meeya insisted that Galla be kept secret.

"I'll not let her get out in the world," Meeya would say, whenever Cuz would suggest taking Galla to the nearest town to interact with other people. "She'd bring danger to us."

"But what about *her*?" Cuz asked, over and over. "Why not ask Galla what *she* wants?"

"We're taking care of her and straining ourselves in the process," Meeya would snap. "I'm telling you, if she gets out into the world, there will be trouble."

And Cuz would mumble each time, "There will only be trouble if we hold her back."

Not knowing why, Galla woke mourning each day. Still, she tried her best to be of help. And when she could, she spent her free time outdoors. She loved most the winds before a storm. And on the vast plain stretching south of the mountains and away up west, any storm could blossom into a dangerous behemoth. She would watch the western horizon darken and gaze up at the high anvil fanning out into the blue sky. The wind excited her, and she wished she could fly into it. But she could not. No sky-craft worked in this area. So she would hold her arms wide and run into that wind, and pretend for those moments that she could belong somewhere. Because she knew, deep down, she did not belong *there*.

She was bald for years, and quiet. She eventually became curious enough to want to go to the town, but Meeya refused to allow her. Eventually, Galla would steal out of her room at night and hide among the long grasses. If the nights were clear, she would watch for meteors. Sometimes a soft green shimmer painted the night sky to the north, or sometimes it was faint reddish-orange, or it might be purple. Sometimes she fancied that in the green bands, one lone emerald flash was winking at her. That green light comforted her. She enjoyed the auroras, but the meteors made her wonder.

"Nobody makes it through unless they're allowed," Cuz had said long ago.

One pocket of the planet's atmosphere allowed spacecraft through, and that territory ranged over part of the northeast of their continent, Orboaanya, and across the sea to the east. Galla had come to understand that many of the meteors were ships burning up in the atmosphere. Like little pushpins trying to penetrate a great iron ball, they met a poor end. Finding the right slot to enter safely proved to be one of the greatest challenges of Quopeia, at least until one made it to the surface. Then a host of other issues awaited.

Half the time mechanical devices malfunctioned, if they ever worked at all. When something worked well, great care was taken to protect it. So Cuz and Meeya did not like Galla working on their equipment. But they did rely on her considerable physical strength, so she toiled away each day and helped them run their farm in near solitude. The cuybaaf farm was a dull and hot and mostly sun-bleached expanse, oppressive without and within except for that beloved wind.

It changed when the Huntrens adopted Dek.

Galla remembered fondly the days of Dek's arrival. She loved him instantly, with his sleek dark curls and big brown eyes and his chubby little legs, which liked to kick at any opportunity. Meeya had fallen ill, and Galla helped more and more inside the home until Dek grew bigger. She cuddled him whenever she could, and marveled as he grew so fast.

Time seemed to pass more quickly with Dek around.

Lume, glowing ruddy low in the sky outside Galla's window, seemed the only constant here, besides herself. She sat up in her bed and wrapped her arms around her knees, staring at the setting moon. She had had an odd dream, one that she imagined might have been a memory. It contained people and places she did not recognize.

Dreams like this had come seldom over the years for her. Always, however, they left her shaken and in agony from their realism.

In the last few months, since Dek's fourteenth birthday, the dreams began coming in torrents. The nights of waking in confusion and frustration were increased from about three times a year to two or three times a week. And always, despite the great emotional struggle she felt in each dream, she could not recall all of the events or the people. Mostly she awoke with feelings of dread or sadness, rather than with images left over from the dreams.

She had for years felt as though nothing about her ever changed, but when Dek arrived, everything shifted. Her hair began to grow for the first time. She bore a fuzzy, short hairstyle with patchy colors, copper and gold and burgundy and purple, none of them uniform. And as Dek grew older, and Galla's hair grew longer, it shot straight out rakishly in all directions. Meeya became concerned, and would chew on her lower lip whenever she noticed Galla's hair getting longer or more unruly.

"Cuz," she heard Meeya whisper one night, after Galla had read Dek a bedtime story about flying bikes, in which he roared at the absurdity, "she's changing more and more now. What do we do?"

And Galla had stared up at the ceiling from her bed and felt tears roll down her cheeks onto her pillow. Her chest heaved as she tried not to gasp out loud. She pulled at her hair and cursed it. She did not reveal that she'd overheard Meeya. Despite their gruff treatment of her, she loved Cuz and Meeya, but she sensed her time with them was limited, and that one day she should finally leave. And in the morning, she built a wall against her pain, and only Dek could break it down with his jolly laughter and pranks. She tried to figure out what her life had been. *Before.* Dek became the one consistent joy Galla had.

She was dutiful, and she worked hard, and she was always polite. Never once did Galla complain or take advantage of the Huntrens' generosity. Eventually, even Meeya, in her weakened state, finally saw that Galla had been a great help to them. In fact, she had always been a perfect farmer: up early, never shirking. But they, simple folks as they were, isolated on their farm, could see that lately she had grown distant and restless.

Cuz and Meeya watched the skies more, as Dek grew older. The auroras had grown more vibrant and intense. Galla stole more looks at them too. She sat alone outside in the chilly air, while the ground remained warm from the day before. Eventually, Dek found her there, and would sometimes join her. He would grow sleepy and lean his rumpled head on her shoulder until he fell asleep. Those quiet nights with the shifting light curtains and rays above them became Galla's happiest moments on the farm.

At last Dek had reached the time to sign up for secondary school. Cuz and Meeya came to Galla.

"We think it's time, Galla," said Meeya, chewing her lip. She twitched a hand through her short, grey hair. Cuz shoved his hat back on his head, displaying a bulbous red nose covered in age spots.

"We know you'd never leave us if we didn't ask you to," he said gruffly. "But it's time. Dek is all registered, and we want you to take him to the City. Now, I've got everything arranged…"

But Galla's eyes glazed over, daydreaming.

The City was Allurulla, on the other side of the Talonii Mountains. The capital. Galla had never set foot there. But the mere talk of it thrilled her. Aircraft! Spacecraft! She felt as though something in her moved forward, took a step into the present and future, when so much of her seemed closed in a past she did not know.

When moving day came, Meeya and Cuz were in a state. They fussed over Dek until he lost his temper and snapped, and immediately felt bad about it. He implored Galla with his eyes to rescue him from his parents' hovering. She merely smirked. She was only too happy to leave, and glad she did not have to move away from Dek.

But Meeya surprised Galla.

"I don't know what we would've done without you," she said, her eyes rheumy. Cuz approached her and held his hat in his hands.

"You did a fine job, Gal," he said stiffly, avoiding looking in her copper eyes. He sniffed loudly and cleared his throat.

And in that moment, sadness pierced Galla. After all, they were the only family she knew. Now it was time to leave them. She quickly kissed each of them on the cheek.

"Love you," she whispered, averting her watering eyes. "Thank you."

They had called for a transit to the shuttle station. Presently it rolled up, billowing dust behind it in coiled clouds. The driver jumped out, lean and jaunty and weathered from the sun, and swiftly grabbed Galla and Dek's few bags. Galla's hat and dress flapped in the incessant wind, and she held her hat down with one hand and waved with her other one. And then she and Dek left the rolling golden prairie hills of the Huntren farm, watching it fade and waver in the afternoon heat, until it seemed a smudge of a memory.

EINDYNN WAS the last way station of the West. It lay at the base of the Talonii Mountains, shadowed in morning and a glory of sunset in the evening. A few resorts and many quaint shops kept transient visitors distracted during their brief passage through Eindynn. The Whoe-naat shuttle system stationed there carried folk through the perilous Talonii chain, and thus it was the only midwestern hub in the entire continent. Dek grew animated, realizing that for the first time he was free of his parents.

Galla and Dek bade farewell to their kind driver, Deorn. She and Dek stood in silence for several minutes as the sun sank toward the horizon, casting colors of rose and amber and mauve to the snow at the tops of the mountains, and creating dusky violet shadows beneath the juts and crags of indomitable stone.

As dusk fell, auroras burst forth overhead. They watched in awe as green and purple light rippled high above.

"They are getting more intense," Dek muttered. Galla wondered why.

Their shuttle arrived then. It was sleek and capsule-like, and fit smoothly within the great clear tube, which curved through the mountains and was supported by great pylons lodged into the mountains themselves. As they stepped aboard, Galla and Dek noticed that the shuttle did not bob or rock, but levitated within the tube as if it rested upon invisible rails.

They found a seat by a large panoramic window and bickered over who would get the window side of the plush seat. Dek won, as Galla resigned herself to the fact that he would better appreciate the sight of trees in the East. The shuttle bore only a few other passengers, and she understood again why Dek was eager to leave. The West meant emptiness, and he wanted to experience something more.

By dawn, the shuttle slid into a dock in Allurulla. The pair fairly stumbled away from the shuttle, looking up in delight at the cerulean and coral-colored spires of the City's tallest buildings, which emerged from treetops of late summer green tinged with gold. All other buildings were hidden below the canopies and only city streets were kept free of the graceful trees. Lakes and rivers, ponds and brooks glistened among the foliage. The alluring City was an eruption of lush vegetation and resplendent artistry; Dek and Galla stood enraptured.

And studying the landscape, Galla tilted her head, with its wild, many-hued hair, and thought, *I have seen this city before, but I have never been here.*

2

———

ON BEING ALLURED

Their taxi dropped them off at a cul-de-sac at the edge of a wood. Galla checked the directions Meeya had given her and shook her head in wonder. There lay a stone walkway, leading through a small grove of slim trees. Beyond these, next to the thick woods, a wee stone house crouched away from its neighbors and hid from the shiny City buildings behind a high border of greensward.

The house was low and round, with grey stone shingles and deeper grey stone walls. This was an ancient structure, its face weathered smooth. Ivy traversed its base and part of the pointed roof, as if the very woods were trying to pull the structure into their secretive depths.

They advanced to the walkway, which consisted of round, flat slabs of stone placed a short distance apart. Dek preferred to walk on the fluffy blue-green grass, but Galla chose the walkway. Her heels rang as she took each step. She looked around and breathed in deeply. The air was laden with sweet smells and moisture; it was all so alive, so colorful and vivid in every sense compared to the Huntren farm in the Southwest. The two travelers dithered where they stood, in awe of such beauty and such peace. Galla's footfalls echoed as she climbed the short stairway to the door.

The door was a simple slab of rock, etched with the patina of immense age. Nothing about it resembled the other structures in Allurulla. The sign that hung above it on a small wrought-iron pole intrigued Galla more, however. She could not make out what it said; she could only see that it bore an inscription that time and weather had made fit to hide from her.

She clasped a gloved hand around the iron door knocker and brought it down with a *clang* three times. Silence. She stepped back, appraised the old door, and glanced over her shoulder at Dek. He screwed up his mouth and rolled his eyes and set his bag on the ground. She waited a few more minutes and tried the knocker again.

"Maybe nobody's home," he said. "I'm hungry. Why don't we go get something to eat and come back?"

"You're *always* hungry," retorted Galla. But he might be right. She sighed and turned away from the door.

It opened.

And she swirled around, her skirt spinning, and turned to look up into a young man's face. His eyes were so dark, she thought at first they were black. He was quite tall, tan-skinned, with a smooth face and with dark hair falling just above his shoulders. He swept his hair back behind his ears and stared down at Galla's copper eyes.

Galla blinked at him, but this man seemed unable to blink, and his steady gaze made her feel uncertain. Dek cleared his throat. That broke Galla's confusion.

"Hello," the man said, a small smile forming.

"Hi—hello," stammered Galla, extending her hand. "We're here about the—we're here—"

"We're renting two rooms," announced Dek.

The young man took her hand. Galla's hair picked that moment to begin misbehaving, and drifted and coiled. She snatched at it to pull it down and heard Dek cough-laugh.

She said, "I'm Galla, and this is Dek...Huntren," she added.

The man nodded to Dek, and his smile broadened. "Hello, Galla and Dek Huntren," he said, and his dark eyes flashed. "I'm Deming. Please come in."

And Deming quickly stepped forward and took their bags before Dek could protest. Galla entered the odd little house, and found the inside was not quite as small as she had imagined. When she stepped onto its honey-hued wooden floors, they groaned and popped from great age. The sound of her shoes on those floors echoed into curved hallways on either side of her. The staccato of her steps made her feel self-conscious. She walked into a simple foyer and turned on her heels to take the place in. Pale mint walls and warm wood frames met her, but this was a spare entrance otherwise.

Deming set their bags down next to one of the hallways.

"Please," he said, gesturing to a little podium in the foyer. "If you could sign in, I'll get you all settled."

On either side of the podium little sconces sizzled. The podium itself stood just at Galla's waist in height. On it, a cracked and ancient book sat open, with a quill marking its place. Her footsteps again echoed as she stepped forward and took the quill. The book revealed a list of names, but they were faded and smudged to the point that she could not read them. The quill appeared dry, but when Galla looked at Deming, he simply nodded for her to go on.

So she bent over the low podium and wrote "Galla Huntren," and found the quill did indeed have some kind of ink. She held it out to Dek, and he signed the book after her. They looked at each other and shrugged.

From somewhere down one of the hallways, Galla could then hear music. She turned her head to listen, but it was too faint to make out. Deming watched her, with the tiniest smile at the corner of his lips and his dark eyes intense.

"I'll show you to your rooms," he said then, and he hoisted their bags.

He led them down the hallway to their right. It curved around, and more of the little flaming phyron sconces met them on the rounded walls. They passed three antiquated wooden doors, and then Deming stopped at a fourth to the left.

"Dek," he said, his voice clear, "this is your room."

The boy sighed in relief. "Good. I was afraid I might have to share with *her*," and as Deming opened the boy's door, he rushed in and promptly shut it behind him.

"Dek!" Galla groaned, exasperated.

"Tell me when there's food!" his muffled voice called out, and she heard him fall onto his bed.

Galla then faced Deming, who tried hard to stifle a laugh with his hand. Her warm eyes studied his face again, and finally he blinked. They stood awkwardly in the hall, staring at each other, until Deming finally held her bag up and pointed to another door on the opposite side of the hall from Dek's, farther down the hall on the right.

Deming inserted an old iron key into the door's lock, and it made a satisfying click. He turned the old bronze knob, and the door opened with a faint squeak.

"I hope you like your room," Deming said quietly, setting Galla's bag inside.

She walked in and the floors creaked as if greeting her. This room's walls glowed in palest butter yellow. The floors shone in the same pleasant, weathered amber as the rest of the boardinghouse. Her bed stood high on bronze posts, with a curved headboard decorated in bronze vines. On the bed, an embroidered white quilt lay, smooth and welcoming. There was a little chaise under a large window, whose white curtains barely shielded a glimpse of a small garden enclosed with a great hedge. Off to the left, a simple little closet and a small wooden desk beckoned. To the right, a small bathroom door stood open.

Galla breathed in. There was something so warm and sweet about this room that she felt relaxed and peaceful just looking it. She walked to the desk and took her gloves off, and then brushed her fingers across the white quilt on her bed. A hint of some flower haunted the little room. She could also smell the old wood and its polish, acrid and layered with age. Everything about this room seemed both familiar and new at the same time.

She had forgotten about Deming, until he shifted his feet.

"If—if this doesn't work for you, there are other rooms," he said in a friendly voice. "And if you need more blankets . . ." He stepped in and pulled a little chest out from under her bed. He opened it and paused, and then gently lifted its contents: an old but beautifully hand-stitched quilt.

She watched Deming's expression change as he held the quilt up reverently.

"This was my mother's," he said softly. "Her mother made it for her. Please, feel free to use it. I keep it in here because . . . well, it seems like it belongs in this room. And so . . . I thought this was maybe the right room for you, too."

He set the quilt back into its case, closed it with a click, ran his hand across the chest and slid it gently back under the bed. He rose and walked back to the door.

Galla took a deep breath and then walked across the room to the door, where he stood patiently. She gestured behind her, and then held her hand out to him, and said, "I love it so much."

Deming took her ungloved hand to shake it, but in that moment, they held their fingers together just a bit longer than one might with a stranger. Vibrant warmth coursed through Galla. She drew in her breath at the sensation, and she felt her cheeks staining. Deming's dark eyes lingered on her russet ones, and she released his hand.

"I'm glad," he said.

Deming then stepped farther into the hallway and said loudly enough so Dek could hear, "The kitchen is back down the hall beyond the foyer. Help yourself to anything you want."

A fumbling sound met their ears, and a door swung open. Dek leapt out of his room, shut his door, and walked swiftly away from them. Galla turned to Deming, and they both laughed.

"He's a growing boy," she remarked. "Thank you, Deming."

Deming dipped his head. "You're welcome, Galla. I'm going out back to the gardens, and then back to work. If you need anything, let me know."

"I will, thank you again," said Galla, and she leaned out of her room to watch Deming's slim, tall frame walk away down the hall, his hair swaying.

Galla then shut her door and took her shoes off. She walked to her bed, lay down on it, and stared up at the ceiling. What was it about this Deming? There was something so familiar about him. She closed her eyes and listened to the wind in the trees outside her window, which had been left open a few inches.

It's so quiet here. I can't hear the City at all!

But before she could wonder why, the swishing of tall trees lulled her to sleep.

When she woke, she smelled something good. Some mix of savory and sweet smells. Yawning, she slid off her bed, slipped her shoes on, and stepped out into the hall. She knocked on Dek's door but found it ajar.

"Dek," she called through the crack, "are you ready to eat?"

No one answered. But Deming showed up at the end of the hall.

"Oh hi!" he called, grinning. "If you're looking for your brother, he —well, he found dinner. He seems neck deep in it. I was just coming to get you."

Galla bit her lip. "Sorry about that," she said, cringing. "He *used* to have good manners. I'm not sure what happened."

"Well he *is* a teenager," Deming pointed out, walking beside her back the way he had come. "And anyway, it's fine."

Galla felt a little less embarrassed, but a tiny crease formed in her forehead. *I need to have words with that boy!*

She shook herself out of her growing irritation with her foster brother and noticed they had crossed the foyer, and were heading down the other hall. A large, open doorway led into a simple dining room, and it was open to a kitchen. In the dining room, Dek was busy scooping up seconds of everything on the table. Several platters were filled with dishes Galla did not recognize, but everything looked and smelled tasty.

"Did you make all this?" Galla marveled. Deming avoided her eyes.

"Some of it," he admitted. He shoved his hair behind his ears and sat across from Dek. Three other chairs sat free. Galla chose a seat at one end, so that Dek sat to her right and Deming to her left.

"Is there no one else staying here right now?" she wondered aloud.

Deming, after plucking a golden roll from a plate full of them, said, "No, not right now. Well, other than us, and Gindoo of course."

"Where is Gindoo?" she asked. Dek hesitated his inhalation of food long enough to listen as well.

"Busy, as usual," Deming said, his mouth twitching at one corner. "That's pretty typical. I usually take him his food."

And as if in answer to Galla and Dek's curious eyes, Deming added, "To his study."

They fell to eating then, and Galla found herself reaching for seconds along with Deming. Dek shamelessly filled his plate with thirds.

"You weren't kidding!" laughed Deming to Galla. "Growing indeed."

Galla blushed.

"It's good," said the teen, with a shrug.

"Thanks," said Deming.

"It's more than good," Galla declared. "It's the best food I've had in years!"

One tiny spike of pain flickered in her forehead. Surprised by it, she held her fingers up to her head. Dek glanced up briefly and then returned to his food.

Deming noticed Galla's fingers. "Are you all right?"

"Yes," she said quickly. "Fine."

"There's cake," Deming announced, just as Dek pushed his plate back. Deming brought out a large, glossy, rich brown cake, round and swirled with frosting. He served them each a tall slice, revealing its several layers. Dek's eyes bulged.

Galla and Dek took bites at the same time and closed their eyes in bliss. Deming snickered.

"So you both like cake," he said, his voice light. "Good to know. I'll make sure we have plenty of it."

Dek finally finished and sighed. "That was the best meal of my whole life."

"I'm glad. School starts tomorrow, yes?" Deming asked.

"Yep. I guess I'd better think about how to get there."

"Oh, it's easy—the academy is a few blocks over," Deming told him.

"That's reassuring," Galla said. She had been trying not to think about Dek being away from her, all day almost every day, but at the same time, she knew he was excited. So she would try to be excited too.

"I'm gonna go review my schedule and read," said Dek, rising and pushing his chair in. "Don't mind Galla tonight, by the way," he added, about to leave.

"What?" Galla asked, the furrow in her brow returning.

Dek rolled his eyes. "You know, the crying thing," he answered.

"No, I don't know," said Galla, growing hot. Her hair began rising a bit, and Dek and Deming raised their eyebrows at her.

Dek sighed.

He turned to Deming and said, "She cries every night in her sleep, but she's fine. It's been a bit worse these past few months. She's always done it."

Galla stood, pushing her chair back with a screech. "I do not!" she exclaimed.

"Yes, you do," Dek snorted. "I've heard you. And Mom and Dad said you've done it every night since they found you. Anyway, good night."

Galla stared at the back of Dek's curly head as he left, her mouth open.

Deming busied himself by clearing dishes, to avoid her turbulent gaze. She shook herself out of her outrage and hastily brought plates to the kitchen.

"He likes to joke," she said wanly.

She felt shaken by what Dek had said. Was it true? And if it was, why had they never told her? The little spike of pain came back.

Deming took a platter from her. "You don't have to stay and help. Really. This is part of my job. You're our guest."

"Please," she said, looking at his profile as his hair swayed. "I want to help. You've been so kind."

Deming smiled at her. "All right then. Thank you!"

They cleared and cleaned the dishes by hand, Deming washing, Galla drying, and he asked about her trip across the mountains. He asked about life on the farm, and about her background.

"I—I—don't remember anything before living with Meeya and Cuz," she confessed. Deming glanced sideways at her. They stood close to each other, working in tandem. Galla suddenly set down a plate she had dried and slapped the towel onto it.

"I didn't mean to pry," Deming said quietly.

"No, no, you didn't pry," she said hastily, and she touched his arm, just barely. She snatched her fingers away. "Maybe I should go."

"Thank you for helping," said Deming. She nodded and turned to leave. "I hope you sleep well tonight," he added. She almost ran out of the kitchen.

She walked swiftly down the hallway and stopped at Dek's door, with every intention of giving him a piece of her mind, but she halted. There was no light shining under the crack of the door. The hall sconces were glowing warmly, but otherwise the light in the hall was dim. There was nothing for it but to go back to her room and try to get a full night's sleep.

But she could not. *Were they right?* she kept wondering. She wanted to talk to Dek more about it. But as it was the night before his school started, she did not want to get into any major discussion with him. *How could I not know something like that?* The little lance of a headache bothered her again.

She tossed and turned and came close to dozing off. A creak brought her out of her tired state. She heard soft footfalls outside in the hall, and after a few moments, she heard a door open and close. She looked at her legs, outlined by moonlight spilling through the curtains. Lume was growing fat and full, and its creamy light would soon wane again.

She cast aside the covers and grabbed her robe from the end of her bed. She opened her door and gently closed it behind her. In bare feet she walked down the hall, until she met a door at its end. Solid and made of the same material as the front door of the boarding-house, it bore old scratches around the bottom, as if from some animal long ago. She turned the bronze knob and found herself at the top of a little set of stone stairs that led into a round yard surrounded by tall hedges and a few trees. The light of Lume spread all around the little yard, and off to her left, she could see a shape bent over. It rose and turned to her.

"Hi!" called a calm, quiet voice. It was Deming. He said softly, "Did I wake you?"

Galla walked down the steps and across the cool lawn, the dew wetting her toes.

"No," she told him. He was looking down at her with eyes so dark, she felt magnetized by them. But the light of Lume twinkled just a bit in their depths.

He held out a basket to her, and she then looked down to see that it was full of huge, trumpet-shaped white blooms. Behind him, she noticed vines with these fragrant pale blossoms twining all along the back of the hedge.

"What are those?" she asked him.

"Radiant nightshades," he answered, and he took one from his basket and held it in his palm. "I collect them at night, when they bloom. Gindoo needs them for his tinctures. Here, take one! There are plenty."

Galla took the immense bloom into her small hand and tucked it behind her ear.

"That's perfect," said Deming, and then he looked away from her. He bent to pick more of the blooms and said, still averting his eyes, "Maybe Dek is wrong."

"What do you mean?" Galla asked.

"I didn't hear you crying," Deming replied.

They were silent for a long moment. Then Galla knelt beside

Deming and asked, "Do I pick them like this?" She turned one of the attached blooms so he could see.

"Yes," he said. "I'm sorry. It's none of my business. But...I just wanted you to know."

Galla's cheeks burned. She plucked some of the flowers and put them in Deming's basket. "I'm glad you told me. But then, I wasn't sleeping, so...who knows?"

After several minutes of quiet harvesting, Deming rose. "I think Gindoo will be very happy with these." He held his free hand out to help Galla up.

She was flushed, although in the pale light he could not see.

"That was fun!" she said eagerly.

"It was!" agreed Deming. "We made a good team."

And they smiled at each other under the light of Lume, and Galla felt a warmth flood through her, welcome and pleasing yet unsettling to her.

"You know," Deming said, as they walked slowly back to the door, "Gindoo knows many things. I could ask him if he could help you... with...what's bothering you."

Galla opened the door gently and said, "Maybe. I—yes. I suppose it wouldn't hurt. Thank you."

"I'll ask him then," said Deming firmly.

He stopped at her door, and the sconce light flickered and lit their faces. Deming watched its warm light catch in the several colors of Galla's mercurial hair. Her hair looked alive to him, and he marveled as it drifted slightly toward him. To his surprise, his fingers tingled with a sudden desire to touch her hair. He resisted the urge. She tried to tame the unruly coils and looked down in embarrassment. He whispered to her, "Thank you for your help. I hope you sleep better."

Galla whispered in a rush, "You're impossibly nice. Good night, Deming." She slipped inside her door and shut it quickly, her heart pounding. But she did sleep then, dreamlessly, peacefully, and with no tears.

. . .

Deming, meanwhile, stayed awake late. He had taken the flowers to Gindoo, below the main floor of the house, and walked slowly back up to his room. He had said nothing to Gindoo at all. His thoughts were elsewhere. They were drifting off, around the curved hallway of this house in which he had spent most of his life, and into the room where Galla lay sleeping.

His own room looked different to him now. It looked smaller, and somehow emptier. He took a deep breath. Deming loved his home. He had liked the quiet solitude of his room, where he could make things in peace and write. But now, for the first time, he felt like he could leave this place and not miss it at all. He sat at his small desk and tidied up his various collecting logs. He brushed the dust off the cover of a small notebook and took a pen in his hand.

Today I met someone. Two someones, really. Galla and Dek Huntren. Dek is her adopted brother. A normal teenager. But she is not like anyone else. She helped me with the nightshades tonight. I already forgot what that was like before she arrived. It was nothing, a boring job. And now I want to do that again, with her. I don't even know what to say about her. I just know it wouldn't be enough.

He felt sweat forming on his hands, and the pen slipped out of them. He closed the notebook, lay down in his bed, and stared at the ceiling. His thoughts kept walking down the hall.

3

———

ANAMNESIS

She did not cry in her dreams, because she had no dreams that night. It was, without her realizing it, the best sleep she had had in many years, since before her arrival on Quopeia. She had felt safe and at ease in one night in a manner she could not fully understand. So the next morning, she felt blissful at first, waking in the soft twilight of the dawn. She looked around her little room with adoration. It felt like a home.

Then she sat up with a jolt. Today Dek was going to school! She quickly dressed.

Galla fussed over Dek's hair and his clothes, and then she did start crying.

"Ugh, stop, Galla," Dek groaned, raising his hands in protest. "I'm only going to school. And it's just a short bit away."

"I know. I *know*," said Galla, dashing her tears away with her fingers. "Big hug," she said, and she squeezed Dek until he said, "Oof!"

"Love you," she called, and he sighed and called over his shoulder, "Love you back!" and then he was off, walking in the golden morning light.

And then she really did feel destroyed.

She stood on the stairs of the boardinghouse and watched him until she could no longer see him. Then she sighed and entered the house. She sauntered to the kitchen, where Deming had left them breakfast treats, sat at the table, and nibbled at a small hand pie. She let her head fall in her hand and wondered what she would do with her day.

Deming shuffled in then, and brightened at the sight of her.

"Good morning!" he said. "Is Dek off to school?"

"Yes," said Galla. "Oh! And good morning," she added.

"I'm sure it will go well," said Deming, reassuringly. *I think she needs a distraction*, he thought.

She nodded, avoided meeting his gaze, and returned to her room.

She felt so disoriented, not having Dek around. The first day seemed eternal, and when he finally returned from school, he groaned when she peppered him with questions.

"Not *you*, Galla!" he whined, flailing his hands. "I'll have to sit through *all* the questions from Mom and Dad tonight."

Galla frowned at him. "Well, at least tell me this: did you like it at all?"

Dek rolled his eyes. "Sure," he sighed. He opened his door, tossed his backpack in, and pulled the door shut with a bang. He and Galla both winced.

"Sorry," he muttered. "Can I just eat now, please?"

She sighed and followed him to the kitchen, to his great annoyance. To her surprise, Deming was there already, and he turned to them both. He glanced at Galla and smirked.

"I had a feeling school worked up an appetite," he said casually.

Dek blinked at him, and then opened his eyes wide as Deming lifted a platter in each hand and set them on the table. Dek gave him a closemouthed smile and a grateful thumbs-up and dove into the spread of snacks before him. Galla felt her shoulders drop immediately. Her stress streamed out of her, and she tried a few of the snacks herself.

The next day, she waved Dek off again at the door. He quaked in embarrassment. He did not look back, just shot a hand up as he left.

She felt the tension in her shoulders form again. Then she heard footfalls behind her in the foyer. It was Deming, and he looked at the little crease in her forehead and bit his lip.

"Would you be available for something today?" he asked, and he looked excited to Galla.

"I guess so," she said slowly.

"Well," said Deming, "I want you to know, I talked to Gindoo. He was a bit evasive—that's Gindoo for you—but he did suggest I ask you to help me go sampling."

Galla raised her eyebrows. A tiny sting in her head marred her curiosity. *Sampling.* Her thoughts rolled over the word.

"Sampling what?" she wanted to know.

Deming told her, "There's a grove of trees on the other side of town with these spiky fruits. They're ripe only in early autumn, and now is the time to get them. Gindoo needs some for his work. After that, we can hike up into the forests and gather some other things. And," he added, his smile broadening, "you would get to see more of the City! Oh, and fresh air, exercise, and all that."

Galla felt torn, for again she felt so bound to Dek that doing anything without him felt strange. But she *did* want to try new things, and explore this new land.

"Yes," she said, convincing herself then and there.

So they set off in the cool morning, with the shadows growing longer and the dew glinting in the sunlight on the tips of the trees. It had rained in the night, too gentle a rain to wake anyone. And again, she had slept soundly and dreamlessly. She felt more awake and alert today than she could remember feeling. She breathed in the damp smells and looked at the sparkling trees, and looked sideways at tall Deming, who strolled beside her.

He wore a backpack, and had given her a smaller one so they could collect plants and other items on his list for the day. His dark hair swayed forward in his face sometimes, and he would push it back behind his ears. His face was smoothly shaven. Galla noticed he had a very fine nose, and his eyes in the sunlight were a rich, dark brown, though they looked black in shade. He was a lean young man, with long legs. She watched him adjust his vest and its many pockets, patting some to check that he had everything. His hands looked a little worn, and his fingers were stained, but they were deft and their thumbs very flexible.

"Do you do a lot of work outdoors?" she asked him.

"Yes," he said, smiling at her. "I think I prefer being outdoors. I get a little cooped up in the house. Although I do love to write."

"I don't think I could imagine a better house to get cooped up *in*," said Galla, and he laughed.

"True. But wind, and sun, and even rain, and green things," Deming said as he paused and breathed in the autumn air, "and autumn—they all draw me out. I spend so much time in Gindoo's study. I get starved for light."

And he looked at Galla then, with the flickering, dappled light of the trees in the street sparkling on her hair in bronze, auburn, almost-purple, and gold, and the amber-copper of her eyes shining, and he swallowed. *She's autumn personified*, he thought, and he finally took a breath. He breathed out, and it came out in a puff in the chill air.

They wound their way around the streets of Allurulla, and Galla gazed up at its tall towers, with various crafts rising and falling among them. After so many years on the southwestern prairie, with a bottomless sky and an empty undulation of grain, the City woke her up, made her more alert. She wanted to see everything, and ask what everything was, but at the same time she held back. There was that part of her again, tightly binding her within, a protective barrier. It frustrated her. She could not even really put into words why. Something was missing, some vital part of her, and even looking at the shining surfaces of the skyscrapers, she felt an odd sense of déjà vu, like she might have seen something similar, somewhere, once. *Or am I imagining it?*

Then they reached the end of a long avenue, arched over by reddening little trees and phyron streetlamps, and on one side a café gleamed in the morning sun, its windows steamed up. On the other, a very interesting being inspected the outside of a shop that Galla, squinting, could see was some kind of salon. She felt drawn to both, but detoured to the salon first, Deming in tow, bemused at her attraction to and distraction by so many common shops in the City. But that salon was anything but common.

Its peculiar keeper turned and saw Galla, backlit by the sun, her hair twisting like flames in a wind. As she approached this being, she found herself wondering what species it belonged to. She felt her mind straining to sort it out, but came up with nothing. For the being was spectacularly coifed, with teal and ultramarine and green hair coiled skyward over a meter, and within the hair there were moving shimmers and little designs that curled this way and that. The being bore a long, slender nose in its pale chartreuse face, with large, deep-set golden eyes and pointed pupils, a tiny full-lipped mouth painted several colors from white to pale yellow to deep orange, a long, thin neck, and two slim arms ringed by countless bracelets that clinked when they moved. Its body was dressed in a gauzy material that was deep mint green, and its lower body curved outward over large hips. But Galla could not see its legs, so she did not know if it had any.

The being said in a hooting voice, "We aren't open yet, love, but come back later, hmm? Magnificent hair, love, truly. You won't be needing our anti-grav, that's for sure!" and the golden eyes watched Galla's hair move. "Maybe a deep conditioning, though," and the being tutted.

Galla bent her head back a bit, perplexed and confused, but the being said, "My name is Pear. I know, I know—but none of you can *ever* pronounce my true name. You don't have the vocal cords for it, love. Come back later. Ask for me."

And Pear leaned a bit to one side to look at Deming, and back at Galla. Pear nodded, then turned and set about unlocking the salon. Galla twisted around and looked back at Deming, whose face was creased with a lopsided grin. She shrugged, and he did as well.

"Bakery?" he suggested. "I saw you looking at it."

"Yes," she answered with gusto, and they set across the avenue to the steamy bakery, where the smells set them sighing.

Deming opened the door for her, and they were met with a line of customers, and even more delicious smells. The bakery was all golden and ornate, with marble and other valuable stone lining the floors and counters. Behind the counter, both humans and other beings worked quickly to serve the customers. The ceiling behind the workers was hung with little rails, and pastries traveled along them like little edible trains, sliding down like the Whoenaat shuttle tubes through the mountains. Galla could have stared at those in pure delight for hours, but she noticed something else, and became fixated.

Behind one of the glass cases, a stack of purple turnovers leaked caramelized juice from their ends. *Those...I know those...I know their smell; I know their taste. Somehow. How?*

She gazed at them for long enough that Deming cleared his throat.

"It's our turn to order," he said, bending down to where she crouched to look at the tarts. "Would you like some of those? We can get them to go, and eat them before the hike. I'll also get some sylcaah. They'll go great together, I think."

She arose in a reverie, her head swimming, and tried to focus on his face. By instinct, he caught her by her elbow, and looked at her seriously with his dark eyes.

"Are you all right? Should we go?" he asked.

And then the person behind the counter spoke.

"What would you like?" and Galla turned and stared at the being. It was a blue-grey being, with several arms, and she glanced from the purple tarts to the being's face.

"Very well," said the cashier curtly. "How many?"

"Two, please," Deming said, "and two cups of sylcaah, with that sprinkle on top, please." He paid, and gently herded Galla off to one side. The being reached behind itself to grab two purple tarts with one arm and handled money with another. A third arm reached for a mug, a fourth arm seized another mug, and a fifth arm shook a jar of something over each. A sixth arm then brought forth a little box, and all the arms together tucked everything in the box. Deming picked it up and thanked the being.

Galla glanced over her shoulder at the cashier, and then noticed it was staring directly at her as well. *Who is that? So familiar...*

"Is that someone you know?" Deming asked, and he grew more concerned by the minute. *Is she in a fugue state?* he wondered.

She shook her head and walked absently out of the warm, steamy bakery into the crisp autumn morning air. Everything seemed to snap back in place for her. She looked up at Deming and blushed deeply.

"I'm so sorry," she said, sweating even in the chill. "I'm not sure what happened to me."

"You okay?" he asked.

"Yes. I am *oakay*," answered Galla, and Deming took a breath.

"There's a park bench. Why don't we eat there? Then we can circle back behind the park and start heading up the trail."

She followed him, and they gingerly sat on the edge of the old stone bench, for its seat was damp from dew. She reached eagerly for one of the purple tarts, and turned it over and over in her hand. Then she smelled it, taking a long, indulgent whiff, and her cheeks rose and her eyes half-closed, for she loved that smell. She *knew* that smell. And it made her happy. So she took a bite, and the deep, richly colored fruit, still warm, gushed onto her tongue.

Deming laughed. "I have never seen someone so blissed-out by food as you. Well, maybe your brother."

She laughed in spite of herself.

He handed her a go-mug of the sylcaah. He pushed his swooping hair behind his ears and watched her take a drink. She put it under her nose first, breathing in a buttery-sweet yet spicy fragrance. She took a sip.

"Mmm," she said. "It's delicious! Thank you."

Deming looked triumphant. "I thought you'd like it! It should give us plenty of energy for today."

They sat and ate their treats and finished their sylcaah, and by then Galla felt fully refreshed and hyperalert. She looked back at the avenue, and at Pear's salon and the little café, and she felt wistful. She could not understand what had happened to her back there. She felt caught between two worlds, or two times, she was not sure which.

4

AUREATE

Deming led Galla to an old orchard of gnarled trees between the edge of the City and a large park. The trees bent over, like dancers bowing to each other, their boughs heavy with ripe fruit. She could see little white spines sticking out of each garnet-hued fruit. She reached up to pluck one, but Deming quickly blocked her reach.

"You need these," he said, holding up a pair of thick gloves. "Don't ask me how I know."

In fact, his first experience with geelybans made him wince even now, after almost twenty years. He had been a major fruit lover, he told her, and when Gindoo had taken him and his brother to this very grove, he ran full tilt on his little legs and immediately found a windfall of geelyban before Gindoo could stop him.

"Let's just say," Deming said with a grimace, "Gindoo swears he can still hear my howls over picking up one up barehanded to this day."

Galla snickered and donned the gloves.

"Go for the really dark red ones," he told her, and they moved between the trees until they found the best ones. They were surprisingly lightweight to Galla. After picking a few dozen, their packs still felt light.

They then hiked on among the parkland and reached a trail-head. It bore deep ruts from summer rains, and a tangle of autumn-crisp vines flickered over it, like a veil to some secret passage.

"This is it," Deming announced. "It's a bit of a haul from here. Are you up to it?"

Galla felt the thrill of the trail calling. "Oh yes," she said, and they each drank from their water bottles and clinked them together before stowing them.

"Up we go," said Deming. And he felt a deep excitement and plea-sure, having a trail mate like her.

At first the going was easy, up a slow incline through the forested trail. Then the trail became more rugged, full of broken boulders and limestone overhangs. The roots of trees bulged up into the trail, and the landscape grew more primitive. The season had progressed higher up as well. When they reached a broad clearing, the gold leaves of some of the deciduous trees were drifting off, gently falling all around them. Deming walked into the shade of the trees and knelt down near the base of their trunks, and began to dig for roots and fungi.

Galla looked up through the gilded canopy at the turquoise sky above, and a leaf fell and brushed her face like the hand of a lover. The blue of the sky and the autumn colors stirred some old part of her that she did not recall. It left her in a trance.

She said very quietly, "Love fallen, as your leaves in autumn."

Deming's feet shuffled through leaves as he walked over to her. Her face was upturned, and her eyes now closed.

She looks so far away right now, he thought.

"What did you mean?" he asked her.

She shook herself, and her hat slid off her coiled hair. She turned to look at him.

"What?" she asked.

"Just now," said Deming. "It was like a poem."

She felt dazed. She blinked several times, opened her mouth and closed it. She shook her head.

"I don't know," she said, and she could not even remember what she had said.

"It was beautiful," said Deming. "You should write it down."

Galla lowered her head. "I should be helping you. What should I look for?"

Deming pushed his lips together and thought, *It's like she didn't know she was speaking at all. I hope Gindoo can help her.*

Aloud, he said, "If you could look for more of these, I need a sack full." He showed her the fungus. "They're under the soil of the trees with the gold, jagged leaves."

"Sure," she said.

Deming approached a small brook that bubbled along the hill.

"I'm going to check under and around the stream rocks for ailfern," he told her. "There are two kinds. Each has healing properties, and they make a vapor that clears the lungs. Gindoo can't keep up with demand in the fall and winter, so I hope to find them. Usually they grow in the Northwest, but the higher elevations here are similar to that climate, so you can sometimes find them here."

Galla nodded, and as she turned to forage, she asked, "And what are these fungi for?"

"Oh!" Deming laughed. "Those are for dinner."

Galla snickered and went on her way to harvest. They worked through the area for over an hour, and finally Deming's shadow emerged next to her. She looked up to see his face shaded from the noon sun.

"Hungry? There's an overlook where we can eat."

She shook her bag of fungi, shouldered it, and joined him. They stood at a gap in the trees, and Galla could see all of Allurulla spread in the valley below, its little blue lakes cobalt, its coral and turquoise spires shimmering.

"It felt like we were so far away from the City," Galla remarked, "but we aren't."

"That's why I like coming up here," said Deming. He gave her a wrapped savory pastry, and they watched aircraft lower into the City. "I prefer wild places, wild things. I don't get up north as often as I'd like, and I never have crossed the Talonii Mountains."

"One day," said Galla, smiling up at him. "These are so yummy," she said after taking a bite. "How is your food so good?"

Color erupted on his face, and he shrugged. "I don't know. Fresh ingredients?" and he nudged her bag.

She laughed loudly, scaring little animals in the undergrowth. She covered her mouth then, and Deming stifled a laugh.

"Ready to head back down?" he asked her when they'd finished. "We've done well. I couldn't have got all this myself, without being here all day. I'll get you home in time for Dek."

Galla breathed in the sweet air of the old mountain ridge and thought about the strange ache inside her when she looked at the falling leaves. She pulled her hat back into position, ignoring the unruly locks that insisted on flying back out.

"I'm ready for anything," she said.

"I believe it," Deming said, with an admiring grin.

As they made their way back to the City, a number of slate-grey craft streamed overhead. They both watched them veer off to the south and arc back around. She heard Deming sigh.

"Those looked official," Galla remarked, and she thought, *Why is he frowning?*

"Big events in the coming days," he muttered. "It's that time of year. I kind of forget, working like I do, but holidays sneak up on you."

She shielded Siloxxa's rays from her eyes to see if any more ships were incoming. She did not see any.

"Come," he said. "I'll take you back along the river trail this time," and she followed him, still noting the furrow in his brow.

5

BROTHERS

Later in the week, Galla woke with a start. The front door of the boardinghouse had shut with a loud bang. She blinked and slid out of bed, into slippers, and walked out of her room and across the hall. Dek's door was closed. She put her ear against the wood and heard him snoring. She frowned. Deming never made much noise coming in and out; in fact he made a point to be as quiet as possible. And she knew by now that Gindoo would never slam a door, because he was never outside of his study, wherever it was.

Curiosity got the better of her, so she dressed and walked down the hallway to the foyer. There she stopped, hearing voices: one of them was Deming's; another came from a man she did not know. She wavered there, half tempted to turn back and return to her room. But she felt the urge to investigate.

She walked quietly over to the hall that led to the kitchen and Deming's quarters. She halted. They were in the kitchen: plates were clinking. Deep laughter rang out, and then a shushing sound followed it.

Well, she thought, *it* is *breakfast time. I'm just going to go ahead.*

So she smoothed out her shirt and pants and sighed in frustration over her feral hair, which felt coarse and wild this morning, and walked forward.

At the door of the kitchen she heard Deming say, "Let them sleep! You're going to wake them. Well, Galla, anyway. Dek will sleep in until he smells food."

The deeper voice of the other man replied, "So considerate! You must really want to make an impression."

"Would you stop?" hissed Deming.

More deep laughter. "It's no good, you can't escape me."

"Of course not," muttered Deming, and Galla could hear a note of bitterness in his voice that surprised her.

"I could find out for you," said the man, in a teasing tone.

"Find out what?" snapped Deming.

"If she—"

"*No!*" cried Deming. "Never. Never do that to her!"

Galla blushed. Were they talking about *her*?

Unable to bear it any longer, she swallowed, and then breezily swept into the kitchen with a radiant smile and said, "Good morning, Deming!"

And she found Deming next to a tall man, not much taller than Deming, but larger. He turned to her and she felt the force of his gaze like a shock. He was almost unbelievably attractive. His skin was a deep bronze, his wavy black hair was cropped very short, and his eyes! His eyes glowed an ethereal green. Galla felt almost dizzy looking at him, and when he smiled his teeth shone brilliant white, and she realized she was gawking openly at him.

Deming shifted where he stood and said with downcast eyes, "Good morning, Galla. I would like you to meet my brother, Paul. Paul, this is Galla."

But Paul had not stopped staring at her either. A crease formed above his nose, and his smile froze on his face. Nevertheless, the two stepped toward each other and shook hands.

"Nice to meet you, Paul," she said. She felt as if she had slid off a rooftop and landed on her back. Who was this man? His eyes...what was it about his eyes?

"Very nice to meet *you*, Galla," he replied, and he held her hand and stared into her copper eyes.

Galla felt as though she were being examined under powerful lenses.

She gasped, "Likewise."

"I've heard so much about you already," said Paul, his voice quite deep and his peridot eyes mesmerizing. "You're unlike anyone else who has been inside this old place, I can tell you that."

He broke his gaze and looked at his brother. Galla followed the look and felt a stab of shock at Deming's face. It had gone pale.

"Are you all right, Deming?" she asked, and she stepped forward.

He smiled faintly at her, his dark eyes barely looking at her. "Fine. I'm fine."

Paul grinned. "He's anything *but* fine," he chuckled. Deming glared at him. "Oh, relax. But I'm right. Galla here is unique. I can't read her at all!"

"I told you—" Deming began, and then he shut his mouth in a thin line. Color burst into his cheeks then.

"Don't worry," Paul scoffed, looking back at Galla. "I didn't try very hard; I didn't need to anyway. She's completely unreadable! Unlike anyone else I've come across. So. Can't help you there, little brother."

Paul stared at Galla's face again until she felt her cheeks grow warm, and she lowered her eyes and walked over to Deming.

"Very unique," she heard Paul mutter. She glanced back and saw him looking at her with that crease in his forehead again. His smile had faded. They looked at each other as if across a long bridge. *Who was he?* And by his expression, Galla felt some instinct deep down that told her he was thinking the same thing about her.

He *was* attracted to her, at least superficially. She recognized *that* look. The look Deming had so far never given her, incidentally. She exhaled after realizing she had been holding her breath.

"Can I help with breakfast, Deming?" she asked. He blinked and looked at her then, and gave her a true smile and a nod. Galla was aware that Paul watched them both.

"Wow, Deming," he laughed. Galla shot him a sour look. She could see Deming tense up.

Paul poured himself a large mug of tea and sat at the long table, back erect. He was quite muscular through his shirt, with large biceps and chiseled forearms. *A powerful man*, Galla thought.

"What is it that you do, Paul?" she asked.

Paul yawned and rubbed the short, wavy dark hair on his head. His green eyes glinted over his mug as he blew on the hot tea. "I work for the government," he said simply. He turned to look at his brother, who brought a plate of toast to the table. "You know, that's a bit hard, little bro. Maybe you should say it out loud."

Deming's jaw clenched and his face and ears went bright red. Galla frowned again, looking between the two brothers.

"What is going on?" she demanded.

Paul set his mug down and looked up at Galla, who stood next to him with arms crossed, her hair bouncing in every direction.

"Well, Galla, your new friend Deming here has a lot to think about, though he says very little," Paul said quietly.

The wild hair and stern expression on this young-looking beauty bemused him. He wrestled a bit with his feelings, because he found her staggeringly appealing, with her fine figure, elfin face, and shining eyes. But on some level, he held back from thinking about it further. It didn't seem proper to him, somehow, to lust after this lady. And Paul was known for lusting after just about everyone and everything.

"That's vague," snapped Galla.

Deming cleared his throat. She turned and retrieved a platter of fruit from him and set it on the table.

"Just tell her," Deming said, in an exasperated voice.

Paul sighed and rubbed his face.

"Galla," he said, "I'm a telepath."

She blinked at him. Finally she and Deming sat down, with her at the head of the table, between the two brothers.

"So," she said slowly, "that's what you meant by...reading me, then?"

Paul nodded. "It's fascinating. I can't read you...not at all. That's pretty uncommon. Some species have natural blocks, but no human does: blocking has to be learned, and it's not always successful. Gindoo seems to have it down pretty well, but then again, sometimes I wonder if he's human or not. Sometimes he'll leak music from his thoughts, though. With you, when I try to read you or listen to your thoughts, there's nothing: absolute quiet."

He sighed. "Honestly, it's a nice feeling. Looking at you is like taking a break."

Deming scooted his chair noisily. Paul glanced at him, and a grin curled at one corner of his mouth. That seemed to Galla the only similarity between the two of them: their wry grins. *Well, they're also both quite tall*, she realized.

"Who's Dek?" Paul asked suddenly.

Galla opened her eyes wider. "That's my little brother. He's going to school here in Allurulla."

"Lucid dreamer," said Paul. "He's broadcasting far and wide—"

Deming cleared his throat again. Paul rolled his eyes.

"But he's not like you, Galla," Paul went on. "He's just a normal kid."

"He's a great kid," she beamed.

"Sure," said Paul with a shrug. "My point is—and I mean no offense—he's human. And you, well...you're obviously not."

Deming dropped his fork and it fell off the table to the floor with a metallic twang.

"Paul! For fuck's sake!" cried Deming, and then he blushed.

Galla stared at him.

Paul guffawed. "So chivalrous!" he cried. "Well? I'm right, aren't I?" and he turned back to face Galla.

Galla squeezed herself with her arms, not knowing what else to do.

"Yes," she said. And there again, that feeling—the sharp little pain in her head, the sudden fatigue. The feeling of that barrier inside her rose again.

"Galla," said Deming, "I'm sorry my brother is so *goddamned rude*."

She and his brother stared at Deming with huge eyes.

"Whew..." whistled Paul. "Bro, you're pretty worked up. Maybe I should head out for a bit."

"No," said Galla suddenly, deathly calm. The brothers turned to her swiftly and she stared at each of them with glints in her russet eyes.

"Stop this, whatever this is you're both doing," she said quietly. "Eat the meal that *Deming prepared for all of us*. And Paul, maybe you should have a conversation with Gindoo. He seems to be a source of wisdom in this household, after all."

Paul pushed out his lips and raised his eyebrows. "I think I may do just that," he said seriously. But he cheerfully lifted his mug and said, "To the Queen—*that's you*," and took a swig, and started eating.

Deming's obvious turmoil brought out a pang of sympathy from Galla, but at the same time she was furious as well. Finally, Paul rose and took his plates to the sink.

He turned and said, "Well, now that I'm here, I may as well say it: there's a President's Ball coming up in a few weeks. Deming, they'll want you back for that. Galla, of course you're invited."

Deming took a deep breath, and she watched him stab at his food.

"Thank you," she said awkwardly.

Deming's jaw muscles twitched.

"I can take a hint, *bro*," Paul said then, and he grinned at her.

He said to her, "I'm impressed. I didn't know he had it in him, at all, for anyone. I've never been more wrong." And he left to go to his own room.

Galla and Deming then sat next to each other and ate quietly without speaking for several excruciating minutes.

"What was that?" she asked him finally.

Deming closed his eyes.

"Paul lives a very different life than I do," he told her. "His skills make him...valuable. So he's not around very much and—well, as you can see—we don't get along that well. Usually I just avoid him but, well, today—I—I don't know what came over me. I apologize."

"There's no need for that," said Galla, and she reached over and pressed her hand on top of his. Her touch brought him out of his reverie, and they looked at each other. Galla felt warmth making its way through her. Deming squeezed her hand gently and quickly and released it. She realized she wished he hadn't let go.

"Do you—Deming," she said, shyly, nervously, "do you care? That —that I'm not human?" And she held her breath, for she realized she had wanted to ask him all this time, ever since she had met him. She had been afraid of his answer.

"Why would I?" he asked her in return, with quick little glances at her. "That's nothing to be ashamed of, after all. I don't care what you are, or where you came from. And there is nothing wrong with you. Not a single thing. Not even one."

He abruptly stood.

"Good morning, Dek!" he called, for there stood Dek in the doorway, sleepily looking from Galla to Deming and back again. "Breakfast is ready."

She turned away from them both, her cheeks ablaze, and she hastily cleaned up after herself and bolted out of the kitchen without looking at either of them.

6

AN INVITATION AND A GOWN

Galla spent the next few weeks in a new routine: she would see Dek off to school, but a little less each day. Then she would meet Deming, and they would trek off to collect plants, and she would marvel at the City. He showed her little secret side streets, where he sometimes found enormous bulbenberries and other treasures. She listened to him talk about the properties of each plant, and watched him carefully store everything in his pack. He occasionally brought out a little notebook as well, to jot down where they found things.

So meticulous and patient, she thought. *Except when it comes to his brother.* Every time Paul's name came up, Deming's entire demeanor changed. She puzzled over that. She barely saw Paul, who left early for work and returned late, but each time they did see each other, he made a ridiculous, deep bow until he could get a smile from her. And somehow it worked every time.

They did not return to the avenue with Pear's salon or the bakery with the purple tarts. Something steered Galla off from wanting to go there again. But she did want to see Pear again. She wondered if she would have any reason to.

Finally, school let out for a small break. Dek took advantage of the scenario by sleeping in. So Galla dressed for breakfast, slid down the hallway, listened to see if anyone was in the kitchen, and tiptoed in. For once, she wanted a quick, silent meal. Finding the kitchen empty, she sighed in relief and pulled down a plate.

The floor popped behind her, and she whirled around. It was Paul. Looking...sheepish? She found his expression peculiar. He stood in the doorway holding something in his hand.

"Good morning," he said to her cheerfully, his eyes evasive. Then he made his deep bow, nearly touching his head to her feet. She laughed, and he looked victorious.

"Good morning, Paul," she answered.

Paul looked to his right and left in the doorway, and then entered the kitchen.

"I have a question," he said, twisting the object in his hand absently. Galla crinkled up her nose and squinted at him.

"Yes?" she asked.

"Well—the thing is—there's a ball coming up," he began. "The President's Ball. Only the biggest social event of the year. Fall holidays, and all that."

"I remember your telling me," Galla said, holding her plate in her left hand.

Paul cleared his throat and swept a hand through his cropped hair. "I'm expected to attend. And I...I need a dance partner."

Galla could feel a tingle growing in her cheeks. She set her plate down and looked at him with clear, warm eyes. His eyes fluttered and finally looked at her, and he smirked.

He made a show of it then, and got down on his knee. "May I have the honor of your company to the President's Ball?" and he thrust the paper at her, which she took and stared at in confusion.

She smoothed the crumpled wad and found an engraved invitation for the President's Ball. Galla found his antics amusing and she could not help but snicker. He looked up at her with a quizzical line in his forehead.

Have I ever been to a ball before? she wondered. *I don't even know if I can dance! But I want to.*

"I'm sorry," she said. "You just—you caught me off guard."

"So...is that a..." he began.

"Yes," she said emphatically. "Yes, I'll go."

Paul rose and sighed with relief.

"I'm sorry for the short notice," he told her. "It's in one week. The dress code is formal."

She tapped her chin with her finger. "I don't have any formal clothes at all," she realized.

"I'll pay for them," said Paul enthusiastically, stepping over to her. "Normally I'd have a date by now, but I was on deployment, and I've been busy with work. And there's *nobody* there I want to ask."

She smirked. "You make it sound like I'm a desperation date," she said.

Paul raised his eyebrows. "You! What! A desperation date? *Hell no.*"

Galla blushed and laughed. "Thank you."

And at that moment, Deming walked into the kitchen, and found Galla and Paul laughing. Paul knew Deming had arrived without seeing him, and he stiffened, and his face looked worried.

What is going on? thought Galla.

"Good morning," said Deming uncertainly. "I can come back later..."

But Galla stepped forward and seized Deming by the hand and drew him into the kitchen. Paul glanced at her.

"Paul just invited me to the President's Ball," she said quickly. "And I've accepted. But I have no dress! So...I have to figure that out."

Deming nodded slowly, not looking at either of them.

Paul's face look pained. "We'll come and find you at the Ball," he said, holding his hands out.

Deming's lips stretched into a thin half-smile. "Of course." And he turned to Galla. "I always assist with the bar, every year," he explained. "On account of my laboratory—or in this case, mixology —skills."

"Oh!" said Galla. "So you will be there? Good!" and she puffed out a relieved sigh. "I'll definitely come to see you."

"Great," said Deming simply, and then he ignored both of them, got his breakfast, and left the kitchen.

Galla looked at Paul uncertainly. He shrugged and sighed.

WHEN GALLA TOOK her humble funds to the boutique district later that morning, she realized she could not afford anything she saw. Gindoo, who she still had not seen but was fairly certain she had heard playing music, had arranged for Deming to give her a stipend for her sampling help. Still she could not justify the expense. She chewed her lip and wondered idly if she could make herself a dress. She could imagine any design, and liked to draw, but had no dressmaking skills. She sauntered by Pear's Salon, watching the anti-gravity hairstyling and cosmetic artistry of this maestro. Her own hair began lifting skyward as she watched the display. She self-consciously pulled it down. Off to her right, she noticed someone in a dark robe. She turned to look at the shape, and it was gone.

She felt perturbed. Something seemed amiss about today. The awkward invitation by Paul, Deming's strange reaction to it, and now this.

Maybe I should call it for the day, she thought irritably.

She walked back to Gindoo's boardinghouse, and again noticed something unusual. Something rippled behind her, like a shadow. When she called out, "Who's there?" she heard a strange fizzing in the air.

Unnerved, she walked more quickly. She had just walked down the cul-de-sac to home, and saw the door of the boardinghouse shut. Glancing behind her once more, she darted ahead and slipped inside. She banged right into Deming in the foyer.

"Ugh, sorry!" she howled, as he held his lip from where her forehead had struck it.

"I'm fine," he mumbled, rubbing his mouth.

"No, you're not, you're bleeding," gasped Galla, dabbing his lip with her finger. "Come, I'll help you."

Deming protested, but she pulled him along to her room. She stared at what sat in front of the door: an ornate box.

"This just came for you," Deming told her. "I was on my way back to my room after putting it here."

"I didn't order anything," mused Galla. She opened her door, picked up the box, and stepped inside. "One thing at a time," she said, and she found a small cloth in her bathroom, wet it, and returned to Deming, who stood shuffling his feet at her door. She cleaned his lip, and he stood patiently as she did, his dark eyes soft in appreciation.

"Thank you," he said gratefully. They stood close together, and Galla felt a bit of heat working its way through her, so she stepped away from him.

"Galla," he said quietly, blinking rapidly, "I have something for you."

She turned away from the mysterious box to look at him. She noticed then that he had a hand in his pocket.

"I thought about waiting until the Ball," he said, shifting his body weight from one foot to the other.

Galla felt intrigued, and Deming watched her hair float up a bit. "What is it?" she asked.

He pulled a small, dark green cloth bag from his pocket and held it in his palm. She looked at his inky eyes, shy yet open, and with her fingers trembling, she took the little bag. She opened it to find a small woven bracelet, made from shining threads of several colors.

"Here," he said, and he took the bracelet and looped it around her left wrist. "I made it from thread saved by my grandmother. She had a little sewing kit. It was part of the few things we have left from our family. She was quite the crafter, and quilter. Now I'm the one who patches things up. I...picked up some of her habits, I think, even though I never met her."

Galla felt overwhelmed. Her eyes began filling with tears. She could see he had taken considerable time with the tiny threads to make the bracelet, and for it to be woven from something so special, she did not know what to say.

"Do—do you not like it?" he asked, worryingly, and he carefully reached to pat her cheeks with his sleeve.

Galla shook her head and clasped his hands. "Oh—I'm sorry! I'm crying because I love it so much," she told him. He sighed with relief and laughed softly. They avoided each other's eyes then.

"Let's see what this is," she said at last, and with a sigh she approached the box on her bed. On its lid, an elaborate silver design curled.

"It says 'G-D,'" Deming noted. "I'm guessing the 'G' is for Galla, of course. But what's the 'D' for?"

"That's unusual," she murmured.

She traced the design with her fingers and shivered. Something about this seemed so familiar to her.

"Maybe I shouldn't open it," she said quietly.

He gave her a sidelong glance. "Why not?"

Why not indeed? she thought. *I'm being silly. It's just a box!* But she felt quite certain that it was not just any box.

She bit her lip. "Fine. I'm opening it," she said, and she worked with the engraved lid until she could lift it off. He stood next to her. She found inside a silver satin cloth, tied with a silver cord. She pulled the cord and pulled back the cloth. Something shimmered there, in deep blue. She lifted it out.

It was a blue gown, sleek and shining, with starburst patterns all over it, and it reached to the floor from where she held it up to herself.

"Oh!" she cried. "It's extraordinary." And then she said, "Turn around. I'm going to put it on!"

"Wait, I should go—" Deming began.

"Oh stop," sighed Galla. Deming turned to the door. She shimmied out of her clothes, and they fell around her feet. She slipped the dress on...

And it fit like her own skin. Her heart began racing. Something in it—some incense, or whiff of something—made her light-headed. She had a wild moment of wondering if she had ever worn this dress before. She steadied herself.

"Well?" she said finally. "How does it look?"

Deming carefully turned back to her. He caught his breath. The blue gown did look as if it were made for her; it hugged every curve. In her excitement her bright, living hair undulated to and fro as if underwater. Her eyes were large and vivid amber, and she smoothed the dress with her hands over her bodice and waist. He was floored. And he feared what to say next, but he managed to speak.

"God da—" gasped Deming, then he turned deep scarlet. "The dress is—it's—it's fine," he said finally.

Galla tilted her head at him and laughed.

"I wonder if I should keep it," she said seriously. "Do you think Paul ordered it? He did say he could buy a dress for me."

Deming shook his head, as if enchanted. He turned away from her a bit.

"I'm sorry," he said, with what he feared was a too-loud swallow. "I have no idea. But yes, that is a *good dress.* You should keep it."

Galla snickered at him and gave him a sunny smile. "I will," she said. "Okay, you can turn around again."

And Deming bit his own lip while turned away from her, knowing if he peeked, he would find her nearly nude. *Or totally nude?* he wondered. And he broke into a sweat. He fought himself. *She's my friend. What the hell is wrong with me?* And he realized then just how glad he was to have a new friend like her in his life. *What if she had never shown up at our door? My life is already better with her in it.* He sighed.

She set her dress aside, and the tiny pain formed in her forehead again. She followed Deming out of her room, and when they reached the foyer, Paul entered.

"Paul!" she said. "Thank you for the dress."

He stared at her. "What dress?"

"Oh," said Galla, turning pink. "I guess it wasn't from you. Someone sent me a dress."

"Weird," said Paul.

"Well, that's sorted anyway, I suppose," she remarked with a twist in her smile. "Is there anything else I need for the Ball?"

He shrugged. "Not that I can think of. Shoes might be a good idea, though. Deming, you look a little bit out of it," he said, and then he cracked up. "It's a good thing I'm the only telepath in this household right now." He guffawed.

Deming looked flushed. He touched Galla's elbow. "I'm headed back downstairs," he told her. Paul's eyes twinkled at them.

But at night, in her room, the gown beckoned to her again. She could not sleep. *How do I know this thing? Because I do know it. Somehow. And it scares me.*

When she closed her eyes in her bed, she imagined the dress on her, with hands sliding it off of her. Hands that worked their way over her body, caressing. Lips that nuzzled her. In a dreamlike state, she imagined long white hair falling over her. She felt a moment of being held tenderly, and then a sensation of shock and of pleasure. She slid farther into dreams of someone with silver eyes watching her.

7

GINDOO

She later woke with a start, soaked with sweat. She felt incredibly aroused. This feeling and its power confused her. She jumped from her bed and panted. She stared at the dress box, but it was closed. She snatched her robe, tied it on, and slipped out of her room. The bracelet Deming had given her slipped down her arm to rest against her hand. She stroked it, liking its familiarity. She slid down the hallway and out the back door. And in the light of the moon, Deming's head was shining as he collected flowers, much as it had her first night in the boardinghouse. He looked up in surprise.

She walked to him on bare feet and found the ground bitingly cold and crunchy. Their breath came out in fog.

"Collecting?" she asked him softly.

"Yes," he said, "the last of the year. The frost will kill them and ruin them. So I'm harvesting now. You're up late."

"I couldn't sleep," she admitted. "It's the dress. I—I dreamed about it. Deming, I—I think it was my dress once before."

"What?" he asked, watching her kneel to pick flowers. She put them in his basket, and their hands touched. He wanted very much to drop the basket and take her warm hands in his.

"I know it sounds crazy," said Galla. "But I think this is some part of the puzzle of *me*."

"Should we ask Gindoo?" Deming asked.

"Maybe so," Galla admitted. She was shivering. It was not the cold that bothered her. It was the uncertainty.

Deming hoisted his full basket, and they walked softly back inside, taking care not to wake Dek. He led her beyond the kitchen, past his room door, and they stood at the door to Gindoo's study. His dark eyes glinted in the phyron sconce light as he looked thoughtfully at her. He opened the door.

She peered in and blinked. At first it was incredibly dim, but she could see several flickering sconces along a curved staircase that led downward.

"Step carefully," he advised. "It's farther down than you might think." He stepped down first so that she could follow him.

He was right: she walked down several curving flights, confused by their direction. Ultimately, they seemed to curve clockwise downward. The phyron crystal lights whistled and popped. One side of the stairs abutted the curving wall, while the other side had no support at all. Galla looked down into the wavering spiral of lights and low-lit stairs. This dizzied her.

By and by the lights increased, and strange music met her ears. At last Deming stopped at a landing, and she looked in wonder at a series of recessed areas inside a vast room. How far under the boardinghouse they were, she could not guess.

"This," she breathed, "is where you work every day?"

Deming watched her keenly, and he nodded and smiled. Galla stood next to him. The music, which had echoed from this great room, had stopped. She blinked. All around the walls, narrow shelves were loaded from floor to ceiling with little glistening bottles. Sconces were crammed here and there to light the place, and their light flashed off those bottles.

"Did you make all those?" gasped Galla.

He smirked. "Not *all* of them. No. Some of them are quite old, from way before I was born. But I did help to make some of them. Gindoo always adds the finishing touch."

"What are they?"

"Potions. Samples. Medicines. Tinctures. Some things I can't guess," answered Deming, sweeping his hair behind his ears. She could see pride in his face, and reverence as well.

"Well?" a voice wheezed, startling them both. "Are you going to bring her all the way down here, or not?" A long, rattling laugh rose from somewhere below them.

Deming stepped down the final set of stairs into the great room. It was a series of smaller rooms, in a way, with little work areas tucked down and around the main floor. Galla wondered if there were another floor below this one as well. Gindoo had to live somewhere, she reasoned. *Unless he sleeps in his laboratory.* She followed Deming and looked all around, but she could not see Gindoo.

She admired the various laboratory apparatus in one of the little alcoves. Simmering, distilling pots bubbled and hissed. Acrid smells stung her nose wherever she turned. Steam rose from one contraption, and her hair felt weighed down by it. Something bumped into her hip and she turned and squawked.

It was a little man, whose wizened head reached her waist. He was stooped low over a cane, and his brow was deeply furrowed like a forgotten canyon. His hair was long and stringy and grey, and pulled back in a tie. His goatee was woven in several long, slender grey braids. He wore what looked like an old grey bathrobe over wide-legged pants, and very worn, ugly slippers covered his feet. Galla could not tell what color this tiny person's eyes were, but they sparkled despite their age.

"Hello!" she exclaimed.

Deming rushed over. "Galla, this is Gindoo. Gindoo, meet Galla."

"Yes, we've just met," chortled Gindoo.

Gindoo stared up at her, squinting, and her multihued hair twisted and coiled up and down and around her shoulders. The light of the sconces and sparkling glassware made them both look somehow not real to Deming, like something from a story he might have read as a child. He gazed in wonder at the two of them: his teacher and his friend.

"Yes, well," said Gindoo in a quavering voice. "I see you got the blooms in time."

"I did," answered Deming, showing Gindoo his basket.

"Good, good," the wee man said. "Go ahead and get them soaking."

The young man walked off to do as he was told, and Galla continued staring at Gindoo.

"Deming tells me you're good at sampling," he noted gruffly, again squinting up at her, as if trying to see her in a different light. "Thank you for helping."

"I suppose I'm good enough," she answered, leaning over. "Thank you for the stipend."

"Come, come," said Gindoo testily, and he waddled off slowly to another alcove.

There he kept a desk, piled high with cracked papers and bottles of glue and flasks of lurid-hued liquids. He waved his cane in a semicircle, and a stool appeared. It abruptly swept over and into Galla's backside, so that she sat in it with a yelp. Gindoo then settled behind his desk, and his own roughly hewn wooden chair rose so that he perched at eye level with her.

"Yes, well," he said, sniffing, "out with it! I knew Deming would eventually bring you down here, or else you'd find it yourself. Better this way. Maybe not quite so impulsive these days. Too skittish? Yes, well. That's to be expected, after everything.

"Now, where was I? Oh yes. Tell me what happened."

Galla blinked in the light of the sconces and candles. She could smell the flowers Deming was infusing, and everything in this warm, dim space made her sleepy. She struggled to focus.

"The dress," she murmured. "I received a dress earlier."

"A dress!" exclaimed Gindoo. "Is that all? Are you generally surprised by *clothing*?" He opened his wrinkled eyes wide. She could see then that his eyes were blue-grey and a little rheumy.

"Not—not usually, no," she said. "I just...it seemed...familiar, somehow. And it had the letters 'G-D' on the box. In silver. Very ornate."

Gindoo stroked his goatee and stared at her under bushy eyebrows. She found him amusing and liked him instantly. But he was less enthusiastic.

"So you received a dress. Yes, well, you're going to the President's Ball, correct? Paul told me," said the little man. "Now you have something to wear. I don't see the problem."

"I—well, it's *because* it felt familiar to me," said Galla, growing frustrated. "I felt like it was mine from long ago, or something. And then I dreamed about it tonight."

She rubbed her neck and glanced over to where Deming was stirring a pot full of flowers. He stole a look at her, and she blushed.

"It was a very vivid dream," she said in low voice.

"Oho!" cried Gindoo, and he cackled and wheezed loudly. "Now I begin to see. *That* sort of dream, eh? Took you somewhere. To someone."

"Yes," she whispered, low enough so that Deming could not hear. *Why do I not want him to hear this, though?* "Someone I must have known."

And Gindoo leaned forward, lowering his eyes to slits. "Go on," he said, and Galla wondered why he was so curious.

She whispered, "Someone with long white hair. We—we...I was... with him. In the dream."

Gindoo leaned back, his gnarled little hands clenched around the knobby head of his cane. He did not take his eyes off her. Several minutes passed. Deming shuffled around and set other experiments going.

"What is it you would like to know, Galla?" asked Gindoo finally.

She blinked, and then furrowed her brow. *Well, what have I ever wanted to know?* she thought, irritated. *Who I am, where I came from, why I'm here. Doesn't everyone wonder those things?* She swallowed.

"Am I supposed to be here?" she asked at last.

Gindoo laughed until he choked. He slapped his chest with his balled fist.

"You *are* here!" he exclaimed. "Bit late for wondering whether or not you *should* be!"

Galla felt her cheeks grow hot.

"I meant...I'm not *from* here," she said, feeling her temper rise. "I know that. I have no memory of my life before the Huntren farm. All I knew was my name: Galla. And I keep having moments, with pain, that make me think I'm trying to remember something. An old life somewhere? I—I am afraid. I feel like I should be doing something. Especially lately. And I'm not doing whatever that is."

Gindoo held up a flask and swirled it. It contained some deep green, opaque liquid.

"Did you have a good life on the farm?" he asked her suddenly. He continued swirling the flask. She watched, engrossed.

"I—yes, I did. I had a family who took me in. I worked for them. They were kind." *Most of the time. Sort of.* "And I helped raise their little boy," she said. *And I miss them*, she thought. *More than I thought I would.* She closed her eyes to remember Meeya's shifting expression, as if the woman tried to resist caring for Galla. And Cuz pulling on his silly, worn old hat and spouting off some gruff remark.

"You were lucky," said Gindoo. "A real family. Maybe it wasn't perfect, but it was real. Something you might never have had, otherwise."

"What?" asked Galla.

Gindoo swirled the flask again.

"You were like this liquid," he said. Deming walked up behind Galla then. "You were amorphous, going from one thing to the next, fluid and volatile and seeking. And then suddenly, you were bottled up. By this world. And it stoppered you. In doing so, it saved you. But it can only hold you for so long. This bottled life of yours has to end, and you have to go back out into the great void. You have to put right the madness afoot, out there. But maybe...maybe not alone, this time."

He set the bottle down. Deming watched him with questioning eyes, then looked back to Galla. The little man opened his desk.

"It's time, now," Gindoo said softly. He brought out a beautiful little box, with a silver design on its cover.

She gasped. "That's the same sort of design as my dress box!"

Deming stepped forward to look, and was amazed when Gindoo gave it to him.

Gindoo sighed. "Well, your brother is out, and this should really go to both of you. I've kept it a long while. And wondered, and waited. But now it is time."

"What is this?" Deming asked, holding it gently and touching the silver design.

"It's a little box, given to your mother long ago," said Gindoo. "There was not much left with you and Paul. They didn't have much time."

And the little fellow sighed again, and looked deeply ancient, and sad. "Your father was a fine lad. I wish he could have stayed here, but he was a seeker. You are like him more than you realize. Implacable. Ah, but there's that bit of your mother in you, too. Stubborn."

And he looked at Galla. "You're correct about the box," he told her. "They're by the same maker. Now, when Deming opens this little box, he won't understand much of it. But his brother might."

"Can I open it now?" asked Deming. Gindoo nodded.

Deming opened the little box next to Galla, for he wanted her to see it, for some reason. They watched as images of a bearded man and a dark-haired woman flashed before them. They were exploring a wooded planet, and its seashore. Eventually, young children accompanied them. And over time, they aged, and their children grew. One day, the man, by then quite aged, began walking toward the woods behind a cabin. He turned and waved, then entered the woods. There was a light shining somewhere beyond the trees. He did not return. The images stopped.

Deming looked at Galla with a puzzled face. Then he turned to Gindoo. "You're right, I don't understand this," he admitted.

"That," Gindoo said, "is just as well. But that man was one of the first humans to venture across the stars. And your mother helped him do it. In fact, she named you after him, partly: Linden Deming Forster."

Deming's eyes popped wide open.

"I've never heard this story!" he exclaimed.

Gindoo ignored him and went on, almost to himself: "They did not know about us, here, because that is the way of this world and its mysteries. Quopeia is selective. The President figured this out very quickly."

"The *President*?" asked Deming. "I'm really confused, Gindoo."

"Likewise," said Galla. "What has any of this to do with me?"

"You are bound up with this family," said Gindoo quietly. "That much is clear. It also is clear that you must go in search of a friend, and gain access to Quepahi."

"Quepahi!" they exclaimed together.

"Yes, well, the very place, yes," said Gindoo, shrugging. "I think the sooner the better, what with winter on the way before long. There are too many convergences happening. Now I see it: your arrival, the dress, perhaps even the Ball is in some way a trigger. I am not sure you should even wait for that! No. It is clear. Deming, you will guide Galla on her journey. Take her to see Caxxius Caxx, who lives in a cave above the Rift. He will help you across."

"But," Deming protested, "Quepahi is a sealed land, a completely wild place. Nobody ever comes out of it alive."

"So the stories tell us," agreed Gindoo. "Which makes it a good place to hide something."

"Like what?" Galla demanded. "What's this to do with me? Why should I go to a Quo continent? We couldn't even fly into it! The electromagnetism would fry anything!"

"Again," said Gindoo, putting a finger to his lips, "very good for hiding. No. Go there, together. As soon as possible. After the Ball, or before the Ball. But decide quickly. Maybe go to the Ball, so as not to arouse suspicion. You're already on the books to attend with Paul. Things are afoot. Quopeia's defenses are strained, clearly. Otherwise that dress would never have got in."

Galla put her hands to her cheeks. "I don't understand *any* of this!

You thought the dress was pretty harmless, earlier. How does the dress have anything to do with Quopeia's defenses?"

"Yes, well," sighed Gindoo, "I changed my mind. Someone got it through, and got it to *you*," Gindoo told her. "That means you must plan to leave. But tell no one."

"What about Dek?" she asked suddenly. "I can't just leave him!"

"You can, and you will," said Gindoo firmly. Galla shot up off her chair. He held up his cane at her. "He will be under my care, do not worry. I'll give him such protections as I can offer. And he can learn from me and assist while Deming is away."

"I do *not* want to leave my brother with a stranger!" she shouted. "To go on some...mission to find some Caxxius Caxx or whoever!"

Gindoo stood, held his cane high, and marched up to Galla to stare up at her.

"Do you want your brother to live?" he demanded.

"Of course!" cried Galla.

"Then do as I advise. The time has come. If Quopeia falls, so goes the galaxy. It is the last fortress. Dek will only be truly safe if you stop the threat. I have done what I could." And Gindoo looked fondly at Deming. "It is time for the children of Ariel and Dagovaby to enter the fray. In many ways, Paul already has. But now, Deming, child, you must as well."

Galla pressed her fingers to her head, which throbbed. Deming looked stunned.

"I don't know what to say," Deming stammered. "I'll go with Galla, though. You can trust me."

Gindoo took one of Deming's hands and squeezed it.

"I know," said Gindoo. "Now take the box, and show your brother. And get some sleep, both of you! I have a feeling things will start to happen very soon."

8

MYSTERY BOXES

Paul did not at first seem moved at all by the little box. He stared at it at the dining table, with one hand supporting his chin and the other one holding the box. He opened and closed it a few times, turned it over, inspected the design, and his face grew stony.

"I don't know what to make of this," he admitted at last. "I don't know the tech, but it seems familiar somehow."

Galla jerked her head upright. "Yes," she said, her breath coming quickly. "And Gindoo said it was from the same maker as the dress box."

"There's nothing threatening about the box," Paul muttered. He glanced at Galla with his bright green eyes. "Nor the dress, honestly. But Gindoo is right about the delivery. He's not saying who this person is, but he knows. Funny old fellow. I can't really go to my department with this, if Gindoo won't give me more info. But now I will be even more on alert than before. As if we didn't have enough on our hands..." and he trailed off.

Deming walked in and handed his brother a folded jacket.

"Best I could do," he said, and Paul unfolded it.

He looked up at his younger brother. "Excellent work. As usual. Thanks, baby bro."

Deming rolled his eyes, and Paul grinned.

"He patches things up for me," he explained to Galla, who watched the interchange nervously. He glanced up again. "What do you think? What's that glowing thing he's going into?" He gestured back at the image of Forster. "Christ, he looks so familiar to me."

"Well," Deming reminded him, "Gindoo did say he knew our mom. Do you think she left some kind of image of him with you?"

"Maybe," muttered Paul. He rubbed his forehead. "I wish I could remember."

Galla locked eyes with him then.

"Yes," she said simply. He nodded.

"Sometimes you don't need telepathy," mused Paul. He reached around and slapped his brother on the back. "Sometimes it's obvious."

Deming sighed. "Well? What's your plan?"

"I don't know. I'll have to think about this. See if I can dig a bit in my own mind, maybe," said Paul thoughtfully. "I'll pay closer attention to everything, though. Don't worry, Galla, we'll be all over that Ball."

She shrugged. "I'm not worried at all."

The brothers looked at each other. Galla could not decipher the look and did not try. They weren't hostile toward each other at the moment, and that was all she wanted to know.

"Here," Paul said suddenly, and he pulled two things from his pocket. One, a small, pearlescent oval, he gave to her first and said, "Get whatever you need for the Ball. Only four more days."

Then he handed her a little box. "Something for your neck," he told her.

She took them from him and said, "Thank you. There's only one more thing I need. I hope there's a slot available."

She left them and returned to her room.

9

———

THE ADVENT OF SOCIAL GRACES

The day of the President's Ball began cloudy, and rain threatened.

Golden-eyed stylist Pear finished tucking a last jewel into Galla's feral hair, and said, "If it rains, I'll murder the sky. I will. Because this? This is my masterpiece today."

Galla looked in the mirror and watched herself smile in delight. She was dressed in a very plain shirt and pants, but her hair had been transformed by Pear into a confection of curls and swoops, with little winking jewels set among the locks of gold, auburn, magenta, violet, copper, and all the other unnamed colors.

"I don't know how long it will hold," she said to Pear. "My hair... does strange things."

Pear looked at her with catlike eyes and said, "It will hold. And if it does not? Then I will have met my match at last!"

"Thank you, Pear," said Galla, and the two hugged briefly.

She received many odd looks as she walked back to Gindoo's boardinghouse. But she felt buoyant. She felt as though anything were possible on a day like today. She walked into the house, went to her room, and stared at the dress box.

Someone knocked at her door, and she opened it to see Paul. He was in a dress shirt and pants, and bare feet. He stared at Galla's hair.

"Well, *that's* different," he said.

Galla rolled her eyes. "Different? Really? That's what you say to your date?"

"Sorry," Paul said with a shrug. "It looks great. Hey, I've arranged for a ride, so you have about one more hour, and then we need to make our way over to meet with Deming. He's going separately."

"Oh, he is?" she asked, finding herself disappointed.

"Yep. We'll meet up with him later. Meet me in the foyer in one hour, okay?"

"Got it," answered Galla, and she closed her door. Another knock sounded.

She opened it, and this time it was Dek.

"Hey," he said, and then his eyes made their way to Galla's hair. The look on his face made her laugh out loud.

"You don't have to say it," she said, "I know it's ridiculous. It'll look better with the dress."

"Okay then," said Dek, and then he said, "Hey, Gindoo wants to meet with me while you're gone. He said he has something important to talk about."

Galla went pale.

"Oh?" she asked, turning away from him. "That's...interesting."

"Yeah. Look," said Dek, rumpling his messy dark, curly hair, "he's not gonna turn me into an animal or anything, is he?"

Galla looked over her shoulder at him and rolled her eyes.

"Not if you don't deserve it," she snapped.

"Do you need anything?" Dek asked, his voice breaking high.

She looked at him with adoring eyes. "Sweetie," she said. "Just a hug."

And they hugged, and Galla felt a stab of regret. Gindoo would tell him something that would change things for them, maybe forever. Dek looked at her as if trying to figure out her expression.

"Well," he said, "have fun! I'm going to raid the kitchen while I can."

She snorted, and Dek grinned and left. She could hear him walking on his lanky legs toward the kitchen. Another knock. She blinked.

This time, it was Deming. She took a deep breath. He was fully dressed in his tuxedo for the Ball. His hair was combed, and his outfit smooth. She had never seen him so polished, or so handsome.

"Come in," she said, and he did so.

They stared at each other. He looked at her hair.

"I love it," he said, and she sighed in relief.

"Thank you."

"I'm leaving soon," he told her. "I just wanted to see if…if you needed any help getting ready?"

She considered. She lifted the lid off the dress box and pulled open the satin coverings. "It's time I dressed. And then, if you could help me with the necklace Paul gave me? I would appreciate it."

Deming turned around while Galla pulled the dress out of the box. He heard its little starbursts tinkle against each other, and the sound of sliding as she let it reach the floor. He could hear her place it softly on her bed. And then he heard her undress, as she had before, with little soft thumps as each item fell onto the floor. She pulled a drawer open with a scraping sound of wood, and shut it, and then he heard a snapping of undergarments. Then the hiss of the dress fabric again, and finally she said, "You may turn around."

So he did, and he was a man staggered. Deming had never felt such an urge in his life as he did right then to take hold of her, lift her in his arms, carry her back to his own room, and shut off the Universe while he kissed every part of her. His hands started shaking.

She looked shyly at him and tried to decipher the emotions flickering across his face, for he said nothing. *Say something,* she thought. *Dammit.*

She bit her lip and said, "Can you help me with my necklace?" and she handed him the little box his brother had given her. He opened it and brought forth a silver and diamond necklace, set with large sapphires that glittered darkly in the fading light. The largest sapphire was worked into the shape of a beetle, surrounded by little diamond legs and antennae.

"He chose well," Deming remarked, and he took it out with trembling fingers. Galla turned her back to him and held up her hair. It took every shred of his willpower not to brush his lips on that smooth neck, where little curls gathered at the nape. Yet somehow, he managed it, though his telltale fingers threatened to drop the necklace as he fastened it. Then he found a gauzy stole on her bed and draped it around her shoulders.

She faced him then, and said, "He did. But it's not my favorite," and she lifted her wrist and stroked the little rainbow-hued bracelet Deming had made for her.

"You're wearing it," he said, beaming.

"I never take it off," said Galla, and they stood very close together.

A loud chime rang out in the room, and they both jumped, and laughed at each other.

Deming sighed. *Damnation!* he thought. Aloud, he said, "That's my ride. I'll see you later?"

"You will," said Galla, and when he left her there, she felt the urge to run after him and tell him...*Tell him what? "Hi, you're my best friend!" How's that?*

She shook herself, then went to her vanity, put on her makeup, slid her shoes on, and waited, fidgeting. Finally, it was time, and she walked to the foyer. Paul met her there, looking model-perfect, and he bowed to her, though not to his usual overblown depth.

"Nobody's going to have a better date than I tonight," he said, smirking indulgently. "Damn!"

She laughed at him. "Come on. Show me your dance moves, mister."

"Gladly," he said, with an impish look in his bright eyes.

THEIR LITTLE AIR taxi whooshed quietly along like a high-speed bubble, and when it stopped, they stepped out into the night. It felt oppressive and sultry, but so far, no rain fell.

Pear won't have to murder the sky after all! she thought.

Galla admired all the various people, humans and non-humans, heading up the broad steps to the brilliantly lit state mansion. There were many elaborate fashions, far more outrageous than hers, but nobody's hair looked like hers, so she stood out in that regard. She held Paul's arm as they made their way up, passing through various security checkpoints with ease. It helped to have someone in the government as your date, she mused.

Inside there was a din of voices, and vibrant faces and outfits and gowns and capes of all sorts. On one hand, Galla adored this colorful display. On the other, she longed to steal away from it all and watch it from a distance, rather than be part of it.

Paul introduced her to so many people, they all blurred together in her mind. She felt a little out of it, and he seemed to sense it. After they'd danced through two songs, he squeezed her hands.

"Let's go find Deming," he suggested. "Get the fuck away from these fake people."

Galla laughed until her shoulders shook.

"You sure you can't read my mind?" she asked.

"Oh God, I wish I could, Galla, I really do," he said, his voice velvety. "But your face really does say *everything*."

They made their way out of the ballroom and through hallways to the end of one long one, at which one of the bars was stationed. There stood Deming, politely and deftly pouring drinks and handing them to guests. He looked up, and she could tell even from that distance that he was relieved to see them.

"I'm already exhausted and the night is young." Paul leaned his elbows on the bar and rubbed his face, then looked up at his brother and groaned. "Hook me up."

Deming poured him a glass of water.

Paul nodded to him.

"Three drops ought to do it."

And Deming pulled something from his jacket pocket. She could see it was a little bottle, and turning away from the crowd, he took out its dropper and let three drops fall into Paul's water.

Galla looked pointedly at Paul. He winked at her, a too-dashing gesture that she noticed had a powerful effect on others. As for her, she grinned.

"I can't have anything traceable that affects my mental state," he explained. "Tonight I needed heightened skills. Sometimes having a tiny wizard in your basement comes in handy. Even better, when his apprentice is my brother."

Clever rogue, she thought.

"What is it like, especially in a crowd like this?" Galla asked in a low tone that only the brothers could hear.

Paul glanced at her, and then turned his dark-lashed, leaf-green eyes back to the ballroom. He brought himself to a ramrod-straight position then, and those eyes swept over the crowd.

He's on the hunt, Galla thought, and she shivered.

"Their thoughts are like a layer of haze or smoke," he said. "I sift through them. One learns to, for the sake of sanity. Sometimes certain thoughts disturb the haze, so I sense waves or ripples through it all. Then I know something's up."

He paused then, staring ahead, grateful for Galla's absent mental signals and his brother's disciplined mind. A tiny twitch moved in his jaw.

"One more dance," he whispered to them.

Galla glanced at Deming, who also watched the crowd. She met his gaze. He looked troubled but said nothing.

"Are you ready?" Paul asked more loudly. "Last official dance, then the speeches. After this dance, you're relieved of duty."

He looked down at Galla with an inscrutable face. She looked up at him uncertainly but set her mouth in an elegant smile. She straightened and took his arm and nodded.

But before they walked away from Deming, Galla said to him, "Save a dance for me." He raised his eyebrows and gave her a nod. His expression was level, and she closed her eyes for a second. *Does he not want to dance with me?*

Paul pulled her away from her thoughts by making a display, sweeping into the crowd again with her on his arm. They made a stunning pair, him in his full formal attire, his flawless bronze skin, green eyes, and bright smile charming everyone, and she in her sapphire gown with moving starbursts, crystals in her elaborate hair, and proud posture. The murmurings increased as everyone in the room turned to watch them. It did not take telepathy for her to realize they all wanted to know who she was. And she was heart-glad they did not.

The musicians signaled the song for the final dance. The guests ceased their chatter. The notes began slowly, then gained momentum, and Paul waltzed and spun Galla over the dance floor with perfect moves.

Which is well and good that he's leading, since I'm a complete dunderhead at this!

"Make small talk," he whispered. "Keep it neutral."

Galla dipped her head as if he'd told her she looked ravishing, and smiling, she said with an uplifted face, "Thank you."

He looked at her then, and said, "Oh believe me, the pleasure is all mine."

"Maybe not all of it," and she made herself coquettish, lowering and lifting her eyebrows.

"*Fuck!* You're good at this," he said, softly into her ear. "You sure you don't want to sign up with us? God, the damage you'd do."

Galla blushed then and let out a high trill of laughter. She whispered back, "I may need you more than you need me, one day. Something to keep in mind."

"I like the sound of that," he said, his lips curving. He tilted her back in the dance, pulled her back up, and whispered, "I hope to God Deming's not watching too closely."

She turned into his neck to hide her face then.

And then the music ended. He bowed to her and kissed her hand.

"My lady," he said, with the smallest wink of mischief.

He nodded, and Galla understood he had someplace to be. Fanning herself delicately, she made her way out of the crowd. A waiter approached with a tray.

"A beverage for the most beautiful?" he asked.

She barely glanced at him, for she strained to watch for Paul's movements as she searched for a route back to Deming.

"Thank you," she said absently, taking the drink. It was deep ultramarine in hue, held in a crystal goblet. She sniffed it and thought it smelled divine, like every summer fruit she'd ever loved, mixed with sun-warmed flowers. She took a sip.

She began walking out of the crowd but was stopped constantly by others.

"What a lovely gown!" one said.

"Look at her hair!"

"Magnificent dancing," and so on.

She felt on edge. So she drank more of the heady, delicious cocktail. Finally she made her way out of the civilized bedlam and took a deep breath.

She felt a little dizzy. Everything took on a blue-tinged hue. She stood in a dim hallway, with little alcoves, and dark curtains and pillars. Some of the alcoves hosted trysts, or people chatting quietly. She walked more slowly, really feeling more euphoric by the second. She even waved at one trio in an alcove, and they quickly drew a curtain for privacy.

Then she found herself dancing along, repeating in slow motion some of the dance moves Paul had shown her. She took another drink.

Where is Deming? For that matter, where am I?

And she swayed and made her way carefully to an alcove that shone with pale light. The air made cracking and snapping noises. She felt drawn to that light. And then she stood before something, or someone, made of the pale light itself.

It was a person, tall, all in black despite the light, but his hair was long and white, and he reached his arms out to her.

She looked down at her drink, then up again, and a laugh bubbled out of her.

And the person spoke: "Have I found you, Galla-Deia?"

And she felt as though everything spun. It was the person in her dream, the one she had made love to. She felt frightened then, and the glass slipped from her hand, smashing onto the floor. She turned away, and felt as if everything had slowed: time, herself, and reality. She dared not turn to look behind her, and she tried to run, but her legs were now numb. So she staggered away, vision blurred, scared.

"Deming!" she cried. "Deming, please!"

She could not see him, could not find the bar. Tears formed in her eyes.

Help me! she thought wildly.

And then, gentle hands caught her arms, and she looked up, and there he was, his kind, dark eyes full of dismay at her state.

"Galla! What's happened?"

He led her back toward an exit, not far from the ballroom. Security was pressed in tight at the entrance for the ballroom, for the President was now speaking.

Not knowing what else to do, Deming thought, *Paul! Something's happened to Galla! I'm going to try and help her.* He hoped his broadcast had worked.

There was a disturbance, and they could not hear the President's voice anymore.

Then, a shout.

A man held his hand high in the ballroom and said, "It is over! We will make it better!" His face sweated, its expression steeped in madness. And he made a symbol with his fingers, and then clenched his fist.

Deming seized Galla's hand and they ran out the door.

A great clap ripped through ballroom. Galla could see the blossom of white and blue and orange shred everything in sight. She turned rapidly to Deming and jumped onto him to shield him, and they were flung several feet by the explosion. She covered him with her whole body, even her hair spread out around him, and felt glass and stone pummel her back.

He screamed below her, *"Galla! Galla, no!"*

10

———

DRAUGHT

In the chaos, with sirens blaring and his own hearing muffled from the blast, Deming carried Galla in his arms on back streets and away from streetlamps. *I wanted to carry you. But not like this.*

He stopped once, when they were far enough away from the carnage. He leaned against a tree, with her pressed up against his chest, and he openly wept then. *Paul. Paul.* Nothing. Not that he expected anything. Paul did not have a habit of tampering with his brother's mind, except to read his thoughts and tease him.

You can tease me forever. Just be okay. Please.

After resting, he pushed on, and did not stop again until at last he saw his own familiar street. As soon as he set foot upon it, all its lights winked out. His shoulders relaxed. Gindoo knew he was coming, then.

He made it to the walk at the boardinghouse, and a slim shape darted out of it. It was Dek. The boy's face contorted at the sight of Galla, but he took hold of her legs, and the two of them brought her inside. Gindoo stood inside the foyer, wobbling on his cane, his eyes now wide.

"Take her down."

At the command, Deming and Dek carefully carried her down and down and down, in dim flickering sconce light, and the stairs seemed to stretch for leagues. Deming's legs trembled and threatened to fold. Gindoo, remarkably, kept nimble pace behind them. He nipped past them somehow, and Deming thought idly, *Did he float down?* but his mind was too imprisoned in its torment to think much about it.

Gindoo raised his cane, and all his papers and samples and books swept into one high arc and settled on the floor in stacks, leaving his wide desk clear.

"Put her on her side, so I can see her back," he said, and they did so.

Dek looked frozen. He stared at Galla, not knowing what else to do. He was too stunned to focus.

Gindoo lifted Galla's hair and undid her necklace, and it slid onto the desk, then onto the floor below. Dek reached down for it and closed his hand around it in a fist, then shoved it in his pocket.

"Deming," Gindoo said, "help with her dress, lad."

There was no time to dwell on anything but helping her, so Deming tenderly peeled back her shrapnel-shredded dress to reveal her back. He gasped in shocked relief: there was no blood spilled. Large, red-purple bruises stained her skin.

"Hold her in place," the little man said crisply. Deming held her still.

Gindoo brought forth a magnifying scope that fit over his eye and studied Galla's back, her spine, her skin, and stopped above her pelvis. Then he pushed the strap of the scope onto the top of his grizzled head.

"None of her skin is broken," he announced. "She has deep bruises. She took the full bore of the blast."

Deming shook violently. "She shielded me from it."

"Like father, like son," muttered Gindoo, and Dek blinked at him. Deming did not hear him.

"Is she going to die?" Dek asked abruptly. "Don't hide it from me!

Is she?" His face looked stern, and Deming could see in it the strength of a growing man.

He's holding it together better than I am, he thought with affection.

Gindoo squinted up at Dek.

"Not today, boy," he answered. He folded his arms. "I think she's concussed. But, mercifully, she seems to be a little anesthetized. Deming, what in Siloxxa's fire did you give her to drink?"

It all came back in a rush to him then. He answered, "Nothing. She had nothing from me. But when I found her, she was staggering around, completely out of it."

"Drunk?" asked Gindoo, raising his eyebrows.

"Absolutely smashed," agreed Deming. "That, or poisoned. She seemed frightened by something, too."

"Poisoned!" shouted Dek. Then he broke into tears. "This is too much."

The old man walked around to look at Galla's face. He pushed her lips aside to see her teeth and took a swab and wiped them. He held it up, grimaced, and then hobbled over to a shelf. He looked up.

"Deming, can you get me the 9-4-7?" he asked in his wheezy voice.

The young man reached above him and brought down a vial. Knowing his teacher well, he found a small dish. Gindoo nodded at him, and Deming poured a bit of the clear liquid out of the vial labeled "9-4-7" into the dish. Gindoo stuck the swab in and swirled it around. The liquid turned deep blue, almost black in the flickering light.

"Is that..." Deming began.

"It is!" exclaimed Gindoo. "Stroffy liqueur."

"But *you* make it!" said Deming.

"Yes, well. I do. And one other," said Gindoo. He tapped his chin. "Yes indeed. Only two of us, in the whole galaxy. Of course, the bulbenberries are native to Quopeia. How long has it been?" And he stared off with his rheumy eyes, into the past.

"Not poisoned, then," he announced. "It was deliberate. I do think that. But it was meant to *protect* her. She took a bit too much of it, and that's partly why she's out cold now."

He looked at Galla's still face, pale and thin. Some of the little jewels still shone in her hair, but the rest of her hair lay in all directions, not moving. He wiped his ancient hand across her brow.

"This lass," he said with a sigh. "So much already, and so much more to come. Don't let it harden you back to stone, lass. Yes, young Dek, too much indeed. Given the state of her, I'll need your help, boy. Get her things ready. As soon as she's able, Deming, you have to take her."

"I understand," said Deming. He ran his hands through his hair, and then tucked it behind his ears. "Any news from Paul?"

Gindoo glanced up at something across the room. "Not yet," he answered, but they watched him as he waddled over to a little dark globe in a recessed shelf. "Still black."

"What is that?" asked Dek, and only now did he feel relaxed enough to take in his surroundings. He had a feeling he would get to know everything in that room very well, before long. And he thought he liked the idea.

"A communicator, after a fashion," Gindoo replied, and he chortled. "I'm glad it's black, let me tell you!"

Deming sagged onto a stool next to Galla and looked simultaneously exhausted and relieved. "So he's alive." He found her hand with the bracelet he'd made for her, and he held it in his. *And she's alive.* He thought he could sleep for years, just then.

"Can we take her to her room?" he asked.

"Yes, well, why not?" answered Gindoo, pulling on his goatee braids. "Nothing more we can do. She has to sleep it off. She won't like how she feels in the morning, oh no! But I daresay, that special Stroffy is the best, and maybe the only, painkiller that will even work on her. They knew what they were doing. Yes, things are moving fast indeed. Get her up to bed. Then the two of you need to sleep, yourselves. I've had enough drama tonight! Get out of here, will you?"

Dek snickered at that, thinking he was in for quite the experience as a pupil of Gindoo. Deming gave him a sidelong look and shook his head. "It's not all *that* fun," he whispered.

"I heard that!" called Gindoo as they carried Galla up the stairs.

When they reached her room, Dek pulled back her bedcovers, and Deming laid her down on the soft bed. Dek reached in and kissed her on the cheek.

"I'll tell Mom and Dad everything," he said.

Deming said, "They'll be glad to know you're all right. I don't even know if the President survived. I guess we'll know soon enough. You've got some strange days ahead, my friend."

"I've never felt more alive!" said Dek.

"I know the feeling," replied Deming, watching Galla's chest rise and fall slowly as she slept. "If she's awake before dawn, we'll leave then. I don't think we can risk staying another night. She'll want to say goodbye."

"Better get to sleep then. Wake me up, will you?" Dek asked, and he turned and left with a sigh.

Deming heard him shut his door. He sat carefully on the bed next to Galla and plucked all the jewels out of her hair, setting them in a little bowl on her vanity table.

"It's probably good that you don't leave a little trail of jewels behind you on our trip," he said in a low voice. She stirred then, and turned on her side to face him, her dress slipping off one shoulder. His hands twitched from a desire to set the strap back on her shoulder, but she looked comfortable now. Her color had come back. He bent his head into his hands and said, "We never had our dance."

And she stirred again, and her eyelids fluttered, and he froze. She blinked a little, moaned and touched her forehead, and then fell back asleep. He left her and slipped back around the house to his room to start packing.

11

RUNAWAYS

The pen scratched in the little notebook, and driblets of ink dotted the lined page. *"This is my last entry in this notebook. I'm leaving it behind, and taking a new one with me. Still no word from Paul. Paul, if you're reading this, give me some kind of sign, will you? I am going with Galla to Quepahi. I don't even know what to say. I'm just writing to calm myself. I forgot what life was like before I met her. I don't care where, I don't care what happens. I'll go with her."*

So Deming placed a fresh notebook and his pen inside his backpack, and checked and double-checked his supply list. His pack was ready.

A staccato rattle on his door told him it was almost time to go. He opened it, and Dek said, "She's as ready as she's ever going to be. *Oh man.*"

The floors creaked and popped as he made his way to the foyer, where he let his pack slip onto the floor. He had already stowed part of their food, and he had another supply for Galla's pack. She walked out then, and stood facing him with haunted eyes. She set her pack beside his, and they let the moments pass. Then she ran at him, and he caught her in his arms, and they both let out something between a sob and a laugh.

She spoke into his neck. "Dek says Paul is alive. Do you know anything else?"

"No," he said into her hair.

They separated then. The floor squeaked behind Deming, and Gindoo appeared. He gave a little bottle to Deming, who stowed it in his vest. Dek joined Galla. She stepped forward and bent to hug Gindoo, and she kissed his forehead. He swayed a bit, and held fast to his cane, and pulled on his goatee, but his eyes squeezed together like two little smiles.

As for Dek, Galla felt heavy in every step that took her back to him, and she hugged him tightly and tidied his hair, her face shining with tears.

"Tell Cuz and Meeya that I'll be in touch with them, someday. I don't know when. But I promise that," she said with a quivering lip. "I love you."

"Love you, Sis," Dek muttered, tears runnelling down his cheeks.

She zipped up her jacket, and they opened the door. Gindoo stepped out first, and waved his cane around, and the air grew very still. It had rained, finally, and the lane was a dark, slick band curving out of sight, all its lights again extinguished. So she shouldered her pack, and she and Deming set forth, turning back to wave to the people they loved, both sending outward all the hope they had that Paul was safe.

They walked for several blocks in the darkness, melding into the shadows, and toward the orchards and the park. The air was damp and cold, yet not freezing. When they reached the end of the park, Deming finally spoke.

"I think we can risk our mountain trail," he said, "but we'd better hurry. Another two hours and the sun is up. Can you do it? Are you all right?"

She felt steady enough to feel a spark of mutiny. She swept her escaped hair back from her cheeks and said, "I am as far from all right as you can ask, right now. My body hurts *everywhere*, my headache makes me want to break a tree in half, and my heart, well. I think I left it behind, somewhere back there."

He lowered his head and adjusted the straps on his pack.

"Dammit, Galla," he muttered. "At least you're alive."

"At least *you* are." And she kicked the fallen leaves at the trailhead.

"I can thank you for that, I know," he said. "Why did you do that?"

"Are you *serious*?" she hissed, but really, she wanted to scream it.

This is not going to work, she thought. *We're arguing and we've barely started.*

Furious, she started marching up the trail, and he made a frustrated sound with his throat, but she pushed ahead of him anyway. He caught up with her, and she sped up more.

"What are you doing?" he asked her, puffing again next to her. She kept trudging.

"You don't have to go with me," she said, halting suddenly.

His eyebrows crinkled up.

"Yes, I do," he responded.

"No, you don't. You almost died. Hours ago. You'd be safer if you stayed."

Deming took hold of her chin and lifted her head up. "Bullshit," he said. "You *saved my life*. How am I any safer back there, without you, than I am here? I don't have any special powers of any kind. But I know my way in this country, and you don't."

"Impossible man," she said, not looking at him. She backed away from him and started hiking again. Her head raged and her stomach protested. She felt too much just then.

Then she stopped and realized they had reached the clearing where they had sampled before. And she moved forward and found the overlook to the City. Behind it, a thin, ember glow of dawn threaded the horizon. Lume had already set. Deming walked up beside her, and they looked at the lights below, shimmering among the remaining leaves. The wind swished the high canopy and shook off the earlier rain down onto their heads. They both donned their hoods. They turned to each other.

"I'm sorry," said Deming. "I know, deep down, you don't really need me. But I really do want to help. And if I went back there, not knowing about Paul, and having you out here alone...no. I'm going with you, to the very end."

Galla felt as though the mountain would slide out from under her.

"I'm sorry," she said, blinking her aching eyes, and then wincing. Even if she wanted to cry anymore at the moment, she could not. "I don't know what to say. I feel terrible, responsible for what happened. I can't stand putting you at risk. But you seem to be beyond hope, as far as your stubbornness."

"Mm," said Deming, his mouth twitching. "I've heard that one before. And also, what? How are you responsible for a terrorist attack?"

"Something happened to me, right before the explosion. I was given a drink, and then I saw something. In one of those weird little alcoves in the mansion. Something glowing. And I went over to look at it, and—" and here she stopped, and leaned over, dry-heaving. She waved off his concern. She stood back up. "There was a man, or—or —a being, and he spoke to me, but it was like he was a hologram or something. And he said, 'Have I found you, Galla-Deia?' And I...well, truth be told, I panicked. That's when I went looking for you. Deming, that person? He was in a dream I had when I first got the blue dress. I know him, somehow."

Deming looked thoughtful. Then he said slowly, "Galla-Deia. The G-D on your dress box, then? Okay, that's all very strange, I understand that. But in *no* way do I think this is related to the attack. We saw the attacker. And let's hope he was the only one. But this other person? He doesn't sound like he was a threat. In fact, I think he was trying to help you."

"What?" she asked, startled.

"Gindoo said you had a glass of Stroffy liqueur," he said, "and while it's rare—he's one of only two people who make it, apparently —he thought this person knew how it would affect you. That it might protect you. And it did! It numbed you before the blast."

"But wouldn't that imply this person knew about the blast?" she asked, feeling unease crawling up her very sore back.

"Maybe he knew something would happen, but there wasn't anything else he could do about it?" pondered Deming. "After all, it was an image you saw, not the person himself. It's obvious he's a mage, like Gindoo. Mages do weird things, what can I say? I've worked with one my whole life. But no matter what, this wasn't your fault. Things are happening out there, Gindoo says, that we've so far avoided. And now that's over."

Galla shivered. "That's what the attacker said."

Deming grimaced. "Why don't we put some mileage between us and that situation? It's almost dawn."

"Agreed."

They hiked on in silence, stopping only to relieve themselves or to eat, and they walked for several miles without seeing anyone. They were well beyond the outer borders of Allurulla by mid-afternoon, and in fact the trail had begun winding downward toward the sea. Deming chose a fork of the trail that went northward.

"It's best if we head for the Strait," he told her. "Then we can at least sail across that instead of going all around it to the south."

"Sail!" exclaimed Galla. "Sail in *what*?"

"Gindoo has an old boat up there, though it's been years since I've used it."

"Wait, you *sail* too?" Galla looked at him with awe. "What can't you do?"

"Too many things to list!" he said, brushing off the compliment. "I don't have any real powers, like Paul."

"I don't think you need them," she said seriously. "Your skills are powerful enough!"

He looked at her with a tolerant sort of disbelief in his dark eyes, and went on, "Anyway, if we sail the Strait, and cut across, it'll cut off an enormous amount of time to get to the Rift and Quepahi."

"You make it sound easy," she marveled.

"Oh, it won't be."

It started to rain, and they entered the lowlands of the mountain range, and could see in the distance a broad, hilly, rocky land, and beyond that, the palest sliver of the sea. She thought about what she might have done, had she gone on her own. She had not thought at all about sailing. *I might have walked forever and never got very far.*

"I guess I do need you, then," she said.

12

STITCHES

Late in the day, the sun broke forth, and they were cheered and energized by it. Both of them were sore from the blast and fatigued from stress and the hike. The initial thrill of a new adventure had worn off, and having Siloxxa appear at the right time set them on a final burst. Deming directed them to a large set of boulders, away from any settlements, and found a good spot for a tent. It was then they realized, finally, that staying in close quarters every night would be their new routine.

They raised the tent, and Galla spread out a blanket on its floor and unrolled their sleeping bags. Deming started the fire and set a little pot going over it. He added water, herbs, and some dried foods from his pack's supply. Soon the soup was bubbling, and he tore up a dried, long bread loaf he had made a few days prior, for dunking in the soup. Galla stretched her sore muscles and winced at every twist. He watched her as he stirred the soup, his thoughts tossing back and forth, but he said little.

"The least we can do is eat well, for a little while anyway," he said finally, holding out a bowl to her.

She sat across from him in front of the fire and ate the soup slowly, savoring every sip. It filled her with warmth and soothed her in a very different way. It was as if he were saying to her, without speaking the words, *See, I am of some use, after all. I can't read minds, but I can make you feel better, and that is what you really need.*

And she did not know how to repay his kindness, except to praise his work. She cleaned the bowls and tidied up, and they banked the fire with what wood they could find. Then they sat next to each other and stared into the flames, their faces roasting and the sparks spinning skyward into a cloudy, dark night. The pain inside Galla faded, and the worry as well, at least a little. They seemed far from any trouble, and soon she grew so drowsy that she crawled on hands and knees into the tent. She stripped down to her undershirt and leggings and coiled up in her sleeping bag. Soon Deming crept in next to her, settled into his own bag, and they said nothing, just listened to the dying fire pop and crack.

They woke at the same time the next morning and turned on their sides to look at each other. Deming's hair was flattened on one side from heavy sleep, and the other side flared up. Galla laughed at him, and he pointed at her own hair, which was tangled and frizzing from the humidity.

Sitting up, she said, "Did something wake you up? I thought I heard something. Like thunder, maybe?"

"I thought I felt something," said Deming with a wide yawn. "Like a shallow earthquake."

"There aren't usually earthquakes here, are there?" she asked. He shook his head.

"Not until you get out to the Northwest, near the Rift. These are very old, worn mountains, and they aren't geologically active."

The sky hung low and grey and dark, but no rain fell. They packed up, buried the evidence of their fire, and set forth. She felt uneasy for some reason and kept looking over her shoulder, as if expecting someone to be following them. Deming noticed, and occasionally did the same. The ground sloped slowly downward, but the going was rough around the huge glacial boulders. Still, they felt the urge for speed. The strange sound or boom or quake that had awakened them put them both on edge, and they said little to each other for hours.

After they'd stopped for a snack lunch, the wind shifted, and Galla could smell a hint of salt air from the north. The air was also much colder, and that did not excite her in the least. Still they pressed on. Neither wanted to talk about the Ball again, but it was close in their minds, and Deming thought again of Galla throwing him out of harm's way and shielding him, even with her hair. He sensed that she did not know she could do such a thing, and he wondered what else she was capable of. There seemed to be so much about her that remained hidden, and he wanted to learn all of it.

Where did she come from? Are there others like her? He had so many questions, yet he knew she could not answer them. He hoped they would reach their destination so they both could get answers.

The sky remained a hazy pewter into the afternoon. The wind grew fiercer and colder, and soon they would need to find a place to camp for the night. The sea was no longer in view as the land flattened a bit, but they could smell it more strongly all the time on the north wind. They reached a small valley, and Deming could see off to the south some low buildings that looked weather-beaten and damaged, like old barns.

Galla followed his gaze and felt a chill. Everything about this place seemed derelict, but why? Was the land infertile? Was it just too difficult to build, with all the boulders? Working the land in this world was harder than on other worlds, because of the problems with electromagnetism. Machinery would work occasionally, but not consistently. They had adapted in the Southwest, and obviously Allurulla had the benefit of being a stable pocket of Orboaanya. Here, though, on the northern edge of the continent, the influence of the Quo continents must already have an effect, she guessed. That still did not relieve her of her crawling sense of unease.

A loud *shiff* sound came from their left. And off to the north of the valley, they saw a line of beasts staring at them. They were huge and covered in red and black fur. She heard a series of growls and turned swiftly to Deming.

"What are those?" she asked, her mouth agape.

He was staring at them, his arms out and down. "Technically they're called kayalhaas. Colloquially? Shavers."

"Um," said Galla, holding onto her pack, ready to run, "why are they called shavers, exactly?"

"Because they can shave your face right off," said Deming in a cracking voice. And the beasts bound toward them at high speed. "Oh, *fuck*! Run!"

They started running, and Deming shouted, "Drop the packs! We'll get them later!" *Maybe*, he thought, but he shoved that panic down.

They dropped their packs and ran for their lives, but the beasts were much faster and soon overcame them. They passed Deming by as if he were invisible and bounded in full pursuit of Galla. He saw their eyes, and there was something in them as they lunged past: desperation, and madness. Where had he seen that look before? This was not normal. And they were converging on Galla.

She shrieked, for the pack had jumped upon her, and the horrible sound of ripping and tearing met Deming's ears and made him enraged. He ran at the beasts, screaming and waving his arms to distract them, but again they ignored him. Galla's cries became more muffled.

Deming then panicked fully. He brought out a packet from his vest and rubbed it between his hands. He ran at the pack and yelled, "Hey!" and when they did not respond, he blew on the packet and threw it into the air toward them. It burst into green flame with a loud boom and set the fur of the animals ablaze, and they let out howls that bounced across the countryside and back again, echoing from the boulders and chilling him to his marrow. And they ran off then, driven insane in their burning agony, in all directions, but away from him and Galla.

He ran to her and found her clothes shredded to ribbons, hanging off her, exposing bruised, but once again unbroken, skin. She lay immobile from the pain, and he could see the marks of teeth all through her, denting and bruising her face and her arms and neck. Letting out a desperate moan, he picked her up and carried her back to where they had dumped their packs.

"I'm sorry, I'm so sorry," he said to her, convulsing in horror and rage.

He set her down, and she fell onto her side and seized up in a fetal position. She could not speak through her pain. She shook constantly. He quickly set up their tent and built a fire. Then he picked her up again and held her in his arms as he sat before the fire and rocked her, for he did not know what else to do. She let out a yelp of pain, and he readjusted her. Then he felt the little bottle in his vest that Gindoo had given him, and he pulled it out. It bore the words: "Stroffy. Two or three drops, as needed, under the tongue."

He looked up at the sky and then closed his eyes. "He thought ahead," he murmured. To Galla, he said, "Can you sit up and drink something?"

She nodded, though it was hell for her. She could barely focus through her pain and shock.

"First, water," he said, and gave her a flagon. "Now, a little bit of Stroffy, not too much."

"Again?" she asked in a hoarse voice.

"Just a tiny bit," he said, holding the dropper. She leaned forward and opened her mouth, and he dispensed three drops of the liquid under her tongue. Then he lifted her up, set her down on her sleeping bag, and lit phyron lamps.

"Oh, ow," she hissed, straining to sit up.

"Wait," said Deming, handing her a blanket, "get under this, and take your clothes off."

"What?" she asked.

"They're in pieces," he answered, and she finally looked down at her body, and winced at the sight. "I'm going to fix them."

"How are you going to do that?" she croaked.

"I'm prepared," he muttered, and he brought out a little envelope with needle and thread.

She managed to think, *Is he real? Am I imagining him?*

"I'll take care of this, and you can sit back and relax."

"It hurts too much," she said faintly. "I can't sleep right now."

"One or two more drops, then?" he asked, pulling the vial from his shirt.

She made a raspberry sound. "No more, please. I'll let myself shriek all night, but I've had enough of *that*. How did you scare off those animals?"

He felt his muscles relax. She was well enough to talk, though obviously still in great pain. The Stroffy liqueur was taking effect, and her cheeks pushed up her mouth into a tipsy, wincing sort of grin.

"Gindoo's training has its advantages," he said with a shrug. "Like I said, I'm prepared."

She managed to sit up on one elbow and stare at him.

"How can I thank you for this?"

Deming shot her a stunned look. "Um, you did just save my life the other day, in case you forgot. There's no thanks needed."

"Not...not anything?" she asked, and then she blushed. *Where was I going with this? Ah...I hurt too much to think straight. But I do feel better now.*

"Um," said Deming. He cleared his throat tactfully. "You could tell me a story, if you're up for it. But no pressure. It might be best if you just slept."

"I think I can manage, for a bit," she said eagerly. "What sort of story?"

"The only one I care about," he murmured. "The story of you."

They sat in silence for a moment. The logs on the fire outside their open tent sagged and shifted and hissed. Deming began to work on repairing her shredded garments.

"So...what was your life like ...before Dek?" Deming asked her.

"I lived on the Huntren farm, before he was adopted." Her eyes glazed over, reaching back in her shattered memory. Everything seemed to hit the same wall in her mind, and it hurt her head to try to push that wall. "Cuz—the farmer—said that I was burned, that he and his wife, Meeya, found me completely naked and hairless, buried in the ground. The only thing I could even say for a long time was my name." She smiled ruefully.

Deming's face fell. "It sounds like you crashed. That's so awful." Galla closed her eyes.

"The Huntrens took me in without question," she went on. "But I think, when I try to remember now, they must have been afraid at first. And they didn't know what to do with me. But they found out I was strong enough to help them. All I ever wanted to do was to help. So that's what I did. I stayed on the farm for years, never leaving."

"So...you hid from everyone?"

"I don't know if I hid," replied Galla. "Not consciously, anyway. For a long time, I just really didn't want to leave. I was afraid to, for some reason. And Meeya refused to let me go far. I was comfortable, but at the same time, I didn't feel like I belonged. But I stayed, and they adopted Dek. I was like a nanny to him at first, and later like a sister." She blinked in fatigue. "And of course, as he grew, I didn't change much. Another mystery of me. I think..."

Deming sighed. "I keep thinking there's this barrier with you," he mused. "Something keeping you from whatever came before."

"A wall?" she asked.

"No...a box, maybe," said Deming thoughtfully. "A box inside you that needs to be opened. Right now, it's closed, and you can't open it."

"I never thought of it being a box," she said, "but maybe you're right."

Galla glanced at his kind face, with its new stubble making him look much more mature, and she bit her lip. He bent over the sewing work, drawing the thread in and out of the fabric of her ravaged clothes deftly, carefully. His focus on it impressed her, as did the work itself. *He has so many talents,* she thought. *But he doesn't really show them to anyone. Except me.*

She felt so at ease with him at that moment that she wanted to tell him anything and everything, even in her exhausted state. "You remember Dek saying I cried every night? I don't remember ever doing that. But I trust him. I think I'm afraid to move on with my life."

Deming set the repair work down. He leaned over, brushed away her hair from her forehead, and said, "Forget about all that for now and get some rest."

She nodded off, and in her sleep, she wept. Deming, startled from his notebook, moved closer to her. He was wracked with indecision and sympathy. *I don't know what to do for her.*

He touched her cheeks as lightly as he could. She stilled, and breathed deeply and softly, now in a calm sleep. Even in the low light of his phyron lamp, he could see that her dried tears shimmered pale purple. He drew his fingers back and tilted them under the lamp, watching the tiny violet crystals twinkle in the light. Every part of him shook, and he looked at her with almost unbearable feeling.

He took his pen and scrawled into his new little notebook: "*Universe, you brought her to me. I believe that. She doesn't know this, but I would do anything for her. And I've never felt so helpless at the same time.*"

He looked over at her again and extinguished the lamp.

13

TEAK

Will the wind never stop? Galla splashed water on her face, and the chilly air woke her senses. Every muscle hurt, but she had no headache, so that was something. She thought over the day before and shook her head. She considered every possibility, but the fact that Deming was ignored while she was attacked looped over and over in her mind. It seemed so deliberate.

Deming looked grim-faced. He pulled out a slender packet of something and poured a bit of it into two mugs, and then added hot water. A smell of spices rose, a comforting scent, and she walked over to investigate.

"I was going to wait and surprise you with this another time," he said, looking up at her with a half-smile. "But I think you've earned it today." He handed her a steaming tin mug.

"What is it?" she asked. "Not sylcaah?"

He tilted his head in agreement.

"It won't be as good as fresh, but it's the best I could come up with."

"You really are a mage, then," she said, taking a sip and enjoying the warmth and strength of it. She held her mug up to his, and they tapped them together.

"You seem much better today," he said.

"I feel somewhat better, but I'm so sore it hurts to move. Maybe once we get going it won't be so bad, but I dread the backpack especially. It's not been the best few days." She stretched her back and winced. "I just don't understand it. I mean, I'm glad they went for me and not for you. But why did they do that? Why did they attack at all?"

"I've been thinking about that, and I can't come up with any good explanation. Shavers can be vicious when provoked—hence their name. But I've never heard of a wild pack just attacking someone before. There was something in their eyes…"

Galla shuddered. She had seen it as well, for their snapping and ripping faces had bitten right onto hers. There was a strange, glazed gleam about them. Not simple madness: something else.

"They seemed possessed," he said.

"Or driven to it," muttered Galla. Deming looked at her, alarmed, and reached over to squeeze her hand.

"I hope that's the last we see of them."

"No doubt they'll remember not to mess with a mage," said Galla with a smirk.

"I'm not really a mage," Deming said, his head bowed. "I just make things."

"Things that save lives, yes, so maybe you're a doctor?"

"Then you are as well," he said, nudging her with his elbow. He sniffed. "Maybe you can get rid of this cold for me?" She squeezed his hand back.

They broke down the camp in much better moods, although when Galla shouldered her backpack she swore for a few minutes. Deming hid his expression, for her verbal gusto made him want to laugh, and it relieved him as well. The going was tedious, with the wind ever in their faces, and the sky was mottled silver and pearl. Siloxxa refused to show itself directly. Their way took them downward in elevation, and finally around midday the sea covered the horizon. They hurried through lunch and set forth, and other than small flocks of animals winging above them, they saw little wildlife that day.

For the first time in a few days, Galla felt buoyant. She could tell Deming did as well, although she did not know how much of that related to his relief at her recovery. She began to feel confident that they would be able to get to Quepahi without much incident. A stray pack of insane wild animals would become less likely in the colder Northwest, or so she hoped. She pushed that potentiality aside and focused on the sea, which she had never been to, and charged ahead. She gritted her teeth at the pain all over her body and face and soldiered on.

They made it to the shore by late afternoon, and Galla let slip her backpack and sprang ahead at a run. Deming caught up with her and set his pack down, and watched her shed her boots and socks and roll up her pants.

"That water is frigid even in high summer," he called, but she ignored him and walked across a painfully stony beach and into the small bay with its little gentle waves.

Galla sucked in her breath at the bitter cold of the water but did not let him see her reaction. She faced north and tried to make out the distant Quo land on the other side, but the far shore was shrouded in fog, and the fata morgana effect was strange, as if tall castles loomed into the sky. She watched red-beaked shorelets run along the dark grey sand and rock, darting their bills into the tidal barrier, then snapping up the creatures that tried to scurry down into the wet sand. She wondered what made the great splashes farther into the bay and she breathed in eagerly the briny scent of the air. The rocks at the shore were draped with seaweed, and here and there little clumps of red and brown and yellow algae were heaped on the beach. She turned back to the shore, where Deming was watching her, and she felt her cheeks burn and her insides quiver. She turned her head to look up and down the shore, and she strained her eyes, trying to make out distant shapes to the east.

She waded back in and said, pointing, "Are those houses, down there?"

Deming walked out onto the beach to follow her gaze, and said, "Those are old fishing huts. In summer, sometimes people still use them, but they're mostly abandoned. It's not an easy living up here, so only nomads tend to come. Are you ready to move on? The sailboat is just a bit to the west."

She nodded, and sat to dry and brush the sand off her feet and put her socks and boots back on. They walked forward, along the edge of the shore, with the high, rocky hills to their left and the bay to their right, and by and by the fog out on the Strait moved in toward them. The light grew dimmer and more diffuse, and Galla wondered if they would make it to the boat before sundown, when suddenly a wooden structure rose in the distance.

"That's the boathouse, where it's dry-docked," said Deming. And again they felt a burst of energy and picked up their pace.

But Galla noticed soon the scent of smoke. They reached the boathouse just as the sun began to set, and they could see a small fire on the other side of it. Deming raised his hand for them to stop. He bent over and sneezed into his elbow, and then tensed up. They watched and listened, but saw no one, only the little fire, bounded by a ring of stones from the beach.

Galla put her hands inside her belt and felt for a knife, just in case.

"Hello?" called Deming, and they stepped forward slowly, looking all around. The mist crawled toward them off the bay, and everything to the north was completely obscured in fog by now. The little fire smoldered and fizzled.

They heard a crunching sound, and then a figure appeared just ahead of the fire and stopped. They stared over the fire at this being and stood uncertainly.

"Hello?" said Deming again, keeping his voice level and clear.

The figure then approached, cautiously, and finally they could see it was a human, short and wrapped in bundles, with a striking red and white shawl. And Galla could see, upon looking more closely, that it was a woman.

"Hi!" she called back. "This your boat?"

"Yes," answered Deming, remaining still.

Galla stepped forward, marched around the fire, and said, "Hi! I'm Galla, and this is Deming."

"Teak," answered the woman, and she rubbed her hands on her pants, and then extended her hand to Galla, which she shook. The woman was probably in her late fifties, Galla guessed, and her straight black hair, bound in a ponytail, was shot through with streaks of white. Her face was reddish-brown and broad, her eyes were brown, and her cheekbones were high.

Deming stepped up beside Galla then and extended his hand, but Galla could see in the line of his jaw a twitch of caution.

"Are you camping here?" asked Galla, trying to defuse things.

"Yes," answered Teak, "just for tonight. Hope you don't mind. I'm getting some kombu and smoking clams, then I'll be headed back east again."

Galla could see now a basket full of seaweed, and she smelled the clams where the woman had placed them near the fire. That reminded her that she was hungry. Teak saw her look and smiled.

"Come, have some," she offered, and Galla leaned her pack against the old, grey wooden boathouse. It was dark inside, so she could not see the boat very well, just a dark mass.

Teak spread out a blanket and Deming brought out what dining ware they had.

"Do you camp up here much?" he asked.

Teak scooped up some of the smoked clams and put a little on each plate. She placed a dark green strip of seaweed next to them. Galla added crackers on the side.

Teak said, "I forage along here in the fall, and sometimes in the winter, but mainly the fall. Good clams up here."

"Where do you live?" he asked next.

"I used to live outside the City, but moved to the shore years ago," said the woman. Deming sneezed and coughed. "Want some tea?" she asked him. "I have a little brewed."

They accepted her tea gratefully and ate the delicious clams and kombu and crackers. Their moods improved, and soon Teak began asking questions as well.

"Are you going sailing?" she asked. "Weather's not been great for it. Maybe better tomorrow."

"I hope so," said Deming.

"Where you headed?" she asked.

Galla watched the little movements in Deming's face, as if he did not know what to say. So she spoke up.

"We're headed out West, to see the land, and look for a friend," she said.

"Out West!" exclaimed Teak. "Not many people out there. Have you seen this friend lately?"

"No," said Galla simply. Deming gave her a relieved look. She stretched and scowled, clutching her back.

Teak looked back and forth between them and said, "Well, good luck." Then she turned to Galla and said, "Are you hurt?"

Galla tensed up. "A little bruised; it's nothing."

Deming asked then, "Teak, have you had any problems with animals out here? Seen any large packs of shavers or anything?"

She raised her eyebrows. "No, nothing like that. I mainly keep to the shore, though."

They finished their meal, and Teak went over to a rucksack and pulled out a rectangular little tin. She tossed it at Deming, who fumble-caught it and stared at her with a crinkled brow.

"Put that on her back," she said.

"I—what?" said Deming, swinging his hair forward in a double take.

Teak rolled her eyes, went over to him, and opened the tin for him. "It's a salve. Rub it into her skin. It'll help her."

"I—we have painkillers," said Deming in a faint voice.

"It's fine, Deming," Galla said, and she felt warmth crawling up her neck and into her face. And she abruptly sat in front of him, facing the fire and Teak. Galla raised her shirt, undid her bra, and bunched her shirt in her front and left her back bare. Teak chuckled.

"Touch is healing," she said to them, as Deming dipped his fingers into the thick salve and wavered over Galla's bare back.

It's not like I didn't just see her back the other night, he thought, angry at his shaking hands.

"Go ahead," said Galla softly, and she jumped a little as his hands met her skin and he began rubbing it in. "Urgh," she said, clenching her teeth against the pressure on her wounds. He froze. "Keep going!" she hissed.

The ointment soaked in and felt warm to her, but her bruises were very painful, despite the care Deming took. Finally she relaxed, and then she began to enjoy the rubbing. She could feel herself breathing harder, and an odd mix of sensations coursed her body. Deming stopped, and she readjusted her clothes. She turned and gave him a look that made him shiver. He abruptly rose and walked away from her, into the darkness near his pack.

Teak laughed. She said to Galla, "I thought you were a couple!"

Galla wanted to dive right into the dark water and hide her face.

"No," she gasped. "He's..."

And at that moment Deming walked back toward them.

"...my best friend," and they looked at each other, and at Teak.

The woman's entire face was creased in a smile.

"Well," she said, "good night, *best friends*."

And she went over and lay on a blanket, where she curled up and fell asleep.

In the darkness of their tent, Galla listened to Deming's breathing until she knew he slept. He coughed occasionally but did not fully waken. Then she opened the door of the tent and sat on the shore, listening to the last of the fire die down and the lapping of the water. She felt too excited to sleep. When she finally lay on her sleeping bag, it took her hours to settle down, but all she could think about was the sensation of him touching her, and how much better she had felt when he did.

Maybe Teak is right.

14

ROILING

Teak went on her way the next morning, but left them some of her kombu. Deming took it gratefully and stored it with the foodstuffs. Before she was out of sight, Teak turned around and called, "Remember, touch is healing!" They heard her laugh and laugh.

Faces enflamed, Galla and Deming avoided looking at each other, and began uncovering the boat and getting it ready for launch. It was not a glamorous boat by any means. It was painted white, but the paint had begun to chip, and dark green stains of algae covered its hull. Its sails were likewise filthy. Nevertheless, it was their only boat. They loaded their gear into it and dragged it off its little ramp and into the water, then tied it off on a rock at the shoreline. On its side, a faded gold word puzzled Galla.

"What does that say?" she asked, not recognizing the language.

"It says '*Pamlico*' if you translate it, but it's written in Gindoo's native language. He said my father named it."

She mouthed the word over. Then she climbed up the little ladder on the side of the boat, and Deming cast them off and followed her. On board, there were bare seats that covered cabinets below. He opened one of them and hauled out a musty life jacket. He coughed and sneezed explosively.

"Do you swim?" he asked her, and she shook her head, so he shoved the thing over her head.

"Mmph!" she said. "Do *you* swim?"

"Yes, quite well," he answered. She stepped over to the seat, opened it, found another life jacket, and pushed it down over his head. She glared at him with large amber eyes. He made a protesting groan but said, "Fine."

There was not much wind, so they took turns rowing the boat. The fog had slinked back far enough to give them a view of the hills to the south, and eventually the wind turned in their favor and they raised the sail. That set them skimming along at a good pace, and with the spray of the sea on her cheeks, Galla felt elated.

"I love this," she said, and Deming nodded.

He glanced at her.

"Best friends," he said casually, and she pulled her billowing hair down to her neck to hide the flush creeping up it. "I'm glad."

"Same here," she said, in too high a voice.

They watched the landscape change as they sped onward, and it became an undulating sort of moraine. They saw no one else, and eventually they moved the *Pamlico* farther into the Strait. The brisk wind set them racing along, but Deming's cough was getting worse, and Galla wondered if they should stop and camp.

"No, keep going while we have the wind," he called over the foaming surf. The waves had picked up, and the boat rose and fell. "We can take shifts."

Galla nodded uncertainly. She helmed the *Pamlico* until late afternoon, when at last Siloxxa broke out in a sky of shredded clouds flashing overhead. Then a terrific *crunch* met their ears, and Galla flew face down onto the deck.

"What the hell was that?" Deming asked, helping her up, and Galla looked at him in concern. His eyes were red, and his cheeks were redder. She held her wrist to his forehead.

"I don't know, but you have a fever, and so I think we should—"

SLAM! Something else struck their bow, and gripping the side rails, they looked down into the water. Huge, dark shapes swirled below the boat, surrounding it. They were chasing the boat, and one of them swerved over and smashed into the side, sending Deming onto his back. Something lurched underneath them and made a sickening crack. He looked down into the depths, sweating, and saw an eye look back up at him. He jumped back.

"Shit!" he said.

"What are they?" Galla shrieked, as another one struck.

"They're wakeroamers," he said, "but they never attack anyone! They're huge gentle gia—"

WHAM! An ominous crack ripped through the air.

Galla dared a glance at the enormous creatures bent on smashing the *Pamlico* to smithereens, and one of them rose up to blow, and she faced its eye. It looked coated in something grey, and Galla shuddered. Something was very wrong with these animals.

They're acting like the shavers did!

She turned just in time to see the tail of one of the wakeroamers strike the other side of the boat, and Deming flew overboard.

"Deming!" she screamed, and she held onto the railing and looked through the darkening water, whose whitecaps glinted in the late sun, so innocuous in the sky and so useless to her at the moment. She did not see him, and she went cold. Another pummeling right beside her, and another crack. Then she saw the life jacket, and the wet head of Deming as he emerged from the water, choking, and then he was thrust back under by the sheer weight of the wakeroamers.

Frantic, she seized the oars and slapped at some of the creatures with them, and turned the boat around. *He's under too long,* she thought in agony. She saw him bob up again, and then flail, and she screamed, "Grab the rope!" as she tossed a coil at him. He seized it, but he was coughing and sputtering and weakened. She pulled him closer, grabbed his armpits, and dragged him over the side.

He was pale and shuddering and she had to help pump water from his lungs, all the while enduring the constant pummeling by the wakeroamers, clearly driven to madness. She tied him to her then and rowed as hard as she could toward the shore. The deck of the *Pamlico* now sloshed with water.

We're taking on water, she thought bleakly. *Not sure if I can make it without having to try and swim in this.*

But she pumped the oars with her arms and yelled in fear and fury, and finally the bottom of the boat scraped on the rocky shore. Shaking all over, she untied Deming, jumped out with a rope, and tied the boat around a rock. Then she tugged and pulled on him so that he managed to stand, and helped him over into the shallow water. She looked behind them and watched the roiling water flatten out in the Strait. Then she saw three blows in succession, and the light faded.

Deming coughed constantly, and at one point he vomited multiple times within a few minutes. His skin looked greenish, and Galla helped him to dry land farther inland. She realized then their packs were in the cabinets on the boat, so she hurried back to pull them out. She hefted one on each shoulder, amazed that she could do that. One side of the boat's cabinets had remained dry, but Deming's pack was soaked thanks to the gash on that side of the boat. Pressing her hands to her temples, she concentrated, and ran up and down the shoreline gathering anything she could for firewood. Most of it was driftwood or low shrubs. She built a fire, helped him sit in front of it, and gave him her dry blanket.

"Get out of the wet clothes," she urged. He did, and he shivered uncontrollably in front of the growing fire. She laid out all his wet clothing and gear in front of the fire.

"Some of your stores are ruined, I'm afraid," she said, picking up limp packets of herbs among the supplies she had laid out.

"I should have waterproofed them better," he managed to say through chattering teeth.

"Never mind that now," she said. She set up their tent and urged him to drink from his flagon. His cough grew worse and his brow was hot, and she wondered what to do next as she kept vigil in the darkness in this new land. She stayed up all through the night, urging him to drink, but he coughed uncontrollably at times, and she did not know how to help him.

She lay down next to him and tossed in her wretched sleep, counting his breaths and listening to them worsen. Dawn seemed forever away.

15

UNVEILED

The rattling in Deming's lungs terrified Galla. She had been around bad coughs before. When Dek was younger, he suffered from croup every winter for years. This was different. Deming was slipping in and out of consciousness. He would not eat.

Galla, trembling constantly, tipped his canteen into his mouth whenever he came to. At one point he sank deep enough into sleep that she made a decision. She would have to leave him alone and look for one of the herbs he had taught her about.

Ailfern, she thought. His dried store of it lay disintegrated on the ground by the fire.

She knelt over Deming, laying her head on his chest and listening to the slow beats of his heart. *Too slow*, she thought. His fever had lowered a little and his heart had slowed, yet his breath crackled deep in his lungs. *He's going to die*, she thought. And she felt her tears seep through his shirt. She lifted up and looked at him, with his fine nose, his face too pale, his short beard making his face look even slimmer. She smoothed back his hair and took one of his limp hands into both of hers. She kissed his fingers.

"I have to go," she told him. "I'm going to look for ailfern. You're a good teacher. I know what to look for. I just hope I can find them. Deming," and she squeezed his hand, "please...please wait. I'll try to be fast. Please wait."

She leaned in and pressed her cheek against his and let her tears spill onto his face.

"Deming," she said in the softest whisper, "I love you."

And she pulled his blanket up to his neck and tucked it all around him. She slid another phyron crystal into the lamp and hoisted a mesh sack onto her back. She glanced at him but swallowed the lump in her throat and left the tent. And she ran.

She ran in the grey-green moors, tripped over countless rocks, and looked everywhere for a stream. And as soon as she knew she was out of earshot, she lifted her voice and shrieked. She sobbed openly, unable to hold it back any longer. And she felt inside her a fire building, something ancient yet familiar. A magma bubble of pure, clear rage burst forth.

"Don't take him from me!" she shouted, nowhere and everywhere. "How dare you! *How dare you!* Help me! *Help me!*"

The rage felt cozy, like old clothes worn for comfort. She could feel strength building from it. It made her savage and tireless, so she ran farther and kept running. Finally she could see a line of shrubs descending on the horizon. She burst forward at a sprint. *There! A stream!* A small brook among the shrubs tumbled down over dark grey stones. She got down on all fours and crawled along its edge, searching among the rocks. She snatched plant after plant and laid them all out to survey them.

It might be that one. Or is it this one? One was silver, the other bronze. My terrible memory! Why can't I remember this? Her temper had worn down and she felt a slide into despair. She rubbed her hot tears away with her forearm.

She heard a *snick* and whipped her head up. A shape stood above her, under the bushes. She could make out two large, dark violet eyes staring at her.

"Who are you?" she yelled.

The shape leapt into the air and then dashed off.

Some kind of animal, she thought. *Please, no more animal attacks! Not now!*

She gathered up the plants.

"Dammit. I'll just bring them all. Hopefully I won't poison him."

She thrust the plants in her sack, filled up the canteens, shouldered the load, and bolted back north and east. The sky had darkened, and the clouds hung low. The shrinking day length made everything darker faster at this latitude. Every once in a while, she thought she saw something out of the corner of her eye. She would abruptly turn to look and see nothing. She frowned but ran on.

Finally she reached the tent just as drizzle spilled down from the sky. She shoved her pack through the door of the tent and turned around to see if anything had followed her. She could hear creatures far off, flying in to roost or nestle in for the coming night. She scrambled inside and pulled off her dirty outer clothes and cleaned her hands. Deming lay perfectly still, not having moved at all. The phyron light, normally warm, cast a sickly glow on his face. Galla gasped. Deming's lips were blue.

Fighting her own anguished sounds, she gritted her teeth and laid her head on his chest. A slower heartbeat met her ears, and a whistling breath. He was still alive, but not for much longer. She pulled the bruised plants from the pack and stared at them.

"Deming," she said, choking, "you're the only person who can tell me which is which. And you can't tell me. I'm sorry. I'm going to use them both."

He lay motionless, not hearing or seeing.

She bit her lip and set to work grinding the plants into a paste, and set their small pot over the phyron just outside the tent. She poured her canteen water into the pot, added the paste, and pushed the phyron with twigs until it pulsed with heat. It seemed like ages before the mixture in the pot began to bubble. Raindrops fizzled in the heat of the little fire. The mixture smelled powerfully volatile to Galla, so much so that her eyes stung. But she could feel, leaning over the mixture, a sharp clearing of her sinuses. She took the pot off the heat and poured the contents into a thermos. Then she climbed back inside the tent.

She held the thermos under Deming's nose as best she could, not knowing what else to do. The steam flooded his face. He made sighing, gasping noises, but still remained unconscious.

Galla clenched her teeth. *I don't know what to do.*

Something rustled behind her, and she jumped, almost spilling the thermos. A nose poked through the tent door, a moist, pointy nose, and after that, two large, almond-shaped violet eyes shone. Delicate legs stepped in. It was the creature she had seen earlier.

"Go away!" Galla cried.

But the animal stepped farther in, and its fur glowed dark amber in the phyron light. It had long, upward-pointing ears and a thick, long, curling tail. A creamy patch of fur graced its underbelly. The animal bowed its head down to its feet, looking up at Galla the entire time.

"Shoo!" shouted Galla, lunging. But the animal stayed bowed. Then it raised its vivid eyes to her copper eyes and made a motion with its mouth. She watched as its tongue came out and lapped the air.

Galla pinched her eyebrows together.

"Are you wanting something to drink?" she asked, her curiosity getting the better of her. *So far it doesn't seem too insane. And its eyes are clear, and beautiful.*

The animal then stood again, and raising one paw, pointed at Deming. Galla's eyes grew large. The animal bowed again and lapped at the air.

"You...you mean he should *drink it*?" she cried. The animal hopped on all fours. "Well, I don't know if he can drink anything. I hoped he could breathe this in. And I don't want to poison him—"

But when Galla saw the blue expanding in Deming's face, she hushed.

"It's too hot for him," she murmured, but she thought quickly. She drew out a cloth from her pack and dipped it into the thermos. "Deming," she whispered, "I want you to drink this. I'm going to drip this into your mouth. Somehow."

She pushed his lips open and squeezed the mixture in. Some of it spilled out the side of his mouth, but some did go in, just a few drops as far as she could tell.

"I don't think I can get any more in without choking him," she said, as much to herself as to the animal behind her.

The animal padded in, around to the other side of Deming, and lay down against him.

"Are you...do you think I should lie down too?" she asked the beast, feeling ridiculous, but desperate. The animal sneezed and then tucked its chin around Deming's left shoulder.

So Galla set the thermos down. She hoped against hope that a few drops of the liquid would be enough. She lay down next to Deming and turned on her side toward him. She draped one arm around him and nuzzled her chin into his arm. Exhausted, she fell asleep.

The sound of panting jolted her out of her fitful sleep, and she shot up. The animal was sitting up a bit, on the other side of Deming. Galla bent over and listened to Deming's heart. It was beating faster. A percolating sound in his lungs confused her. Was this worse? The phyron lamp had dimmed, so she kindled it again. She could not see in the dim light whether he looked better or not.

"Now what?" she said aloud.

And he coughed. A great, rasping, crackling cough. The animal on the other side of him jumped to its feet and stared at Galla. It dipped its head and lapped at the air. Galla quickly retrieved the thermos. She set it next to Deming and pulled him up, and he coughed again. His eyes flickered open for a few seconds, and then he coughed up a rope of phlegm and groaned. Galla wiped his face.

"Deming," she said softly. "Can you drink?" and she held the thermos to his lips. He was very weak, so she tipped the drink into his mouth. He swallowed and coughed again. She could see the color had come back to his lips. She blinked back tears.

"Gross," he whispered, and Galla gasped in relief at hearing his voice. She then gave him water. Then he sank back to his sleeping bag and slept soundly, and while his breathing rattled still, his heart beat steadily.

Galla could not stop her tears from flowing, and she shook. She looked over at the animal, and it blinked at her lazily and lay back down next to Deming. So she followed suit.

A flapping sound woke her this time. It was daybreak, and the tent door whipped in and out in the wind. Galla felt warm and content, and then with a start she realized Deming was turned toward her, awake, and pushing her wild hair away from her face.

"Deming!" she cried, seizing him. "You're awake! And—and you look better! How are you feeling?"

Deming smiled at her; his eyes almost closed to slits. "Terrible and fantastic, all at the same time," he said in a hoarse voice.

Galla sat up swiftly and looked around. "Where did it go?"

"What?" he asked.

"The animal that was in here last night," said Galla.

Deming's eyebrows lifted. "Um," he said, "there's no animal in here."

Galla shook her head and stared at the tent door. "No, I'm telling you, there was a furry animal, and it helped me out with you, and it slept on that side of you, and I was on this side."

"Ohhh," Deming drawled, and he coughed. "Maybe that's why I was so cozy this morning. I was surrounded!"

Galla instinctively handed Deming the thermos.

He scowled at it. "Must I?"

"I think so, yes," said Galla, not meeting his eyes. "Until your cough is gone."

Deming reluctantly took it and swallowed a large swig. He gagged.

"What...*what* did you put in this?" he wheezed. "It's literally the worst thing I've ever tasted!" He coughed some more.

Galla blushed and began straightening up the tent. "It was the best I could do. I'm not the genius forager you are, after all. And it seems to have worked, so..."

"Galla," said Deming quietly. "Maybe you are the genius. I think this—well, this horrible stuff saved my life."

She continued to avoid his eyes and blinked away tears. She handed him a water canteen, and he drank deeply. Then she turned her back to him and gathered up the rags she had used.

"Galla," he said. "I'm a little weak. Can you come over here so I can thank you properly? I'm feeling better very quickly. And that couldn't have happened without you."

Her cheeks burned and her insides felt hot. She shoved her pack to one side of the tent, glanced around outside for the animal, and then turned back to Deming at last.

He stared at her with his dark eyes wide open—but Galla jumped.

"Your—your eyes!" she exclaimed.

Deming crinkled his brow and smirked. "What?"

Galla approached him and sank to her knees next to him. He gazed up at her with his dark, velvety eyes, but around their pupils, a gold ring shone. Galla felt a wave of something inside her, a confusion, or a recognition.

"You're—" Deming began, rising up a bit. He gasped. "You—Galla. I—I feel you. I feel what you're feeling!" and his voice rose. He trembled.

"What is happening?" she asked, almost afraid of the answer.

"Galla," he said urgently, reaching out to her. "Do you mean it? Do you?"

She felt her cheeks flame, and she breathed quickly.

"Do I mean what?"

"Tell me," pleaded Deming. "I can feel it from you. Like a bonfire. Oh God—it's incredible. But please—please tell me."

"Tell you—" Galla began, but her copper eyes and his dark, gold-ringed eyes met. She could not hold back. "I'm in love with you."

Deming gasped again, and his eyes shone. "You told me last night, didn't you?" he asked her, and she took his outstretched hands.

"Yes," Galla said, terrified. This precious, impossible man, her best friend: she loved him more than anything. She knew in that moment that he was everything to her.

"I love you, Galla," Deming told her, and his shaking arms pulled her to him. Their noses touched and he said, "Oh God, I've loved you. Immediately. Beyond anything. I love you, I love you—"

"But you're my best friend," she gasped. "How can we—what if it doesn't—I can't stand the thought—"

"I feel everything you're feeling," he said, his arms around her waist now. "Don't be afraid."

Galla felt as though a wave had crashed into her and soaked her to her soul, warm and welcome and extinguishing her old rage and her new fear then. She sank into Deming's arms and met his lips with her own. His lips felt warm and healthy, and soft and delicious.

"Are you all right?" she asked him suddenly, pulling away.

"I'm stronger by the second," Deming said, his eyes glowing. "You saved me. Again." He kissed Galla again. "I want you."

"I want you too," Galla answered, and Deming's lips journeyed over her cheeks, her nose, and her chin: a breathless exploration.

Their tongues met, and their hands wandered, and soon they pulled and pushed their clothes away. Only the little bracelet on her wrist remained. Deming held her out to look at her, and he smiled. He kissed her breasts and gripped her small waist, and her legs squeezed him. She ran her tongue along his broad shoulders and nuzzled the fine dark hair on his chest and tasted his sweat. She could smell on his neck a whiff of woods and spice, and thought, *Home.* And he sat up, and with gentle hands but strong arms, he lowered her onto him as he held her. They both cried out, never looking away from each other, lips and bodies moving slowly.

Deming could feel everything Galla could, and she felt an explosion of desire and power she did not think possible. Spikes of pleasure surged through every part of her, building and building, and tingled through her almost to the point of unbearable pressure and ecstasy, and then fractured all through her so that she screamed. They rose and fell again and again, crashing into each other's bodies and souls. Clenching each other, entangled and rapturous, they broke through the barriers of fears and friendship. And they collapsed together in a heap, in luscious oblivion to time or anything else.

Galla and Deming stared at each other, reaching out to touch each other as if they could not believe what had happened, as if wanting to prove again it was real.

"We should probably drink something," she finally said, grinning. "You are recovering, after all."

"I feel pretty damn recovered," said Deming with a wry smirk, moving in to kiss her neck and her breasts, and soon she ran her hands down the hairs of his abdomen and he laughed.

They made love again, and not long after, a third time.

Finally Deming said, "Fine, I'll eat now. I'm starving." So they laughed, and ate, and fell back to exploring each other more.

Galla looked briefly for the animal, but it was gone. She was grateful for it. It had helped her; she was certain of that. Her love had lived.

16

THE GRAVEYARD

A long and slow trek across windy moors led them to a wilder place, a shrub-steppe of old, glacial moraine inter-mixed with black basalt. They were entering the far north-western lands of Orboaanya, and with Deming recovering, Galla took no chance in rushing them. But both of them felt greater urgency. On clear nights, the auroras burst forth with astonishing intensity, an incredible sight of looping greens and purple veils. Sometimes the light from them cast shadows. On one night, they camped at the edge of a lake surrounded by short trees. The aurora splayed forth above them, reflected in the lake. But there were other wonders in the heavens.

Galla spied a strange set of streaks high above.

"Meteors?" Deming wondered aloud, but she shook her head.

"I don't think so. It's hard to see them, but there are crafts up there of some kind. Very high up in the atmosphere, low in orbit. Do you see those?" She pointed so that Deming could follow her finger.

"Very faint," he said. "But I do see them. They're ships, then?"

"I think they are," she agreed. "And I think...maybe they're fighting."

They watched from a rock next to their campsite lake, with a fire burning in a stone circle. Their stores were running low, though they had foraged what roots they could. The wind was noticeably colder during the day. It died down at night, but the edge of the lake would soon freeze, they knew. Autumn waned quickly. Deming made the soup that evening, out of cut-up tubers, dried slips of kombu, and a couple of drops from what were left of his bottles. Galla took a cup of the soup gratefully, and they sat next to each other and stared at the fire.

Far in the distance, some animal yipped in the night. Galla kept her eyes out for the furry companion who had helped her with Deming, but she had not seen it again. They had found no people at all, but occasionally there were herds of ungulates, and small animals that peeked their noses out of burrows to watch them in silence.

Deming put his arm around Galla and stared up at the night sky, with its vivid auroral arcs and the splinters of lights that she thought were ships.

"You're meant to be up there," he said softly. "Fighting with them. I feel sure of that now. I wonder if Paul is already there."

Galla stared at him. "Why would he be?"

He squeezed her hand. "He wasn't just a spy, Galla," he said. "He was a soldier as well. It's possible he's defending us up there, right now."

She looked up and then covered her face with her hands.

"I want him to be alive, but I hope he's not up there," she whispered.

"He knows the risks," he told her. "And so do you. Maybe you don't remember them, but you wouldn't be out here if you didn't understand on some level."

She sighed and leaned her head on his shoulder. "I'm glad I'm here with you, then," she said, and then she glanced up at him. He kissed her, and they entered their tent.

Every morning and every evening now, this was their ritual, feeling each other's bodies collide, a constant desire fulfilled whenever they rested for long enough. The tug of what they felt seemed as natural as the moons' pull on the sea.

"I don't know how you can excite me and relax me at the same time," Galla told him that night.

"Maybe," Deming murmured, working his way down her body, "we"—*kiss*—"just"—*kiss*—"fit"—*kiss*—"well together," and he let out a long, enraptured sigh as she placed her ankles on either side of his neck and grinned at him.

"*Very* well," laughed Galla, swiveling a bit. They said nothing more that night.

But in the morning, she sat upright in surprise. Their tent door was flapping open. The air in the tent was frigid. She reluctantly looked back at Deming, with his eyes closed, cocooned in their sleeping bag, and began pulling on her layers. She would have preferred staying with him, and felt herself growing hot with desire, but she felt also the pressure to get going with the day.

I don't want to wake him. But how did our tent come open by itself?

She crawled outside the tent. The wind had picked up, and she felt the sting of small pellets of ice strike her face. *Not the best trekking weather ahead*, she thought grimly. The little glacial lake bore many ripples and looked tarnished silver in color.

"Deming," she called softly, "we should get going."

She began cleaning their campfire site and then stopped. There were footprints in the ash all around it. They were smaller than her palm, with little nail tips. Her neck prickled, and she looked all around the lake and their campsite. She thought about their open tent and looked at the ground near the opening. Sure enough, there were a few shallow prints.

"I think our friend came for a visit," she said, as Deming exited the tent and grimaced at the wind. She pointed at the prints. "Our tent was open this morning, too."

His eyes closed halfway, and she could just barely see the new, gold rings around their pupils. He bent to look at the tracks.

"Those could be anything," he said with a shrug and a rub of his growing beard. He kissed her temple. "Keelhearts, short-tailed cabalaries," and he rattled off a list of animals she had never heard of before.

"This had a long tail. And are any of those animals sentient, with large, violet eyes?" she challenged him.

"Well, no..."

"It's a wild land out here," she said. "So there could be some kind of interesting species that no one in the East knows about. Especially the closer we get to the Quo continents."

"That's true, but—"

"Oh Deming, you really don't believe me, do you?" she sighed, exasperated.

He looked cornered. "I want to, I do. But...I've never heard of anything like this before. It's just...you were under a lot of stress."

Galla rolled her eyes. "Well, no kidding. What with your nearly dying and all. But I didn't hallucinate that animal!"

Deming raised his eyebrows and his hands at the same time. Irritably, Galla snatched up supplies and packed them away. She stuffed her wild hair into a cowl and wrapped a scarf around that. Still, coils of her hair escaped, as if revealing her desire to flee this place. The wind was burning her cheeks, and she could see (though at the moment she was avoiding his eyes) Deming's cheeks redden and his eyes squint. They broke down their campsite and hoisted their packs and headed into the wind. There was nothing for it: it was going to be a savage day ahead.

Still, she watched for the creature. They saw little wildlife that day. And then the snow arrived in earnest, and it was a dry, granular snow that lashed them as they trudged forward.

"We can't do this much longer," she called in a muffled voice through the whistling wind. "It'll be nightfall before we know it."

"We'll have to find someplace to shelter," Deming agreed. "Maybe we should've stayed one more night by that lake."

"Too late for that now," said Galla. But she was worried.

She worried incessantly, now, about Deming's health, lest he relapse. But his coughing grew rarer, and all she could do was hope he would be fine. *I wish I could switch off this part of me that worries about him. But then maybe I wouldn't love him as much either. And I can't even imagine that. So.*

Thinking along those lines distracted her enough that she could cope better with the wretched weather. She moved closer to him and they stopped briefly to rub noses, and then quickly covered their faces again. The light was growing dimmer, and the snow squalls lessened. It was miserable going, and Galla began to grow uneasy about their long-term chances. If it were this challenging now, what would it be like when winter truly set in? She did not know her own limits with cold and did not want to find out. But the pain she felt from the cold wind told her that she would not enjoy worse conditions. They both had to survive this.

She realized, now, that she could not send Deming back, even if she wanted to. He was a good tracker, despite his stubbornness over that animal. She would need his guidance to get to Quepahi, and also, she began to understand, to keep her sane.

For not only did she worry about him, she thought endlessly about what to expect when she got to Quepahi. What would be there? What if it was a dead end? The anxiety over how best to help in the fight above this world made her dizzy. Gindoo had spoken as if she had a major role to play in the galaxy's struggle. And this world, her home for over twenty years, had seemed so safe and sure to her, all while she felt she did not belong in it. It seemed grievous to think of Quopeia suffering at all. And yet if it was truly a last bastion, what was the rest of the galaxy enduring? She would swallow her suffering and try to find out.

They were slowing down, the sky was darkening, and there was no shelter to be found...at first. But by and by, they saw something on the horizon. The snow stopped, and as the sun sank, the clouds opened briefly. Siloxxa shone deep red, like an eye, as it sent out a last blast of light before setting. The light caught on several objects that looked to Galla like they were set in a deliberate line. Deming saw them as well. They glanced at each other and burst ahead in a scramble toward them.

As they approached and the light quickly faded, Galla could not at first get her head around what she saw. They walked up to the formations, finding them several feet tall, and Galla touched one: it was made of warped metal and composite.

"They're *spaceships*," she breathed.

It was a line of destroyed ships, of several different makes, stretching over at least half a mile, all lined up on a ridge.

"Someone *put* them here!" Deming exclaimed. "A graveyard of spaceships!"

Galla turned, with one hand on the mangled ship next to her, its nose buried deep in the ground, and saw something move close by.

"Look!" she hissed, and Deming followed her gaze.

There, down the hill from them, an animal sat on its haunches and gazed from Galla to Deming and back again. It bore large, violet eyes, long, pointed ears, and a fabulously bushy tail.

"Hello again!" called Galla. She glanced at Deming, who sheepishly grinned back. She smirked, victorious. The animal dipped down, as if in a long bow. And behind it, in the distance, little shimmering lights shone. Someone lived there.

17

PRILANNA OPTISON

The animal ran ahead, stopped, and turned back to look at them. It hopped into the air on all fours as if to say, "Follow me!" Galla and Deming looked at each other and decided to approach.

"Yes, I concede you were right," Deming told her.

"Wise," she responded, gleeful. She playfully bumped her hip against his.

"It's rather stupid," Deming admitted. "Because I could feel that you were right, but I was too stubborn to admit it."

Galla stopped for a moment and looked at Deming solemnly.

"Do you regret this new ability?"

Deming's golden eye rings shone brightly. "God, no," he said. "It just means I can't come up with any excuses around you." He laughed then. "For the first time, I kind of get what Paul must feel like." And then he sighed, and they both instinctively looked up at the skies.

A high yip jolted them back to reality, and the foxlike animal jumped in the air again. So they continued their trek over the barren land, past more broken ships, to a valley filled with low, round structures, all lit with wavering ropes of lights that the cold breeze set dancing. The couple paused before entering the village, as the beast had met a pack of others of its kind, and they all turned to look up at Galla and Deming.

"I wish I could feel more than just you," Deming told her, "but if that is not my ability, then I'm fine with that. Still, look at them! They look like they're talking about us. In silence...like—"

"Like telepaths," Galla finished. Deming nodded.

He said, "There are people coming from the village. Should we go on?"

Galla lifted an eyebrow at him. "It's cold, and they have light, and presumably heat. I think we've earned it; you certainly have! Yes, we go on."

And as they approached the village, Deming said softly, "Ah, Ildions! I've never seen so many. A colony?"

Galla shrugged, not knowing enough about the beings to say.

As she and Deming walked up to the group of animals, who stared at them with unnerving, gorgeous violet eyes, and sat primly on their haunches behind the one who had helped her, Galla could see the Ildion people more closely.

Two of them advanced, and like the rest of their species, they were shorter than humans. Their skin ranged in hues of pale lavender, and the two who walked forward seemed related. While most of the petite beings were slender, one of these two was rather rotund of cheek and midsection, and flushed nearly magenta even in the lights strung between the buildings. This fellow's arm was looped with a much younger Ildion, whose brown eyes flashed back and forth between Galla and Deming. Galla could see that this female was quite clever, and had likely made up her mind about them instantly. As with all Ildions, there were groove marks in their faces, which from a distance looked like gills. Up close, they were merely folds. Older Ildions' folds were more prominent.

With a lilting brogue, the plump, older male said, "Welcome! Nalag tells us you have had a long journey, and you need a place to rest."

Galla and Deming stared at each other, and Galla's forehead crinkled up.

"Who?" she asked.

And as if to answer, the beast who had led them there made a deep bow, and sneezed.

"Oh!" said Galla. "You're Nalag?" and the animal's tail twitched back and forth.

"I am Birannon Optison, chief of our community," the fellow said, "and this is my daughter, Prilanna."

"I am Galla," and she at first wanted to say Huntren, but then stopped herself. It didn't feel right anymore.

"I'm Deming," her companion said.

Prilanna stepped forward, bowing. She assertively placed her hands on her hips.

"Welcome, and follow me. I will give you a place to stay, and you can unpack your things. And clean up," she added, looking askance at Deming, whose eyebrows shot up. She glanced over her thin shoulder at Nalag, who trotted up alongside her.

Prilanna's hair-like extensions were combed back into a tight twist, and deep blue-grey. With her lavender skin, the only warm features on her were her large, bright brown eyes. Again, Galla felt that Prilanna's eyes were calculating everything about her and Deming constantly.

Prilanna led them to a smooth, round, pale grey house, essentially a more rigid yurt. She opened the arched door herself, and lit phyron sconces once inside. She gestured for Galla and Deming to enter. Nalag waited by the doorway without entering, still as stone. But its mesmerizing eyes watched the two of them.

The little house was more than adequate, with a round bed of sorts on the floor, piled with cushions and blankets. Galla and Deming let their packs slip off their weary shoulders and looked gratefully at Prilanna.

She said, "There is a bath through that little door," pointing to one of two doors in the small structure. "And in that one, you'll find fresh clothes. I am sorry, but they will not fit you well. Let us take what clothes you have, after you bathe and change, and we will clean them."

All this time, Prilanna stood as tall as her height could allow, and ramrod straight. But after her last statement her shoulders fell.

"I forgot!" she exclaimed suddenly. "You're to dine with us. Ah! You'll have to bathe quickly, and I'll have to—I'm sorry, I have to go! I'll come get you later, or Nalag will," and she muttered the entire way out the door and into the street, with Nalag glancing back.

"So she's rather young, then," said Galla with a smile. "A teenager, like Dek, maybe? Or the equivalent."

Deming grinned. "Naturally she came around to food, so I think you're right." And he looked pointedly at the door leading to the bath. Galla blushed.

"Together?" she asked. And Deming nodded, his cheeks creased with a broad smile. And so one by one, each item of clothing fell, and they ran shivering through the door to find a steaming tub. Deming gave a shout when he stepped in, and Galla laughed at him. But they soon encircled each other, floating in the hot, bubbling spring water, and soaped each other's hair and splashed around.

Galla felt a moment of extraordinary bliss, as she and Deming held each other and kissed in the water, and she slid her legs around his waist while he looped his arms around her and held her gently backward, letting her hair float about her.

"You are so beautiful," he said, shy even still. And they quickly dried and made their way to the round bed and tested it out with gusto.

Draped across him, Galla said lazily, "You know, if we had to stay here, this wouldn't be so bad."

"We could for a bit, if they'll let us," Deming suggested.

Galla rose up a bit, her still-wet hair beginning to twist in moodiness, and said with a sigh, "We have to keep going, even though it's tempting to stay. Maybe one more night?"

"As many more with you as I can have, thank you very much," said Deming, and then they tested each other's limits of ecstasy to the point Galla wondered if the entire village heard them.

Afterward, they found their temporary clothes, and roared with laughter at the sight of each other. They essentially wore pale grey robes that only reached their knees, and their sleeves only reached their elbows.

"The draft is going to be *unpleasant*," Deming remarked, wincing at the thought of going outside. "Good thing we already had our moments back there, because I would have shru—"

A tapping on the door stifled their giggles. It was Prilanna, with Nalag accompanying her. The animal lolled a tongue out at the sight of Deming and Galla, arm in arm, underdressed for the cold.

I swear, that beast is laughing at us, Galla thought, feeling her lips twitch.

"Right," said Prilanna, and Galla could see dismay in her eyes as she took in the truncated outfits on the guests. "I'll have them speed up the laundry. Now, if you can follow us, we'll dine at my father's home. A bit late for us, but you need to eat. And Nalag says you have spent yourselves."

Deming began coughing uncontrollably to the point that Galla grew alarmed, but his eyes shone, and he covered his mouth and cleared his throat.

"Thank you," Galla said to Prilanna. "We would be honored," and she nudged Deming with her elbow. He had to look away from them and take a deep breath.

They found themselves in the Optison home with bare legs and blushing faces, to the point that Prilanna, embarrassed herself, dashed off to seize a couple of blankets that they could wrap around their lower bodies. They sat at the low table, and Deming, with his stature, banged his knees instantly and grimaced. Prilanna looked agonized. Clearly, she had wanted to make a good impression, and she felt her chance slipping away.

Galla sympathized with the awkward teen, and she said, "You've been just wonderful, and you must make your father proud."

Prilanna served Galla and Deming herself, as her father boomed on about the town, its history, and the ship monument. Galla watched the girl's face react to everything her father said, and she could tell that Prilanna had heard every story many times over; at times she would stop and reminisce, while at other moments she would look irritated. Deming glanced whenever possible at Galla, who alternated between nodding politely at Birannon and furtively observing Prilanna.

How is she doing this? he wondered. *Galla is really skilled at diplomacy. What was she like, before? What did she do? I wish I could have asked Gindoo more. But then, he didn't really know her. I wish I could ask anyone.*

Galla said, then, in answer to Birannon's question, "I'm seeking answers to my past. I was injured many years ago, and I am apparently important to some kind of mission. But I don't remember it, because of the accident. I'm told there is someone who could help me out here."

"Out *here*?" Birannon and Prilanna said simultaneously.

Prilanna made a chirping sound. "There's nobody out here but us," she said.

Nalag nudged its pointed nose into her thigh after she sat down.

"But-but," Prilanna stammered, taking the hint, "we would be happy to help you in any way we can."

"Yes!" agreed Birannon, tucking into the feast. "Prilanna is correct, though. We get wanderers out here, looking for things, or driven mad by the strange phenomena here at the edge of the Quo continents. But they're rare, and they never pass by again."

Deming watched Galla touch her forehead and realized she had experienced a stabbing pain. He squeezed her hand, and her face flooded with color. She smiled up at him.

"That always makes me feel better," Galla said softly. "It feels right."

"Then I'll never stop doing it," said Deming simply. But he pulled his gaze away from her and asked, "What about Caxxius Caxx?"

And Birannon choked on his food until he wheezed. Prilanna fretted over him, but he waved her off. She looked at Deming as though scandalized.

"Caxxius Caxx!" the older fellow hollered. "By Lume! A nutter, that one! We tell the deengynes to stay away from him, but they still prance off now and then." And he pointed reproachfully at Nalag, whose eyes lowered halfway.

Prilanna looked agitated, as if she wanted to say something, yet could not.

Deming said carefully, "Well, my mentor, Gindoo, said he knew him, or knew of him, and that he could help Galla with her quest."

Galla said, "It's crucial that we find this...mage, or whatever he is. Because while it may be peaceful out here, there was an attack at the capital, and there is a battle above us."

Birannon snorted. "As if the capital ever gave a snot about us out here! We live our own lives, same as we have for many decades. Even before the sky changed and the aurora arced. That was before my time, mind. Certainly, before the *President* and his kind showed up."

And he swore in another language for a solid minute in disgust.

Prilanna hissed, "Father!"

Birannon bowed his head. "I didn't mean *you two*. You're different."

Galla and Deming exchanged quizzical looks.

She said, "Either way, I have some role to play in the war, and if I don't find this person, your village will never be safe again."

That stilled the room.

"So," said Galla, and Deming felt ripples of some inner power reverberate from her, and could only watch in admiration, "I must find him, and soon. Will you help us or not?"

Birannon leaned back and took a long look at her, with her hair curling upward and outward and shining in the warm light in vivid colors of copper, gold, magenta, and violet. "You're definitely not like them," he observed. "But we don't deal with that crank in the mountains. He lives by the river of fire, in a high cave. And *officially*," and he turned to look sidelong at his daughter, who sat still and aloof, "nobody is supposed to go there. The deengynes are hard to control sometimes, as they do have minds of their own." He clucked, and Nalag slid over to him, where he could stroke the beast.

"What do you think, Nalag?" Birannon implored the creature. "I'm not sending my own. Would your kind take them?"

The animal looked back at Galla and Deming and made a chuffing, "Ah-ho!" sound that was neither bark nor yip.

"Well, that's on you, my friend; I want no part of it, understand?" Birannon said, and Nalag reached up to touch its nose to Birannon's chin.

Birannon looked back at Galla and Deming, whose shoulders touched.

"Stay a bit longer. Nalag tells me Deming here was ill," he said, and Deming lowered his head a bit.

"I'm much better, and I don't want to delay," he replied.

"One more night," pleaded Birannon, beseeching Galla directly. "I fear if you go that way, we'll never see you again. And I like you both. And so does Prilanna, I can tell. Take a rest and enjoy our village a bit more, before you go."

Deming turned to Galla, and all eyes were on her.

Galla took a deep breath. "One more night. You are kind, and it is comfortable here, and we appreciate your hospitality. After that, we have to leave, for everyone's sake. I feel a pull, something I can't explain. An urgency. And it's been stronger every day. It's not that we don't want to stay; it's that we can't. I would rather see you safe, and never see you in person again, than to know I delayed too long and caused your people to suffer."

Everyone then stared at her in awe. They were witnessing something Galla could not understand, but they did: she was becoming a leader, before their very eyes. Prilanna absorbed every mannerism Galla made and rolled every one of the woman's statements over and over in her thoughts. And then she made up her mind.

18

UNCIVILIZED

As she pulled the fabric up her legs, Galla let out a massive sigh and said, "Pants! I don't think I could do without them ever again!"

Their laundry stowed and their own clothes back on their bodies, she and Deming felt relieved after a couple of days without them. They were used to packing up and moving on, and only into their second day in the Ildion village, both grew restless. Galla felt a renewed energy the night before they left, watching an extraordinary, roping aurora overhead. She could sense that this aurora was not typical.

Listening to Birannon talk of the past, she gleaned that something had happened in this region, decades prior to his birth, that changed the atmosphere and the landscape of the area. Anyone who had borne witness to that event no longer lived to tell the tale, however. Galla found it odd that there was little record of it, other than word of mouth.

"Something in the sky bent the sky itself," was all Birannon could really say. "A great storm, maybe, and it changed the aurora forever, made it stronger. Of course Quopeia was always resistant to anything that entered its atmosphere. So I do not know just what happened. A crash, perhaps? But we've not ever been able to find anything other than the ships you see lined up out there. And I don't see those having as much of an effect on anything. So now it's a legend. We don't know, but we can spin all the tales we want about it."

Their final night, Galla and Deming were serenaded by the trilling songs of the Ildions. Prilanna sounded almost mournful, her shoulders shaking with great emotion.

Galla held her hands out to the girl.

"You'll make a fine leader one day," she said. "You've been so kind and helpful to us, and we won't forget. We wish you and your village well."

Prilanna held Galla's warm hands and watched her lustrous copper eyes gleam. She looked to Galla as though she wanted to say something, but the words halted in her throat.

Galla had cared for Dek long enough to know that eventually the words would indeed spill forth, in their time. So she lowered her eyes and smiled to herself, with a feeling of hope within.

Nalag and its fellow deengynes gathered at the end of the village, and each animal's body pointed northward. The sky in that direction looked leaden, and the horizon was wreathed in fog.

Galla and Deming bowed to Birannon and Prilanna, and they turned to set off behind the foxlike deengynes, who made little soft sounds to each other. As their steps took them farther away for the Ildions, however, the creatures grew quiet, with only the lightest footfalls on the tundra.

Nalag slinked back to Galla and Deming, and its head found Galla's hand, and she stroked its fine, amber fur and looked at it affectionately. She glanced up at Deming, and back down.

"You've already done more for us than we could ever have hoped," she told Nalag. "I'm so happy you're coming with us!"

Nalag nudged in between her and Deming, and leaned its head into his hand as well, so that he could pet the beast. Then Nalag galloped off to be with its cohort ahead, and so they made their way over steeper, rockier terrain all that day and the next. At night, they circled Galla and Deming's tent, and after falling asleep curled against each other, the couple would wake to find Nalag at their feet, and one or two other deengynes lounging around on either side.

"You make it very hard to want to get up," Galla mused one morning, yawning, speaking generally at Deming and the deengyne contingent taking up every space in their tent. "It's too warm and cozy to want to move. But move we must! Off you go!" and she rose to get on with the day.

As they walked that day toward an ever-darker horizon, Galla noted Nalag's ears swiveling this way and that. Its nose lifted to the wind. And then it looked up. Galla followed Nalag's gaze and saw shapes wheeling high overhead, too high to see what they were. She shivered.

"Deming," she said quietly. He looked up as well.

"I don't like that," he said, the gold rings in his eyes bright. He pushed his hair behind his ears.

"No," she agreed. "They're not ships, obviously. But something doesn't feel right, not after"— and she shuddered, thinking of the wakeroamers and the shavers.

"Let's stick closer to the base of the mountains," suggested Deming. So they changed course on their way northward, and for all that day, neither of them spoke. The deengynes sank low into the craggy brush and rippled over the landscape like one great, stealthy creature.

One of the animals finally stopped, and all the others followed suit. Nalag made a low, gurgling sort of sound, not quite a growl. The other deengynes reciprocated.

"Are they communicating telepathically *and* vocally?" Galla wondered aloud.

"Maybe," said Deming. "Sort of like Paul." And he took a breath and closed his eyes. Galla found his hand and interlaced her fingers with his, reveling again in the powerful sensation of rightness in the act. Deming opened his eyes and looked deep into hers.

"If you hadn't been there..." he began, but she held a finger to his lips.

"It's over," she said in a murmur.

"You saved me more than once," Deming told her, "and I would do the same for you, over and over, until the last star in the Universe burnt itself out."

"I hope you never have to," Galla said, leaning her face up to kiss him. But the deengynes let out a long, high note.

She shivered, and she and Deming looked down at Nalag, whose ears whirled. The fur on Nalag's back stood up. It licked its lips and glanced up at them, and Galla saw an unmistakable emotion.

"You're afraid," she said softly. "What is it?"

And before any of them could react, a great, dark shape shot down from the sky and plucked a deengyne shrieking into the air.

"Fuck!" Deming pulled at Galla's hand to get her to run with him.

"Nalag!" Galla screamed, holding tightly to the animal, who wanted to join its companions. "No, please don't go, there are more—"

And the screams of the beasts rang in her ears as more and more winged nightmares arced down like whistling torpedoes, long, jagged talons lacerating and butchering them.

Galla held Nalag in her arms as the beast whined and shook, and Deming took her pack with his, and they ran toward the boulders at the feet of the mountains. They had almost made it to a crevice in the rocks when a broken cry rose above the carnage. Deming threw his packs down and turned, and Galla shoved Nalag into his arms and ran off.

"Galla!" Deming shouted.

"Deming, it's Prilanna!" shouted Galla. "I'm going to get her!"

Deming yelled, "No!" but Galla ignored him. She looked up. The sky swirled with the strange creatures, winged and eyeless and without remorse. Galla could see Prilanna running toward her, and her arms were covered in blood; another deengyne's entrails hung off her. Prilanna's look of pure panic set Galla into a rage.

She ran as fast as she could, and seized Prilanna, and picked her up and ran back, just as the winged terrors above turned in a long arrow formation and dove right at them. Pumping, Galla jostled the poor Ildion girl, but she did not stop and did not look up.

Deming's face told her everything she needed to know, that those creatures were coming for *her*, and there was no time to lose. With a skid, Galla crashed on her knees before Deming, and nearly threw Prilanna into the small cave with Deming and Nalag. Then Galla turned and walked back out.

"What the fuck, Galla!" screamed Deming. "Come back!"

Galla called out so that any remaining deengynes might hear, though she did not see any. She ran out into the open space, and one of the flying creatures opened its talons and its great maw and dove right to her, its companions swirling behind it, ready to tear apart anything below it.

She could feel the heat of its foul breath, and see its bloodstained teeth, and that set her screaming in fury. The beaklike mouth stabbed, but she seized it, and twisted and wrestled, even as the animal tried to fly upward again. Galla turned its head and shoved its beak deep into the ground, where it flailed, trying to break free.

Then she faced the next animal. She waited until it almost pierced her, then darted aside, and it struck the ground. Then the swarm was upon her, and she kicked and punched and grabbed and twisted and shrieked, enraged and flushed in awe of her own strength. A high ringing in her ears muffled Deming's own shouts of anguish from where he watched...but then she realized it wasn't so much a ringing as a strange tone...

The winged animals let out a collective, scraping cry, nearly metallic, and sickening to hear. Then they leapt into the sky and fled at high speed up and away, out of sight. The tone rang for some time after, and Galla covered her ears, as did Deming and Prilanna. Nalag yowled.

Then it stopped.

Gasping, Galla looked down at herself. Her clothes were ripped in parts, but mostly intact. She wiped the dirt off her hands and fell to her hands and knees. Her wild hair snapped and coiled all around her. She breathed heavily for a few minutes, then finally she rose. Deming looked ready to spring toward her, but she held up her hands, gasping.

"I'm all right, I'm—I'm—" *What's that word?* she thought. Then her head shot through with a pain so great that her legs buckled, and she held herself as she staggered toward her friends.

As soon as she made it into the cave, Deming's eyes radiated, and she lifted her chin high.

"Why in the hell did you do that?" he said, half-crazed from anxiety, and he seized her and held her up. She looped her sore legs around his waist.

"I wanted to let them know," panted Galla, "that I wasn't going to give up. Not now, not ever."

"But they were like the shavers, and the wakeroamers," protested Deming.

"Deming," said Galla solemnly. "I may not know my past, but I know enemies. And these creatures are driven by someone who wants me gone. Who wants all of us gone," and she slid away from him and approached Prilanna, who sat traumatized, stroking Nalag. She stared with her huge, brown eyes not really seeing anything.

"Prilanna," said Galla warmly, "oh, it's all right, we are safe now. But why did you follow us?" She sighed. "Never mind that now. Let's rest and recover, and drink some water."

She then placed her hand on Nalag's head and said sadly, "I am so sorry, Nalag. I don't know if there are any left. Can you tell?"

Nalag lowered its head onto its paws and let out a long sniff. Galla felt her eyes begin to fill with tears. Deming put his arm around her.

"I'm going to see how far this cave goes back," he said. "Just in case those things come back, maybe we should put some distance between ourselves and that opening."

"Be careful," cautioned Galla. "Who knows what's farther back in the cave, too? I can go."

"You can't do everything yourself, Galla," Deming said, and he looked at her with his inky-dark eyes, with those strange golden rings piercing the shadows he stood within. She nodded.

"I'll stay here, then," she agreed.

Galla sat between Prilanna and Nalag, with one arm around each, and pulled them gently to her, not knowing what else to do.

Deming soon came back, and his eyes were wide, but he had a wry smile on his face.

"What is it?" Galla asked.

"Something really cool," he answered. "Kind of creepy? But it's worth hearing. Come on, you three!"

Wearily, Prilanna stood, and Nalag stretched. They reluctantly followed Deming, with Galla bringing up the rear. The ragged path Deming took them through darkened at first, but by and by they could see light.

"What's that light coming from?" Galla asked.

"Wait and see!" Deming replied, his voice a pitch higher than usual.

They squeezed through a narrow slot, and then the cave opened up into a broad cathedral of sorts. Encrusted all throughout where long fingers of golden-orange light.

"Phyron!" gasped Galla.

And as she said it, a voice rippled back, "PHYRAXIUS PHYRAX PHYRAX!"

"What the—" Galla began, and a voice answered, "THAXIUS THAX THAX!"

Galla, Deming, and Prilanna stared at each other in the warm light. Nalag's ears went high and swerved this way and that, and then it gave a leap into the air.

19

CAXXIUS CAXX

Galla held her hands over her mouth.

Before any of them could say anything, Nalag sprang forward, tail high, no longer despondent to their eyes. It leapt up along a crude stairway and turned every few steps to look back at Galla, Deming, and Prilanna, who were at a loss for words.

Galla stepped forward and followed Nalag's path, and soon they were all climbing up the stairs higher and higher in this great crystalline hall. After several minutes, they reached an outcropping of the phyron crystals, and there they found a flat surface. A carved doorway met them.

Nalag stepped lightly on its delicate feet forward, until finally they heard a shuffling sound. Nalag scooted back into Deming's legs. A figure walked slowly toward them all.

"What the fuck is going on out here?" the voice bellowed. *"Haven't I had enough disturbance today? Had to call off the goddamn crazy bird-things already, didn't I?"*

And they beheld a grizzled old fellow with a wild, long beard and grey hair that shot in all directions. There was a strong but not unpleasant smell encircling him, akin to varnish. He wore a long outfit, of some drab color in the warm, dim light, and it was streaked with what looked like paint of several colors. On closer inspection of his beard, Galla could see bits of blue and yellow paint lodged here and there.

Galla was ready to introduce herself and her companions, when she felt Nalag rub her thigh. She looked down, and its radiant violet eyes shone up at her. She looked at the man. He looked at her. He rubbed his crinkled, hazel eyes.

"I...you...I know you; I know you..." the man said, and his voice trailed off, his hazel eyes watching her emotions flicker on her face, and her hair billowing. Some of the coils of her hair drifted toward him, which surprised her. "You! Is it you? Galla?"

And his face was like shafts of light breaking through a leaden sky, his mind stirred from a long, dark slumber. He let out a moan, and fell to his knees, and bent over and wept, and then he seized her about her legs. She stared at him with enormous amber eyes, not comprehending.

Deming swept forward to pull the man away from her, but she held her hand up.

"You're...Caxxius Caxx?" she asked him, her eyebrows high.

The man stilled and wiped his nose on his sleeve. Then he looked down at his sleeve, and she watched his face turn red.

"God, I'm a mess. I'm sorry."

"Well?" she repeated, and he stood to face her.

"Yes. But no," he said, and then he laughed raucously, and Deming whispered to Galla, *"He's nuts."*

Galla felt her temper simmering, and she clenched her teeth.

"Then who are you?"

The man laughed again, and then said, "Yes, I am Caxxius Caxx. Or that's what they called me. And after so many years, why not! Sure, I'll just be Caxxius Caxx!"

And then he saw her quizzical face, and he nodded.

"From the echo out there."

Galla's eyebrows twitched up and down. "Oh!"

"You don't recognize me. But," he quickly said, rambling, "of course, of course you wouldn't, I've been here so long...Holy shit!

What I must look like to you. And I was asleep and then I wasn't and then...why am I awake now?" And at that moment, he looked at the glowing golden rings around Deming's pupils.

Tentatively, he thought, *Are you a telepath?*

Deming tilted his head a bit at the wizened man. "Are you trying to...communicate with me? Telepathically? I'm not a telepath so much as...well, I suppose I'm not a complete empath. Only with her," he said, gesturing toward Galla. "Or maybe she's so powerful with her emotions, everyone else is quiet?"

"You...you triggered me, then," the man gasped. "I can hear your thoughts in my mind...wow! Wow!"

And he sat down on the ground.

"Wait, who are *you*?" Caxxius asked him. And he leaned back to see Prilanna behind him, but he seemed incurious about her.

"I'm Deming," the young man said, his brow quizzical.

Caxxius scrambled to his feet.

"No! What? It can't be!" and then he threw back his head and cackled. "Deming! *Deming!*"

Deming and Galla blinked at each other.

She stomped one foot and said impatiently, "You're raving. What are you going on about?"

The bearded fellow pointed at Deming and said, "Your name. Is Deming. As in *Linden Deming Forsler*. My great-grandfather!"

Deming gasped. "What!?"

Galla felt another ferocious stab of pain between her eyes.

"I don't understand," she said.

"It's me, Galla! Kein!" he said urgently, excited.

And his eyes looked suddenly youthful and buoyant, but the next moment they sank with sadness.

"What happened, Galla?" he asked, reaching out to her. "It's like you don't know me at all." She stepped away from him.

Deming touched her elbow. "Are you all right?"

"No," she gasped. "I'm in pain. And I don't know this man."

Deming said softly, "He does know *you*, apparently. You knew each other. I can't feel his emotions like I can yours, but it's obvious. He loves you. And he's frightened that you can't remember him."

And Kein said, "That's not all. Oh my God. How long? How long has it been? And…and why are you named after Forster? And how long have I…" and then he held his hands over his mouth. Tears poured from his eyes.

"I…" he said, choking, "I need a few minutes. I'm sorry."

Galla felt a frustration so great, she could have screamed. *This man knows me. Why can't I remember him? Why? Oh, help me! How can I fix this?*

Deming held her, but she stood stiffly, her face frozen.

He said, "Look, Kein is clearly feeling intense anguish. Even if he knew you, I'm not sure how he can help you like this."

"No," Kein spoke up, returning. "I made a promise. I promised Rez, I promised… I came to find you and help you. And something happened… My ship was…grabbed, I don't even think it was the right ship, I'm not sure. And then I ended up here. And I…I think I went mad.

"Galla, you were right about everything. Back on Perpetua. I had to be around another telepath, or in this case an empath. I'm awake! But you! Why? All those years, you can't remember?"

"It's gone," she said, feeling numb and frightened in a way she had not in many years.

Kein looked at Deming, his eyes darting over the young man's face.

"You can sense *her*, but I can't read her thoughts…I can only read yours. I'm sorry, I won't prod," he said quickly.

"You can also just talk to me," said Galla, cheeks aflame. "If you knew me…before…maybe you can help me *now*. I was told to seek out Caxxius Caxx, and here you are, except, now you're not really Caxxius Caxx, you're Kein?"

"Yes," said Kein. He took a deep breath, and exhaled. "I am Kein, the first human you ever met."

Galla shook all over.

"Help me," she murmured, and both men moved to her, one on

either side. Prilanna joined them and looked with great sympathy up at her. Galla said, "You're supposed to help me get to *something*, something beyond the border of Quepahi. Can you do that?"

Kein spoke as if from an ancient memory. "Now I think I understand. The voices. The voices beyond that border, that veil separating this land from the Quo continents, from Quepahi. They kept telling me to keep watch. *'Watch for her. Bring her in.'* And I...I kept hearing that, over and over, for *years*, and I didn't know where I was or whose voice it was...and I...was devastated. I...I went to some dark well in my mind, Galla, and I am so sorry." He swallowed and wiped his tears from his eyes.

He straightened, and looked into her confused, teary copper eyes, and said, "We've waited long enough. We'll go together."

20

THRESHOLD

Kein led them back into his home. He had made a series of rooms inside the catacombs of the mountain, and given the abundance of phyron crystals, most of the rooms glowed of their own accord. But Kein was forever a craftsman, and a tinkerer, and he had found ways to cope with a lack of reliable electricity near the border of Quepahi.

He had fashioned his cooking equipment from the phyron crystals and other found objects and could focus the phyron for higher-temperature baking and grilling. He watched Galla constantly as she, Deming, Prilanna, and even Nalag cast curious eyes about his unique home. He twitched a great deal, having developed a sort of tic, and he pulled on his long-braided beard while describing different equipment.

"I hauled some of this crap up from the shipwrecks," said Kein, and he jerked his head toward Prilanna. "The ones that didn't become sculpture."

At that Prilanna flashed, "They're not sculptures! They're memorials!"

Kein rolled his eyes. "Okay. Sure, memorials. You've all put a lot of work into them, I can see that."

"I never thought Caxxius Caxx was a scavenger," sniffed Prilanna indignantly.

Kein laughed.

"You probably never thought Caxxius Caxx was just an old crank trying to survive either. Oh, I've heard the stories, as much as one can, living alone as a semi-lunatic in the craziest land there ever was."

He turned to Galla again. "Apparently I am something of a wizard." He snickered, awaiting some response in her, something familiar. Galla wrinkled her brows at him, and his smile faded, replaced by a sorrowful expression.

"Right," he said. "God, what have we lost? How long has it been, and what's happened?" He began pulling out pots and pans, and he continued, "I never gave a shit about anything outside my home on Perpetua. Rez was my home."

And he paused and leaned over his makeshift stove and stood silent for a few minutes. His shoulders trembled.

Galla stepped forward and reached toward him, but Deming caught her arm and held her gently back. He looked at her, his lean face full of concern. He shook his head.

"Anyway," Kein finally continued, "the Ildions hyped up my arrival, and I'll never understand how *that* started. I sure as shit didn't start it, I'll tell you *that*. Can *you* tell me?"

He stared pointedly down at Prilanna, who looked confused and angry.

"No," said the girl. She squeezed her lavender hands together and declared, "It's all I've heard my whole life. That the wizard Caxxius Caxx lived in the mountains by the Rift, that only he could enter the Boundary, and that all who ventured to find him would be haunted by nightmares for the rest of their lives."

Kein snorted.

"Clearly that didn't stop you," he said, his beard wagging.

"What do you mean?" Prilanna demanded.

"I've seen you and your friends sneaking over here for years!" Kein said with a cackle.

Prilanna gasped. "How'd you guess that?"

Kein's hazel eyes twinkled. "Your guilty thoughts are shooting out like little fireworks, first of all. Kind of cool! Secondly, I did see you kids from time to time. You never made it up here, so I guess that's a credit to the legends. Kept you scared enough. Whoever came up with them."

Deming cleared his throat, and Kein looked up at him.

"I think I know how they started," said Deming, and the corner of his mouth dimpled. He pushed his hair over his ears and said, "I'm pretty sure it was Gindoo's doing."

"Gindoo!" Kein exclaimed. "How do you know him?"

"Wait, do *you* know him?" Galla asked, finding this entire conversation fascinating yet perplexing.

Kein lowered the heat on a pot he was boiling and folded his arms.

"You know, it's weird. I don't quite remember." He rubbed his temples. He looked fondly at Galla and said, "I guess we're both a little broken, aren't we?

"But what I do remember was, after coming here, I woke up in my ship and found its door open. And I walked out, and it was night, and the auroras! Spectacular auroras. Cold as hell. I could smell sulfur"—his eyes glazed over—"and I thought there must be some sort of geothermal activity close by. I looked all around, and I saw a strange haze to the west, and these mountains to the east. A clear sky I didn't know. I'm staring up at these new stars on this new planet, and somebody says something, and I nearly pissed myself!

"I look all around, and finally down, and there's a *fucking man there*, and he's tiny, and he's got this crazy-ass long hair and beard"—and then Kein looked down at his own beard and guffawed. "Oh shit! I'm turning into him, aren't I! Anyway, then the little guy says, 'Yes, well, took you long enough, didn't it?' And I'm like, 'Who the fuck are you? And where the hell am I?' and he leans on his cane and looks at me like I'm an idiot. And man, did I ever feel like one!"

"What was Gindoo even doing out here?" Deming wondered.

Kein shook his head.

"He says to me, 'You're supposed to be here, and you're supposed to help Galla-Deia when she comes to you.' And I said, 'Look, I don't know you; how do I know you're not the enemy?' And the little fucker—sorry, Deming, clearly you know him..."

Deming and Galla laughed out loud.

"Anyway," Kein went on, "the guy says, 'My name is Gindoo, and I am the most powerful person you've ever met, *aside from Galla-Deia*'—and I'm thinking, no fucking way, I've met Aeriod, and—"

Galla started shaking, and pressing her fingers to her forehead, and she cried, "Oh!"

Deming looped his arms under hers before she slid to the floor of the rustic stone abode.

"Who's Aeriod?" Deming asked. "Galla's having a strong reaction to the name, she feels like she needs to run away, but there's more than that..."

Kein knelt before her and took her hands. "Galla, Galla, I'm so sorry, I didn't mean—*shit*. We won't talk about him. It's okay. It's okay, Galla."

Kein met Deming's gaze and the two communicated in their own way. Kein could read Deming's thoughts, though Deming could not reciprocate. And Deming said quite clearly in Kein's mind, "She's triggered by the name. He must have been important to her." And Kein nodded in silence, knowing better than to discuss that history with him.

Galla, for her part, felt embarrassed, and helpless, and furious at her own lack of self-control. "I'm fine," she said, vehement, standing and dusting herself off. "Go on, Caxx—Kein."

Kein sighed, and continued: "So Gindoo has introduced himself as this super-powerful being, I guess," and Galla and Deming snickered. Kein smiled in relief at Galla's return to humor. "Okay, so he's established he knows his shit here on, oh yes, Quopeia. Which I had never heard of, by the way, not that I had a planetary list lying around...but he made it clear it's obscure for a reason. And then it dawns on me that this place is hidden. And I'm thinking, well, I sure hope Galla can find it, and I want to ask Gindoo more questions, and he—just—disappears!"

Deming laughed indulgently. "He likes to do that! Did he come back?"

Kein sighed again, and he sounded angry.

"He did, but not for a long time. So I was stuck out here, not knowing anything about the place, and waiting. I met some Ildions down in the village, and we bartered for a bit, because I was handy. So I helped them build some of their homes and fix their electrical grid. Such as this godforsaken place allows, that is. I was lonely, and I started unraveling a bit. I was depressed, and missing Rez. I basically started to become a recluse. I built this place," and he waved his arms around. "And I waited. And waited. Gindoo came back occasionally and vanished again. I don't remember everything he said, because, well, frankly, I was just losing it. I didn't care anymore. You never showed up."

And Kein reached out to Galla, and she took his hand. She wanted desperately to remember him. She liked him; he seemed safe to her, and kind, and witty, in his twitchy, eccentric way.

"Finally I asked Gindoo, had something happened, and he said" —Kein trembled, and his eyes filled with tears—"he said the war was over. You were missing. Aer—a lot of folks had disappeared, or were injured, or killed. The seat of galactic government was sacked. Paosh Tohon had a key new player and used that person's power to break into some of the last barriers left. Whoever it was didn't know about this place. But Galla, how did you find it?"

Galla squeezed her arms around herself and Deming stroked her hair for a moment.

"I don't...know. I think, maybe, it found me," she said. "I apparently crashed here, and was jarred badly, and lost my memory... It was a long time before I knew my name. I didn't remember the 'Deia' part at all. I don't know where I came from."

"So," Kein said, and his audience could almost see his thoughts forming before their eyes, "you *did* make it here, obviously, sooner than now, and Gindoo didn't tell me? Why?"

"He didn't know where I was," said Galla, and she felt her teeth clench, remembering Meeya's strictness and poor treatment of her in her early days.

Kein whistled. "Wow. Well, maybe that's a good thing…or a really terrible one, I'm not sure which yet. The galaxy needed you, but it had already fallen, and you couldn't have done anything to stop that. And now, finally, you're here. And I think it's time we did something about it. But first: dinner!"

Deming helped Kein serve Galla and Prilanna, and Nalag was given a special plateful of goodies as well. Kein looked back and forth between Galla and Deming, and he held his hands under his chin and reminisced.

He then said in a soft voice, "I'm happy for you, Galla. And for you, Deming," and the young man blushed and glanced at Galla. "This…this feels right. I wish…but no. I can't think like that. I know Rez would have been happy too."

He lowered his head and focused on his food.

Later he said, "I feel more clarity now than I've felt the entire time I have lived here. I don't know if it's the familiarity with Galla, and even Prilanna here, or Deming's empathy, or Nalag's own telepathic abilities. Shit, maybe it's all of you together. I feel…repaired, for lack of a better word. For that, I thank you. And Galla, it's time we got you where you need to be. I'm cutting all this shit off," and he pulled at his beard and long hair, "and we're heading out first thing tomorrow."

"Quepahi," breathed Galla, feeling excited. Prilanna met her gaze, and the Ildion girl lifted her chin in satisfaction. Deming squeezed Galla's hand, and Nalag rested its head on her knee.

Yes, thought Galla. *This does feel right.*

21

ALLOTROPY

In the morning, after filling their packs anew, a newly groomed Kein led them all upward through the pathways in his home until they could smell fresh outside air. Soon the dawn's light met them as they walked onto a large ledge overlooking the valley below and the fog-cloaked Quo continent to the east: Quepahi.

Prilanna Optison told them, "It is said a city of copper exists on the other side of the boundary, and my people have sought it for years. It is called Trozzhia. And those who looked for it never came back."

Kein slapped his thighs. "That's a good one! Almost as good as my being a goddamned *wizard*. I guarantee you there's no truth to that one. I'd have seen it!"

Prilanna looked quickly up at him, her eyes narrowed, and snapped, "Really? When's the last time the fog lifted? Do you check every day? Do you check at night?"

Kein made an exaggerated rolling of the eyes. "Okay, so I may not have much of a life here, but no, I have not spent my every waking hour looking for a lost city that doesn't exist. Look, I know you believe it with all your might: that's okay. I just...don't."

And he shrugged, while Prilanna looked both stunned and irritated.

"I'll stick to my own beliefs," she retorted. "And you still *might* be a wizard. After all, Ildions can't communicate through thoughts, only deengynes can."

Nalag said, "Awf!" almost as clearly as a spoken word.

Prilanna went on, "Or so we thought, but then you're able to do this too. Maybe you're able to do many more things, and like Galla, you can't remember."

"I seriously doubt that," Kein muttered.

"You seem to doubt a lot of things," sniffed Prilanna.

"Are you going to argue this entire trip?" Galla asked them, and they both looked at her and then at each other. Kein shrugged, Prilanna tossed her head. But they both quieted, and so the journey continued.

Kein led them across the spine of the peak they had stood upon, and gradually they began to zigzag down to the valley. They looked to the sky occasionally, wary of any of the vicious beasts that had attacked them before. None of them appeared. So their spirits lifted a bit, and the excitement of travel returned to each of them.

Galla could smell strong puffs of sulfur, and to the north, she could see thick columns of what looked like steam.

"What is that?" she asked, pointing.

"That's the Rift," Kein answered. "It's a split in Quopeia's surface, spilling up part of its mantle. There's a great river that has tributaries that flow into the Rift, and it sends up a lot of steam. You'll see the Rift soon. We'll have to cross it to get to Quepahi."

Deming stared at him. "How are we going to do *that*?"

Kein replied nonchalantly, "Oh, there's a big stone bridge."

"A bridge?" Galla, Deming, and Prilanna said in unison.

He looked at them in surprise. "What? There are such things as stone bridges, you know."

"Have you been across it?" Prilanna asked breathlessly.

"Nah," said Kein. "Never had any desire or need to do that, until now. I heard the voices from it, long ago...but it was too much for me. I sure didn't want to go and find out anything else."

"How can you be so incurious!" the girl exclaimed.

"Oh! So you really didn't know there was a bridge! Guess you don't know everything about this area, then, after all!" Kein cried victoriously.

Galla covered her mouth to hide her grin. Prilanna only looked intrigued, with her eyes massive, and she picked up her pace. Everyone else followed suit, and Nalag trotted along for some distance ahead. Then the beast abruptly halted, lifted its snout, and jumped into the air.

"What is it, Nalag?" called Prilanna.

The animal's tail flicked back and forth like a flame. Then it took off at a charge, up and over a hill, and out of sight.

"Is it hunting?" Galla wondered.

"Nalag doesn't usually hunt like that," Prilanna replied. "I don't know what's going on."

They kept walking, and then a ripple of chattering little voices met their ears. And up from a little curve in their path bounded several deengynes, with Nalag leading the pack.

Prilanna cried out and ran to Nalag and embraced the deengyne.

Galla quickly followed. "Oh!" she said joyfully, "thank goodness, oh...I am so glad there are survivors."

Suddenly all the animals encircled Kein and sat down on their haunches to stare at him.

"Good God!" Kein exclaimed. "It's like an attack of cuteness!"

His face moved between amused, perplexed, and awed. He sat down among the circle of animals.

"They're all speaking with me in my mind!" he said to his companions. He closed his eyes to concentrate.

"What are they saying?" Galla asked.

Kein focused. "They're saying they hid, that the things we saw flying normally don't live here and were taken over by something. That other animals were being taken over, and they were looking for...Galla, they're looking for *you*."

Galla felt icy prickles march up her back. "Again!" she whispered. "Why? Why do these creatures keep coming after me?"

Kein grimaced. "If I had to guess? I would say maybe Quopeia isn't as safe anymore. That the enemy is here."

"Agreed," Deming said. "There was an attack in Allurulla. Gindoo told us to leave the city and come out here and find you. We don't even know if the President survived."

"Oh shit!" said Kein. "Well, something's afoot, even out here. That...doesn't bode well. So, let's get to Quepahi and hope for the best. I don't think anything is getting into that place. Not the enemy, and maybe not us, either!"

The smaller pack of deengynes, with Nalag at their head, swooped up and down over the hills, and circled back, ever on the move, and much more cautious. Their ears swiveled, their tails twitched, and if one of them yelped, every animal and person ran to hide. This happened three times, but nothing came of it. Everyone felt on edge and exhausted when they set up camp for the night in the shelter of huge, ancient glacial boulders.

As twilight faded, the auroras burst forth, and everyone stared in awe. Coils and curtains and starbursts of brilliant greens and violets arced overhead, beyond the sky, into space. Yet Galla could see a strange bending of these silent ripples of light in the darkness: they seemed to stretch from the fogged-in land of Quepahi and to the far north, but they converged over a concentrated area beyond the boundary they sought to cross.

"It's *really* crazy tonight," Kein noted. "Look at how they're so focused over there!"

Galla asked, "So it's not normally like this?"

"Nowhere near this vibrant, and not so...focused, I should say," Kein remarked. "It's almost like...they're being brought down to the surface!"

"We noticed in the Southwest that the auroras kept getting brighter, what we could see of them anyway...which wasn't much," said Galla.

"They have been," Prilanna said. "We've been recording the

increase for many decades, and before that it was just a normal aurora, based on Siloxxa's activity."

"What mythology did you cook up for that?" Kein quipped.

In the darkness, Galla could not see Prilanna's face, but the young Ildion's little disgusted tutting noises told her everything she needed to know.

She considered the changes, and Deming scooted next to her as they all sat and looked into a small fire. The wind, stronger in the day, began to die down, while the light shows above them twisted.

"It seems like everything is converging," she mused. "I'm—I'm a little scared for what it means."

"Let's get some rest," Deming suggested. "No matter what we face tomorrow, you're not alone. And we will all be better after a proper sleep."

22

THE CITY STONE

Thrashing in her sleep from fitful dreams and anxiety, Galla threw off her sleeping pack and sat up in the dark hours before dawn. She could hear the distant crackling and hissing from the Rift, as the magma rose from below Quopeia's surface and met the rivers and other tributaries that flowed down from the snowy mountains of the North. The smell of sulfur rose and fell with the presence or absence of the wind. Once in a while, a deengyne let out a cautious, low howl, and its friends responded with snorts and soft yips.

Nalag had chosen to sleep between Prilanna and Kein's encampment, but the deengyne glanced over at Galla, with the fading campfire's embers reflecting in its haunting, violet eyes. Deming stirred, having slept soundly despite Galla's movements, and in his half-dozing state, he stretched his long hand along her back to soothe her. It worked, a little.

I dread what's coming, she thought. She felt relieved that no one seemed to be able to read her thoughts, despite her emotional outpourings. *I don't know why, but I am afraid of what we will find. It's pulling me toward it, though I do not want to go. It's stronger than gravity. What is it?*

She stared up at the spectacular loops of the aurora, and they shone in a vivid, mesmerizing green. And even its hue stirred some feeling of familiarity in her. The night had grown still, and the ground began to freeze. She curled up behind Deming and wrapped her arms around the tall young man, and pressed her nose into his neck, and breathed in his scent. She thought of the comforts of Gindoo's boardinghouse, and for some reason, she thought of the quilts in her room. She wished she had one of them now. Deming's grandmother's, he had said. He had a family he had never known, and she wondered if she did as well. She stroked his dark hair and kissed his neck.

I am afraid for him also. And she felt her tears collect on her cheek, and slowly fall, until she finally fell asleep.

SHE WOKE TO A ROARING FIRE. Kein had rebuilt the fire at some point and was cooking breakfast for them all. The cadre of deengynes had hunted already and lay in circles around the fire, panting and content. Nalag rose and stepped delicately over to Galla, nudging her and Deming. Deming rose on one elbow and scratched Nalag's head. The creature reached for his hand and lowered it to its chest, and Deming laughed and began scratching there instead.

He sat up and put his arm around Galla.

"Try not to be nervous," he said to her, with his rich, dark eyes offset by quite brilliant gold rings.

"Did I keep you awake?" she asked, sheepishly.

Deming rubbed the short but rapidly growing dark beard on his chin and grinned. "It was worth it for what you did after. Keeping me warm, as always, you little furnace."

Galla whispered, "I wish we had more privacy," and Deming responded by taking her small face in his hands, looking into her warm, copper eyes, and letting her vibrant coils of hair twist toward him.

"I'll love you publicly," Deming told her. "At any time or place. I don't care who knows it, I don't care who sees."

Galla blushed and laughed in spite of her anxiety, and kissed him profusely on his lips, his nose, his cheeks, and for good measure, his neck, in front of everyone.

"Unabashed," Kein said in a low voice, but they all heard him, and the smile on his face and the tears in his eyes said more than he dared to say aloud.

He cleared his throat, looked down at his worn and stained hands, and looked up again, blinking, toward their destination: the stone bridge. He said, "I think we should get going, just in case we have any more unexpected visitors from above, or wherever the hell else."

So they broke down their makeshift camp, doused the fire, and set their packs on their backs. They could see the outline of the bridge in the thick fog. It was enormous, easily seventy feet high, and looked as if it were part of the landscape of surrounding basalt. It rose through the fog, and where it ended, they could not see in the blankness beyond. It was a broad bridge, much to everyone's relief. The deengynes began climbing the rough rocks above them. Nalag pranced up ahead of the others and made little hoots down at them.

Kein said, "Nalag says the other side is still invisible, but good and stable. It's pretty huge, though I've never been across it. And it may be wide, but you sure as shit don't want to fall down into the Rift."

The heat from the magma current of the Rift, along with the noisome stench, would have sent most people back the way they had come. But Galla would not be deterred, having come this far. The others watched her. The deengynes parted where they perched on the bridge.

"Onward," she said, and set forth and upward as the great black bridge stretched above the licking flames of molten rock.

It was slow going, for the fumes and the steam and the fog set them all coughing and straining to see. The deengynes served as another sense, in a way, communicating in their little chains of thought, which Kein could pick up and decipher. After an hour, they all halted and panted as they sat on their haunches. Nalag whined.

"They've reached the top," Kein announced.

Galla watched her team wipe sweat from their brows. Prilanna looked miserable, having covered her mouth and nose with a scarf to avoid the strong smell. Deming's eyes streamed tears from irritation. Kein coughed other every minute. Galla marched forth.

"Keep going," she told them. "We'll be down again soon and...and then, well. I guess we'll know what we're really dealing with."

But she could not escape the increasing sense of dread from the night before, and by the looks of her companions, they too were growing uneasy. Slowly they moved closer to one another. And by and by, the deengynes slinked back, rather than prancing ahead of them all. Tails down, they began to congregate and wait for Galla.

"What is it, Nalag?" she asked, for the creature had lowered its head and approached her, making high-pitched squeaks.

"They're afraid," Kein said simply. And the bulging of his large, hazel eyes told Galla that he was, as well.

Galla drew in a shaky breath and walked ahead of the animals and her friends. She turned and looked back at them all.

"You don't need to come with me," she told them. "Something is wrong here...or at the very least, strange. And I don't want to endanger any of you. Why don't you all head back and make camp? I can go on, see what it is, and find you later."

Nobody budged.

"I'm going with you everywhere," Deming said flatly.

"Seconded," Kein said. "I have *nowhere else to go*. This is what I signed up for. *This* is why I am here."

"I will follow you," Prilanna declared.

And the deengynes all tipped their noses high, and some of them sneezed.

Galla nodded, the left corner of her mouth curling in just a bit.

"Onward it is," she said.

She turned and set forth, and the black bridge began to descend. It sank into ever-thicker fog, until she could barely see anything. She stumbled on the rough surface under her feet and slipped. She felt herself falling, and she grasped desperately for any hold, and that the handhold she reached crumbled. Soon her legs dropped over the side of the bridge, and she hung above the crevasse of fire below.

Her breath came in shallow gasps, and she strained on her elbows to lift herself back up.

Where are the others?

"Guys!" she called, trying not to sound panicked. She could feel the heat beneath her feet and heard the strange flow of magma pulsating below. *One more slip, and I might find out just what will kill me.*

Nobody responded.

Finally, she cried, "Help!"

Still nothing. She pulled at the rock bridge, which was damp and slippery from the steam and fog, and strained, feeling more weakened every second.

All this way, and I fall off a bridge? The thought made her laugh, and it made her furious. And then she felt strength again. She felt a hot rage, and if she could have seen herself from above, she would have seen her hair jerking back and forth in all directions, reflecting her explosive fury. She pulled and slipped and pulled again, and finally she swung her legs with all her might and caught hold of the bridge. She pulled herself up and stared up from where she lay on her back.

What was that?

And she found herself alone.

"Deming!" she called. "Prilanna! Kein! Nalag!" No one answered her.

Her fury dissipated and she felt a cold fear creep back into her.

What if they fell off the bridge? she thought in a sickening horror. *No, no, no. I will not think this. This does not help me. They're lost in the fog, that's all. I'll keep going.*

But this was not a simple task. She could see almost nothing, and the descent grew steeper and more treacherous. She called for her friends repeatedly, and received no response.

Am I meant to take this journey by myself after all?

Then Galla felt horribly alone. Her eyes stung from suppressed tears, for she did not want to hamper her vision any more than the fog had seen fit to do. She felt as if she were on the verge of something, some ghastly moment, a moment of pain and ending and beginning. *A first memory or a last one?* For in it, she stared up at a bright orange moon from a crater on a prairie...*But where did I fall from?*

Someone yelled, an agonized and jagged sound, and Galla sucked in the smelly air and listened. She called out, "Deming! Kein! Prilanna!" but no one answered her in words. Instead she heard a higher-pitched scream, looping over and over.

What's happening to them?

The fog lifted just enough to allow some visibility, and she ran ahead. But the thick fog returned, and she slammed into a black stone wall and slid down on her backside. A shape moved to her right and fell onto her. It was Kein. He gripped his temples as though he might tear into them.

"My mind!" he cried.

Another shape formed, to her left, and it was Prilanna, and she fell weeping onto her hands and knees next to Galla.

"Help me, help me!" the girl screamed.

And then a tall form appeared and fell down and forward, and it was Deming, reaching out, and he held onto Galla's waist and whispered, "I can feel all of them," and then he sagged to the ground and lay still.

"Deming!" Galla cried. "Kein, Prilanna! What's happened?"

Each of them twitched and moaned. Kein ultimately crawled away and vomited, and he must have been leaning over the edge of something, because the vomit never struck anything they could hear.

Galla sat numb and helpless. Deming held her legs, and she leaned her head back against the stone she had struck earlier and looked up. The fog began to dissipate a bit, and she saw the bright arc of an aurora, so bright a green that it almost hurt to look at. She had never seen a more vivid green. She breathed in the pocket of fresher air and stared up at the waves and ripples and curtains.

"Look," she managed to say in a hoarse voice.

One by one, they each looked up.

Seeing them come out of their reveries, she asked her companions again, "What happened?"

They shuffled a bit. And little shapes emerged from the fog to crowd around: the deengynes, their tails lowered, their backs bristled.

"I could feel...everyone," Deming croaked. "I mean *everyone.* Everywhere."

Kein cleared his throat. "I could hear everyone's thoughts."

Prilanna shifted around so that she sat beside Galla. "I could see something terrible. Black and twisting and reaching for all of us."

Galla listened and tried to still her anxiety by watching the green aurora.

"I nearly fell," she whispered, her eyes fixed on those high, brilliant curtains of light above. "I felt so alone. As if there were no one else that could ever understand how I feel. But I'm watching the green above...as if it matters, somehow. And I don't—I don't feel so alone now. I don't know why that is. It's not just that you're all back here. It's—it's as if someone else out there *does* understand."

She swallowed, closed her eyes for a moment, and then she gently stepped away from Deming's arms. She stood tall and confident. "We've each experienced something very strange," she said to them. "But we can't stop. Come on, we have to keep going."

Kein groaned, Deming sighed, and Prilanna shook herself. They rose to their feet.

"Before the fog comes back, let's try to find our way to the top of this rock wall," said Galla, drawing her hands across the basalt surface she had slammed into earlier. Nalag trotted up to her then and nudged her knee with a wet nose.

Galla looked down at its luminous violet eyes and watched it bounce on its front feet. She could not help smiling.

"Very well, Nalag," she said, stroking between its ears, "you're nimbler than the rest of us. Show me what you found."

Nalag dipped its head down to its paws, and then lifted it up again and sneezed, and pranced a bit in place before stepping off to the left of Galla and Prilanna. They followed the animal, and Deming and

Kein joined, as did the rest of the deengynes, flowing between the humans' legs, much to Kein's dismay.

"I don't need to trip and fall down into the lava chasm," he chided the animals irritably.

Galla and Nalag led the way up a steep crack in the rocks, and after several slips and slides and scrapes, the others joined them. Galla halted on a mostly flat surface and stared at what lay before them all.

A sleek, shimmering surface rose in front of them, stretching left and right as far as they could see, and it arched upward, curving out of sight. The enormous domelike structure resembled a bubble. The flickering green aurora above their heads not only reflected on the surface of the bubble, it also seemed to extend down into it, somewhere within the structure.

"What the hell is this place?" Kein said in a low voice. He lifted his head and stared in awe. "God...it seems so familiar, though..." and the aurora swirled in his hazel eyes as he took it all in.

Galla felt chilled. "You're right," she murmured. "It does."

"What's on the other side?" Prilanna wondered aloud what everyone was thinking. She moved closer to the bubble, but Galla threw her arm in front of the girl to stop her.

"Don't touch it," Galla warned them all. "It could hurt you, or worse. Let me do it."

"Galla, no," Deming urged her, putting his hand on her shoulder. "It could hurt *you*."

Galla turned and looked up at Deming, his gold-ringed eyes glowing, the aurora shining on his dark hair in the northern night, and she brushed her fingers along his fine nose and his high cheekbones, and around his short beard. She grinned at him.

"I'll risk it," she said to him.

And she turned before he could stop her, dashed forward, and placed her hands on the surface of the bubble. It felt like glass at first. But then she felt a shiver in the surface, and it began to soften, and little ripples fled from where her palms touched it. She pushed a bit, and the surface bent with her.

"Hold onto me," she told Deming, "and if this works, hold onto the others and bring them too."

Galla pushed as the surface warped inward. It was stiff yet supple at the same time, like a thick rubber, but reflective. She pushed harder, and Deming held onto her waist from behind, and it yielded to both of them more, so Kein and Prilanna quickly ran up behind Deming. Nalag gently nipped Prilanna's leg, and the five of them fell forward into empty air, and the bubble snapped shut behind them. They were met with silence and a marvel.

Galla found herself on a sleek, downward-curving surface, which looked like new copper, stretching in a great crater for miles before them, underneath the dome they had just entered. Far from them, a lone copper tower rose, nondescript, and from its top great electrical arcs rose to the zenith of the dome. The green aurora appeared to originate from the top of the huge dome.

The brilliant copper floor beneath Galla's feet shuddered then, and she and her friends began to slide down into the huge bowl below them. But the bowl began to flatten a bit, as if it were rising. Galla skidded to a halt on the flattening surface. She looked behind her, at Deming, Kein, Prilanna, and Nalag. Her multihued hair began rising in all directions as if from static electricity. The copper surface below her mirrored the color of her eyes.

"What do I do now?" she asked them. Her eyebrows were raised, and her eyes huge, and she felt quite out of her depth.

"Look!" cried Prilanna, and they all turned. Something was bulging out of the great copper floor. It was a small bulge, and soon it popped out, and they all found themselves staring without comprehending what it was.

It was a round, silver object, about knee high. It sat still for a moment, freed from its copper entrapment. Then it began rolling toward Galla. She could hear voices behind her, the two men protesting and cautioning her. But she stood absolutely still.

It rolled right up to her feet, and a little bright sort of eye-light shone up at her. It squawked, and a little piece of its top panel opened. And out of that emerged a sparkling, violet object, about the length of Galla's hand, hexagonal, and it began to glow. The little round presence trilled and extended the purple crystal up closer to Galla.

Kein gasped.

"It's yours, Galla!" he cried. "Take it!"

Galla took hold of the stone.

23

PHOENIX

The stone burned Galla's hands, and she screamed, but she clung to it, while her friends watched in horror. She shook violently, and as brilliant violet swaths of light emerged from all of the stone's facets, she struggled to hold on to it. With a shriek, she found herself flung high into the air. She began spinning over and over, and those below her could not tell if the brilliant violet light they beheld came from her, the stone, or both.

"Galla!" Deming shouted up at her. He could feel turbulence building in her, even from that far below her, and he half dreaded what was happening to her. Still, he stood firmly. *I knew she would be a journey. And here's a twist in the road.*

Hearing his voice, Galla fought with herself and the stone. For in her mind everything had tumbled and crashed together, expanded and contracted, and it became too much for her for a moment. She let out a long, haunting wail, and her companions shivered, hearing it. But she stopped spinning. She looked down at them all, and she closed her eyes as she held tightly to the purple crystal. She then hovered down to them, her hair aloft and shimmering, and her feet met the surface again.

Deming rushed to her, but she held her hands up at him, still gripping the stone. The look in her eyes chilled him.

"Don't," she said, her voice hard. "I remember."

Deming's face fell, as he could feel every emotion churning in her. So he understood her sudden caution. But he set his jaw.

"What do you remember?" he asked her carefully.

Galla turned and looked at Kein, and said softly, "I remember you, Kein. My dear friend," and her eyes shone with tears. Kein stepped forward as well, then stopped, and knelt before her, his face streaming.

She turned back to Deming, and he flinched, for it seemed to him that she looked at him as if through a telescope, from a long distance away. He could feel her trying to push him back.

"I remember everything," she said. "I remember Bitikk. I remember everything there. I know what they did to me. And...and I know what I can do," and she began trembling.

"It's all right, Galla," Deming told her.

She could not bear to look at him.

"I remember Rob," she said, and she shook with sobs for several minutes.

Kein, Deming, and Prilanna exchanged looks of confusion. Nalag slinked up to Deming's legs and nudged him. Deming looked down at the animal, and then at Galla.

"Please don't shut me out," Deming said to her.

Nalag dared to slip next to Galla, and its violet eyes reflected her violet stone. Some of her tears fell on its fur. But she looked down, and she managed to smile a little, and she stroked the gentle animal.

Deming looked at her desperately.

Galla sank down onto the surface and looked about through her tears, and she called out, "Pliip! I remember you too," and the little silver bot who had given her back her stone whirred and buzzed and rolled slowly over to her.

"You're a little slower now, Pliip," she said, stroking the silver bot. The bot piped out some indignant noises. Galla patted it.

"Galla," Deming said, breaking her reverie, "may I hold you now?"

She blinked up at him, and she blushed.

"I know you," she said.

Deming smirked then and said, "Um...yes, you do. Very well."

Kein snorted.

"Not that," she said, her cheeks aflame. "I know who you are, really. I knew Ariel and Dagovaby...your parents," and her tears poured forth anew. "I'm so sorry. I tried to stop Ariel from going and she wouldn't—" but Kein shot her a warning look.

"I don't understand," Deming replied, not quite equipped to deal with the emotions radiating from Galla, but unable and unwilling to step away from her. "What are you saying to me?"

Galla held her stone to her chest and said, "Ariel and Dagovaby decided to go to Paosh Tohon by themselves, to try and stop it. Obviously, that didn't work. And the minute you met me, I set you on a dangerous path. It's obvious Paosh Tohon has been trying to stop us, even though this planet has protected us for so long. I can only think that the reason it got through at all...is that Ariel was used to find us."

Kein sighed. Deming did step back then, and Kein reached out and put his hand on the young man's shoulders.

"It's all right, Kein," Deming said warmly. "I can handle this. My parents made a terrible choice. That isn't your fault, Galla. And...you lost...someone you loved, named Rob. I'm sorry. All that pain for so long. You were badly injured. And now I know what that little box was, that you kept buried in you. It protected you. It's gone now. You don't need it anymore. Let yourself grieve. I won't stand in your way."

Galla looked at him with fire in her eyes, which surprised him.

"Yes, I lost people I loved. I loved Rob, and he died before my eyes," she said quietly. "The Huntrens found me, gave me a home, and I recovered after a fashion. I think I really didn't start the healing process until Dek came into my life. I may never have left the Huntren farm, had it not been for him. I think Meeya and Cuz knew that. But Dek grew up, and had to leave, and so did I. It was time. But what did we lose?

"I knew I was running out of time to stop the Event. I was told there were only two chances. I lost the first one. I can't lose the second. I need to track down the telepaths and seal off the Event before it's too late."

Galla met Deming's gaze and stood and took hold of his left hand with her right.

"Deming, I love you," she began.

"Do not ask me, Galla," Deming interrupted her. "I won't do it. I know what you're going to ask."

Galla tossed back her violet-copper-gold hair, but it still drifted toward Deming.

"I won't put you at risk," she told him in a firm voice. Every word she said now had an edge to it, for her long memory was full now, and much of it hurt. "Go back to Allurulla, and stay there, hidden. Let me finish my Task. I won't lose you too."

Deming stood proud and clear-eyed.

"My parents were taken by this thing," he said. "If there's any chance they're still out there, in any form at all—dead or alive—I want to find them. You need telepaths. Well, I'm an empath now, and Paul is a telepath. So we have to help you."

"I don't want to lose you! Either of you!" shouted Galla, an old, seething rage boiling in her. "I've known for a long time that Paosh Tohon wanted to defeat me by killing those I love. I won't allow it again!"

"You don't have a choice," said Deming firmly, his own eyes flashing with their newly golden rings. "I'm never leaving you. There's no going back. I knew that from the beginning."

Galla crinkled up her brow. "What?"

Deming took hold of her wrists gently, and she looked down at the bracelet he had woven, and at her stone in one hand.

He kissed her and said, "I've spent my life training for something. I never knew what it was. All the repetition, the tests of patience, the frustrations Gindoo put me through. He was helping me get ready. Gindoo told me many times throughout my life that one day I would face a choice to go forward, or to hide. And once I made the choice it would be final. He said, too, the choice would be easy and difficult at the same time. But he was wrong about that part. It's the easiest choice to make, because it's the right one."

Galla watched him in surprise as he took hold of her crystal and, wincing at its heat, slipped it into one of her pockets. Then he took both her hands in his. She opened her eyes wide. Galla felt a current of warmth flood her. It was the feeling of solace in darkness that she had felt long ago, and yearned always to feel again.

"It was *you*," she gasped. "When I first went into a Device on Rikiloi. And then later, on Bitikk...where I spent over half a century. I had visions of you!"

It was Deming's turn to be amazed. "Visions of *me*?"

"Yes, but...they still don't make sense," and as she searched these old memories, she remembered a feeling of sadness in the visions. This sent a chill through her. "I know now it was you, though, because..." and Galla took his hand, "of the feeling when we hold each other. I knew it in those visions, and I wanted it so badly to be real. And it is."

He looked at his beloved friend, in this silent, copper place with its strange humming. Kein watched him with a mix of joy and sadness, for he knew the pain of leaving the person he loved. Galla was making the same choice Kein had made for Rez, but this time, it was different. Kein could hear the young man's thoughts: *She is a goddess and I am only a man. I don't know how or why she loves me, but I will never leave her.*

Galla felt confused and conflicted, her thoughts whirling with myriad memories, both good and bad, spanning a length of time far longer than Deming's life. She remembered her time with Aeriod, she remembered Meredith's death, and she remembered the goodbye she had never wanted when Rob was killed.

She said to Deming, gazing into his dark, gold-edged eyes, "Meredith's grandson, Ariel's son...how could it be that we would find each other now? But you mean more to me than anything. I have fallen onto a planet and survived. Losing you would kill me."

The tears on her cheeks glistened in the softest hue of purple. Deming met them with his lips and tasted them.

"We all die someday," he said quietly, kissing her neck. "But with you I feel more alive. I want to help you, always. I know what you need. I know what you want. And I will give it to you."

Galla shook her head under his chin. "But what if—"

Deming grinned at her and shook his own head.

"Stop catastrophizing. I want to marry you."

"What!" cried Galla. And she couldn't help it. She laughed.

Deming lowered down to his knees, and kissed her belly, and laid his head against it. He held onto her waist and sat there for several moments, and she stroked his hair, and occasionally swept tears from her eyes with her fingertips.

"Deming, are you serious? Are you—are you ready?" Galla asked, feeling so much turbulence within...but overriding it were long waves of growing joy, despite all her worries.

"I was ready when you walked in my door," Deming said, lifting his head and locking eyes with her.

Kein, enough out of earshot not to hear every word, caught the power of Deming's thoughts, and he shouted, "Did you propose to her?"

He and Prilanna moved closer to Galla and Deming.

"Yes," Galla and Deming called out in unison.

Kein threw up both arms and stared at Galla. "Well?"

To Deming, Galla whispered, "So was I."

And he rose and picked her up and held her close and breathed her in. Their tears intermingled, and because he could feel her, their happiness did as well. Prilanna squealed and Kein whooped.

But a whine from Nalag broke the moment. Prilanna turned swiftly to look, for Nalag's ears had flicked back in alarm. Prilanna held out her arm and pointed, her already large eyes flaring wider, and Kein followed her gaze.

"Uh—what the hell is *that*?" he exclaimed.

Galla could see something shimmering before them. The copper surface beneath their feet glowed, as if becoming molten, and something bulged in the bright, liquid mass. It was the shape of a man, or so Galla thought. And it changed from copper to blue-silver. Its eyes shone a deep bright blue. She covered her hands with her mouth.

"Oni-Odi!" she cried. And she ran to him, weeping, disbelieving.

"My daughter!" said the gentle android, and he embraced Galla-Deia.

24

TROZZHIA

Galla clung to Oni-Odi, while Deming, Kein, and Prilanna looked on, mystified. Pliip and Nalag approached each other. Nalag sniffed Pliip, and Pliip beeped, which made Nalag jump high into the air. Then Nalag bowed deeply to Pliip, and the two cavorted on the smooth copper floor, chasing each other in circles. Galla laughed through her tears of overwhelm.

Oni-Odi turned to face Deming with his unblinking, cobalt eyes. Deming stood steadfast, his eyes wide, his chin high, his expression hopeful.

"The Associates did not plan for you," the android told him. "The Summoners knew Galla-Deia would be essential for the Event. They did not know exactly how. Now it is clear. She needs you and Kein, the descendants of two divergent lineages of telepaths.

"Daughter, you are the prism of minds," Oni-Odi declared.

Galla bent her head.

"I don't know how to do what I need to do next," she admitted. "I know that I must make sure all the telepaths we recruited long ago are even still alive. And then they need to be put into place on every Device world, their own stones awakening those waiting for them. After that, I would need to channel my own power from...from here, somehow, maybe? Here, at the apex of the Horseshoe. There are so many questions I have. I don't even know the status of the rest of the galaxy! Is there a way I can find out? And how would I find everyone? If Paosh Tohon and Valemog are so powerful after all these years... how can I face such a thing, and win?"

"You will need strong minds to help you," Oni-Odi answered placidly.

Galla started. "I've heard this before, but not from you," she murmured. "From beings...on Perpetua, and on another world filled with giant creatures underwater, that looked like neurons—"

"What?" cried Kein. "Are they the same as the ones on Perpetua?"

Galla tapped her chin with her finger. "They seem related somehow. I don't know if they're exactly the same. But they're connected to this."

"The Innervation!" Kein smacked his head. "That has to be the answer. Whatever this...this place is, my great-grandfather Forster told me before I came here, 'You're in the Innervation,' and it seemed like crucial info."

"What *is* the Innervation?" Galla asked. "I've heard of it before as well. Oni, do you know?"

Oni-Odi stood straight and tall, silver and blue. His unwavering, cobalt, glowing eyes showed no emotion, as ever. He bent his head down to look at Galla, and his eyes glitched for a moment, and sparked. Galla jumped.

"What is it, Oni?" she gasped. "Are you...are you *oakay*?"

Prilanna stepped close to Galla, her face grooves flaring in anxiety and wonder, her great brown eyes shining.

"It is the effect of the Quo," she said to Galla. "Nothing electronic can work for long."

"But," Galla began, and then she watched as Pliip slowed and halted, even after Nalag nudged the little bot with its nose. "But Oni, you've been here...how long? And what has happened to Demetraan? And the other bots?"

And Galla felt a cold burrowing in her soul then. She almost did not want to know.

Oni-Odi said in his calm voice, "You have been delayed long enough from your Task. I have worked in that time as best I could to prepare for you." He turned to look at every one of them. "Each of you must play a part as well. She needs strong minds to help her: yours. And your brother's," Oni-Odi added, turning to Deming.

"I don't know if—" Deming began. Then he looked up again. "I think I would know if Paul had been killed."

"Gindoo would know," Oni-Odi declared impassively.

Deming made a sound in his throat. "Does Gindoo just travel everywhere when I'm not around? How do *you* know him?"

"Gindoo allowed me to enter Quopeia, to hide Demetraan."

Everyone stared at him.

"What?" Prilanna spoke for all of them.

Oni-Odi looked upward, with sparks in his robotic eyes, at the great aurora above them. It was fading a bit, as the glow of dawn edged along the horizon.

"Gindoo is a mage. Mages are good for hiding things. Planets, people," he said, and he turned his bright eyes to Deming. "Perhaps some mages are good for training, like Gindoo. Perhaps others are not," and he looked upward again.

Galla knew of a silver-eyed, silver-haired mage who might fall under Oni-Odi's latter description.

"Has Aeriod been here?" she asked.

Oni-Odi's eyes shone clearly then. "He has not been *here*. I think he may have attempted to enter Quopeia."

"Yes," Galla said. "He—at the Ball in Allurulla, he appeared to me, almost like an apparition. I didn't recognize him exactly then, as I couldn't remember him. It triggered a fear response in me, and I ran, and then the explosion happened, and—that was a terrible night. I do hope Paul made it out. And Deming, I hope you are right.

"But Oni—what do you mean, he attempted to enter? Why would he not be able to enter? He's a powerful mage."

Oni-Odi tilted his head down to look at her.

"He was unable to enter because Gindoo did not allow him entry."

They all made confused and surprised sounds.

"That doesn't make sense," Galla said. "Does Gindoo allow terrorists to enter?"

"That is highly doubtful," Oni-Odi remarked.

"I agree," Deming said emphatically.

Oni-Odi said, "This planet does have its own defenses. Gindoo knows how to use them for his own purposes. But if the enemy found a way in, it was not Gindoo's doing, and this portends that Paosh Tohon is more powerful than the Associates anticipated. Quopeia was the last fortress of protection, which is why I chose to hide Demetraan here."

"But...this isn't Demetraan," Galla said, looking about her.

"It is," said Oni-Odi. "But it is made new. For you. And for your Task. As my purpose has changed, so has Demetraan's. The city is your own now. Once it is launched away from this planet, Paosh Tohon will know of it again. So I have prepared."

"But Oni," said Galla stubbornly, and she did not notice Deming approaching her slowly with vivid eyes, "Demetraan is *yours*, not mine."

Galla could not quite comprehend that the surface she stood upon was the same Demetraan she had been raised in. That was another time and place, sleek from the Seltra legacy, and full of trees and green spires and so many robotic beings all around her. She held her stone, cooled now and dark. She looked out at the jagged mountain ranges, the carnelian thread of the Rift, and the long undulation of the landscape to the west and north. This was a wild land, carved and broken and untamed, and she felt a kinship with it.

She did not like the emotions roiling within her, as her past and present collided. She closed her eyes for a moment and found herself remembering Allurulla. She could hear her steps ringing on the wooden floors of the stone boardinghouse, and the quiet mornings, laughing with Dek and listening to Deming. She even missed the bickering between Deming and Paul, for that felt normal and relatable to her. That felt like home to her, in a way Perpetua had, but more so. Even more, she realized, than Demetraan had, long ago. And

Demetraan was burnished anew, malleable. What would become of it? And dear Oni-Odi: at last she could be with the closest thing she had to a father. But she was troubled.

I left long ago. I grew up, in my own fashion. I thought for so long that I could not function well without Oni-Odi in my life. But I have lost too much to cling to someone I once was. Aeriod's touch and visions of Rob's beautiful eyes and their last kiss pierced her. *The best way to honor Rob, and Oni-Odi, is to move forward, always.*

As Deming moved closer to Galla, Oni-Odi said abruptly, "My daughter is going to be married," and his voice sounded just a tad higher. They all looked at him. He opened a panel in his chest and brought something forth. He stepped toward Deming. Deming gawked at the object. Galla, realizing what it was, laughed loudly at his expression.

"What's...this for?" Deming asked, taking it in his hands.

Oni-Odi said in a serious tone, "She will need this. Be gentle with her. There are always many tangles. It is called a hairbrush."

Galla took a deep breath and sighed. She sensed a change but did not want to accept it. She looked up at the only father she had ever known.

"I missed you so much, for so long...sometimes not even realizing how much, not remembering," she said with little choking sobs. She held onto Oni-Odi's chest tightly and did not want to let go. "I wish I could have been with you all this time."

Oni-Odi held Galla back gently and looked at her with his cobalt eyes. They shifted a bit, and so did his face, and he seemed closer to human in appearance, and an old human at that.

"My beautiful daughter," he said to her, "I waited, and I was glad to wait. I knew you were working hard to do everything you set out to do. I anticipated challenges keeping you from stopping the Event the first time. I would never have asked you to give up the bonds that you made, and the battles you fought, and those you will fight going forward. I was given a purpose, like all androids, my daughter. My purpose changed when you were born. I am no longer the last guardian of the Seltra race. My purpose was to become your father."

Galla shook, not understanding. Deming watched her, and he ached with sympathy.

Oni-Odi went on, "Daughter, you have made me proud every day. I did not know what it meant to care for anything beyond duty. With you I knew that I had someone to love. I wanted to provide for you, and for your future, and help you when you were ready. Now you are ready. And it is time for me to leave."

Galla threw her head back.

"What?" she cried.

Oni-Odi held his arms wide, and Pliip rolled up slowly alongside him. "Demetraan is yours now," he said. "I have altered it. It is everything you will need, for your Task, for your battle. It will become what you wish now. But for it to work, I must become one with it, and with the Universe. I will always be with you. Goodbye, my daughter. I love you."

Galla reached for Oni-Odi, but he vanished in a hiss of countless glittering bits of silver, along with Pliip, drifting into the air and merging with the copper surface of the new city.

Galla fell to its surface, her face and hands reaching for any remnant of them. She let out a wail that pierced her friends and echoed across the vast copper expanse.

Deming threw his arms around her. Kein and Prilanna and Nalag squeezed together, Kein in tears, Prilanna covering her eyes. Nalag lifted its nose into the air and let out a high, mournful call.

"No!" Galla screamed. "Come back! I want you back! Oni-Odi! Father!"

Deming felt all her pain, and let it burn through him. He held tight as she thrashed in grief and shock. He smoothed her hair back from her face.

"I just got to him; he was just here—how is he gone? Why?"

No one could answer her.

Prilanna said quietly, "It really is Trozzhia now."

And Galla curled up on the floor of her city and let her diamethyst tears pool on its copper surface.

25

ACTUATION

In the dreadful stillness of the dome-covered copper landscape, broken only by Galla's anguished cries, dawn broke at last. Her friends had encircled her and clung to her in her pain. And so, they sat in exhaustion and worry and confusion and sadness, as Siloxxa's rays penetrated the dome and reminded them it was morning.

Kein touched Galla's shoulder.

"Galla," he said fondly, his eyebrows downturned in sadness for her, "I don't want to bother you. But it's daybreak, and some of us need to eat. Can you eat, too?"

Galla shook her head and lay on the surface with her cheek pressed against it, as if on the chest of Oni-Odi himself. Prilanna and Deming consoled her in their own ways.

Prilanna had been shaken by Oni-Odi's death. She trembled, thinking of her own father, and for the first time, she wondered whether or not she should even be here. But she shoved that feeling down and decided that was not what she would allow herself. Galla needed help; she needed her friends. And Prilanna found in Galla someone she could look up to, despite the woman's flaws. She had sensed something that Galla could not fathom about herself, and Prilanna wanted to be part of whatever that was. It was all well and good to live a secure and peaceful life in her village, and to be assured that she would lead one day by her own blood right. That did not interest her much before, and it did so even less now.

Prilanna inhaled and held onto her breath, her cheeks turning bright purple. She risked it and said, "Galla, I know if it were my father, he would have wanted me to take on the village and rule in his stead. He knew I didn't want that, though. Do you want it? I think a lot of people need you right now. And maybe my father does too. If Paosh Tohon is here now, my family is at risk. All of us are. I hope you'll take the city and fight with it."

Galla propped herself up on her elbow.

"Demetraan was never a city for fighting," she said. "It was made for preserving the Seltra race, the last of them. Well, Oni-Odi was what remained; he was the last of the Seltra."

She took a few minutes to wipe the tears from her face with her sleeve. She wished she did not have to get up.

"But Galla," protested Prilanna, not unkindly, "the Seltra are gone. And if he was the last, then it's no longer the Demetraan you knew. It's Trozzhia, it's your city, and he gave it to you to help you. So, it's not for preserving the Seltra anymore. It's for—for preserving the rest of us who are still out there. It's for—"

"The Questri," Galla finished. "It's for us."

She rose to her feet then. She was exhausted and devastated, but she knew she had to keep going. They all looked at her, with sunken, tired eyes. She heaved a long, shaky sigh, and said, "Trozzhia, then. Come with me."

She set off walking down the sloping surface, now brilliant in the morning sun, to try to reach the nadir of this new place. Deming, Prilanna, Kein, and Nalag followed behind her, their paces quicker despite their fatigue.

"Where are you taking us?" Deming asked.

"I'm not exactly sure," Galla confessed. "Trozzhia doesn't look like Demetraan. I have no idea where anything is, where Oni-Odi put anything. I intend to find out. The place is huge. I can't imagine everything that existed before has been destroyed."

"You'll have to leave Quopeia to deal with the malfunctions," Kein said. "How the hell can that be done? I can't believe something this big can even be *landed*, much less launched!"

"I have no idea," said Galla, and she felt her hair drift and snap in irritability. That sight actually relieved Kein.

She's not altogether ended, he thought.

Galla reached the bottommost point of this great copper bowl, and she turned and looked all around her. She shielded her eyes in the reflection of the metallic surface of orange, pink, white, brown, and myriad other colors that could also be found in her own copper eyes.

"This is where I have to be," she said to them all. "I don't know how to describe it. It feels like I'm meant to be *here*, when the time comes for...whatever the hell I'm supposed to do to stop the Event. I need Prince Hazkinaut—no, you don't know him. I hope he's alive. I need everyone. I need help. I—"

And she noticed that the last remnants of the green aurora had vanished.

"Green," she murmured. "I need Coniuratus. And no: you didn't know him either. But he's like me. He looks human and he's not. He's another Representative. I think he's been trying to communicate with me, but Quopeia didn't let him in."

"Well, this planet *is* an ass," Kein said, rolling his eyes.

"It protected you, at least," Galla said to him, trying to smile. "It protected Deming, and Paul—we hope. Now I know. I know what Ariel and Dagovaby wanted. They wanted their children hidden. I can't think of a better place for that than Quopeia."

She stroked Deming's cheek.

"We've got to find Paul," she said to him. "And we will." He nodded.

She looked down at her feet.

"I'm not sure what to do here," she said to the copper surface, feeling ludicrous. "I'm just going to ask you, my city: how can we find Paul?"

Something arose in molten form from beneath her feet, and she stepped back. They all watched stupefied as a pillar rose there and grew, mushrooming out and around them, until they were enclosed in a round capsule of sorts. The center of the pillar began separating into something like panels, and beneath them rose smaller objects.

"Holy shit!" said Deming. "They're *chairs!*"

They found themselves surrounded by what looked like a large cockpit, with chairs circling the paneled pillar in the center. The panels began winking and flickering. The humming in the city began to rise in pitch, and a great shudder buckled underneath them.

"Get in the seats!" cried Galla.

"What's happening?" screamed Prilanna above the ear-shattering noise.

"I hope you're ready, Questri," Galla shouted to them all. "We're launching!"

26

ATOMOSPHERIC

"Nalag!" Galla cried, holding onto her seat. The sounds around them all were deafening, as Trozzhia shook. "Can you tell the other deengynes to run clear?"

Nalag tossed its nose.

"If you want to stay, you can, but otherwise you need to leave now, before we are in the air!"

Nalag sneezed, and Kein said, "It's signaled to the others. They're falling back and taking cover."

Galla exhaled in relief. Nalag sprang into Prilanna's arms, and they all held on.

"Can this be quieter?" Galla yelled, and instantly they were met with a quiet cockpit. She looked at the others and raised her eyebrows. "I don't suppose it can be less bumpy?" and she was answered with a terrific shudder then, as the city wrenched itself from the ground of Quopeia. Everyone lunged for something to grasp hold of.

"Can't have everything," Deming said.

"What must this look like from the village?" Prilanna wondered. Her eyes grew in size at the wonder of it. "Now it all makes sense...the auroras were never like that years ago. I think my people must have seen the city landing!"

Galla caught in the girl's face the innocent awe of everything, and for a fleeting moment, she recalled her own youth—or the closest thing she had to youth—and felt a fierce protection of Prilanna, as she might have for Dek.

Deming looked at Galla, heat in his gaze, and she blinked at him.

"He'll be fine," he said to her. "Gindoo is training him, and Gindoo will protect him better than any of us could."

Kein said, "Hey, is this thing going to make it? It's shaking badly. Is the planet too much?"

"I hope we can make it," Galla said, gritting her teeth, determined. But her hair betrayed her, and it bounded every which way to reflect her rising anxiety.

As if in answer to her, the thrust of the city increased, and they rose swiftly upward, charging faster and faster, and through the protective dome they could see swirls of plasma forming. For a few seconds they experienced weightlessness, and then the artificial gravity of the immense city engaged. The turbulence ended.

"We're in orbit," Galla breathed. "I think we just need to get a bit farther away from Quopeia, and we'll have better control. And who knows what else?"

Deming exhaled, and Galla glanced at him.

"Are you sure you want to marry me?" she asked him, and his eyes flashed to hers. "After all, I've never piloted a star-city, we're going to take on a powerful evil being and its lackeys, and there's a galactic natural disaster to fix. Chaos is a near-certainty with me."

"You sound like you're trying to convince yourself," Deming pointed out with a wry grin. He reached out to clasp her hand. "You came to my door: *my* door, not some other unfortunate person's, who will never know the pleasure and the awe and the exquisite mystery of you. Your hair drifted toward me. Your eyes shone like fires mirrored in my soul. How would I ever not want to be with you, always? If it's chaos to be with you, Galla, I'll take that over order. I'll hold your hands in hell, and I'll love you in the heavens. Now. Are you sure you want to marry *me*?"

Galla did not answer with words, and cared not about her audience, but leapt into Deming's waiting arms and met his lips with her own.

Kein then cleared his throat and said, "Uh, Galla, that was grand and passionate and everything, but...what's that on the panel, flashing?"

Galla settled back in her chair to look away from Deming, beyond the starlight, beyond Trozzhia's shield, and her moment of thrill vanished. She bit her lip. An amorphous group of shapes shimmered in the darkness of space.

"It's a fleet of ships," she said. "They're headed our way."

27

SELTRA

The fleet looked as discordant and menacing as the force it represented, a jumble of different spacecraft, all with one unifying feature: a red symbol on each livery, like a bloody gash from claws.

"Valemog," said Galla. The crew stared at the enhanced images as she commanded scans.

She turned to Deming. "I know you can feel *me*, and a bit of others' emotions...but now that we're in space, can you feel Paul at all?"

Deming gazed outward into the oncoming fleet, unflinching, his golden eye-rings shining, his brow furrowed in focus. He pulled on his short beard.

"I can't feel him," he said.

Galla nodded.

"Trozzhia," she said, "find Paul Ambrono."

I hope this works.

A new image appeared, separate from the fleet, and Galla squinted. Kein leaned in. "What is that?" he asked, mirroring her own question.

"It's a rock," said Prilanna, looking reproachfully at Kein. "A rock in space."

Galla felt a flush of excitement but realized quickly that it was not her geode, the source of her diamethysts. *One mystery at a time*, she reasoned.

"Trozzhia, what am I looking at?"

A hissing sound met their ears, which blended into a strange chorus of voices, and then that all settled into one, as if it were trying itself out.

"Paul Ambrono," the voice said.

Deming protested, "That is a rock. That is not my brother."

Galla, eyebrows lifted, decided on another approach. "Trozzhia, where is this...object?"

"On the far side of Lume," came the resonant voice. The image of the great copper-hued moon shone before them on their bridge.

Galla tossed her multihued hair and breathed a sigh of relief.

"He's hiding in plain sight."

"So now what?" asked Kein, rubbing the space between his mustache and his nose.

Galla considered. "We're in a huge star-city, and to approach Lume might invoke some chaos and draw Valemog toward that rock. We need a rescue ship, something small."

Valemog's fleet wasted no time in pushing Galla's decisions. Trozzhia came under fire from long stabs of light, which reverberated through the city's protective dome, but did not penetrate it.

Kein said, "Can you just...destroy them all?"

Galla turned her head to look at them all and said with a stern voice, "Maybe so, but there might be prisoners or refugees on board. We can't risk taking an innocent life. And I have a top priority right now: find Paul. With a small ship that can go undetected and bring that rock on board, or something."

The Valemog ships descended all around them.

"We still should move, I think," said Deming, uneasily watching the swath of ships swarming toward them.

Galla smirked. "I thought you were raised by a mage!" she said, nudging him with her elbow. "What do mages like to do the most?"

Deming closed his eyes for a second and laughed. "Hide."

Galla nodded.

"Trozzhia," she said more loudly, "hide the city from Valemog's forces."

The immense star-city looked the same to her and her crew but had vanished from all of Valemog's sensors. One, two, three ships soon collided with the invisible dome and exploded.

"Such a shame," Kein said, shrugging.

"Well, that's one approach, not quite what I had mind," admitted Galla. "Now for another request. Trozzhia, make us a small ship, easy to maneuver, but large enough to bring that rock on board."

She glanced nervously at her companions. "I don't know if this will work, of course."

She scanned the area below her command tower, and something began stretching out of the surface of the copper bowl of a valley. Kein leapt to his feet.

"It's one of Demetraan's teardrop ships!" he cried. "Just like a larger version of the one that took me from Perpetua!"

And Galla watched as the newly made craft indeed took on a teardrop shape.

But she frowned.

"It's not quite what I'd like," she said, and she sighed heavily. "I was rather fond of the *Fithich*," she continued, and her crew looked at her quizzically. She looked at them and smiled sadly. "One of Aeriod's ships: it became mine. Anyway, I want something sleeker, more streamlined."

She tapped her chin with her finger. "Trozzhia, can you change the ship so that it looks more like one of Aeriod's space planes? Only... only I don't want a black ship. I don't want it green, either. I want it to be mine. I want it sharper. My legacy is fire. Make it a blade of fire."

Galla felt a rush of excitement, watching the ship morph and twist. Its surface altered, with copper and scarlet and vivid flame hues, and it stretched and warped and gained four wings and a tail. Galla bounced on her heels.

"Thank you, Oni-Odi," she said under her breath, and she fought down her feelings.

"That's a damn fine ship," Kein remarked, whistling. "What will you name it?"

"I'll keep it simple," Galla replied, "and honor its legacy. That is the *Seltra*."

28

MOONDANCING

Galla stood and pressed her hands against the windows of her command tower, overlooking Trozzhia and the *Seltra*, which hovered above the city's shimmering surface. The ship blazed in its many bright colors. There was no looking away from such a striking vessel, with its ever-changing fiery livery.

I will fly again, she realized, and that gave her a deep thrill.

She cleared her throat.

"Okay, here goes," she muttered. "Um...I command you, *Seltra*, to come to me," and then she blushed at the awkward order.

Kein snorted, and Deming bit his lip; both cringed in sympathy. Prilanna, however, watched rapt and excited.

"It will work!" she exclaimed, and Galla smiled fondly at her.

Prilanna was right: the *Seltra* rose and sleekly shot over to the tower and hovered outside of it. Galla looked over her shoulder at everyone.

"Kein, Prilanna, Nalag," she said to them all. "Stay here. Trozzhia, obey the commands of each person here."

"Acknowledged," came the clean voice over the speaker.

Then she turned to Deming, copper eyes shining.

"Let's go get your brother," she said.

. . .

GALLA COMMANDED the tower to open, and for the *Seltra* to approach closely enough for her and Deming to board its bay.

"Hold tight," she called to the rest of her crew on Trozzhia, and she and Deming settled into the cockpit.

"We need better seats," she said to the *Seltra*, "shaped for humans —softer, more supportive. I need a shield all around the ship to protect us from attack. I need a command table in the midsection of the ship, and passenger quarters, and escape pods. I need weapons. And I need a medical suite. I don't know what we are going to find on the other side of Lume, and I need this ship to be ready."

Deming watched in amazement as the malleable ship altered itself, morphing sleekly this way and that to accommodate Galla's commands. Galla took a deep breath and watched the ship do its work. Again, she thanked Oni-Odi under her breath.

If I had had this ship long ago...but he wasn't ready. And neither was I.

Deming reached over and clasped her hand.

"Thank you for this," he said.

"We've not found him yet," said Galla, with a sense of unease. "And we don't know what to expect."

"I know," said Deming, and he sighed. "I'm ready."

"Then let's do a little moondancing," Galla said wryly. "Trozzhia: release us into space."

The *Seltra* rose to the top of the star-city's dome and seemed to absorb easily through it.

Galla tilted the ship and looked beneath it, and only empty space and a field of stars shone. They could see nothing of Trozzhia. Its shield held fast.

"Your plan is working so far," said Deming. "But are we hidden? Because...those ships out there look like they've seen something."

He was right: the Valemog ships began their advance, but again, some of them struck the invisible surface of Trozzhia and shattered. Confounded, the fleet encircled the *Seltra*, but Galla was ready.

"*Seltra*," she murmured, "whatever they fire at us, send it back to their propulsion systems. A debilitating blow, not a lethal one. Can you do that?"

It was Galla's turn to be amazed, as each volley from Valemog's ships pulsed back into each craft's own body, soon disabling a dozen or more ships. They hung in space, but glorious Quopeia loomed close by, only too ready to seize them with its gravity...a force Galla knew all too well. She shuddered, remembering her fire-fall. And now she could fully remember slamming into the planet's surface.

With the distraction of their ricocheting firepower to throw the enemy ships off course, Galla quickly turned the *Seltra* and powered it toward the great, copper-colored moon, Lume. It arced up to meet them, and Galla skimmed its surface, looking for anything resembling the great rock her star-city had shown her. She piloted in low gravity, but still she loved it, flying again at last.

"Do you feel anything, Deming?" she asked the young man gently. "I know it's a long shot. But your father's range was broad. I think you can feel more than just me."

"You tend to eclipse everything else," Deming reminded her. "But I am trying. He is my brother, after all."

They crisscrossed in low orbit over the surface of Lume, with its many peaks and craters, yet no successful outposts for any civilization could be found upon it. That was the working of Quopeia again, protecting its own satellites. A number of rocks could be found in orbit around Lume, and this frustrated them.

"Which rock?" Galla asked impatiently, and the ship showed them a broad swath of them. Irritated, she asked, "Do any of them show life signs?" And then she wished she had not asked the question.

"No life signs," answered the *Seltra* blandly. Galla bit her lip and glanced at Deming. He looked resolute.

"We will search every rock, then, one by one," declared Galla.

No sooner had she said this when Deming sat upright. She watched him keenly.

"One of those," he said quietly, eyes gleaming gold and dark.

"Any idea which one?" Galla asked.

Deming swallowed. "Yes. That one," and he gestured.

Galla could not discern much difference in the rock Deming pointed at from any others they had seen, even having been shown the image by her ship.

"Are you sure?" she asked, desperate for Deming to be correct, hoping against hope.

"As much as I can be," he said, reasoning, "there's something in that rock. And it's very, very weak. But it's familiar. I have to know."

Galla noticed that Deming was trembling.

She stood and said loudly, "*Seltra*, seize that rock, gently, and bring it into the bay. Rest it carefully on the floor of the bay."

With a number of scraping thumps, the rock was brought in by Galla's ship, and as soon as the bay closed, she pelted down the halls, Deming fast on her heels, to examine the rock.

It was utterly nondescript, a grey-brown hunk, but larger than her diamethyst geode had been. It left little piles of Lume-dust on the floor where it had settled.

Deming's brow crinkled while he appraised the thing.

"There's something more to this," he said.

"What do you mean?' Galla asked.

"I can detect two beings inside that rock. I think—but I don't know—that one of them might be Paul. As for the other, I have no idea."

Galla swallowed. Something about this disturbed her. If Paul was indeed in the rock, and something else was with him, what could it be? Paosh Tohon? A member of Valemog?

"I think you should go back to the cabin," she said to Deming softly.

Deming creased his brow and tilted his head at her, incredulous.

"What? Why? I want to see my brother!"

She looked up at him with her radiant eyes and clasped her hands under her chin. She knew this had an effect on some people, though she still did not understand why. And she watched, amazed, as Deming blinked and slightly lowered his eyelids, and then reached down to her, cupped her face in his hands, and kissed her.

"I understand," he said. "You don't want me to get hurt. But I'm not leaving from this spot. *I need to know.*"

Galla, in turn, knew Deming well enough to see what she was up against: a stubborn man who would do anything for her, but also for the rest of his family.

"He's basically my family too," she said to him. "I'm duty-bound to protect him. But if something with him is hostile, I won't risk losing either of you. I will ask you to run while I take care of whatever it is."

They both shivered. Deming nodded.

Galla turned to the great rock.

"Well," she said, "all things in turn, I suppose. I was born from a rock. Your mother was rescued from one. Now it's my turn to open this one."

Deming moved forward with her and pushed on it, to test its surface, but Galla snorted at him. She pulled back her arm, balled a fist, and thrust it with all her might into the rock, and it split into several chunks. They stood back to let the dust settle. Galla stepped into the pile.

Deming shook his head in stunned admiration of her strength.

"There are two pods," she announced, brushing dirt off of one, and seeing little lights flashing faintly. "Stasis pods."

Deming waited no longer and dove in toward the other pod. He swiped its surface and then pressed his cheek upon it, as if listening for a heartbeat. Galla felt her eyes sting, watching him, as his own eyes closed, and a slow smirk formed at the corner of his mouth.

I do love this man, she thought. *It's really damned unfortunate. I think I love him too much.*

Deming opened his eyes and sighed, and she felt her shoulders release. He didn't need to tell her, but he did anyway: "It's Paul."

Satisfied, he then stepped over to the pod Galla had uncovered first. He leaned his head against it as well. He worked his mouth into a funny line while he concentrated.

"I can't really tell much from this one," he said. He stood. "I think it's human, though. This person is in a very deep state of consciousness...injured, maybe?"

"Paul may know," said Galla. Deming nodded, and looked back at her.

"How do we get him out of this safely?" he asked.

They both puzzled over that, until finally Galla asked the ship, "I need these pods opened without damaging the people inside. Can you do that?"

She received no answer.

She cleared her throat. "Well. I guess I can't get everything. We're on our own. Deming, I leave it up to you. Do you want me to open it, despite the risk to Paul?"

Deming stared down at Paul's pod. *How long have you been in there? Why were you put there?*

"Yes. Please open his pod," he said, and Galla looked at him with her large eyes, full of worry and love.

She fiddled with the pod controls, but they would not open the pod. She then tried to twist her ferocious hair into a bun so she could concentrate, and she felt with her fingernails for any rim to grab hold of. There was an extraordinarily tiny crevice, something Deming might never have been able to detect. She pushed her fingernails into it and then a great *CRACK!* startled them both. A hiss erupted from the pod, along with a strange, sickly-sweet smell, which quickly dissipated. Deming hovered by her side, pushing his hair behind his ears.

She knew she could easily remove the top of the pod by herself, but she also knew the importance of letting others help her. That had taken her many years to find out. And although she remained fiercely independent, something in her felt strongly that Deming should help remove the cover from his brother's pod. So she motioned for him to stand on the opposite side, to help her lift.

Their eyes met across the pod, and a flash of recognition coursed between them.

"Thank you," he said.

"You're welcome," she replied, smiling, but with a little brow furrow of worry above her nose.

And they lifted the pod cover and set it carefully down.

Within the pod, another cover could be found, some sort of full-body seal over a tall, muscular person. They could not see his skin.

"What is this?" Deming asked.

Galla leaned in. "I'm not sure. I think it's some sort of barrier, providing him food and water? Deming...Paul will be very weak, I think."

"We have to get him out of this!" Deming said.

Galla pulled delicately at the material and it shrank in, responding to her touch.

She felt an irrational little spark of anger, and said, "That's it. I'm tearing this off. Sorry, Paul."

And she seized the filmy substance with her nails and tore it open. It fought to repair itself, but it could not match her strength, and certainly not her temper. So she shredded it and pulled it off, balled it up, and threw it behind her.

She and Deming stared down, beholding the person within. He was frozen in a dreamlike state, his arms folded across his chest, his normally bronze skin much paler, but it began to change color. Slowly his complexion returned to normal, and his closed eyes twitched back and forth. Galla and Deming leaned closer.

His arms flailed out and snatched them both, and Galla shrieked. He pulled them both into his pod with him, in a pile of arms and legs and muffled voices.

Galla lifted herself from his strong grip, and copper eyes met green ones.

"I knew you'd find me," said Paul, and his trembling arms held on to his brother and Galla with all his might.

29

COMMANDER

Galla soon turned her attention to the other pod.

"Paul," she said, eyeing him as he sat up and rubbed the long sleep from his eyes. "I know you're tired. But if you can tell me who or *what* that is, I would appreciate it."

Paul glanced at the pod, grimaced, sighed, then cleared his throat. Deming raised his eyebrows at his brother.

"He's alive, then," remarked Paul, yawning. "Well, I've done my job, I suppose. And he's done his." He grunted.

Galla turned her chin down and looked at him with eyes like amber lanterns. Her hair coiled in bronze, gold, and violet to and fro, impatient.

Paul sighed again. "That," he said, pointing, "is the President."

Deming cried, "What?" and Galla crinkled her forehead.

Paul held out a hand to Deming, who took it, and shakily stepped out of his pod. His skin was deeply creased from his slumber. He brushed off his pants and smoothed his shirt, pulled a bit of it to his nose, and recoiled.

"First thing I want is a shower. Then, food."

He looked expectantly at his younger brother, who snorted. The two embraced where they stood.

"So...want to tell us what happened at the ball?" Deming asked.

"You survived," grunted Paul, smirking, and he winked at Galla, who shook her head and grinned despite herself.

Then Paul stared into his brother's eyes. Galla watched his bright green eyes open wider, and then tears formed in them. He took hold of Deming's face, and shook.

"Your eyes," he said. "They're...they're like..."

Galla stepped up to them and pressed her hand onto Paul's shoulder.

"Do you remember, then?" she asked him. "Because I do. They're like your father's."

The Ambrono men turned and looked at Galla in amazement.

"What?" and "How?" erupted from them.

Galla lowered her head. It was her turn to sigh.

"I have my diamethyst now," she remarked, cupping the sparkling violet stone in her small hands. "My memory is restored. All of it. I was there when you were born, Paul," and she smiled at the memory. The smile drifted away, though, as she thought about Ariel and Dagovaby.

Paul gave her the same look he had when they had met on Quopeia.

"I knew you, then, when I was small," he said, his voice reverent.

"You did, and yes, you were a toddler when...when your parents sent you off," Galla said slowly. "I'm sorry. They were trying to save you. And now...now we have Valemog at Quopeia. And obviously they were at the Ball. I'm just glad you're safe. As for keeping you that way? We have work ahead of us."

She held up the diamethyst to their eye level. "This stone is the only thing outside of Quopeia protecting you from the power of Paosh Tohon. There were more diamethysts...but the geode they were in was lost when I...when I fell..."

She sucked in her breath, remembering the escape pod, Rob having set the *Fithich* to blow with a dead man's switch. The geode had bobbed inside the pod before it ruptured, sending them all sundered from each other. Rob had already died when Galla fell in flames. *He took a bit of me with him, I think.*

Deming stepped forward and looped his arms around her, looking down with his gold-rimmed deep eyes. She leaned forward, her forehead on his chin.

"We have to find that geode," Galla said. "Somewhere out there, I *hope*, there are still telepaths like you, Paul, who were given their own diamethysts by me long ago. If the keepers survived...if those in the Devices survived...then I have to bring them together. I have to stop the Event."

"*You?*" Paul asked, incredulous. "How can you do that?"

Deming looked at him with a devilish grin.

"She's far more than Gindoo's tenant, brother," he said, and he stood a little taller, considering his beautiful lover with pride.

Paul's eyes bulged, looking between the two of them, and he read his brother's thoughts, which broadcast like starbursts.

"Holy shit!" he yelled. "You're engaged? How fucking long was I *out*?"

Galla and Deming laughed.

"Long enough," said Deming.

Paul took in the two of them, and for a fleeting moment, he felt wistful. But he also felt the rightness of it, and he smiled at them. "This is the best thing I've ever heard in my life," he said, and gave Deming a loud slap on his back.

Galla lifted her chin and looked pointedly at the other pod.

Paul rolled his eyes. "I guess we have to wake him up."

"And then what?" Galla asked. "Once we get within view of the Valemog fleet, it's going to be a firestorm to get back to Trozzhia."

Paul tilted his head. "What's Trozzhia?"

Galla smirked. "You have some catching up to do. For now, get hydrated and take it easy. Wake the President. I'll take the helm."

PRESIDENT TANANAAT WAS A WIZENED, ancient man, but ferociously alert the moment he regained consciousness. He sprung up in his pod and barked at Paul, "What's our status?" before crawling out on his own and standing with surprising agility.

"The status, Mr. President," Paul answered slowly, "is that we were rescued by my brother and Galla."

"What?" the old man exclaimed, confusion twisting between his white brows.

Tananaat straightened his outfit and twitched his wrinkled collar.

"Take me to the cockpit," he demanded.

The two made their way through the sleek ship, glinting in copper streaks, its controls utterly inhuman in appearance until they reached Galla's cockpit. There she sat in one chair, looking quite human to the President's eyes at first, and Deming in another next to her. The couple gazed out at the arc of Quopeia, and a line of ships amassed above the planet, with red markings on their livery.

"Valemog!" gasped the President.

"So you know of them," Galla said dryly.

"Yes," the President replied. "But I do not know *you*. Who are you, and why are you here?"

"That's a fine thank you," Deming said with an edge to his voice.

"I beg your pardon, young man," spat the President, "but show some respect to your President."

Deming stood up, and Paul's eyebrows lifted. "First of all, you're not *my President*, as I have never voted for you, nor will I. You've held the office for decades. At what point do you get your crown? Or is Allurulla your crown?"

The President's mouth opened in awe at Deming's open hostility.

"My brother served you and saved your life," Deming went on. "Galla-Deia saved *mine*."

Galla stood and faced the President.

"No, you do not know me officially," she said, her hair rising, her cheeks hot. "I am Galla-Deia, daughter of Demetraan, keeper of the diamethyst, a Representative, and a Questri. And I'm here to save this planet, and any others that I still can."

"I do not follow your authority," said the President bitterly, gawking at the brazen lady, her arms crossed, her stone gleaming and sending darts of purple-violet-magenta light in all directions.

"And I will never follow yours," Galla said, smiling at him. "Now that we understand each other, would you like a ride home, or would you like me to let you off right here, for Valemog's pickings?"

Tananaat wheeled to look at Paul. "Get me back to the City!" he bellowed.

Paul saluted him.

"Can you take him back to the City?" he asked Galla, his voice as dry as ash.

Galla frowned.

"Eventually."

She sat back in her seat, turned away from them all, and said, "*Seltra*, where is the last known trajectory of my geode?" Her console screen began projecting images of space and a pattern of ship tracks, satellites, and other noise from the past couple of decades.

Then she looked over her shoulder at the President, who looked laughably out of his element, his eyes darting between her, Paul, and Deming.

"This is outrageous!" he cried. "I'm in charge of a country, not a rock expedition!"

Galla stood again and marched up to the man. Deming and Paul instinctively backed away from her.

"Do you value your life?" she asked him.

He set his mouth in a tiny line. "Are you threatening—"

"*Do you?*"

"Yes," he answered.

"Do you value your country?"

"Of course!"

"Do you value this world, which you have adopted as your own?"

"Yes!" and he looked most bewildered.

Galla lowered her eyes to fiery slits. "Then I suggest you let me find this geode. It might mean the difference between your destruction by Paosh Tohon and your survival. Yours, your country's, and that planet's." She leaned in toward him and hissed, "*Your choice.*"

The President's mouth opened and closed, and finally he threw his hands into the air and shook his head. He stalked off barking various nonsense orders at Paul, who followed him only at a slow pace.

Galla settled into her rage and shaped it in her thoughts, choosing to aim it at the ships beyond her window.

"*Seltra,*" she said clearly, and Deming put his arms behind his head and watched her with intrigue and powerful attraction. "Disable every Valemog ship. Set them adrift with no power. If Quopeia takes them, so be it."

The svelte copper ship made a high spinning noise and set off volley after volley of bright golden bursts, which launched at every ship in sight. The bursts found their appropriate quarry and pummeled the ships, but did not destroy them. Galla watched in satisfaction as some of them spun over and over, unable to stop.

Deming applauded.

"Now, back to the hunt," she said under her breath.

She soon found something that she did not like, as the ship discerned the fate of the geode. It had survived...but it had landed in one of the planet's oceans.

She swallowed and glanced at Deming.

"I guess we really test this ship now," she said, taking a deep breath and letting it out slowly. She called on her intercom, "Buckle up. We're going to attempt to enter Quopeia. And...um...we're going underwater."

She could hear profanity from the President, but as he did not appear, she nodded to herself and patted her chair's restraints. She looked sideways to Deming.

"You're *sure*?"

"Never surer," he said, his mouth wry.

"When this is over, you're going to be one very tired man," said Galla serenely. "Because we're going to have to make up for all this lost time outside of a bed."

"I'm ready whenever you are," Deming replied.

With that, Galla soared among the disbanded Valemog fleet, and called out to Trozzhia, "We've made it out, and we're headed to the planet's surface, for a search-and-retrieval mission. Stand by up here and let me know if anything pops up."

"Aye-aye, Captain Deia," Kein called back.

Galla dipped the *Seltra* lower toward Quopeia's atmosphere, intent on the search mission. Valemog drifted, Trozzhia hovered in orbit, and for her it was a matter of dealing with the atmosphere... and whether or not the planet would let her into it.

She was not overly surprised to meet resistance. But she did not expect the form it took. In front of her, on her descent, something wavered into view. It was a great iridescent black ship, with ornate silver markings, much larger than the *Seltra*, and it blocked her path.

She sucked in her breath.

"Aeriod!"

30

THE WIZARD AND THE PRESIDENT

The screen in the cockpit shimmered, and Galla's hair twitched in all directions as she watched the face appear before her. Pale, sharp, noble, arrogant, framed by long, straight white hair and pierced by silver eyes, he shone clearly, unlike her previous encounter at the ball in Allurulla.

"Galla-Deia," he said smoothly, evenly.

She tried to still her shaking. She began breathing deeply to calm herself. Deming watched her but said nothing.

"Aeriod," she said back to him. Her voice at the end of his name rose just a tick.

She could see that a long, silver chain still hung around his neck, with a small, oval purple stone affixed to it. Her own stone warmed, and she could see his glow in response.

"It is...good to see you whole again," the mage governor said quietly.

"Likewise," she said simply.

"Do you think you can break through the defenses?" he asked next.

Galla glanced at Deming. "I intend to try."

"Then I have a favor to ask," said Aeriod.

She swallowed. "And what is that?"

"It won't let me in," he told her, "but if we went together, perhaps then…"

"I'm not so sure that's a good idea," Galla said nervously.

"Suppose we piggyback?" Aeriod suggested.

"Er, what?" said Galla.

"We hook the ships together. Maybe it'll let you in, and therefore it'll let me in. If not, my ship detaches, and so be it."

He looked at her so coolly and with such a neutral expression that she felt more confused about him than ever.

"You mean, I would ride on top?" she asked.

Aeriod's eyes sparked. He threw back his silver mane and roared with laughter.

"Always a favorite," he said.

Galla turned nearly purple in embarrassment. Deming squirmed in his seat, cringing, feeling her profound mortification with sympathy.

Derailed for a moment, she gathered herself up, straightened her back, wrangled her hair away from her face, and said crisply, "I'll allow the attempt."

His eyes glistening with impish delight, Aeriod nodded his head.

"I'll position myself under you," he said, grinning.

Galla switched off her screen and held her burning cheeks.

She looked back at Deming. He deliberately pushed his lips together and leaned back, arms behind his head. He had lowered his eyes so that she could only see gold glints shining out.

Galla then turned back to her console and watched as Aeriod's ship maneuvered beneath hers, and a jolt and a tremor reverberated through the ship.

"He's attached," she murmured.

"Quite," answered Deming.

She closed her eyes and fought the urge to groan.

"I'm steering us down," she said next.

Aeriod paged her.

"What's your course?" he asked.

She did not turn her viewscreen back on. She said flatly, "Southern ocean, to find my geode. It would appear to be several hundred feet down."

"If we can get past this barrier, I would like to help."

"Fine."

Galla navigated down into the upper atmosphere, and the coupled ships were met with intense turbulence. Aeriod's ship buffered the worst of it, for which Galla was secretly relieved. The plasma flares all around them gave her flashbacks to her first arrival on the planet, and she began feeling nauseated. That had not ended well. She did not want a repeat of that, for any of her crew. She sat back in her chair and closed her eyes.

"You're going to be all right," Deming said. She opened her eyes and looked at him. He shook his head at her doubts. "You will."

Paul paged her and said, "So, we have a traveler?"

"Yes," she replied. "You met him, decades ago. Mage governor Aeriod."

"I'll bet the President will *love* hearing that," Paul said quietly.

"Stay strapped in. We're not through yet," Galla cautioned.

And as if in answer, the great ship beneath them whined and bucked, shaking everyone. But it held fast to her ship, so she hoped Aeriod was right.

"It's doing its damnedest to tear us apart," Aeriod called.

Galla could barely speak through the vibrations. "We have to keep trying."

And with a final, sickening jolt, the coupled ships were flung into the air above the cold, roiling southern ocean. Aeriod's ship thrusters roared just before they could impact the water.

"You got us in," he called, his voice relieved. "Now, the geode. My sensors are a mess thanks to this precious planet. Can you detect it now?"

The *Seltra* was also affected, its sensors haywire.

Are we going to be stuck out here? she wondered suddenly. She did not like the prospect of their ships collapsing into a cold sea with no land in sight.

A few blips on her screen gave her a rough indication.

"Trozzhia?" she called hopefully. "Can you improve the mapping?" Trozzhia did not answer. "I guess we're on our own."

She turned and brought Aeriod's image up. For once, she was grateful *that* worked, at least.

"I see something. I'll fly us over it," he said.

The joined ships hovered over the foaming sea. Galla said, "This is as good as I can make it. Now what?"

Aeriod nodded. "I'll see what I can do."

She watched him close his eyes and concentrate. She was reminded of a long time past, in which he controlled his own captured asteroid on Rikiloi, where he had built his keep.

Galla adjusted the *Seltra*'s sensors to watch for anything in the ocean, and soon a boiling, bubbling area burst forth to the surface, and up rose a great, round rock, covered with debris. It hovered in the air.

"Where do you want it?" Aeriod asked her.

"On my ship," she said.

"We'll have to separate, then."

"Yes, we will." And Galla did not hide her emphatic tone.

The two ships slid apart, and she opened the bay of the smaller copper-colored vessel. Aeriod steered the geode into the bay, and Galla shut it. She rose to go straight for it, when a loud band of static struck her ears.

A flickering image arose before her and Deming, of a diminutive figure bent over a cane, wagging his long goatee.

"Gindoo!" they both exclaimed.

"Yes, well," the vision responded. "Who else? Now that I have the attention of all of you, would you kindly stop meddling about and bring the President back to the Capital?"

Galla's brows wriggled over this statement. Then, to her shock, Aeriod answered, "Well met, Gindoo. Thank you for letting me in at long last."

The look of contempt on the little wizard's face startled Galla.

"Yes, well," he said, "there is much to discuss, with each of you."

He pointedly turned to Galla as if in the same room with her, and said, "You may park in the cul-de-sac. I'll take care of it."

And his form vanished.

Bewildered, Galla shook her head. "Off to Allurulla, then."

And mercifully, both ships sped unhindered over the frothing seas, toward the continent of Orboaanya.

GALLA HAD to admit that the descent into the City enchanted her, with its coral and turquoise towers shimmering in the muted afternoon, and the remaining late autumn leaves quivering in gilded hues. She navigated over a more wooded area and spotted a tiny, low roof among trees, with a cul-de-sac along the road outside.

"You're only seeing it because he's letting you," Deming told her. "Otherwise, no one could. He hides it."

"I believe it," said Galla, thinking back to Rikiloi again, and the Device on that world. "Mages do like to hide things!"

As soon as the *Seltra* touched down, Galla pelted down to the bay and beheld her geode. Deming followed closely behind, and Paul emerged with the President in tow—the latter looking rather wan and relieved at the same time.

Galla and Deming stared at the great rock, split open on one side. It was completely covered in barnacles, which proved tough to remove. Galla pulled at them with her fingernails to scrape them off. They smelled atrocious to her.

"They just don't want to let go!" she said, feeling her temper rise.

Deming looked at her slyly.

"Somehow I don't think you're really talking about barnacles," he said with his wry calmness. "You can talk about Aeriod, you know."

At that remark, Galla felt a wave of some terrible sensation pass through her, and she flailed wildly, and quite suddenly vomited all around herself. She gave a small scream and vomited again.

"What's happening?" she cried.

"You're vomiting," Deming said, approaching cautiously. "It's normal."

"No! It isn't normal!" she gasped, collapsing onto her knees for another spasm. "I have never vomited before!"

Galla felt frightened and vulnerable as Deming helped her up, and he suggested getting her some water.

"Wait," she gasped, and she crawled back to her immense geode and pulled at several of the stones within. They broke off more easily for her than the barnacles, but no one else could have pulled the diamethysts off at any strength.

She thrust one of them at Deming, and rather unceremoniously she said, "Here. Keep this with you at all times."

She approached Paul and the President, looking flushed and a tad feral, and gave them a stone each. "For your protection," she said. "Don't lose them!"

The President nodded at her. "Thank you, Captain Deia," he said, a note of admiration in his tone. "That was quite a mission you pulled off. We certainly could use your skill, if you're interested."

Galla pulled back her vivid coils of hair and managed to laugh despite her extreme nausea.

"I have a galaxy to save," she said to him, "but thank you just the same."

She noticed the ramp to the ship stood open. Then she turned about and jumped. Gindoo stood next to her, leaning on his cane, considering the geode.

"It's smaller than I imagined," he remarked, his eyes glassy. "But big enough."

Then Gindoo turned to the President.

"Mr. President," said the little man, "it's time we had a long overdue chat. If you'll all join me in my home." And he pointed his cane to the ramp and shuffled down it and out of the ship.

President Tananaat looked confused and a bit alarmed to Galla. Paul held the tiniest smirk at the corner of his mouth, and if she guessed correctly, he seemed rather satisfied about something. The group followed Gindoo out into the cul-de-sac, where Aeriod stood waiting. Their ships then disappeared from view.

"You?" Galla asked.

Aeriod looked down at her and shook his head.

"Him," he said, gesturing toward the ancient little man who held open the immense stone door to his boardinghouse.

31

A PAST REVEALED

A lanky figure appeared behind Gindoo, with dark curly hair. Galla bounded toward him.

"Dek!" she cried, and she threw her arms around him.

Dek, all limbs and overly large smile, hugged her back.

"I'm so glad you made it! Will you stay here now?" he asked.

"No, dear boy," Galla said, with a regretful sigh. "It's only temporary. I'll be heading back out. But tell me, how is the training going?"

Dek rubbed the back of his rumpled, dark head and squeezed up his face.

"I...well," he began.

Gindoo turned and gave him a look that made him stand stiff and straight.

The little wizard said to Galla, "Your brother has skill enough," and he pulled on his goatee thoughtfully. "But Deming is the better cook. Deming, would you mind...?"

Deming laughed. "Sure. I'll cook dinner. Quite the crowd, this time! But first: how is it that I can sense Galla now? Why didn't I have this...empathic ability before?"

"Yes, well," Gindoo said, eyes narrowed, "you must have almost died. Yes?"

"Yes," said Deming, brow twisted.

"The same thing happened to your father, in his youth. I guess you needed a trigger."

"Could love also have done this?" Deming wondered.

"Probably," Gindoo said. "For anyone else, being able to sense Galla's powerful emotions would lead to insanity. I did give you a lifelong lesson in tedious work, so it's clear you can handle it." And he said nothing more.

Deming swept his eyes over Paul, Dek, Galla, Gindoo, the President, and Aeriod, who stood off at the end of the walk, his black cloak wrapped around him. Deming caught his look at him and shivered. He could not fathom what the next hour would bring, but he would find himself thinking back to that moment and realizing it might be the last time he faced any moment in peace.

Galla cleaned herself up and found one of her simple gowns in the closet of her old room. She breathed in the polish of the wood floors and the faint smell of dried flowers. She really did miss this little room, and a large part of her wished she could dwell there forever.

She emerged and found Dek across from her, and he chatted excitedly.

"There's been a lot of talk," he told her. "About the President missing, about invasion...I heard there's a fleet up there!"

"Hmm," said Galla, her eyes shining. "There *is*, technically. But it's powerless."

Dek gaped. "How? What happened?"

"Your sister happened," Paul remarked, appearing in the hallway. "We'll fill you in. Dinner's ready."

It was a strange sight indeed, all of them crowded into the dining room of the little stone house. Aeriod's height towered over everyone else's, as he stood at the end of the room next to the tiny Gindoo. There seemed to pass between them an ancient communication or recognition that Galla could not discern. They knew each other; that much was obvious. It was not clear how well they got along.

The President looked the most out of place, however, and he

folded his hands over his belt buckle and watched in silence as Deming and Dek served everyone food. Galla would ordinarily have fallen upon that food, for Deming never made anything bad, but she found it somehow unappealing just then. She poked at her dish and watched everyone.

At first, they all exchanged cordial remarks, and thanked Deming for the meal, and Gindoo for hosting. Gindoo stood, then, and flashed his gaze toward Galla.

"You should eat, lass," he said to her, his expression gentle.

"Maybe later," she replied warmly. "I...haven't felt well."

"That's because you're pregnant," said Gindoo.

Galla jumped up, and every bit of color drained from her normally rosy face.

"What?" she cried.

The silence that met her made her dizzy.

Both Deming and Aeriod stood as well, looking between Galla and Gindoo.

"How?" Aeriod asked, his voice like iron on stone. His expression was unreadable. But Galla knew he was deeply shocked. For that matter, so was she.

Gindoo grinned wickedly. "Yes, well, it's called *reproduction*, and involves the appropriate bonding of individuals who are...*compatible*."

Deming walked over to Galla.

"Wait," said Galla. She inhaled deeply. "Wait. I was told I would never reproduce. That I *could not* reproduce, as part of being a Representative." Her thoughts spun, and she felt for a moment that she might vomit again; but she had nothing left inside her to bring up.

Maybe the floor could open, and I could slide down Gindoo's stairs to his lab and disappear in a puff of smoke.

Deming reached her, and put his arms around her, and swept her clean but tangled hair away from her face.

"Galla, I...don't know what to say. But I won't leave you, no matter what happens. If...if you want this."

Galla looked down at her abdomen. There was nothing showing

to reveal her pregnancy, but her breasts felt tender. *How long have I been pregnant?* she wondered.

Aeriod could not help himself.

"How is it possible?" He pointed to Deming and said, "This is a human, yes? And Galla is *not* a human, despite her appearance! Explain this!" and he glowered at Gindoo until the elderly man twitched his cane.

"Yes, well," Gindoo began, and he looked at Paul and Deming, "one of their parents was of human descent, and you know that's true. Ariel Brant."

Aeriod wheeled in his cape. "Ariel's children!" he gasped. His eyes at first glowed bright, and then they dimmed in sadness. "And their father, Dagovaby Ambrono..."

"Half human," remarked Gindoo.

Galla noticed something unusual just then, for Tananaat had stood as well, and slowly slinked closer to the door. His eyes darted.

Gindoo cried out, "Halt!" and raised his cane, and the door slammed shut. "You're going nowhere yet," he said to the President, his tone hard.

"Yes," he continued, his voice chilling. "There is more to discuss. Even for your ears, Mr. President. For you see, Governor Aeriod, you are correct. No human could reproduce with a Representative. But while Dagovaby's mother, who came to me in need of aid when he was a child, was human, *his* father—if you can call it that—was not. Dagovaby is a child of the Innervation."

Aeriod's eyes grew huge.

Gindoo went on, "As it was told to me by Nour, Dagovaby's mother," and he paused to glare at Tananaat before continuing, "a being had manifested from the Innervation and become her lover. This pairing would mean her eventual doom, for along with certain *experimentations* on Nour"—his eyes became slits while looking at the President—"her body could not withstand the changes it had undergone. I tried my best to save her. And I will regret forever being unable to help. But I did promise that dear boy that I would help *him* one day, if fate allowed it. And so it did...when he sought to hide his own sons from Paosh Tohon."

Aeriod then also turned to stare at the President, as if almost deducing something, but he had not quite made the connection.

"Humans," Gindoo went on, "obviously aren't native to Quopeia. They've been a blessing and a curse. Now, Mr. President, would you like to educate everyone here about just how, exactly, you came to be here, and forge this shining city? First, though, how did you find him, Galla?"

Galla cleared her throat and said, "He and Paul were inside stasis pods, in a large rock."

Gindoo nodded. He looked pointedly at Aeriod. "Sound familiar?"

Aeriod stepped in a broad stride over to the President and stared down at the old man.

"Who are you?" he demanded. "Who are you, *really*?"

The man shivered where he stood. Where before he had held his head in authority and power, now that cloak fell away, revealing simply an old man, who had succeeded for too long in a lie, and had too many people agree with his every command. He bent his head.

"I never meant to hurt anyone," he began.

"Fool!" hissed Aeriod. "There are people in this room who would not be here, had it not been for your meddling! There are people who might still be alive, not taken by Paosh Tohon! Say your name!"

The man bent his head and croaked something.

Aeriod seized him by his shoulders.

"Say it!"

"Clegg Badenhorst," the man stammered. His shoulders sagged, and he staggered, and looked as though he might collapse, but Aeriod held on to him.

"So, you were never murdered, obviously, and never died in some accident," hissed Aeriod. "You let all your telepaths die in the emptiness in space, all in their stasis pods, while they listened, in service to you. And one of them was found by Paosh Tohon. Which is why the galaxy is torn apart. *You* helped this happen, through what, greed? Pride? And how did you manage to get here?"

Gindoo coughed. "There was indeed an 'accident,' which was convenient to cover up what this man was doing. He had found a wormhole, and kept it secret, even managed to hack into programs throughout the humans' solar system, so no one else could detect it. You knew you'd hit a wall, and that you would be prosecuted for the missing and the dead, so it was the perfect crime. Slip away and find a place to start over. Take more recruits with you...more telepaths who didn't make the first cut for your little pet project."

"Project NEEDLE," Aeriod said, eyes like ice.

Badenhorst's mouth spasmed, and his hands twitched.

"But...but...this planet let me in," he stammered.

Gindoo squinted at him. "You were part of the bargain, yes. And I admit it was a good arrangement, for a while, at least so I could keep an eye on you. And keep those you brought with you safe...except for Nour, sadly. You'd already caused enough havoc.

"You have two choices. Resign your post. Go out there and tell them the truth, about who you are, why you fled. Or you can lead. Stop running from responsibility. I'm not letting you get away with faking your death again, coward. And you'll put no descendent of Nour Ambrono at risk ever again. Paul!" barked the little wizard. "Get this man out of my sight. Take him back to the Capital building and be sure he does what he needs to do."

"With pleasure," said Paul, his jaws working.

Aeriod shook his head. "Now it all makes sense. I had wondered about Dagovaby, for clearly the Associates knew nothing about him, not even the Summoners."

"They were rather useless in many respects," concurred Gindoo, "but not without some merits. They were able to find the two lineages of telepaths most needed."

"Those telepaths are lost, though," said Aeriod sadly.

"Are they?" Gindoo asked, turning to Galla. "Who's on your star-city, my dear?"

"Kein is alive," said Galla, exhaling after holding her breath a bit too long.

Aeriod held his hands to his mouth and closed his eyes.

"At last, some much-needed good news," he said. He smiled in relief. "And we have Paul and..."

"Deming," the young man said, one arm still around Galla.

Aeriod looked at both of them and turned away.

"We'll have to figure it all out. There is not much time in the second window for planetary alignment to seal the Event," he said. "I have tried to figure out who all is left, and as I had my own lengthy... entanglements, shall we say, I could not get as far in the search as I would have liked. But I can return to the mission, and help you, Galla, if...if you feel that you can do this."

Galla tilted her head and looked at everyone in the room. She said in a harsh tone, "I will not have you treating me as suddenly infirm. I have a Task to do, and I plan to do it. We need to find out who among our Device telepaths is still alive. And then coordinate everyone to be ready. I'm to be the focal point, or the 'prism of minds' as Gindoo calls me. I'll do it from Trozzhia. After that, we take on Paosh Tohon."

The room went still. "I don't know how—" began Aeriod, but Gindoo lifted his cane again.

"I'm not finished here. You have your own task. Stop running from it."

"What do you mean?" bellowed Aeriod.

"You have to find *her* and make this right," said Gindoo simply.

Aeriod could not have gone much paler than he was right then.

"That door is shut," he hissed.

Gindoo jabbed his cane toward Aeriod and yelled, "Then kick it open! Go, before it is too late for any of us!"

Aeriod strode back to Galla. Ignoring Deming, he said, "There is more I need to say to you, but now is not the time."

And Galla thought, *We need to talk about the silver diamond that you placed on Rob's arm. Among other things.*

Aeriod noticed the stern little furrow between her brows, nodded, and continued, "I'm going off on my own task...a most unpleasant one, I will have you know. But I think Gindoo is right. It's necessary. I bid you farewell for now, Galla-Deia. We each have our paths before us, but I'll help you again as I may."

He bowed to her, swept his cape around himself, and left.

32

PATCHWORK

After Paul, the President, and Aeriod had left, Dek and Deming cleared plates. Galla put her head in her hands and looked across the table at Gindoo.

"How did you know?" she asked him.

Gindoo put his hand under his chin and looked fondly at her.

"It was a guess," he admitted, "since you had been ill. And since, well, you had spent a fair amount of time with Deming. I know Deming well, having raised him myself. I knew he loved you, and I could see you growing fonder of him before you left. Some things just...naturally occur. And also, Deming knew."

"What?" cried Galla. Deming froze where he stood, dish dripping in his hand. "Did you?" She stared at him. "Did you know?"

Deming looked pained. "I...knew something was different. Because I can feel you. I didn't know what, exactly."

Dek coughed loudly.

"Can you maybe...not talk about this in front of *me*?" he asked, cheeks flushed. "Here. I'll do the dishes. You guys go have The Talk."

Deming nodded. "Sure."

He held his hands out to Galla, who took them with a frown between her brows.

"I need some fresh air," she said, and so he led her down the hall, past her room, and out to the back garden.

The deciduous plants had withered and aged along with the year, with seed pods dangling and animals scurrying about, burying any bits of food they could to prepare for winter. Lume shone as a low, bronze sickle in the night sky, allowing the stars to display in thick clusters. The ground beneath Galla's shoes crunched from frost. She stood with Deming, reunited in the garden where she realized she had fallen in love with him. Their breath rose into the night in little bursts of fog.

Deming began, "I feel like I should apologize—"

"Don't," said Galla, holding his hands, and looking at his fine fingers. "We didn't know. We *couldn't* know. And...and I wouldn't take any of it back."

"I have so many questions, and I'm sure not nearly as many as you," Deming said, and his voice shook. She wiped tears from his eyes with her fingertips.

"I would like it if we answered them together," she said.

She led him back to her room and shut the door behind them. She sat on the floor at the foot of her bed, where the chest of quilts lay. She opened up the chest and pulled out each quilt, running her hands across the colorful squares and careful stitching.

"Your grandmother Meredith Brant made these quilts," she told him. "Now that I can remember, I want you to know. I loved her so much. I loved your mother, too. And there's something..." tears began spilling down her cheeks, "there's something I always wanted. I always wanted a family. It felt like Meredith helped give me that. And when she died, and Ariel disappeared, I felt so broken. And then I... well, you know the rest. I failed at my Task and fell to my doom."

They leaned forward, forehead against forehead, over the quilts.

She said slowly, swallowing tears, "Loving you has given me joy again, and purpose, because I want to fight for you and your family. For every family, and every good thing. And now...I guess...we've started a family of our own. I want to keep going. I want the adventure, with you."

Deming answered not in words, but by pulling Galla up with him and guiding her to her old bed, where he had longed to stay with her many times before. And now he could. It was a gift he could not comprehend fully. He felt reverent. But he was still a man in love, and he wanted her, and knew she wanted him. The blending of emotions and physical pleasure with her was almost too much for him to bear, but he could bring himself to that edge, and with her, he could release, entrusting her with his body and soul.

Everything I ever wanted, he thought amid the electric, raw passion Galla wielded.

Later, Galla watched Deming sleep, his pulse bouncing in his neck, his dark eyes closed, and brushed her fingers along his beard, down his chest, and she kissed the area over his heart. Fatigue took her at last, and she lay draped across him, in dreamless sleep until dawn. As the morning sun filtered through the curtains, Galla tried to hide a growing fear within her, though, and knew that he would still sense it. He was a mortal, and she was not sure what she might be anymore. Taking the time like this was precious and she knew it would be fleeting. That made it even more powerful.

She did not want to leave their moment of bliss, nestled beneath the quilts of his grandmother, in this quiet, ancient house ensconced in vines and flowers, on beautiful, mercurial Quopeia.

33

RELINQUISHED

Galla looked about her in the kitchen the next morning, and felt a hollow sensation spread through her. *I will not sit here again as a guest of this house*, she thought. *Today I leave it for good.*

Gindoo shuffled in just then and found her with her chin propped in her hands, her eyes downcast, her hair limp. He tapped his cane just loudly enough that she sat up straight, and her hair frizzed. She looked over her shoulder at him.

"I know what I need to do," she said, as if in answer to an unasked question...or at least to the little wizard's wriggling eyebrows. "Is anyone still alive out there?"

Gindoo scoffed.

"Yes, well, presumably so," he snorted. "Our enemy likes to keep its prey alive as long as possible. The prey, however, wishes otherwise, more often than not."

"Gindoo," said Galla with a sigh. "I mean, is Prince Hazkinaut alive? Are Jana and Guru and Beetle alive? Are the other Representatives—"

"Well, the last question I can answer, to some extent," said

Gindoo, and he scooted on his soft shoes over to a cabinet to retrieve a plate. Helping himself to some scones under a glass cloche, he said, "You knew only one, yes? The one you call Coniuratus?"

"Yes!" said Galla, eagerly clasping her fingers together.

"You did see some sign of him with the aurora," Gindoo told her. "He's not here now. He's trying to hold things together out there, and as a personal favor to me, he's been helping keep watch on the Event. Until you were healed enough to take care of *that*."

Galla considered this. "I can't do that until I know everyone is alive and in place on each Device world. And then what do I do, just...raise my arms and point at the thing?"

Gindoo leaned his head to one side and stroked his long, scraggly goatee.

"Could be. Can't say I've ever done anything like this, mind you. And likely you'll be shot at, among other things, because I doubt the Enemy wants its feeding source extinguished."

Galla took a deep breath and let it out slowly.

"Should I take Paosh Tohon out first, then?"

Gindoo stared at her, and then laughed in a high pitch for a full minute.

"If that were so easy, you could have already done it!" he exclaimed.

Galla rolled her eyes. "I know. Nothing about any of this is easy. And I don't know how I can do any of it at all."

"You keep talking as if you have to do this alone. As if you *could*. Stop that."

Gindoo pointed his cane at her.

"Not one of us can stop this."

"I'm not the galaxy's savior," said Galla under her breath, reiterating what Rob had told her long ago. She sighed in sadness. "I couldn't even save the people I loved. I am just... This is...wishful thinking. That I could go in and take out this...thing. But it's already taken from me, and it could again."

Deming walked through the door then, and said calmly, "I see you found the scones."

"Yes, well, they're better than that rapscallion brother of Galla's makes, that's what," snapped Gindoo. "You could leave a mix or something for that boy!"

"He's not bad, Gindoo," Deming said, with unusual gravity. "Give him the chance you gave me. He's not even been with you that long. And considering his parents...I would give him *more* time. Not less."

He leaned over to kiss Galla on her forehead.

"Where's Paul?" he asked.

A slam met their ears, and Galla grinned to herself. Paul soon entered, filling the room with his presence (she now remembered he had lacked subtlety as a child as well), and everyone turned to him as if compelled. He stood and folded his large, muscular arms, much like his father Dagovaby's, but the vivid green eyes of his mother shone out from his bronze face, ringed with long, dark lashes. With Paul, it was not merely his good looks that commanded others to notice him: it was the strength of his will, without which he would not be so intimidating; but both were part of who he was.

"I quit," he said.

He seized a chair, sat down, and reached for four scones. He wolfed two down while a vein bulged in his forehead.

"What do you mean, you *quit*?" Deming asked, his dark eyebrows twisting.

"I resigned," Paul said between mouthfuls.

"You did *what*?" Gindoo cried.

Paul leaned back in his chair.

"The fucker's delusional," he said, his voice simmering in a growl. "He won't admit the truth. He won't come clean. He won't be accountable for his deceits and his lies. And nobody would believe us; he's got everyone wrapped into his delusions."

Gindoo shuffled over and glared at him.

"Now he'll be insufferable," the old wizard said, scowling. "You might have been the last person in his circle with some reason. If not, he'll fire the rest."

"No doubt," said Paul. "And despite protocols, I caught some of his thoughts. He's scared shitless of you, Gindoo. And of you, Galla."

Galla laughed. "Absurd! Why would he be?"

Paul looked at Galla coolly. "You're new to him. An unknown. And powerful. He knows you're carrying a child with a—well, a mostly human. That might not sit well with a lot of people. But! Before you say it, I know I'm not fully human either. He knew that too...but he also knew me, more or less, as someone he could trust. But I don't trust him, so I'm out."

"I see," said Gindoo, fidgeting with his long rope of goatee. He glanced at Galla. "Take everything Paul just said to heart. You might need it one day."

Galla breathed in and slowly exhaled.

"Thank you for that, Gindoo," she said, her violet-copper-gold hair twitching while she kept her face placid. "I take it they won't let anyone just quit, right?" she asked.

"No," Paul answered with one of his trademark smirks.

Galla lifted her chin, and she felt the thrill of something bubbling within her—that rebellious spirit that had been dormant or pushed down for too long.

She said carefully, "I suppose, then, that you'll want a swift exit. And a new job. And if that's the case, I could use another telepath and a skilled pilot."

Paul flashed his too-white smile, the sort of look that made many people dizzy. As for Galla, it only amused her. He was truly family now, after all.

THE *SELTRA* SAT GLISTENING in the pale sunlight as Siloxxa broke through cold fog. Galla, Dek, Deming, Paul, and Gindoo approached the elegant, fiery-hued craft.

"We're back," Galla announced to the ship. It lowered a ramp to her feet. She turned to look at her companions.

The hardest part was seeing Dek trying to fight his tears, but they escaped along his clenched jaw anyway. *He really is growing up*, she thought.

"When will you be back?" he asked, and his voice cracked into a higher pitch.

Still a boy for now, she thought lovingly. Then she began to blink.

"I don't know," she admitted, and she did not say, *I may never be back.* But she had raised a smart boy. Dek nodded.

"I hope it's soon," he said to her, and they hugged tightly for several long minutes.

"I love you, sweet Dek," Galla said, and she smiled when he mumbled incoherently back. She turned then to Gindoo.

"Thank you," she said, taking his withered hands into hers. Her diamethyst flashed as she bent just a bit to kiss Gindoo's centuries-etched forehead.

"Yes, well," Gindoo replied, and he nodded. Galla could recognize in his face everything that neither of them dared to say aloud in front of the others.

She sensed a mutual respect, something she had not seen in Gindoo before she had recovered.

We are not quite the same, she thought. *But our responsibilities are similar, and our lives intertwined.*

Nothing else needed to be said between them.

Paul and Deming said their goodbyes to Gindoo, then entered the *Seltra*. Galla watched them and looked back at Gindoo. He looked really quite old then, and stooped, and for a moment she wondered if he might crumple then and there on the ground. Dek saw Galla's look and moved next to Gindoo, who then looked up at the teen and brightened. He brandished his cane.

"Yes, well!" he barked, "let's get back to the house. You have your studies."

Dek laughed, and so did Galla, and their diamethysts winked at each other. Then Galla turned away from the boy, her throat aching, and walked onto her ship.

I needed Dek, she thought. *I needed to know what I'm fighting for. For him and all the other children out there.*

She then felt a strong, muscular tug low in her abdomen.

Yes, she thought, patting her belly, *and for you as well.*

The *Seltra* rose into the air but did not ascend above the cloud deck. It began a southwestern turn.

"Why are we going this way?" Paul asked her, looking out the window. "Isn't it safer to go through the main breach?" Deming glanced at him, and Paul nodded.

Galla sat with lips in a tense line.

"I just want one last look," she said in an even, quiet voice.

She steered the *Seltra* along the crest of the Talonii Mountains, remembering how she had once considered them the most magnificent structures she had ever seen. But now she could remember farther back, and all the worlds she had been to. And they were just mountains, after all.

Descending into the shimmering, gold prairie lands of the Southwest brought a number of sensations she had difficulty labeling. A mix of excitement and fear. The distant memory she purposely avoided, of striking the ground with such force that she had left a crater, over two decades prior. The *Seltra* flew in low, sending the cuybaaf shafts swaying in long swaths in its wake. She could see a familiar line of hillocks, and an old homestead, bleached from Siloxxa's rays. A tractor sat abandoned, covered with weeds, in between the house and the silos. Galla circled her ship all around the home.

At last, two people emerged, and looked up with eyes shielded by their hands. Galla swooped around and tilted her ship just so. They could see her clearly through the cockpit, and she stared at them. She swallowed. They made no motion. They did not wave or speak. Nothing. Galla blinked rapidly.

"Do you want to land?" Deming asked, feeling her turbulence.

Galla closed her stinging eyes.

"I spent enough time with them," she said.

And she looked back at Cuz and Meeya once more, then thrust her ship aloft, away from them, and away from that part of her life forever.

The *Seltra* burst out of the atmosphere, gleaming like a molten bird in the sun, and the arc of fickle Quopeia shrank below.

Thank you for protecting us and thank you for letting us go.

She sat at her console, pushing emotions and nausea aside. She turned the *Seltra* toward the immense copper structure of Trozzhia, which hung outside the orbit of blue-green Quopeia. She opened her comms to the City and to her crew.

"Questri," she said, "now we fight."

34

SEARCHERS

With the *Seltra* tucked away into one of Trozzhia's many bays, Galla, Deming, and Paul took a lift to the new central command pillar of the City. When the door opened, Prilanna and Nalag rushed forward to greet Galla.

Prilanna stopped abruptly and cocked her head at Galla.

"What's wrong?" she asked, and Galla looked down at her in wonder.

"I...I'm not sure what you mean," Galla answered, but she clasped her hands in front of her abdomen.

"Your face..." Prilanna began, and then her voice trailed off.

Nalag yipped, and Paul and Deming both knelt down to the beast. Nalag snuffled Paul's hands and whipped its tail around. Paul grinned ear-to-ear.

"It can speak to me!" he exclaimed.

He caught sight of Kein watching him.

"Oh, hi," Paul said smoothly. Kein looked at him with an inscrutable expression that Galla could not decipher.

"Paul," she said, "this is Kein. And you've met Nalag. This is Prilanna Optison."

Paul shook everyone's hands. He and Kein narrowed their eyes at each other. The older man was dwarfed by Paul, but only in size. Kein's own thoughts were as powerful as Paul's, but not as disciplined.

"So it's all come to this," Kein said softly.

Galla lowered her chin and gave Kein one of her large-eyed looks. "What do you mean?"

"Well, I guess I had wondered what the fuck everything was about, why I had to leave Perpetua, and so on," Kein mused. He nodded at Paul, who watched him constantly. "Now I know. We're the descendants. It wasn't about our parents or our great-great-grandparents. It was *us*." And Kein glanced at Deming as well.

Galla said, "The Associates missed the mark by a few generations. That wasn't all they missed," and her eyes narrowed into slivers of amber.

She attempted to smooth her feral hair, cleared her throat, and straightened her back.

"We've seen Aeriod," she announced to the rest of her team.

Kein gasped. "And? Where is he?"

"He's off on some mission, at Gindoo's behest," Galla replied, keeping her voice calm.

Deming looked sideways at her.

"Are you serious?" Kein said, and he clicked his tongue in disgust. "Right when we need him, he's off again? And as for Gindoo—"

"It's fine," Galla said crisply. "We have our own mission before we take on Paosh Tohon. Paul, I don't suppose you remember Jana Okoro?"

Paul half-closed his eyes. "I'm not...sure. The name is so familiar."

"You were a toddler when you last saw her," Galla reminded him. "She and a man named Guru were aiding me before...before my crash, and your parents' kidnapping. I want to know if they survived. And if they did, how we can help them."

"Where were they last?" Paul asked.

Galla sat down in her captain's chair. "Trozzhia," she said clearly, "is it possible to map a trail of the *Fithich* before its destruction? Particularly its tail section, *Fithich 2*? I know the rest of the ship was destroyed..." and she closed her eyes.

"One. More." Rob had asked her for that final kiss before he took his last breath and the ship exploded, sending their escape pod plummeting, to disintegrate in the upper atmosphere of Quopeia.

A soft voice answered, "The ship tracks have long diminished, and the signatures the ship gave out were muffled greatly by design. It may be possible to track junction traffic instead, over the years."

Galla opened her eyes. "Do that," she commanded.

"Meanwhile," she said to her companions, watching Nalag squeeze up against Paul, who stroked the animal's fur, "we have fleet-building to work on. What else might be useful? We can't take Trozzhia everywhere, so it should be a base of operations for us. We have to be able to provide protection to every Device world, and every being stationed inside a Device. So, at least twenty-one ships; likely more. A ship to get them where they need to be, and ships in orbit for defense. What else?"

"People who can actually *fly* ships?" Paul suggested. "Or are all of these going to be drone ships?"

Galla thought back to the swarm of drone ships that had surrounded the *Fithich* in the Mehelkian system.

"Those can be useful, but maybe not as adaptive as having pilots on board," she mused. "Oni-Odi and Demetraan were all androids, bots, and drones. That's not what I want Trozzhia to be. Demetraan was an island of sorts; Trozzhia will be whatever I want it to be. And what I want is for it to be flexible."

"Commander Galla-Deia," a muted voice chimed in around them all.

Galla instinctively looked up and about, and then nodded and said, "Yes?" to her City.

"There were a series of junctions that the tail section of the *Fithich* navigated before its disappearance."

Galla's hair fell flat in dread.

"And?" she asked in a whisper.

"The location of the final junction has been identified."

"Show me," she commanded.

In front of all of them, a simulation formed, showing the *Fithich 2* being chased, and then dropping out of sight near a small planet. Other, unidentified craft descended, and then rose and flew away.

"So...did the ship *land*?" Galla asked, holding her breath.

"It is unclear if the ship landed or was destroyed," the City's voice answered.

Galla glanced around at her team.

"We need to find out," she told them.

"So what's the plan?" Kein asked. "Are you going to take the whole City out there? Or just your ship, or what?"

"I'll leave Trozzhia here in the Siloxxan system," Galla answered. "It's in the right position for me to take on the Event, here at the apex of the Device worlds...the Horseshoe, as we called it. But yes...I'm taking the *Seltra* myself. Who's coming along?"

Everyone stood, even Nalag on all four of its feet.

"We're not leaving your side," Deming told her, smirking.

"I'm getting cooped up in this town, anyway," Kein said.

Prilanna stepped up next to Galla. "I didn't leave my village just to go stay in another village," she said, opening her great brown eyes even wider. Galla looked down at her fondly. "I'm here to help, however I can, and I can't do much staying in Trozzhia right now."

Galla nodded. "Very well," she said. "I don't know what we'll be up against, but it's as good a time as any to find out."

"Trozzhia," she ordered, "send sentinel drone ships all throughout the system here, and give Quopeia adequate warning, should anything decide to drop in for a visit before we're back."

The floor beneath them vibrated, and Galla leaned against the window of her command center to watch little blobs of copper-hued material form on the great bowl shape of Trozzhia's upper surface. Those blobs rose into the air and began modifying themselves into generally teardrop-shaped, small ships. Those then flew through the thin membrane surrounding Trozzhia and shot off in all directions to begin their watch.

"Those look a lot like what brought me to Quopeia," Kein noted. "They're just not green."

"You rode in a Demetraan pod," Galla said, "so some things will remain the same, I think."

I actually have no idea what all this City is and isn't capable of, she thought, *and I don't know how much time I have to find out.*

"Let's go," she said, and she walked toward the lift, followed by her friends and her fiancé, feeling for the first time in a long while that she might be able to get something done without the yoke of her grief and her frozen life for the past two decades. She liked that feeling. She also knew that it would be fleeting, because what lay ahead of them did not subsist on joy. It wanted only suffering. And she was going to fly right toward that vale of mayhem with people she loved.

The *Seltra* took them out of the confines of Trozzhia and off into space, toward the nearest junction. They flew unimpeded, so Trozzhia's disabling of Valemog's fleet had worked for the moment.

I know there will be more, and soon.

She watched the bright spindle form before them and felt the familiar pull of the junction on her. Nalag whined. Prilanna held onto the animal, and when Galla looked back at Deming's face, she realized that half her crew had never done this before. Paul clearly had, as part of his training.

Kein said, "Ah shit, here we go again. Can we shield the lights? I don't need a migraine right now."

"Good point," said Galla, and she commanded the *Seltra* to form a shield for them all, so that the piercing streaks and swirls of the junction's nether-space would not hurt anyone's eyes.

Then she said, "*Seltra*, take us on the projected journey to find the *Fithich* tail section."

As soon as the junction entrance closed behind them, a number of small shapes appeared around them. Their proximity to the ship alerted it, but they were also within visual range. Galla looked at each member of her crew, to be sure their diamethysts were all in place.

"Friend or foe?" Deming asked.

"Assume it's a foe," Paul said with a grunt. "Ran into these things before on a mission. Truth be told, we don't really know what they are. They liked to buzz our ships. I'm guessing they were gathering intel, then they would vanish."

Galla squinted at her console.

"*Seltra*, can you give me an up-close look at one of those crafts?"

"Magnifying," the ship responded, and before them a craft was projected as a hologram.

Galla stood quickly, her hair coiling in all directions. It was an ornate, golden ship, quite small, but its details could not be mistaken.

"They're Mehelkian!" she exclaimed, and her face flushed with relief and delight. "Prince Hazkinaut's ships!"

And she almost commanded her ship to make contact, but one by one, the little ships disappeared.

Paul shrugged. "Told ya," he said simply.

"But it's *okay*!" said Galla excitedly, in one moment reverting to a more innocent look, clasping her hands under her chin. "It means the Prince knows we're out here. I'm sure of it!"

"What do we do now?" Deming asked, bemused by her excitement.

"We keep going," Galla told him. "The Prince has his own ways and means; hopefully we will hear from him before long. If the Event isn't too disruptive for communications, that is."

Paul said, "Oh, it will be," and Galla rolled her eyes.

"Too bad nobody figured out a way around that," she said. "But then again...I guess that's *my* job. Onward, then."

The rest of the journey went smoothly, as they jumped junction to junction with no further surveillance. Galla felt a little suspicious at the ease of it all, but her crew were amiable, cracking jokes, eating lunch, and laughing.

"Final junction," *Seltra* announced. Galla sat upright.

"Strap in, everyone," she called out.

She gasped. The ship had entered a debris field and began to swerve to try to avoid collisions with rock and destroyed ships.

"What the hell happened here?" Kein wondered, echoing her own thoughts.

"A battle?" she suggested.

"One hell of a battle," said Paul grimly. "Not sure anyone won it, either."

Galla swallowed, and took the helm, helping her ship weave through the flotsam that pummeled the craft on all sides. Luckily it was a malleable ship, and it kept adapting protective shields and even its shape to avoid damage.

The *Seltra* then blared out a proximity alert.

"Ships approaching, all directions, hidden," it said.

Galla's hair whipped around her. "Make sure we're hidden too, then," she commanded, and she turned to look back at her crew.

"Remember why we're here," she told them. "We have to know what happened to Jana, Guru, and Beetle. But we also have to survive. This could get rough. We get in, and we get out. Be ready. Paul, help me with targeting."

Paul sat opposite Galla in the cockpit.

Kein and Paul then stiffened at the same time, and Nalag's hair bristled all over.

"Something's here," Kein muttered, his hazel eyes wide. "Something can sense us." He shuddered and fingered the small purple stone around his neck. Instinctively, Prilanna reached for hers as well, and clasped it tightly in her small hands.

"You're not the only telepaths out here, then," muttered Galla.

Another proximity alert made them all jump. "More ships approaching," the *Seltra* announced. "Different origin, partially hidden."

"What is going on?" Deming said, essentially transmitting Galla's own emotions.

Galla looked at the unfolding situation and shook her head.

"We're in the middle of a battle, that's what."

35

SILICATE

Spindles of light revealed more ships arriving from the nearby junction. All around the *Seltra*, space exploded in color and light, as lances of firepower splintered ships.

Paul said, "Not sure who's friend or foe." He looked over his shoulder at Kein, who met his green eyes with crinkled hazel ones.

If we can't figure this out, we need to stay out of it, Paul thought.

Agreed, Kein responded. *Can they both be bad? Whose side are their telepaths on?*

Galla interrupted their thoughts by announcing, "They're distracted. Let's make a run for it."

They could see through the cockpit the system's red star, and one immense gas giant. The *Seltra* said calmly, "There are three gaseous planets and several rocky planets of much smaller size, as well as an asteroid belt. The *Fithich 2* dropped off its minimal signature on one of those smaller planets."

"Take us there," Galla commanded.

The *Seltra* told her, "This planet contains an atmosphere. Adjusting for turbulence patterns."

"Thank you," Galla said, appreciative of the ship, as part of the gift of Trozzhia Oni-Odi had given her.

She soon realized why the ship had warned her, for the small planet possessed a peculiar atmosphere, which buffeted and tossed the *Seltra*. It continually adjusted for the turbulence, but Galla remembered her own flying instincts, and what a certain overly large insect named Beetle had taught her about flying in a storm. She let loose a bit on her controls and let the ship ride the currents.

She heard Prilanna moan and Nalag whimper, for this was not a smooth ride. Their approach to the planet sent a whirlwind of grey sand spinning from its boulder-strewn surface high into its sky.

"Hold tight, Questri," Galla said. "This could be tricky."

The *Seltra* swayed back and forth on its descent, and Galla worked with it to land. It bumped and bounced, and then landed securely, and sent forth landing gear. Galla wiped the sweat from her hands onto her pants and looked at her crew. Paul smirked at her.

"Nice going, Captain," he said, with a roguish nod.

She swallowed. Her mouth tasted quite salty, and before she realized what was happening, she vomited all over the control panels of the ship.

Deming unbuckled and rushed forth, but she held up her left hand to him and clutched her diamethyst with her right one.

"Not the most graceful landing, either way," she said in a crackly voice to her crew. She instructed the *Seltra*, with some embarrassment, to clean up her mess.

Then she turned to Kein, Paul, and Nalag.

"All right, now I need you three to help me search. It looks a bit hostile out there"—and Galla was rewarded with strong gusts thrashing the ship, and the fine pelting of granular silicate—"so I'm thinking we need suits. *Seltra*, can you make three humanoid suits and a—a deengyne suit?"

Kein laughed.

With her mouth twisted, she said, "Deming, Prilanna, stay with the ship."

"At your service, Commander," Deming said smoothly, looking down at her with his gold-banded dark eyes. Her anxiety buffeted his mind more powerfully than the winds pummeling the ship outside. He did not flinch, but instead faced it full on. "Good luck."

She looked at him with her eyes half-lowered, making him shiver. Then she faced her other crew.

You will need strong minds to help you. So she had been told. And here they were; some of them, anyway.

She sighed. *Protect them, Universe. I love each and every one.*

"Everyone got a stone?" she asked, patting her own diamethyst where it lay on her breast. She clasped it gratefully, realizing how much she had missed its presence.

Everyone checked for their smaller diamethysts and nodded.

She walked with Paul, Kein, and Nalag in their various suits out to the bay of the ship. Behind her, Nalag twitched and jumped and snapped in its helmet, until Kein and Paul each reached down at the same time to pet its back. Galla looked over her shoulder at the three of them and felt warmed. She wondered what they were saying to each other in their minds. Whatever it was, Nalag settled into a resigned trot ahead of them all, down the ramp to the surface of the world. The two men looked at each other and laughed.

"Careful, Nalag," she said to the deengyne. "Let Kein and Paul know if you detect any thought patterns. Or if there is anything that makes you feel frightened."

Nalag pranced ahead and out of sight. She could hear the animal's pants inside its helmet, and occasionally it would stop panting, sit on its haunches, and wait for them to catch up with it. After a half hour, she heard a tiny whine, more panting, and then silence. She glanced at Kein and Paul.

"Anything?" she asked nervously.

Paul's bright green eyes shone through his helmet visor. "Something."

Galla felt the hair on her neck rise. She looked at Kein. He shrugged. "Remember, I'm not so good at this. But Nalag was sending quick little thoughts. 'Stay back a minute' and 'be quiet' just a minute ago. Now, nothing."

"I don't like that," Galla said.

"No," Paul agreed.

"Do we stay back?" Kein asked.

"No," Galla answered. "We move forward, cautiously. Paul, hang behind Kein, please."

"On it," Paul said, and he slacked off a bit, nodded to Kein, and swiveled to look behind them, all around. His training gave him an advantage over Kein, but he was not in any mood to boast about it. Of the four of them, Kein might be the most vulnerable of all, he reasoned.

Says you, Kein snapped into his mind. *I'm not that old.* Paul grinned to himself.

"Where are you, Nalag?" Galla whispered into her comms. "Are you safe?"

A soft crackle of static met their ears. And then a growl.

Galla froze and shot a look back at the telepaths. Kein's eyes grew large. But Paul simply nodded and held up a finger in front of his helmet to hush them. He motioned with his other hand to keep going forward. Instinctively, Galla stepped lightly, and they made their way through grey boulders along a sandy path. Nalag's small frame had slipped easily through the trickier parts. Galla, Kein, and Paul had to negotiate their bodies through tight squeezes, and in one stretch, they crawled.

Galla heard Nalag panting, stopping, panting again, and then the tiniest whine, which she felt was for her ears alone, since she could not pick up Nalag's thoughts like her telepathic companions.

"Guys," she said quietly to Kein and Paul, "what's Nalag thinking? Can you pick it up?"

"Not exactly sure. Confusion?" Paul offered.

"No," Kein said, sounding assured. "Not confusion so much as curiosity. Nalag is looking at something and wondering what it is."

"Wait," Paul said, "how can you tell that? I can read Nalag but not to that level. And—no offense—I've done this longer."

In his suit, Kein shrugged. "Might be the only thing you've done longer, then. Maybe I know wildlife better because I grew up surrounded by it."

"Huh," said Paul.

Galla stopped abruptly, and Kein ran into her, and they stumbled a bit.

"I guess we can see what Nalag is curious about now," Galla said. "What is *that*?"

They left their crevasse and witnessed a series of large lumps. Galla could see that one of them was a ship of some kind that she did not recognize. Its hull had been scoured of any recognizable markings, but whatever it had been, something had struck it with weaponry, and it had crashed long ago. Beyond it, however, was a strange, larger object, which from afar would have looked like one of this planet's boulders, if not for its peculiar shape. It was grey and also covered in the silicates, with drifts of them piled over three-quarters high along it. Galla looked at it for several minutes. She jumped when something brushed against her leg.

It was Nalag, and it sat on its bottom and looked up at her through its special helmet with eyes as violet as the stone she had tucked into her suit.

"What is it, Nalag?" she asked softly.

Nalag lifted one paw and pointed at the object, then sneezed inside its helmet, then whined at the droplets that made. The suit soon cleared them, though, and then Nalag jumped off the sandy ground on all fours.

"Nalag wants you to check it out," Paul told her. "But it's a little afraid."

"And very curious," Kein added.

Galla reached down with her hands and held Nalag's pointy, helmeted face. "It's all right, Nalag," she said, smiling. She patted Nalag's back. "I'll go first, dear friend."

Nalag dipped its nose down in a play bow. Kein could not resist and knelt to stroke Nalag's suited back.

"You can stay here," Galla told them.

Kein stood then. "Nope. We're going with you."

Galla sighed and closed her eyes for a few seconds. "Fine," she answered. "But hang back a bit until I know it's safe."

As she began walking toward the object, she noticed something in the sky. The atmosphere blazed for a moment, and she watched as something fell at high speed.

"Deming," she called on her comms. "What was that?"

"The fight's still going on up there," he answered. "Not sure if that was friend or foe."

And the ground shook from the object's distant impact.

"If things get dicey," Galla said to him, "take the *Seltra* and get out of here. I'm not asking you, by the way. It's an order."

"Affirmative," Deming responded. "I think whoever is on our side is still holding them off up there."

"Good thing," Galla answered. "We've reached an object. I'm going in."

"Be safe," he said.

Galla said nothing. She tried to shove down a sudden fit of nausea. *Please...I do not want to vomit in my helmet!* She swallowed, breathed slowly for a few moments, and then walked on. She shuffled through the sand and made it over halfway toward the object when her diamethyst began to grow warm. She stopped and put her gloved hand on her chest. It heated more, until she gasped.

She swiveled back to look at Paul and Kein, and they clutched their chests as well.

"It's hot!" Kein said.

Galla shivered despite the warmth of her stone. She turned back and faced the great object. She bit her lower lip and walked with slow, determined steps. The stone grew hotter. Her eyes began to sting.

She reached the object and looked at it with a puzzled face. She held her hand up to it and brushed away some of the silicate powder.

"Oh!" she cried.

Where her hand had swept, something glistened beneath: iridescent black-purple-green. She felt herself convulse, and tears welled in her eyes.

"It's the *Fithich 2*," she said with a choked sound.

She leaned forward and rested her hands on her knees. She

thought back to the day it had split off from the *Fithich*, when she had wondered if she would ever see Jana, Guru, or Beetle again.

No one here knew them.

"Galla," a loving voice said in her helmet. It was Deming. "Keep going, Galla." He knew, then. He could feel it all coming back to her, even from that distance.

His voice comforted her. She stood again, exhaled a huge sigh, blinked through her tears, and put her hands on the surface of the *Fithich* 2. She walked around and shoved piles of sand away from the crashed ship with her legs. Much of it was mangled on this side. She guessed the nose must be buried in the dirt.

"I don't even know where the door was," she admitted. "I'm going to try to cut through."

She unzipped her suit long enough to retrieve the diamethyst and pulled it forth. Then she zipped up again and grasped the stone in her hands.

She looked back at Kein and Paul, and deciding, she said, "Paul, I need a telepath. Kein, stay with Nalag."

But Nalag bolted suddenly from Kein's side and charged forward to Galla. It galloped across the several meters between them and then slid on the ground. The animal bounced against her thigh and looked up at her.

"You, Nalag?" she said, with a little chirping laugh. Then Nalag looked from her stone to the ship.

Galla said, "Hmm," and looked down at the glowing stone in her hands. "So be it, I guess. Nalag, I want you to focus on the stone, and I'm going to try to use it to cut through. Oakay?"

Nalag dipped its head. Galla held the stone's pointed tip against the iridescent skin of the *Fithich* 2. Testing it, she found the stone would only penetrate so far. She nodded down to Nalag. She watched, fascinated, as Nalag lowered its eyes and gazed at the stone. It began to glow brighter than before, then grew extremely hot. Galla watched her gloves smolder, and then fall away, burned by the luminous diamethyst. Then she gritted her teeth and panted, for it began burning her skin as well. She endured the pain and gasped. Nalag sat perfectly still, completely focused, like a small statue.

She shoved the stone into the ship as high as she could reach. It sank easily through this time, so she dragged it down like a knife. It sizzled for a moment, but the cut stayed. There was no evidence, then, that the ship had any power or capability left for minor repair. She then carved above her across and down another side, making the rough shape of a doorway. Nalag pranced backward a bit. Galla then placed her hands on the door she had made and shoved. It fell inward easily, with eddies of sand whooshing around and then a final great *CLANG* as it struck the floor. Inside lay only darkness. Yet her stone still glowed.

She said, "Kein, Paul, what are your gems doing?"

"Still hot," said Paul.

"Same here," Kein chimed in.

"I'm going in," Galla told them.

"Not without us," said Paul, and he and Kein advanced quickly across the sand.

Static burst in their helmets.

"Galla," said Deming urgently. "Ships are making it through. I'll try to hold them off."

"Great," said Galla. "*Seltra*," she commanded, "recognize the foes and disable them."

"Confirmed," the ship answered flatly.

But something had already slipped through, and lancets of fire-power shot down all around Kein and Paul.

"RUN!" screamed Galla, and she ran out to and past them as they scrambled. She looked up. A ship with a red marking on its side swooped down toward her. "Valemog," she hissed. "Not today!"

And she held her stone aloft, and a column of brilliant, white-violet light erupted from it and burrowed into the ship, which exploded and crashed into the rocks around it. She looked back quickly and saw Paul and Kein had made it to the doorway of the *Fithich 2*.

"What's the situation?" she asked Deming.

"The *Seltra* is disabling the ships. You might have some more incoming, but they're powerless. Don't know where they'll land, but they won't like it."

"No, and maybe we won't either. We need to get in and get out."

She reached her companions at the doorway. She could see their own stones glowing through their suits, but none of them complained. They all looked into the darkness within the bowels of the vessel.

"I have to know," Galla said, filled with dread. She crossed the threshold and entered the dead ship.

36

UNFURLED

"Lights," Galla said, and her helmet responded, as did those of her companions. Even Nalag's helmet shone at a low level into the darkness. In fact, that lower shaft of light revealed a strange structure just in front of their feet.

Nalag whined loudly and darted between Kein's legs, sending him onto his backside. His own headlamp then darted up, and he, Galla, and Paul instinctively scrambled backwards to join Nalag.

"What—the fuck—is *that*?" Kein's whispers came out in panicked spurts.

"It's *huge*," Paul gasped.

Galla stood with her copper eyes bulging, trying to comprehend what she was looking at. It was a large, deep amber-colored *something* that stretched from floor to ceiling and branched in ropy, vinelike tendrils.

"I—I don't know," she answered in a shaky voice. Her diamethyst pulsed with color and light. This emboldened her.

She walked toward the structure.

"No, Galla!" cried Paul.

But Galla ignored him.

"Galla," Deming's voice said in her ear. He said nothing else. Galla took a deep breath and stepped forward once more. She reached her hand toward the thing.

"Shit," Kein's voice crackled.

Galla looked back at them and blinked.

She touched the structure.

A vibration rippled through the floors.

Galla cried, "Get out!" to her friends. They sprinted out the door.

"Deming," Paul called through his helmet, "we found something in the ship. Galla's touched it. Something's happening."

"What can I do?" Deming asked urgently.

"Bring the *Seltra* and hover it close by for an evac," Paul answered.

"On it."

Before they could do anything else, two ships entered the atmosphere, firing at each other. One came in low and began firing at them.

"Not again!" groaned Kein.

Paul looked up.

"We'll have to go back inside the ship," he said.

"Shit!" Kein responded.

"Deming," Paul called, his voice hard.

"I see them," Deming answered. "We'll take care of it."

Deafening strikes of firepower on the sands erupted around them and turned their strike points to glass. The ship firing at them bore another Valemog symbol, and it was a boxy, rough hunk of metal, whereas the ship in pursuit of it was ornated and pearl-colored, with gold scrollwork all about it. A stripe of brilliant blue burst forth from the pearl-hued ship and struck the Valemog blaster in its thrusters, sending it spinning. It tumbled and slammed into the planet's surface about a hundred feet away, sending the men flying and the deengyne running at full speed away.

The pearl ship then landed just to their left. Kein, Paul, and Nalag hesitated, but a vibrant, fire-and-copper-colored ship descended next to the pearl ship. The *Seltra* had arrived. Above them, more ships battled.

"Help Galla!" cried Deming. "I'll ready the ship for engaging this other ship if we need to. I think it's friendly, but I don't know."

"Come on!" yelled Paul to Kein and Nalag, and they ran back into the dark door of the *Fithich 2*. They could see pale violet light emanating from Galla's diamethyst as she held her hands on the surface of the thing inside.

Their own stones grew hotter and blazed.

"Guys," Deming called, "anything happening with your gems? Ours are getting hot!"

"Yes!" Paul answered.

"What's going on?" Deming asked. "Galla? You seem like you're in a trance. You all right?"

Galla's eyes were closed.

Do I cut into this thing? Should I? I need to know!

And then her eyes caught something—a light, the palest, smallest light. Something within the structure. And it was purple!

She cried out, and gripped her own diamethyst, and jabbed it into the structure and tore a gash through it. A gas escaped, and her helmet sensor flashed an alert. She could hear it echoed in her friends' helmets as well.

"Keep your helmet on," she ordered. "The gas will affect your nervous system."

She waited, and looked back at Paul and Kein. Nalag crouched low, its eyes peeking up at the tear. The deengyne growled.

The gas dissipated, and Galla seized the material and tried pulling it, but it wanted to repair itself. She stepped inside anyway, to the dismay of her friends, who yelled at her. Inside she found something enormous, curled and folded and seemingly organic. But amid it there shone one of her diamethysts, tiny yet brilliant, responding to the one around her neck and everyone else's. Then the mass moved.

Galla jumped and scooted away from it, and it stretched and unfolded, creaked and scraped and groaned. She wanted to scream at the thing and run, so powerful was her fear.

I have to face it, she reminded herself. *I'm in command.*

Clutching her stone in front of her, she watched the movement of the object as it turned and then suddenly shot something upward to the top of the structure. A limb!

What is it, what is it?

It twisted again, and she watched the light of the smaller diamethyst wink amid the movements. Her helmet light and the light of her hexagonal stone showed a creature, three times her height, with appendages working and stretching.

Nalag yipped and ran back outside the ship.

"Get out of there, Galla!" Paul cried. "Kein, fall back!"

Galla stood, silent, not knowing what to do, when the light of her stone and helmet shone across something that looked like might be eyes, vast and faceted. Paul rushed in behind her and seized her around her waist.

"Come on!" he yelled.

Then the creature moved its head, and two objects fell in curls down from it. Then they shot forward, and the head bent down quickly, just as Paul turned to look at it.

Antennae, he thought in a rush.

Then a voice boomed from the thing.

"PAUL LARVA?"

Galla and Paul looked at each other in amazement.

"BEETLE!" yelled Paul.

37

T'LEXXA

"The Rynaati T'Lexxa will see you now, Governor," the Fyaldant courier hooted from under its long, shimmering, grey hooded cloak. The courier stood taller than Aeriod, but the latter commanded more attention.

Aeriod gave the being a decorous head tilt, his silver eyes lowered to slits.

Still imperious, he thought, a sneer twitching at the corner of this mouth. *From imperious to impetuous,* he mused, remembering the dancing curls of a certain copper-eyed person beyond his reach. *And now back again. To have to ask...*

But he knew the unpleasantness was imminent, so he began to focus his thoughts elsewhere. He looked at the hoverings, the light beings T'Lexxa had trained to stream overhead. He followed the Fyaldant along hallways lit by the trained creatures flying above his head. The columns lining the halls glowed, and extended high above and out of sight. His silver eyes glazed over as he walked. This was not a place he missed.

But there: something. He turned on his black booted heel, and his long cape, black edged with silver, whirled as he did so.

There was the Rynaati's family crest, woven on a piece of art suspended between two of the immense columns. The crest gave him pause. He had known about it, in ages past, when their marriage seemed promising if not endearing.

There were five facets to the crest. The center portion depicted a creature that humans might have surmised was a dragon, but it had no discernible face, and it bore tentacles as well as legs. The upper left symbol was that of rugged mountain peaks, from the seat of Raexian government. The lower left symbol was that of the sun, Raexam. On the upper right, two cupped hands levitated a ball of fire between them. And on the lower right, a jagged shape puzzled Aeriod. It was cobalt in hue. But if the color were changed to red...

Aeriod stiffened, and held his breath. He looked back at the creature in the center of the crest. He reeled.

There. All this time?

Before he could think more on it, and what it implied, he heard the tinkling of crystals and a chill swept through him. He turned from the crest slowly, dreading the sight. And there she stood: the Rynaati T'Lexxa, who he had not seen in centuries.

At first glance, T'Lexxa would appear stupefyingly beautiful to human eyes. But Aeriod was not human. And upon further inspection, humans would likely recoil the more they looked at her. She was tall, taller than Aeriod by nearly a foot, and her hair appendages stretched in blue-grey crystalline spikes all over her head. Her eyes were deep pewter, her nose was sharp and slender, and her cheeks and jawbone were harshly defined. She opened her mouth by a tiny slit, and her pointed teeth glimmered. Her immense gown stretched in quill-like spikes behind her, to match her head, and her frame was slender and angular, her shoulders nearly spikes in her clothing.

Aeriod could not help himself; he thought of Galla's curves arching over his body and the warmth of her touch, and thought, *How did I marry this person? She's carved from ice.*

T'Lexxa watched him through slitted eyes and let out a deep, cold laugh. She arranged her long-fingered hands at her waist.

"How small you are!" she said to him, looking down her nose. "I had forgotten."

Aeriod knew she was not merely talking about his height. Her glittering fangs told him as much, as did their chilly history. But he smirked, and again thought of Galla making love to him, and held that fiery memory in his mind while looking at her with his own cold satisfaction.

"You never did hold on to memory, as I recall," he said crisply. "And certainly not to love. I suppose those things are indeed small to you. You have, after all, most of our worlds now. A vast reach for your personal empire. Or have they all fallen?"

T'Lexxa's eyes shimmered with deep, cobalt-blue sparks among their metallic depths.

"They were my worlds by birthright, and I deigned to share them with you only during our arranged marriage," she said, her raiment rustling.

"Were?" he asked, his smirk deepening. "So you lost them?"

"I lost *nothing*," she hissed, stepping slowly toward him. "You received your fair share of the settlement."

Aeriod inclined his head a bit. "I know how to take care of what is mine," he said to her. "Do you? How many belong to Paosh Tohon now? Did you strike a deal?"

With a lightning flash, she was before him, staring him down.

He closed his eyes, sighed, and daydreamed of Galla's legs around his waist and her cries of ecstasy. He grinned again to himself.

"Why are you here?" T'Lexxa demanded, her cold breath on his face.

Aeriod held his small diamethyst nodule in his fingers, rubbing it, eyes half-lidded.

"You need to tell me the status of your worlds, for one thing," Aeriod drawled. "Are they gone? Why are you defensive? I have an idea why. But indulge me."

"I have protected *my* worlds from all exterior forces for centuries," T'Lexxa answered in a brittle, low voice.

Aeriod laughed up at her.

"That is, as the humans say, bullshit," he said to her. "I know there is no way you've kept them all untarnished in this fight. And I know why. It's your family. Your brother. Isn't it?"

T'Lexxa seized Aeriod by the throat and dug her fingernails into his neck, her sharp teeth glinting.

"What do you accuse me of? You know my brother is dead."

Aeriod swallowed as she choked him. He closed his eyes and breathed very slowly. She released him, and he stumbled, but recovered, and he swept his black cape around himself and stared up stonily into her dead-cold eyes.

"Your brother was presumed dead," he agreed. "But your family crest in there. It bears a symbol I see on ships that have maimed, killed, or delivered entire populations to Paosh Tohon. It is the symbol of Valemog, but in blue. And the chimera on the crest. He did it, didn't he? He found a way."

T'Lexxa turned away from him, her flinty face in profile.

"You speak madness. My family has never been involved in this war."

Aeriod shook his long, pale hair.

"You can't lie to me, T'Lexxa. I know you too well. You've arranged something. A trade. What was it?" he asked, and he advanced on her and stared up at her crystalline head.

She wheeled on him and bent her head down until the spikes poked the top of his forehead. He did not move.

She said, "What of *your* worlds? Are you still fond of hiding them? I know how it tires you."

Aeriod stepped back a bit.

"So you admit to working with him. With *it*."

"I admit nothing, and you speak in a fool's tongue," T'Lexxa snapped.

"The sooner you admit what you've done, the sooner we can fix this," Aeriod told her, his jaws clenching. "You will not be absolved, mind you. I'll see to that personally, should we survive. Which we won't. Not even you: not even its sister. The arrangement won't stand. And you know it."

T'Lexxa turned away from him and stalked off, her shoes echoing in the vast hall.

"What do you want, Aeriod?" she asked him, turning at the end.

"Tell me more about the chimera. What did he want? How did he do it? We—I—need to know. I need to know a weakness."

T'Lexxa stood still.

"Please, T'Lexxa," he said. "If you ever loved me—"

T'Lexxa laughed in a loop of staccato horror.

"Why should I have loved you, Aeriod?" she asked him, and her eyes gleamed across the distance between them. "It was a fool's errand on my part, I admit. You are a vain simpleton. Good only for property acquisition. And you have no family."

Aeriod closed his eyes and felt supremely happy for a moment.

No family? In that you're wrong. And he felt more determined than ever to do anything possible to save Galla and her child.

"Oh, don't worry, I'm glad it is over," he told her. "You had nothing to offer me. No love, no warmth, no passion, nothing. I wanted to help those worlds. Do you know what that's like? Can you even imagine *helping* something other than a blood relative? Helping refugees build a new future for themselves? I venture you do not, or you would never side with this monster."

T'Lexxa wheeled around and stormed up to him.

"I side with no one!" she cried.

"So you're alone in this?" he asked, heated. The air between them fizzled and sparked.

"Always," she answered in a hiss. "No thanks to you."

Aeriod nodded, satisfied. "Well. Here's your chance. Give me what I need. Redeem yourself in some way. Otherwise you will be known as complicit. And if you think he won't come after you and everything you've built, you're wrong. It is only a matter of time."

She closed her eyes, her spiked-crown head thrown back. She stood that way for a long moment.

"Leave," she said at last.

He didn't hesitate. He bowed to her, more out of shared history than any other decorum. He turned and left.

38

───────

TRANSMOGRIFY

Galla and Paul watched in awe as the creature continued to unfold itself. Then, seeing it struggle a bit with its enormous cocoon, they tried to tear it down. Paul could not, but Galla's strength outmatched his, so she pulled the buttressing of the thing apart, and then what once was Beetle could now stand free. It stooped under the ceiling of the *Fithich 2*.

"Beetle, can you step outside?" Galla asked.

"I...can...try," it said, and to Galla it sounded winded.

"Come on, my friend," she coaxed, and she and Paul stepped back.

"Beetle," Paul said, "you actually used to look like a beetle. Now... what are you?"

Rattling a bit as it walked forward on two wobbly legs, Beetle made it out onto the surface of the planet.

"It is too thin and dry," it told Galla, breathing in.

"I can adjust my ship, the *Seltra*, so that you'll fit—oh!" and she gasped as Beetle stretched.

Great, iridescent green and purple wings stretched out on either side of its thorax.

"Not a beetle," Paul mused, "maybe more like those things I've read about in stories. A moth?"

"What's a moth?" Galla asked. "Anyway, it doesn't matter. You've metamorphosed. I didn't know your species had another form! Tell me more when we get you to the *Seltra*."

The *Seltra* perched nearby and its bay opened. Galla appraised the size of its entry.

"I don't know," she muttered. "*Seltra*, extend the entrance and the interior ceiling to accommodate Beetle here. Please study Beetle and make some kind of appropriate food, until we can get fresh leaves."

Then she turned back to the creature and admired the sparkling of its eyes. Around one digit hung a little diamethyst knob, which flashed in concert with her larger stone.

"Beetle," she said then, tempering her elation at finding her friend with a worried voice, "what became of Jana and Guru?"

Beetle turned and clicked a bit in its old fashion, but there was something more musical in its voice, and it said, "I am sorry, Captain Deia. I stung them."

Galla clapped her hand to her mouth.

"No! Oh Beetle! Oh no! Why?" she cried.

Beetle lowered its head and folded its splendid wings back. "The ship was being attacked. I did not want them taken hostage."

Galla slid down onto the sand and sat stunned.

Taking quick, shocked breaths, she said, "But—but Beetle, what did you do—with them?"

"I cocooned them."

"What!" she gasped. "Where are they? Are they alive?" and she jumped up and swiveled toward the crashed ship.

"I do not know," the creature admitted. "My body was changing quickly. I knew I must enter stasis. I also knew that if I stung them just enough, they might sleep, as I did. Too much, and they might die, but they would not be taken by the enemy. I do not know what happened after I cocooned them, for I had to fend off the attackers. I sent webbing at the enemy and...injured them, and brought down their ships. The cocoons are hard to breach, as you found. You might have been the only person who could open one. I do not know. I am very tired now. May I go into this new ship?"

Galla stood and felt dizzy, and again fought down severe nausea.

"Yes, go," she said, uncertain what to do next. She looked over at Paul, who had stood in stunned silence.

"Do you remember?" she asked him.

"A bit. I remember riding Beetle's back. I can't have been very old. A toddler? It's all a mix in my head. I don't have many memories from my time before Quopeia. But Beetle is coming back to me," he said, and then he winked at Galla. "Explains my interest in those kinds of creatures. Remember the necklace I gave you?"

Galla blinked. "Yes! I didn't make that connection until now."

She turned toward the *Fithich 2*.

"You don't have to go with me," she said to Paul, "but I want to see if Jana and Guru are still in there. And—and—well. One thing at a time."

"I'll go with you, obviously," Paul replied, grinning. "You need a telepath for this one, right?"

Galla nodded slowly. "I hope I do."

Her helmet crackled. "Uh...Galla," Deming called, "there's an enormous creature here who says you're its captain. What do we do?"

"Give Beetle some water," she answered. "Paul and I are going back in the ship to look for my old crew."

"Copy that," Deming responded.

Additional blazes of light crisscrossed the upper atmosphere of the little world. Galla eyed them warily as they walked to the *Fithich 2*. Once inside, headlamps flaring, she and Paul stepped carefully into the husk of Beetle's former cocoon. She could see two strange, dark marks toward one end of the cocoon, and as they walked closer, it appeared to her that these had originally been openings that were since sealed off by Beetle's weaving.

"Do you pick up anything?" she asked Paul quietly.

Paul glanced at her with his bright green eyes, and she met them.

"No thoughts," he answered, his jaw taut.

Galla closed her eyes and sighed.

"The stone," he said then, and Galla looked down. Her diamethyst began to shine again, a low, soft purple light emanating from it. She eyed Paul's chest and could see a glow through this suit.

"Oh please, oh please," she whispered. Paul reached out to her and grabbed her bare hand.

"I'm here," he said warmly. She bit her lip and nodded up at him. He reminded her so much of Dagovaby just now, in his confident reassurance, yet he looked at her with Ariel's eyes.

"I'm going to open those coverings," she told him. "Stand back, just in case."

"Got it," Paul replied.

She bent down, and taking hold of her diamethyst, she used it to pull gently at the webbing over one of the two former holes. It opened, and a puff of gas emerged from it. Galla then took her stone and tore a longer gash. Her light shone down, and she jumped. There lay a curled form, covered in some kind of powdery membrane. Her stone began glowing more brightly. She crawled forth on her knees next to the shape.

"Oh!" she cried.

"What?" Paul asked, his voice a little higher than usual.

"Jana," she said softly, reverently, and she touched a glowing little area on her friend's shape. Jana's stone was responding to hers. "Oh Jana," and Galla began crying.

A blast outside shook the ship.

"Paul, Galla," Deming's urgent voice chimed through their helmets. "You need to get out of there. Looks like some ships got through."

"*Seltra*," Galla said in a shaky voice, "shield yourself and fire into the propulsion systems of enemy ships. Prepare for takeoff as soon as we return."

She turned back to Jana's still form and pulled gently at the membrane covering her.

Paul gasped, and Galla fell back on her heels in surprise.

"Dreams!" he said to her. "I'm picking up broken dreams!"

"She's alive?" Galla whispered. She reached forward and

continued pulling off the membranous substance, revealing Jana's still face. Even in the mixed light, she could see Jana's eyes darting back and forth. But there was something strange about her face that Galla could not discern. First of all, it was quite bony. Her hair had grown over time, slowly, and was thick and cushioning her head on the floor. Galla could see the woman's fingernails had grown and curled very slowly over time as well. But her skin shone in a way that confused Galla. There were shimmers on Jana's dark complexion, veins of something opalescent.

"She's beginning to waken," Paul said, leaning in. "Do you want me to contact her?"

"No," said Galla firmly. "Let's get her out of here." She carefully pulled Jana's form out of the cocoon, and she was immobile, so Paul held her upper body and Galla held her legs.

Another blast ricocheted close by.

"We've got to get her inside the *Seltra* and to its medical bay," she told Paul. "And we need to find Guru."

"I can carry her back," said Paul.

"Wait," she said. "Let's look for him in the other pod over there."

She ripped the other covering open, and they found another figure in a fetal position, with a small pulsing diamethyst shining through the membrane over the person.

"Guru," she said in a low voice. "Paul? Anything?"

"I'm not picking up dreams," he answered. "He's in a very deep sleep, but there is brain activity."

Galla breathed in for one long moment, and then slowly exhaled. Her relief exhausted her.

"Let's unsheathe him from this. We need to act quickly. I know the atmosphere isn't too terrible, but I don't want them exposed to it for long."

And so it was that Galla carried Jana, and Paul carried Guru, and they nimbly crept out of the *Fithich 2* in time for a blossom of shrapnel and fire to knock them on their backs. Up from that wreckage stormed an ornate, golden ship, inlaid with pearl, with a flag emblem she had not seen in over twenty years.

"It's Mehelkian!" she cried.

"Lady Galla-Deia," a voice said, booming through her helmet.

"Prince Hazkinaut!" Galla shouted.

"Hurry," he said to her. "We need to leave, and then you need to follow me out of here."

Galla and Paul did not hesitate one more second; carrying Jana and Guru, they dashed across the grey sand and into the *Seltra*. The fiery copper ship rose, cloaked, and met the Mehelkian ship, which promptly cloaked as well. The Valemog ships pursuing them darted back and forth, but Galla could see on her viewscreen that they ruptured in flame below her, shattered by the Prince's firepower.

"So the Prince is now a battle mage," she said to herself. She felt a tug and knew Hazkinaut's ship had attached itself to the *Seltra*.

The *Seltra* said, "The Mehelkian ship is transmitting coordinates for a safe location."

"Take us there," said Galla, and she watched as the *Seltra* entered the bright spindle formation of a junction and bolted forward; where, she could not guess.

39

PLIGHT

Galla and Paul carried Jana and Guru carefully through the coppery hall of the *Seltra* and to its med bay.

"Give me two human-sized beds, adjusted for the height of Jana and Guru," Galla said, her voice cracking. She watched anxiously as two amorphous surfaces rose from the floor. Once they reached the height of Galla's hips, she held her hand out.

"Stop," she commanded.

The beds, smooth and copper like the rest of the ship, sat ready, simple and bare. Galla held Jana's weak form gingerly over one of the beds and laid her slowly down. She gathered Jana's drooped arms and placed them alongside her body.

Paul followed Galla's example, doing the same with Guru.

"They need nutrients," said Galla. "Hydration."

Deming peeked in from the door of the med bay.

"What do you need?" he asked.

Galla glanced at him and his dark eyes looked concerned.

"Do you know how to treat *this*?" she asked, holding Jana's arm, with its opalescent streaks. Deming stepped closer.

"I don't," he answered, examining Jana's skin. "Maybe ask Beetle?"

"Maybe so," said Galla. "But I don't think Beetle anticipated this.

Much less its own change. I just"— she closed her eyes—"I—we *just* found them. I need them to live!"

Deming nodded. "I'll ask anyway."

Before he left, he added, "Try not to worry. Think about it: I'd never been on a spaceship before I met you. I sure as hell never had a giant winged insect for a crew member! And I never dreamed I'd be with someone like you. So, what I'm saying is, a lot of incredible things have just happened. Don't rule anything else amazing out!"

Galla smirked at that and nodded, giving him the lowered, half-lidded look that always thrilled him.

She turned back to Jana and Guru. Paul was leaning just slightly over Guru and glanced up at Galla. His twitching eyebrow intrigued her.

"What's Guru's status?" she asked him. "Can you read anything, pick up any thoughts?"

Paul folded his muscular arms. "REM sleep, broken dreams. I don't want to intrude. Guru is slowly climbing out of the torpor...so far. But it might not—"

At that moment, Guru jolted on the bed. Then he flailed his arms. He arched his back, bucked where he lay, and convulsed.

"Deming! Kein!" Galla cried.

But Prilanna ran in first. She bounded over to Guru and brushed her lavender fingers around his neck as Paul held him, and suddenly Guru relaxed.

Galla stared at the girl.

"What did you do?" she asked, stunned.

Before Prilanna could answer, Jana jerked on her bed and began her own series of violent convulsions. Prilanna swiftly turned and tapped her little fingers quickly around Jana's bulging neck. Jana splayed out then and stilled. Galla could see her breathing normalize.

Deming entered, followed closely by Kein. Paul and Galla looked up, then looked at Prilanna. The girl stood and twisted her fingers in her hands.

"I—I..." she began. "I applied pressure at multiple points. I didn't know if it would work on...larger beings."

Galla beamed at her.

"I didn't know you could offer medical help!"

Prilanna blinked shyly. "It's part of my training to lead, as it is any Ildion's. Since there are so few of us, everyone learns basic skills. I don't know how helpful that will be on a spaceship; there aren't any herbs here."

Galla said, "You're needed here. I want you to stay with them until they awaken fully."

Prilanna's gill-like facial folds flared a bit, and her skin turned a deeper purple.

"I will," she answered.

Paul looked to Galla and then to Kein.

"There's sort of a confusion to both their thoughts," he said. "I don't know if that's good or bad. What do you think, Kein?"

Kein shook his head. "It's almost like they're fighting something. You know when you're having a bad dream, and then you're aware you're dreaming but you can't wake up? Kind of like that."

"We can't force them awake," Galla said firmly. "Just let them adjust."

A shuffling sound in the hall startled them all. Great, yellow eyes peered in the doorway of the med bay. It was Beetle, too large to fit through the door.

Beetle's former clicks and hoots sounded much more melodious now, as it said, "Are they healthy?"

Galla sighed and crossed her arms, her feral hair lowering down around her shoulders. "There's something wrong with them. Beetle, had you ever stung something before?"

"No," the creature admitted.

"Then have you ever seen another of your kind sting a being?" she asked next.

Beetle flicked its great, sparkling wings behind its head.

"I have," said Beetle. It lowered its antennae, and Galla saw a flicker of its diamethyst.

"Did something like this happen to...whatever was stung?" Galla asked, holding Jana's hand gently and examining the patterns on her skin again.

"No," Beetle replied. "I did not have to give a full sting to either of them. I have not seen the streaking of any being's outer covering before."

Deming suggested, "Maybe because you were undergoing metamorphosis, it affected your sting?"

Beetle lowered its head further.

"It is possible."

Galla's copper eyes watered. Deming walked over to her and held her face in his hands.

"You can't know what will happen to them next," he said. "None of us can. We have to keep going and hope for the best."

Galla sighed and bent her head, but her copper-gold-violet hair twisted upward. *If they don't make it after all this...*her thoughts began. But she stopped. *No. Deming is right.* She turned and marched to the cockpit.

"Contact the Mehelkian ship," Galla said to her console. The screen shimmered and twitched. "Still problems out here?" she muttered.

The ship adjusted as best it could. Prince Hazkinaut's bejeweled head appeared on the screen.

"How are they?" he asked immediately, large eyes full of concern.

Galla breathed in. *He has evolved so much.*

"We...don't know," she told him. "I think we've got to go and hope for the best. It's possible we could drop them off..." Galla let her eyes glaze over for a moment, as she imaged a particular coral-hued space station that looked like a giant conch shell.

"Your Highness," she said suddenly, "how ready are we, and how much time do we have?"

The Prince replied, "Silderay says everyone is ready to proceed to the Device worlds. But we will meet resistance now, except perhaps on Aeriod's world, Rikiloi. We need a good offense, and I fear there are not enough powerful ships left to break through. Lady Deia...

there have been many battles while you recovered. And most have gone poorly."

"But *you* made it," Galla pointed out. "And now I can help. I'll give you all the ships you need. Send me all the information you have on every telepath you've recruited. My ships will need to know who's on our side."

The Prince nodded his great, turbaned head, which she knew to be covered in long, feathery stalks that waved about, though he kept them hidden. He was a powerful telepath and a mage to boot. *Perhaps the only one who's both*, she mused.

He asked, "So you're ready to fight?"

"I was born for it," Galla said, drawing herself up and putting her hands on her hips. "This fight is mine."

40

LINEAGE

Galla brushed her fingers along the console of the *Seltra*. She felt a bit dizzy, standing there, looking out at the stars and wondering how to do everything she needed to do. Swallowing, and feeling with dread an unpleasant sensation roiling in her midsection, she steadied herself.

"*Seltra*," she said, "I need to command Trozzhia to make a fleet of twenty-one ships just like you. And accompanying, smaller drone ships for each of those. They need to have every weapon available, and every defensive capability as well."

The *Seltra*'s smooth voice answered her command: "Acknowledged. Instructions transmitted to Trozzhia."

Galla nodded, swallowed again, and sank to her knees. She felt dreadful.

Deming slipped into the cockpit and knelt beside her.

"Hey," he whispered, "what can I do to help?" and she leaned into his open arms. "I'm so sorry you're sick."

"I wonder," Galla said with a thick voice, "if this will be a fast pregnancy and birth, as it was with your mother?"

"I don't know," Deming replied. "Did you ask the *Seltra*?"

Galla felt well enough to crinkle her brow at him. "How would the ship know?"

"Try it," he offered.

Galla answered by leaning away from Deming and vomiting onto the ship's floor, which began cleaning itself. *How can I command, feeling like this?*

"*Seltra*," she pleaded, "is there any way to know how long my pregnancy will last, and is there anything that can make me...*oakay*? As in, not sick?"

The *Seltra* at first did not answer. But its console glowed, and Galla found herself surrounded with a pale orange light.

"It's scanning you!" Deming exclaimed.

The *Seltra* announced, "Your pregnancy is a singleton, and is developing as a hybrid of its three species. Its rate of growth will be slower than a full human's, but faster than a Raexian's, by my projection."

Galla flung her head back. "A *what*?" she cried.

"Three species?" Deming asked. "What's a Raexian?"

An image formed on the screen of a Raexian for Deming. He took a deep, quick breath. The long, silver hair and silver eyes of Aeriod stared back as if in front of him.

Galla fainted.

"WHAT'S WRONG WITH HER?" Kein demanded, and Prilanna hovered like a little moth around Galla, where she lay on a new platform in the med bay.

Paul's shrewd eyes swept over his brother.

"She's only been with you," he whispered to Deming, "right?"

Deming watched Galla's pale face, her eyes closed, her hair drooped on her bed.

"I—they—she said they had been together a long time ago," Deming said. He took hold of Galla's limp hand.

Paul looked at Galla as well, and carefully swept her hair away from her face. The two brothers stood on either side of her, and Kein stood at her feet.

Prilanna clucked irritably.

"Get away from her, please," she said testily.

At that moment the scraping and rustling of legs and wings met their ears, and Beetle dipped its head into the room. It took a look at Paul and Deming, instantly reading their thoughts.

"A larva!" Beetle cried. "I will be able to make a pupa for it! This pleases me."

Everyone standing turned and stared at Beetle. Paul burst out laughing.

"Oh, Beetle," he said, between spasms, "your timing really is impeccable."

"Is it *your* larva?" Beetle asked innocently.

"No!" Paul said vehemently. "It's Deming's. My brother."

Beetle's antennae shot forward. "Deming-larva! From Ariel and Dagovaby!"

"Yes," Deming said, his face quizzical. "But the—the baby is not just mine and Galla's. It is apparently also Aeriod's."

The *Seltra*'s voice came through the room, startling everyone. "The fetus is approximately nine percent Raexian, forty-one percent human hybrid, fifty percent Galla-Deia, in genetic inheritance."

Prilanna looked excited. "Galla is not a human," she said slowly.

"So," Kein finished, "she has a different sort of reproductive system than humans. She...retained genetic material somehow... Okay, I'm not going there—sorry, Deming. But does Aeriod know?"

Deming stared at him and blinked.

"Ah shit," Kein said. "I'm going to assume Galla didn't either, hence...this situation?" he asked, gesturing to his friend lying on the bed. Then he turned to Deming and stared at him hard with his hazel eyes.

"She'll make a choice to tell him, or not," he said to the younger man. "Respect her choice."

"Of course," Deming said. "But he'll figure it out, right? One way or another?"

"Shit!" groaned Kein. "Of fucking course he will." He shook his head. "Well, this is messy as hell. And is she okay? *Seltra*, what is Galla's condition?"

The *Seltra* cut through the drama in its benign neutral voice and said, "Galla-Deia is resting and will recover consciousness soon. She requires more nutrition."

Nalag crept into the med bay and leapt up on Galla's bed before anyone could stop the beast. It stretched out alongside Galla's left side and sighed, placed its wet nose on her shoulder, and gave a tiny whine. She began to stir then, and her arm nudged Nalag, so it adjusted, and then her fingers found its amber fur and began to stroke its head. It licked her chin, and she awoke, groggy but smiling.

Deming leaned down on the other side of her and kissed her forehead.

"Welcome back," he said warmly. "You gave us a little scare."

Galla stretched, scratched Nalag behind the ears, and allowed Prilanna to lift her hair so as not to have it pulled when she sat up. Paul put his arm around her back to support her. Kein squeezed her feet.

She blinked.

"Whyyyyy are you all staring at me like that? I fainted. I'm *oakay*."

She saw Deming's and Kein's expressions and went pale, remembering her revelation.

"Tell me what it is," she said. "Is the baby—"

"The baby is fine," Deming responded, carefully considering his words.

"Go on," Galla said, her copper eyes large, making her look young and frail.

Kein shot a look at Paul and Prilanna and nodded toward the door. Jana and Guru lay resting in slumber. Galla's crew then left the chamber, leaving her with Deming. But Nalag stayed next to her, and she pet the deengyne affectionately to soothe it and herself.

"Galla," Deming said, with all the care he could muster for the woman he loved more than anything else, "somehow our baby is also Aeriod's, and it's all right. I want you to know that. It changes nothing, for me. But he...well." Deming shrugged and sighed. "It's up to you, what you want to do."

Galla hugged her knees and Nalag pressed up against her until she put an arm around its back. The diamethyst on her chest flashed, as did those around Nalag's and Deming's necks. The stones of Jana and Guru glowed pale purple also. She reviewed what the *Seltra* had said about her child's parentage. She put her hands under her chin and leaned her elbows on her knees.

"I loved him, once," she said softly, looking shyly up at Deming, whose eyes looked soft and warm. "Not like I love you," she added. "Or—or Rob. You're all three so different. But you, Deming...I love you so much that it frightens me a bit. Still, I am not sad to learn about this. I'll love our child no matter what."

"So will I," Deming answered, kissing her. Galla smiled then.

"I will tell Aeriod," she said. She shook her head. "I have no idea how he will react to this."

"He strikes me as a person difficult to surprise," Deming mused.

"Oh..." Galla murmured, "Aeriod will be *quite* surprised."

41

DISPATCHES IN THE VOID

After separating via a junction, Prince Hazkinaut sent a fractured message to Galla.

"Something...happened," he said, but the recording jumped.

She sat in her captain's chair and reviewed the message. "Two...gone."

"I need to get back to Hazkinaut," she said, exasperated. "*Seltra*, what have you got? Can you figure out the rest of the message? Can you get through to the Prince?"

The *Seltra* spoke: "Extrapolating from the message and the damaged portions of it, the Prince sent a warning that two of the telepaths en route to their Device worlds have been killed."

Galla gasped.

"Try to get back to the Prince," she urged. "I need to know which worlds, and what plan he has."

The *Seltra* replied, "I will continue to attempt communication."

Galla wheeled around in her chair and stood swiftly. She called on the comms, "Everyone, meet me at the table."

She walked into the room with the round table and waited for her crew to enter. She looked all around the sleek, mesmerizing copper walls of the inside of her ship, and thought, *Oni-Odi, there is so much about this Task I didn't anticipate. I miss you. I wish I could talk to you. Not something you made.* And she realized then how much she also missed talking to Meredith. *There is no elder to guide me now,* she thought. *I guess that is what it means to grow up. Now it's up to me. I don't know if I like it, or if I can even do it.*

Prilanna entered first and took her place next to Galla. She stared down at the girl.

"How are Jana and Guru?" she asked.

"Resting still," answered Prilanna, looking most self-assured. "I am monitoring them. They seem healthy; they just won't wake up. They seem to be draining their nutrient supply more quickly now."

"Is that...normal?" Galla asked.

"I don't really know," Prilanna answered. "The rate has jumped considerably. I thought that must mean they're close to recovering."

She squeezed her hands together, and by the tiny change in her posture, Galla could see Prilanna was worried and trying to hide it.

"Hmm," said Galla. "I supposed it's good they're getting more food, either way. After the meeting, keep monitoring. And maybe look at any changes in their blood?"

"Oh!" said Prilanna. "That reminds me, there is something strange—"

But at that moment, the rest of the *Seltra* crew entered, including Beetle. Galla appraised everyone and felt for Beetle, who tried its best to crouch near the table without crowding anyone else. Kein scratched his stubbly chin, Paul leaned back in his seat with his arms behind his head, Deming sat on the other side of Galla and pushed his hair behind his ears, and Nalag curled up at her feet and panted.

She announced, "Prince Hazkinaut tried to message us. The Event interference is still hard for this ship to manage. Just as it is for everyone. In this case, we have a big problem. Two of the telepaths who were to be positioned in two different Devices have been killed. I don't have any more information. But I can assume Paosh Tohon is behind it, somehow. It's too coincidental."

"Great," Kein muttered. "Can we get more telepaths? Do we even have time?"

Paul cleared his throat. "Guess it's our turn to take their place."

"What?" both Deming and Kein cried.

Paul shrugged. "Look," he said, green eyes bright, "it's all been coming to this, hasn't it? We'd be needed sooner or later. And by *we*, I mean *you and me*," he added, staring at Kein.

Kein's blood drained from his face.

"Let's not think about that just yet," Galla told him, her voice quivering.

I do not want to send them to their doom.

"We don't have enough information. I don't know what Device worlds they were heading to. These are things we have to find out from Hazkinaut."

"But you can't get through to him?" Deming asked.

"No," Galla said with a sigh. "I think we need help."

"Who can help us?" Paul asked.

Galla pinched her lips together. "We can try for Aeriod."

Deming's eyes met hers. He nodded.

"*Seltra*," Galla commanded, "contact Aeriod. Use any sort of back channel he might have. Or contact Rikiloi."

"Attempting contact," the *Seltra* told her.

They waited. Only silence met their ears across the broadcast. Galla knew her ship had encrypted its message, and that only Aeriod would pick it up. But the delay dragged on. She paced. Her crew got up, made lunch from what stores the ship had, and sat and chatted. Deming fed Nalag under the table.

The *Seltra* then announced, "There is a status change with the two patients in the medical bay."

Galla stopped pacing, gestured to Prilanna, and walked quickly back to her seat.

The *Seltra* chimed again. "Mage governor Aeriod is available."

Galla said, "Prilanna, go see what's going on with Jana and Guru and let me know. I have to take this communiqué."

She swiveled and walked swiftly over the copper floors back to her command seat in the cockpit of the ship. Aeriod's image appeared before her, shining, and she held her hands over her belly. Her hair went berserk.

"Galla-Deia," he said, his mercurial eyes nearly palpable even from whatever distance lay between them. "What is it?"

"Um," she said, fumbling over too many words that threatened to crowd her speech. "We've lost contact with Prince Hazkinaut. Two telepaths are dead. We'll need two more..."

"Ah," said Aeriod.

He watched her.

"What else?"

"What do you mean, *what else*?" Galla cried. "We've lost two people we need for two Devices to stop the Event! We need help!"

"You have two telepaths," said Aeriod curtly.

Galla glared at him. "What the hell is your problem?" she said with a scowl. "I don't want to put them at risk!"

"Galla," said Aeriod sternly, "they're meant for this. You can't shield them from their destiny. The Summoners—"

"Oh, fuck the Summoners!" shouted Galla.

Aeriod's eyebrows shot up.

"Are you going to tell me what else is bothering you?" he asked coolly.

Galla opened her mouth and shut it.

"What?" she asked. Her hair mutinied. She yanked at it furiously.

Aeriod lowered his head and smirked. "After all this time, do you really think I wouldn't notice by your face—let alone your spectacular hair!—that you've got something you want to say to me? I can tell it's something making you uncomfortable."

Galla breathed carefully, for the urge to upend her lunch on his image was powerful.

"We—we need you, Aeriod," she said, gulping. "Can we meet?"

Aeriod tilted his head in surprise.

"I suppose. Where are you?"

"I'd like to go to Rikiloi," said Galla. She had not realized until then how strong the urge to see that world again was with her.

"Really?" Aeriod asked. "Do you know if one of the telepaths was bound for that Device?"

"No," said Galla.

"Then why—" but he stopped. "Yes, of course. I will meet you there."

"Good." Galla exhaled. "I'll try to learn more about the situation. I—I will see you soon."

And Aeriod nodded, watching her various tics and nervous habits, intrigued.

"Very well," he said.

His image vanished.

"*Seltra*—" Galla began.

"Course set for Rikiloi," the ship responded.

Prilanna burst into her cockpit, gasping.

"They—they—they—" she began, and then leaned over, wheezing.

"What?" asked Galla, holding the girl gently. "Prilanna, what is it?"

"They're awake!"

42

ABOVE AND BELOW

The *Seltra* coasted serenely through the brilliant netherscape of the junction to jump across immense distances in the galaxy. Its smooth flight belied the turbulence within its walls, as the hammering of feet running on its floors echoed throughout.

Galla gripped the door edges of the medical bay, darted her eyes about in confusion, and saw nothing at first. Then she looked up and recoiled. Jana and Guru were staring down at her, their backs, arms, and legs seemingly adhered to the ceiling. Their faces were contorted in panic.

The sight of Galla caused them both to groan. They seemed unable to speak or open their mouths. Jana's eyes bulged and her jaw tensed. Guru's pulse visibly pounded in his neck, and his forehead furrowed.

Galla entered cautiously, her arms out.

"It's all right," she said, in as steady a voice as she could manage, but inwardly she quaked in fear and concern. "It's *oakay*."

She looked back at the door, and everyone had crowded to look in.

"Paul, Kein, Prilanna, come," she said. "Deming, please go to the cockpit with Nalag. And do not let Beetle enter right now."

"Understood," said Deming.

Kein and Paul followed little Prilanna into the room. Prilanna trembled, looking up at the two people on the ceiling.

"Talk to me, telepaths," Galla said quietly, looking from Jana to Guru and back. Their necklaces hung and swayed, the small diamethysts responding in a soft, lavender glow to Galla's larger stone.

"They're absolutely terrified," Paul said.

"Super confused, too," Kein told her.

Jana made strangled moans as she looked at Paul, as if she wanted to say something but could not. Paul approached and looked up at her with his large, dark-lashed green eyes. Her own dark eyes grew wider.

"Jana," Paul whispered aloud, and with his thoughts also. "Yes, Jana. I am that little boy you knew. I'm an adult. It's all right. We are here to help."

"Jana, dear," Galla said, aching, "can you come down? Are you stuck up there? Can we help you get down?" and she turned then to Guru and asked, "Guru, can you speak?"

"They can't," said Kein grimly. "They're feeling trapped and terrified, unable to talk, unable to get down."

Galla's eyes stung with unshed tears.

"How did they get up there to begin with?" she wondered aloud.

The *Seltra* calmly said, "Jana Okoro and Guru Pahue regained consciousness, and by their physical reactions to their appearance, a fear response caused them to jump, which sent them to the ceiling."

"Wow," said Kein.

"We've got to get them down," Paul said.

"*Seltra*, give us two steady ladders," Galla ordered her ship.

A bulging from the floor caused her and Paul to step back to avoid tripping over the forms extending upward. They were not detached, but when Galla tried to move one of the ladders, it pulled where she wanted it to go, yet remained adhered to the floor. So she tugged at the mass and placed it underneath Jana.

"I could hover," Galla said, looking at Jana in the eyes, "but I want to try to help you down this way, see if you can take steps."

She looked over at Paul and nodded. He pushed his own amorphous ladder underneath Guru.

"We're going to get you down," he told the frightened man.

"Prilanna," Galla said over her shoulder, "please be ready to help guide them, or still them—whatever they may need."

"I'm ready," the young Ildion assured her. She watched her captain in awe and affection, eager to do whatever was asked.

Galla held her arms up to Jana's waist.

"Jana," she said to her old friend and crewmate, "try to let go, and know that I've got you, I'll catch you. Can you try?"

Jana made frustrated sounds that never left her closed mouth. She did blink, and so Galla readied herself. Jana strained her arm muscles and pulled with all her might.

"That's it! You can do this!" Galla encouraged her. Jana pulled one arm away from the ceiling with a strange *shhhhep* and Galla seized her waist. Jana then tugged the other arm, and it fell too. Galla held Jana firmly, and the woman's arms were too weak to grip her. But she did strain, and pulled one leg from the ceiling at a time. She was sweating so much that her clothes were wet. Her eyes began to water.

"I've got you, Jana," said Galla warmly, and she held onto Jana and tried to get her to stand on the ladder. Jana's knees buckled.

"Very well, we will slowly go down," Galla soothed, and the ladder began to ooze back into the floor of the ship. She held tightly to her friend. "Can you stand, now?"

Jana tried, and the tears flowed, and finally her dried lips parted.

Prilanna ran forward with a bottle of water and held it up to the tall woman to help her drink. Jana sputtered a bit, swallowed some water, choked, and coughed. Galla held her firmly on her feet.

Jana tried her best to stand unaided. Then she wobbled, and she began to drift upward, as if floating.

"Oh shit!" she said, and Galla laughed and sobbed all at once, upon hearing Jana's voice.

"It's all right, I'm not letting you go!" Galla told her. "It's so good to hear you, my friend."

"Gal-Galla," stammered Jana, and the two embraced, as Galla held her in strong arms that would not let her fly upward. "What, where?" And Jana looked down at her dark skin, with its new iridescent, lacelike patterns, and she began shaking and weeping.

"What's—what's wrong—with me?" she bellowed.

Prilanna approached to try to still her trembling, but Jana leaned away from her.

"It's *oakay*, Jana," Galla said softly. "This is Prilanna Optison. She is my medical assistant. We don't have a full medical crew out here, but she's been able to help you and Guru. Prilanna, I think Jana isn't convulsing. She's upset."

"Why—why can't I just walk?" Jana said hoarsely. Her hair was matted and flattened on one side from her repose on the *Fithich 2* for many years. Her several green earrings had fallen out at some point, and Galla wished now that she had looked for them, to give her friend something resembling normalcy.

Beside them, Paul said to Guru, "You've got this."

Guru's lips trembled, and Prilanna gave him sips of water, which he took gratefully, even though much of it dribbled down his chin onto his sweat-stained clothing.

"Thank—thank you," Guru stammered, glancing from her to Paul. He also began drifting upward, and Paul held him down. "Bloody-fucking-weird," croaked Guru. He reached his weak arms behind his head and rubbed a rough area there. Paul looked, and saw an old puncture wound.

"The sting," said Guru, trying his best to keep his feet on the floor. "It's changed us. Didn't kill us, obviously. Yet."

Jana's eyes darted to his.

"If I ever see Beetle again..." she began.

Galla cleared her throat. "Um," she said.

The *Seltra* interrupted with a melodious chime and said, "Now orbiting Rikiloi. Shall I contact mage governor Aeriod?"

Galla closed her eyes and her head spun. Prilanna stepped closer to her and Jana, just in case one or both of them fainted or floated. She was ready for either.

Her captain looked at her then, and with large, nervous copper eyes staring into the girl's reassuring brown ones, Galla said, "Now or never."

43

A VERITABLE MENAGERIE

Deming sat beside Galla and watched her hair dance about while she tried to maintain a smooth face.

"You know you can't fool *me*," he reminded her, smirking. "You won't fool him either. He knows you too well."

"Not as well as you," said Galla, slyly reaching over to take Deming's hand and kiss it. "I think it's fair to say that in all the galaxy, the person who knows and understands me best is you."

"I'll take it," said Deming, "and you. Any way, anyhow, anywhere."

Galla stood, stepped over to him, and let her hair tickle his face as she bent down and sat in his lap. At that moment, Aeriod's image materialized before them, and Deming tried unsuccessfully not to laugh.

The mage's face was still and cold, his eyes half-lidded, and he drawled, "Welcome, Captain Deia and...entourage."

Galla's face flared red, but Deming placed his lips on the back of her neck, out of sight of Aeriod, and she relaxed and grinned.

"Thank you," she answered. "May we enter the fortress?"

Aeriod's cheek twitched. "I suppose you must," he said icily. "But I would like to meet with you alone, before your...team gallops all over the finer rugs."

"Asshole," whispered Deming.

Aeriod heard, and his jaw tensed.

Oh dear, thought Galla.

"Good," she said aloud. "I will see you soon."

His image vanished. She swiveled around and met Deming's brown and gold gaze with a reproachful look.

"Go easy on him," she chided lightly. "He's never had so many people who dislike him under his roof at one time."

They laughed, and Galla returned to her seat.

"Crew," she announced, "prepare to dock."

She then walked to the med bay and found Jana and Guru sitting upright on their beds, with little sensors making their way over their bodies.

Prilanna popped up from a chair, where she was making notes of everything she was doing.

"I've asked the ship to stimulate their muscles," she explained.

"And how's that going?" Galla asked the patients.

"Tingly," Guru answered.

"Painful," Jana said. "Well...okay, not *always* painful. I've had to tell these...whatever they are...to avoid certain areas. No privacy, and all." She grinned, and then she winced.

Guru chuckled at that.

"I think it's working," he said. "I've never felt more tired. But I don't know how much use we will be. And trying to stay put is hard."

"Yeah," agreed Jana. "Sometimes I just want to jump around. And I know if I do, I might end up on the ceiling again!"

Galla approached her and twisted her fingers together. Jana watched her and her telltale hair.

"What is it?" Jana asked. "You look...guilty."

"Well," said Galla, "I feel bad that I didn't come back sooner."

Jana rolled her eyes. "Galla. We know why. Prilanna told us some. And Paul! My God! He's huge...it's so weird. Anyway. Don't blame yourself. Not for what happened to us. And please, please, please: not for Rob."

His name hurt Galla to hear, and she exhaled quickly.

"I only have one regret," Jana went on, and she swallowed. "I want to know what happened to Misun. This ship doesn't seem to have a record of Mandira's population." She heaved a great sigh.

"We might have to go back there," Galla suggested. "For more than one reason. I feel like there are resources there that are unique. I can't quite get my head around it, but I think it's important to do."

Guru sighed then. "I wonder how many are still left. It's been, what, twenty-four years?"

"Do we know it's even still around?" Jana said uneasily. "Did… could *they* have got to it?"

"I am not sure," Galla admitted. "But we're at Aeriod's home. Ika Nui is one of the worlds he governs. So, we can ask him."

Jana nodded. "Do we finally get to see the inside of his castle in the air?"

"Yes," Galla said with a grin. "I think you'll like the food a lot better than what we have here! And the drink," she added, nodding to Guru. "Will you need help?"

"Maybe," Jana said.

"I'll get Kein and Paul to help you. And Prilanna, use whatever resources you can find in Aeriod's home." She stood tall and straight, and her companions could see she was steeling herself. But she set her mouth. "He will give me anything I ask."

Jana's dark eyes widened, and she nodded slowly. "Noted!"

Galla took a deep breath then. "Jana, Guru, Beetle is on board."

Jana's eyes shot open wide.

"Beetle has been hiding until you were well enough to manage the news," said Galla, twisting her fingers under her chin. Her stone bounced against her sternum and sent splintered purple reflections about the med bay.

Jana's chest rose and fell as she took deep breaths.

"I don't want to see—" she began.

Guru held up his arms. "No," he said firmly. "Think about it, Jana. Beetle is an animal. A vastly intelligent animal; maybe more than we are. It wasn't done out of spite. Beetle saved our lives, probably. Made us 'play dead' so the enemy passed us by."

"Decades!" said Jana with a catch in her voice.

"Look," said Guru, "it's decades we could have been tortured by Paosh Tohon. That thing could have flayed our minds for sport. Maimed us—"

"Then what do you call this?" Jana cried, rubbing the lacy patterns across her dark brown skin. They shimmered in the light of the med bay in palest opal hues. "And we're, what, able to jump really high? We're not the same! I—I just—I'm not ready."

Galla bowed her head. "Only you can judge when you are ready to see Beetle. I will say that our companion has changed drastically as well, as part of its metamorphosis. But one thing that remains the same: Beetle's dedication to all of us. Jana, take all the time you feel you need. You too, Guru."

Guru nodded. "I'm okay with it all," he said. "I know my body is different, I'm not sure how. But hell, I'll take it, you know? It beats being used. It sure as shit beats being dead."

Galla turned to leave, when Jana called, "Galla," and then she said warmly, "congratulations. Ariel's son and Meredith's grandson! God, they'd be so happy. And now you're going to have a baby too? You're a brave one, Captain."

"I don't know if that's what I'd call it," said Galla, twisting some of her hair in her fingers in one hand, while holding the diamethyst in the other. "But thank you, dear Jana."

In fact, despite her bravado, Galla felt anything but brave. She felt as small and alone, in some ways, as she had when she first laid eyes on Aeriod back on Demetraan so long ago. What would he do, how would he react? She smoothed her jumpsuit. Her hips hurt, her breasts were sore and had grown fuller, and nausea threatened at every turn. She felt unusual tugs in her abdomen as her uterus tightened gently from time to time. The slightest bulge had begun to appear as well, but it was incredibly subtle. She wondered just how long it would take for her little hybrid to grow.

Of all the things I have been through, pregnancy is the strangest by far!

.   .   .

DEMING, Paul, and Prilanna watched in wonder as their ship entered the atmosphere of Rikiloi. The two amorphous moons loomed pale in the afternoon sky. And below them, the strangest sight met their eyes: a great asteroid, held aloft about a mile above the ground, with tall towers and buildings of sleek black and red carved into the structure. The fortress shimmered, and Paul thought to Kein, who was eating in the kitchen, *Does he hide this too?*

Yep, came Kein's answer. *Among other things. Whole damn planet too, I think.* He had no need to see it on approach, as he had been there before.

Inside the cavernous launch bay, the *Seltra* parked itself among Aeriod's sleek, black and iridescent ships of various sizes and shapes. Galla could see harvesting equipment parked in one corner. She smiled to herself, happy to know the fungus fields on the surface of Rikiloi were still being worked. She wondered whether the Indry-Kol still followed the harvest through the seasons, or if others were invited to live there now.

She soon found her answer, as a row of Indry-Kol she did not recognize had lined up to greet her. A towering shadow emerged between them, and a flash of silver revealed the long mane of Aeriod, as he swept into the bay with a long, black cape swaying, etched all along its edge in silver thread. On his chest, a small diamethyst rested. Galla knew he never once took it off. She felt her copper chain, which he had woven himself before her eyes, that held her own hexagonal stone in place. It had survived her firefall, away from her, and the reentry burn. Eventually found by Pliip somehow, the necklace had endured.

And then she placed her right hand on her left wrist, where the little bracelet Deming had made now rested. One of these things would outlast the other, she realized. She closed her eyes for a moment and shivered, not wanting to think along those lines.

"Captain Deia," Aeriod said smoothly, approaching her. She stood tall and proud, ignoring her feral hair, and he knew that she was at war with herself over something. Deming stood by her side. Aeriod nodded coolly to him, his eyes glinting like mica, taking in Deming's glowing pupil rings. And Galla's copper eyes considered them both.

Silver, copper, gold, she thought, and she held her hands over her belly. *What color will your eyes be?*

Aeriod's power here was palpable in every facet all around them. As Galla's crew left her ship, each member took it all in, and only Kein was unimpressed. He brushed his lunch crumbs off his stained pants and put his hands on his hips. He nodded to Aeriod.

"Governor," he said simply.

Aeriod nodded back. "Kein," he said. "Well met."

Kein nodded. His hazel eyes squinted a bit. It was a lot for Kein to think about, being back here, remembering Rez, and missing him terribly.

"The choices we make," said Kein under his breath. He kept close to Guru, in case the man needed anything. Guru was managing slowly and stiffly along, and stubbornly, Kein thought. Kein had no problem with this.

Paul, meanwhile, stood steadfast next to Jana. They followed along some distance behind the others while he joked with her warmly.

"You must have been quite something back on that planet...what was it you called it?"

"Quopeia," answered Paul with a grin.

"Turned *all* the heads, didn't you?" Jana teased him, happily taking on the role of feisty auntie.

Paul laughed with his brilliant white smile in his bronze face and shrugged. "Maybe."

Jana hooted at him and held his arm. "Attaboy."

As the quiet chatter proceeded, Nalag slinked back a bit, and Prilanna waited for the deengyne. It whined to her and looked over its shoulder.

"Isn't Beetle coming?" the girl asked the little beast.

Nalag sneezed. Prilanna's face fell. She walked back toward the ship, Nalag beside her, and could see the large eyes of Beetle staring out.

"Please come out, Beetle," she said gently. "You're invited too!"

Beetle rustled forward a bit. "I fear I am not welcome here."

"You're as welcome as we are!" exclaimed Prilanna, patting Nalag's head. "None of us really fits in, do we? We may as well make the best of it, *together*."

As Jana moved forward with Paul, Beetle watched respectfully, and gradually exited the *Seltra*. Aeriod turned at the head of the group and surveyed everyone, and noticed Beetle in the back.

"You've brought quite the menagerie with you, Galla-Deia," he said with a smirk. "Come on out, will you, there? I've room enough for all of you, within and without the palace."

Galla beamed at him, and he glanced down at her and at Deming.

"You see," he said quietly to Deming with a gleam in his silver eyes and a tilt of his eyebrow, "I'm not an asshole *all* the time."

Deming exhaled. "Good."

Though tempted to say something about their mutual child, he kept his mouth shut, knowing it was not his place to speak about that just yet.

Aeriod swept grandly forward, past the Indry-Kol, and past the diverse group of species who served as his assistants. He crisply gave orders to show everyone to various rooms throughout the palace, and the murmurings of Galla's crew met his ears. He smiled to himself.

Imagine if T'Lexxa ever saw anything like this, he mused.

To Galla, he murmured, "Your ability to bring together a ragtag team never ceases to amaze me. It's a more valuable skill than you realize!"

He, Galla, and Deming stopped outside a doorway. Galla realized with a start that it led to her old suite from long ago.

"Yours, still," Aeriod said to her, and Deming squirmed as much from their shared awkwardness as from his own. Galla's emotions snapped in all directions, and Deming felt each one.

"Thank you," she said to the mage. She turned to Deming and said, "Go on in, make yourself comfortable. You'll have anything you need."

He took her hands in his, and they touched foreheads. He looked deep in her eyes and squeezed her hands.

"It's going to be all right," he whispered.

She nodded and swallowed. He kissed her and entered the suite.

Now she stood alone with Aeriod in the hallway, much as she had several decades ago. He held his arm out to her, and she took it, breathing in the smoky, spicy scent that enveloped him at all times. It made her dizzy in an unpleasant way, but she focused on her breath.

"Should I take us aloft for everyone?" he asked her. "The sun is setting." And they reached the balcony where the updrafts sent their hair flying.

The beauty of Rikiloi had changed little. She could see that they were moving south in the floating palace, so that winter was coming to the north. She turned to him and said, "There's something I need to tell you."

Aeriod nodded. "I need to tell you something also. Ladies first?"

Galla trembled. "No—no. You go ahead."

He looked at her, with the fading sun glinting on her hair, her face radiant, and unusually flushed. *You are every bit as warm as T'Lexxa is cold*, he thought. He fought the urge to take her in his arms and hold her.

"I was married once," he said suddenly. She blinked at him. "Not anytime recently," he added. "Long, long ago. Centuries before I met you. It was...unpleasant. An arranged marriage. Beneficial for...property, such as Rikiloi. The splinter of that marriage resulted in my retaining a fraction of the worlds I once held. She, the Rynaati T'Lexxa, maintained all the other holdings."

"You never told me," said Galla, watching his inscrutable face.

"I had no reason to," he said. "There was no love remaining; and what little there had been...well, I didn't really know the depth of love I could have until I met you."

Galla gulped in air and hiccupped.

"Aeriod, I don't think this—"

"I'm not finished," he said, and something in his voice gave her pause. "There was something I was not aware of. T'Lexxa had a brother, and they were estranged. He dabbled in strange experimentations, obscene beyond measure; she was ashamed of him, and spoke of him only rarely. I never met him. Galla, what I'm about to tell you...it horrifies me. I don't know if learning about it sooner would have changed anything. But knowing it now, it's too important not to share."

Galla's brow twisted. "Yes?"

"Galla, her brother was trying to make a chimera with creatures very like the ones you met in the underground lake, and those on Perpetua."

"No!" she breathed. "I was told it was a chimera...no, surely not!"

"Yes," said Aeriod, lowering his head. "The chimera was made with her brother, and so that is Paosh Tohon."

Galla stared at him.

"So Paosh Tohon is...is part of your species, then, part...Raexian?"

"Regrettably," Aeriod sighed.

Galla looked down at her diamethyst, which had grown hot, and Aeriod's smaller stone responded. The purple light emanating from both stones cast lavender glows on them that outshone the dying rays of sunlight.

Aeriod noticed her face twist from concern and other unnamable emotions.

"What is it you wanted to tell me? I know it must be important. This other news of mine can wait. Tell me."

Galla took his face in her hands and stared into up into his unreadable silver eyes.

"I am carrying a chimera as well," she said to him. "And the baby is part Raexian. You are a father, Aeriod."

44

——————

OPEN SKY

The sunlight vanished, and the only light on the balcony came from the two diamethysts.

"Mine!" cried Aeriod.

Galla watched him in wonder. His face began to glow, a pale, golden illumination from within, and it beatified him. She had never seen him like this.

"My child," he whispered, putting his long fingers to his lips. Then he knelt.

"I promise you," he said, looking up at her wild hair and the warm, vibrant eyes below it, "I will be there for this child in any capacity you want. Or not. I would like to be part of its life."

Galla closed her eyes and nodded.

"Of course."

From where he knelt before her, he looped his arms gently around her waist and laid his head against her belly. He sat this way for a long time, and Galla stood still, her eyes closed.

"Yours, mine, and Deming's," Aeriod said in muffled voice. He stood then, and the glow on his face remained. "I don't understand it. I never, ever thought it was possible. I can only assume it's something unique about Deming that triggered this in you. I didn't think *you* could reproduce! And certainly not with me!"

Galla swallowed. "It's...it's a lot to take in. I only just found out. From my ship, the *Seltra*."

"I like the name," Aeriod said, "and so would Oni-Odi. I'm sorry. I never got to tell you that before."

She did not answer, but her lips trembled.

Aeriod pulled her to him and held her a long time, and they stood and just breathed. Galla's pale purple tears soaked into his black cape.

"It really is astounding!" he said, eyes shining. "This is a child of you, me, and Deming, meaning it's a descendent of Ariel, Dagovaby, and Meredith! Oh, dear Meredith!" He grew serious then. "I have a true family now. Anything that risks my family risks my wrath."

Galla could not help but chuckle at him. "Now if I can just figure out the nausea," she said, "we can face what's ahead a bit more easily."

Aeriod grinned. "Luckily, you happen to know a mage."

"I knew I could count on you, Aeriod," Galla said.

"Always, beloved," he said to her.

Lying in her old bed, in the opulent suite Aeriod had given her so long ago, Galla nestled onto Deming's chest, one leg draped over his body. His eyes were open, staring at the ceiling. He stroked her hair, which puddled contentedly on his shoulder.

"You had a good life here," he noted. "Do you miss it?"

Galla brushed her fingers on Deming's bearded chin. "A privileged life," she said. "But I would rather be with you in the wind and snow in a tent anywhere else than here without you."

He took hold of her by the waist and pulled her carefully so that she lay fully on him. She looked up at his dark eyes, with their glowing ring around the pupil, and touched his fine nose, and kissed his chin.

"Are you happy?" he asked. "I mean...I can feel your love, but it never hurts to ask you. Because I want you to be happy, whatever it takes."

"I've never been happier," she said, smiling, and then they kissed, and she swiveled up a bit to straddle him, and he gasped with pleasure, and kissed her breasts and gripped her hips.

In their delicious exhaustion afterward, Galla could not help but worry about what lay ahead of them. She did not want to leave the comfort of Deming's arms, and did not want him to leave the safety of hers.

Later, Deming side-eyed Aeriod at the long and food-laden table where he and Galla's crew sat for breakfast.

"Galla," he murmured in her ear, "he's being super weird around me now."

And he was right. Aeriod embraced him outright when he saw him again that morning, which surprised everyone.

Paul, on the other side of Galla, leaned into the conversation and said to his brother, "Maybe I can't read his thoughts, but the guy clearly has had a change of heart. What did you *do*? Fuck! You're definitely *way* more powerful than I am!"

Deming snorted and shrugged. Then he looked at Galla, admiring her poise, her beauty, and her fire, and he said, "If my power is to be loved by *you*, I don't need anything else."

Paul made gagging sounds. "I'm going to be the worst uncle," he hissed, "and by worst I mean *best*, but you will have to endure endless spoiling of that—"

Aeriod tapped a glass.

Everyone turned, and he stood. Spreading his long arms outward, with his black cape flowing, his otherworldly aura stirred everyone there. Even Beetle bowed a bit in deference. Aeriod was of such a great age that he could demonstrate it when he wanted to, and now they knew they sat before someone of immense power. While Gindoo chose not to display the trappings of his strength, Aeriod indulged it.

"This might be the last time we will all sit here at this table for a long while, if ever," he said in a somber tone. "When we leave, we face battles: attacks, subterfuge, betrayal. Paosh Tohon bred legions of enemies in Valemog. Valemog in turn has helped poison worlds beyond count. Should we stop the Event, the chief resource of suffering and challenges will come to an end. We don't have much time to do that. The alignment of the twenty-one Device worlds, including this one, approaches quickly. I'm told that two of the necessary telepaths for activating the Devices have been killed. So we need two more. And I'm not going to wait for replacements. The descendants of Ariel and of Forster sit here now. Will you take on the role you're meant to play?"

Galla gasped and went pale, holding each of the Ambrono brothers' hands in her own. She knew it might come to this but had hoped it would not. Aeriod's calm declaration and question chilled her.

Kein coughed.

"I'll do it, of course," he said. He scooted his chair back from the table. Galla looked at him with tears in her eyes. "What? Did you think I wouldn't? I made Rez a promise. I gave up the rest of my life with him in the home we shared. I missed growing old with him. I grew old in a *fucking cave* on a strange-ass planet and I was *alone*. So don't act like I don't know sacrifice. I'll take Rikiloi's Device, since I'm already here and I know this place decently well. That's all."

Aeriod nodded. "Very good, old friend," he said. "I'll give you provisions for however long this takes."

He turned his sparking eyes to Paul, who stared unflinchingly back at him. Aeriod then blinked. Seeing Ariel's eyes staring at him from the face of Paul made him falter.

"Of course I'm doing this," Paul said, shrugging. "I don't want any other children to grow up without their parents. If this can help put a stop to that? I'm not looking back."

Kein nodded with his eyes closed.

We're in for some shit, you know, he thought to Paul.

I can take it and I can dish it out, Paul responded.

No doubt.

Aeriod sat down, looking troubled. "We need to find out from Prince Hazkinaut where we can place you," he told Paul. "And thank you for your service."

"To that end," Galla spoke up, "we have to get through to him as soon as possible. Have you had any luck?"

"No more than you have," sighed Aeriod. "The Event interference is a continual nightmare. Once we get through—*if* we get through—we'll need to know immediately what course Paul needs."

Galla put her face in her hands. "No. I know where to send him."

Paul and Deming both turned to stare at her, followed by everyone else. Galla made eye contact with Jana.

"You're not sending him *there*?" Jana gasped. "Dagovaby almost died!"

Galla exhaled in a long sigh and said, "Stormworld. That's what we called it. A place that had been obliterated eons ago...and for lack of a better word, is haunted by the emotions of the people who were harmed. Dagovaby's empathic power was tested to the breaking point there. But you, Paul, don't have the same power."

"But I do," Deming said, startling her.

"Not really," she said quickly. "It's just with me."

"No, it really isn't," Deming said. "You're the sun in the daytime sky, and everyone else fades away like the stars. But the stars—others' emotions—are still there."

"I don't want you going," said Galla. Deming made protesting sounds and Paul said, "I agree with Galla. You don't have the experience to deal with this."

"Oh, so you do?" Deming snapped. "You've done all this before?"

"Well, no, but—" Paul began.

"Stop protecting me. Both of you. I'll go," said Deming, face red. He pushed his hair behind his ears and smoothed his beard.

"No, you will not," came Aeriod's cold voice.

"Excuse me?" said Deming. "I don't take orders from you."

"More's the pity," bit back Aeriod, "because you avoid them at your peril, fool!"

"Goddammit, Deming," roared Paul, "I'm going, and that's the end of it."

"Would you stop arguing?" cried Galla, exasperated. "Deming. I need you. Not just because of...everything. But I need you to help me. I need your stability and your guidance. You have something here no one else has: Gindoo's training. I don't know what all it was, or how it will help. But I can't imagine Gindoo would have signed off on you coming on this trip if he didn't think you could help in some way. So please. Let Paul go. I don't like it any more than you do. *Please.*"

Deming looked frustrated and upset. Nalag chose that moment to weave among the legs of the people sitting at the table and came to rest its head on Deming's knee, and looked up at him with its great, deep violet eyes. Deming looked down at the deengyne's eyes, and sighed.

"Fine," he said.

A musical chime sounded then, and everyone turned to see an amazing sight: a being floating on what looked like half a bubble, with dark blue, mottled skin and several arms. Its face was wizened from great age.

It said, "The drama in here is so thick I could fillet it. Now, who wants dessert?"

Galla leapt up from her seat.

"Sumond!" she cried.

She ran to embrace him as best she could, and he lowered his assistance bubble so that he could wrap his atrophied arms around her.

"You're still here," she whispered, crying grateful tears.

Sumond held her face with three shaking hands and said, "Yes, dear, and I knew you were, as a cousin of mine recently told me! She works on Quopeia. We chefs do wield the power in this galaxy!"

"Ah, I thought I recognized someone there at the bakery in Allurulla," Galla said, and she glanced at Deming. Deming smiled at her and nodded.

Sumond recruited several assistants to bring out a lavish spread of desserts and drinks. He served Galla's favorite purple pies to her, much to her delight. Guru took a chartreuse and violet concoction and breathed in its scent with excitement.

"I've got to know what's in this!" he exclaimed.

Sumond laughed, his facial marks deepening in hue. "You really don't want to know!"

And Guru laughed as well, but then a look of dismay came over him as he began to rise out of his seat. "Uh-oh," he said, and he looked over at Jana, who gripped the table while her own legs began to rise.

"So we can't even drink now without flying?" she cried. "Seems like a bad combo!"

Beetle opened its great wings just then and spread them out, covering the entire table, to prevent Guru and Jana from floating upward.

"You are flying!" the great mothlike insect exclaimed. "I would also like to fly."

"But we don't—" began Jana.

Aeriod raised his hands. "I can teach you self-control, Jana and Guru. I think it will help you. But for now...why not? Why don't we all go for a flight? We're already in the sky!"

He opened the ceiling around them, and the bright turquoise sky above beckoned. Beetle stretched its wings and pulsed them a few times, and rose up and up, and swooped and glided, popping and clicking in what could only be the purest of joys. Jana and Guru looked intrigued.

Aeriod said, "Come to an understanding that you have a gift, and not a curse, and use it when you see fit. And should there be other gifts that make themselves known, the same method applies. It's your power to use, but do not give it away."

So Jana and Guru decided to link arms, and they floated up and out of the palace, shrieking or laughing as they did so. Nalag yipped and jumped, watching them and Beetle. Prilanna's cheeks went rosy-purple in excitement. Then Galla got up from the table, and she held her stone, and she shot into the air herself, surrounded by violet light. She hovered near Jana and Guru, and took their arms into hers. And for a few hours, they all forgot about what lay ahead of them, as they each took turns flying, or taking up one of the others with them.

Galla took Deming last, and danced with him among the clouds, with the teal of twilight and creamy glow of the two moons above, and the glittering sky castle below.

45

THE FIRST VOLUNTEER

Aeriod stood at the edge of the Device and unveiled it for everyone to see. A large, gaping circular hole appeared before them, with odd lights and mechanisms along its interior, stretching down into complete darkness. Galla shivered at the sight of it, remembering her first encounter within the strange structure. She turned to look at Kein.

He glanced down into the hole, and the updraft from the Device sent dust upward, some of which got in his eyes. He rubbed them and turned to Galla. His hair was grey, the lines in his forehead deep, and the crinkles at the edges of his warm, hazel eyes belied the tears and anguish of many years alone on Quopeia. He secured the large back-pack of supplies he wore. He shrugged.

"It won't be so bad after what I've been through, you know," he said to her. He could see her large, amber eyes pooling with tears.

She stepped over to him and flung her arms around his neck. He was not much taller than she was, and she was stronger than she looked, so he skipped backward a bit from the intensity of her embrace.

"It's going to be very strange," she warned him. "You may see things. From the past, the future, the present, or something else entirely. I don't know. I've seen all those things. So has Jana, the only other person here who has experienced it. And she's not even a telepath! Aeriod never did, but his mind doesn't work the same way. Just...prepare for anything."

Her diamethyst began to warm, and she looked at the small, rounder one around Kein's neck.

She touched her stone to his and said, "You will find another there, just like yours. I placed it there years ago. I think it'll recognize your stone, and grow bright and hot, and when I am ready, I will aim at the Event terminus and...well, I'm not really sure...but it should be unmistakable that something's happening when I do. And I—Kein, I don't know what the Device will do then. I just hope I see you again. I love you."

Kein buried his face in Galla's hair to hide his tears.

"Shit!" he said. "All right. Let me go, before I change my mind."

He waved to everyone and caught Paul's eye.

Good luck, man. See you on the other side, maybe.

Paul nodded, his face stony. *Here's hoping.*

Aeriod approached Kein on his long legs, his black cape snapping and curling in the wind, his pale hair cast upward.

"My friend," he said solemnly, "once you are in there, I can do nothing for you. And I will have to leave anyway to assist elsewhere in the fight. I know you. I trust in your ability to weather this. And I send you every encouragement I can."

Kein looked down at Aeriod's sleek, black boots, and at his own scuffed shoes. Aeriod had offered him new clothing, but Kein was a simple man, and refused.

He looked at the Device and leaned his head to one side. A scraping, rattling sound could be heard, growing louder by the second. Then a simple platform appeared below the lip of the abyss.

A small voice called, "Caxxius Caxx!" and he looked back to see little Prilanna Optison running toward him, Nalag keeping pace beside her. Her own diamethyst winked and flashed in time with Kein's. She held his dry, aged hands in her small lavender ones.

"You will always be a wizard to me," she said.

Kein took a deep breath, swallowed, and grinned. He could say nothing more, despite the calls from everyone else for his well wishes. He patted Nalag on the head and approached the edge of the Device. He crept down onto the platform and held onto it, and it moved swiftly down, away from the silhouettes of his friends above.

46

TRANSPOSITION

The *Seltra* rose in concert with Aeriod's small fleet of ships, a fiery phoenix followed by a flock of ravens, through the atmosphere of Rikiloi and into space. As soon as they flew past the two moons, the planet vanished from view. Aeriod appeared on Galla's screen. She was startled by his face, exhausted in a way she had never seen before.

"Are you *oakay*?" she asked him.

He nodded sleekly, but his tired eyes were a tell.

"It's a lot of work. The hiding."

Galla thought for a moment.

"Are you doing this for the other worlds too? Perpetua, Ika Nui?" she asked.

"I am," he answered. "And a few...others as well. I find it is...not as easy as it once was. And my resources are already strained. But I will manage, Galla. You needn't worry about me."

Galla nodded, though she did in fact worry about him. But she was relieved that, for the moment at any rate, the other two worlds were safely hidden. She could feel a small wave of nausea make its way through her body, so she took a little silver sphere out of her pocket and put it in her mouth. Aeriod had made her a special concoction, and while it did not eliminate her nausea, it made it possible for her to cope better.

"How goes the signal?" she asked him.

"I think we're going to have to get creative," Aeriod replied. "Given Demetraan's history, I'm thinking we should tap into the resources you now have. Maybe we can build an array with our ships? And try to send and receive a clearer signal with your *Seltra*? But let's get away from here. I don't want to attract any attention to this system. While I've hidden things well, it's not the time to risk the people here. I'll lead the way through some junctions and get us closer to where you need to be."

Galla sat up a little straighter and said, "Proceed."

Aeriod smirked indulgently and disappeared from her screen.

"All crew," Galla announced. "We will be heading through several junctions before we stop. Make yourselves comfortable."

She rose and stretched, and felt a slight cramp. She patted her abdomen and walked down the hall to the round room, so similar to the one on the *Fithich*, but with vivid copper hues and sleeker design. She had grown fond of the *Seltra*, and since it was a somewhat canny ship, she felt a deeper connection to it. She wondered how much of Oni-Odi remained in this vessel and in Trozzhia, and she felt a pang of sadness, missing him.

Beetle entered then, wings carefully folded, and Nalag trotted at its feet.

"Are you friends now?" Galla asked warmly, looking from one to the other.

"Ah-RAH!" Nalag barked, and Galla laughed.

"Nalag and I have been communicating often," said Beetle. "We have been wondering about the rest of the crew, whether they are ready for a battle or not."

"I don't think there's a choice," said Galla. "I'm not sure *I* am ready for a battle. But we must go forward, and never back."

"What will you do, when it is time to activate the Devices?" Beetle asked. "What will happen to your material? And to your larva?"

Galla chewed on her lip, feeling her anxiety rise. With it, so did her hair.

"I don't know, Beetle, but I can't let that get in the way."

"I have woven a pupa for your larva," the large but gentle creature said. "It is full of many colors, like the rest of this new form I have. I hope you will like it. Will the larva arrive before the battle?" She gazed up at it, and admired its rainbow-streaked new wings and its richer, iridescent thorax colors.

"Dearest Beetle," she said, "thank you for the gift. I'm eager to see it. I think the baby is growing at a much slower rate than you saw with Ariel and Dagovaby's children. So...I really don't know when it will arrive. And—as for how the activation will affect it—I admit I am worried, but there is nothing I can do about that right now. Hope for the best, I suppose?"

"That would seem to be an appropriate tactic," Beetle said, clicking and popping.

Galla took hold of one of Beetle's feet and gently patted it.

"Dear friend," she said, "I hope to get you fresh leaves again one day."

"The fungus on Aeriod's world sufficed, and he has given me a store of it. I am fonder of the coffee logs from Ika Nui, however. I think I might have a craving for them now that my body is different. Do you know when I might be able to get more of them?"

Galla's peals of laughter echoed through the ship.

"As soon as it is safe to do so, you may have all the coffee you wish, dear Beetle!"

Beetle flicked its magnificent wings. "Then I will fight harder, so that I may obtain the coffee sooner."

"I think that's a great plan, Beetle," said Galla with a brilliant smile. Nalag nudged itself between the two of them and sneezed. Galla suspected that was Nalag's version of laughter.

Galla watched her crew come and go in the room, on the way to the kitchen. Paul bowed deeply to her as of old, and sat down at the table where she still stood, thinking.

"What's next, Queen?" he asked, winking up at her.

She sat down next to him and folded her fingers together on the shiny copper table. "We need to hear back from Prince Hazkinaut. And tell him we are ready to proceed."

"So when do you drop me off at this...Stormworld?" Paul wanted to know. His green eyes glowed, and when she looked into them, she could feel the rush of meeting his mother, long ago, and then the terror of nearly losing Dagovaby on that strange and broken world.

"Soon," Galla said carefully. They looked at each other. Galla swallowed.

She could not speak.

I do not want to send you to peril.

"It's all right," he said to her. "I can't read you, maybe, but your eyes and your hair...I know, Galla. I know."

She leaned her head on his shoulder. He put his arm around her, and they sat in silence for a long while. Then a pulsing alert made them both jump.

The *Seltra* announced, "Valemog ships have entered the junction and are in pursuit."

Galla rose and headed to the cockpit. "Jana, Guru," she called on the comms, "to the bridge. Everyone else, stay in your quarters."

Aeriod's image materialized in the cockpit, and he said, "Our favorite parasites want to give chase. Shall we lead them someplace they don't expect?"

"Straight to a trash bin?" Jana suggested.

"What do you have in mind?" Galla asked.

"I'll need Paul for this little trick," Aeriod replied.

Galla furrowed her brow. "Very well."

Paul entered the cockpit after Galla chimed him. Just as he did, the Valemog ships surrounded Galla and Aeriod's fleet and began attacking from all sides, creating a kaleidoscope of firepower mixed with the bizarre lighting of the junction.

"Do we engage?" Galla asked the mage.

"No. Paul, we're going to exit the junction soon. When we do, I want you to focus on the stone you have, and I will tell you more after that."

Paul nodded, and crossed his arms. "I'm ready."

"Now, drop out," Aeriod called.

Galla commanded the *Seltra* to leave the junction, and they found themselves in a strange space of warped-looking stars, with an empty void in their center.

"You've dropped us near a singularity!" Galla cried. "Why?"

Aeriod grinned. "We need a signal boost to get past interference. Why not take care of two problems at once? Galla, bring up the images of the Valemog ships. Paul, focus on your stone, and look at those ships."

"Got it," said Paul, and his leaf-green eyes lowered as he looked at the ships and held his diamethyst in his palm. It began to grow bright white-purple, and hot to the touch, but not unbearable.

"See them all?" Aeriod asked.

"Yes," Paul replied.

"Now, focus, *focus...*" and Aeriod's voice mesmerized Paul into a sort of trance. "Think of all those ships. And now think about moving them all into that void out there. Go on. You're just moving them from one place to another."

Galla, Jana, and Guru stared at Paul, whose face had gone very still, but his skin beaded with sweat. They looked out at the ships, which were firing on their fleet without penetrating their shields. Still, the bursts rocked the *Seltra*. They fired nonstop from their ugly gun turrets and violent energy cannons.

"Now!" cried Aeriod.

Paul went stiff, and his eyes went wide, and then he blinked.

"Holy shit!" yelled Jana, and Guru shouted, "Look!"

The ships had been flung into the edge of the black hole, still firing, and a burst of energy shot out from their destruction as they were crushed to infinitesimal bits.

"Got you," Aeriod said, and his ship captured the escaping energy and began to glow. "Transferring energy among the fleet. Use the *Seltra*, Galla! Open a channel to Hazkinaut now!"

Paul slid to the floor on his knees. Guru knelt to check on him. He was conscious but breathing heavily.

Galla quickly hailed Hazkinaut.

The Prince appeared, clear, lucid, and with extreme relief. "Lady Deia!" he gasped. "Finally!"

"Hazkinaut!" Galla cried. "We're on our way. Rikiloi is covered. We're headed to Stormworld next and we have a telepath for that world as well. Get your recruits where they need to be. This clear signal won't last. You might be on your own for a little while, my friend."

"I'm not, fortunately. I have Silderay and the...well, they used to be children. Now they're not."

"One more thing," said Galla, "when you get to the retreat colony —if it's still intact—they've got guardians at the Device. Whoever approaches needs to tell them they're a Questri before they're allowed access. And I'm sending you everything the *Seltra* has on each Device world. Just in case. Got it?"

"Acknowledged, Lady Deia," said the Prince, with relief in his voice.

"You're going to have a fight on your hands," Galla told him. "But I'm preparing a fleet for each Device world, so once it's ready, I'll send it out. I don't know the time remaining."

Aeriod interrupted. "There is no more time. We have days to get in place. Galla, we need to pull free of this system now. The signal will drop. And the gravitational pull of the singularity is immense. We can only hold it off for so long."

Galla sighed. "Hazkinaut, stay safe, my friend."

"You as well, Lady Deia," said the Prince, and he undid his turban, revealing his extraordinary feather star appendages, which swayed and snapped. "We have to succeed, so I can give you a new outfit. Because that one is beneath you."

Galla dipped her head and laughed softly through shaking lips.

"Fashion-shame me again soon, Your Highness," she said, and the signal disappeared.

47

MAELSTROM

"**T**alk to me, *Seltra*," said Galla, pacing her cockpit. Jana looked askance at her, and her new skin patterns almost seemed to glow.

Galla got the hint. She left the cockpit to Jana and Guru's capable hands and paced the longest hallway of her ship. Nalag joined her and jumped at several intervals, nearly tripping her up.

Deming entered the room, and the deengyne ran to him.

"I can feel your anxiety like ocean waves crashing on a rock," he told her, sitting down to rub Nalag's creamy chest fur. The animal sat on its hind hocks and looked at them both with blissed-out, brilliant purple eyes, its tongue lolling. "In this case, I'm the rock."

Galla walked back and forth, her steps growing stiffer and more pronounced.

"Are the ships ready?" she asked the *Seltra*. "Please give me an update."

The *Seltra* did not answer for several minutes, during which Galla nearly made herself sick from impatience and anxiety.

Finally the ship droned placidly, "The ships are assembled and have launched from Trozzhia."

"When will they be at their destinations?" she asked next.

"Varying times," answered her ship.

"And Stormworld?"

"Possibly within twenty-two hours."

Galla huffed out a suppressed sigh. "The best we can do, then." She looked down to where Deming sat. "It's time to get your brother in position. So...if you want to say anything, now's the time. We can hold anything off until my ships get there. Maybe. I hope."

She felt a lump in her throat, and Deming looked up at her without blinking.

"I don't think I have anything left to say," he told her. "I trust him. And he's clearly capable. He moved a fleet of ships into a black hole with his mind! I see, now, why it has to be him in that Device, and not me."

"Deming, I—" Galla began. Paul entered the room then. Deming stood. Galla excused herself and found another area to continue pacing.

The two young men faced each other. The same height, the same smirk, but so different otherwise. There were so many years of words left unsaid. And now that it came to this, neither knew what he should say.

"Take care of her," Paul said, slapping his brother's shoulder. "I really think you're the only one who understands her."

"And if she doesn't make it?" Deming dared to ask.

Paul sighed and shook his head. "Well, then we're all fucked."

They stood in silence, and Paul then seized Deming in a bear hug. "I want to find our mom and dad *together*," he said. "Keep yourself alive, okay, baby bro?"

"You too, big bro," said Deming softly.

The time went too fast, and after terrible insomnia among the crew, for they all liked Paul and dreaded what might come, they gathered as one whole group in the round room of the *Seltra*.

The ship announced, "Approaching target system," and then it and Aeriod's ships dropped out of their current junction.

Paul looked stoic, but Deming could see a tic in his cheek.

Jana kept swallowing and blinking.

"Now you get back with us as soon as you can, young man," she told him. She wiped tears from her eyes with the back of her hands.

Galla felt complete agony, remembering everything—remembering his birth, holding him as an infant in her arms, watching him run to her after Meredith's death. *Universe, protect him*, she thought. She tried her best to seem strong and professional. But she loved Paul so much that it hurt to take him to the place that nearly killed his own father.

The trials I put the Ambrono men through...

The hours dwindled, and Aeriod's voice came through, along with his holographic image.

"I'm afraid we have a thicket of Valemog garbage to wade through at this one," he said with a dour expression.

"So they know what we're doing, to some extent," said Galla.

"Of course," Aeriod agreed, "and it's likely to be this way at every other world. We were fortunate that Rikiloi is mine. None of the others is. And you had already encountered some sort of base at 947 Tauliope in the past."

"Yes," Galla said, remembering the grim planet where she had been attacked while trying to enter a Device. That was where she had realized she could fly, after a fashion. She hoped that whoever took on that Device had a good offensive team. Her ships would help, but only if they made it in time.

"You're the commander," Aeriod pointed out. "What do you order here?"

"Defense," said Galla. "Until the Trozzhian ships arrive, we have to cover Paul."

As if in answer, a volley of explosives went off among the asteroids near the *Seltra*, sending it spinning. Galla calmed her exterior, but inside she was enraged.

"Oh no," she hissed. "No sneaking around for you, Valemog!"

She pelted to the cockpit and pressed Guru's shoulder.

"Let's take them on," she said. "The *Seltra* isn't getting them all."

Guru rose and let her sit in his place.

"Jana, fire at will."

Jana sent a volley of shots into the asteroids, shooting each one, bursting them apart. Valemog ships hid among them, and Jana whooped, picking them off.

"There's a lot," she said, after spending several minutes targeting them.

"There sure are," Galla said, her voice hard. "*Seltra*, what's going on? I can't track and disable any ships."

"Tracking," answered her ship. "The Event interference is jamming the ability to discern all ships from planetoid debris. I am learning."

"Good! Keep learning. What you can't take out that way, Jana can shoot."

"We make a good team so far, *Seltra*!" cried Jana.

The *Seltra* answered, "You possess unique targeting skill, Jana Okoro. I agree."

Jana smirked, full of a glee she had not felt since before her years in hibernation. She felt alive again, and ready for whatever came her way. *And if I get to fly on my own again, I'm embracing it*, she thought. She fired the *Seltra*'s weapons with new fervor.

"Nobody's getting Paul if I have anything to say about it!" she said.

Galla watched and nodded. "Let Aeriod's ships take it from here and cover us, so we can drop Paul. I'll take him down on a sky bike. Oh...*Seltra*? I need a sky bike..."

The blazing starship fled the asteroid field and headed for the atmosphere of "Stormworld," then dipped low enough for Galla to ready herself for a drop. "Suit up, Paul," she told him, and he obliged. She could not help but think constantly of taking Dagovaby down to the surface. Paul was a different man, though.

The *Seltra* made Galla a gleaming, shielded sky bike, and she shook her head in amazement.

"We're getting a lot of action up here," Aeriod chimed in. "Make it quick."

Paul nodded to her, signaling his readiness. They sat on the sky bike, and Galla commanded, "Drop us!"

And down the bike fell, Paul yelling at first, and then starting to laugh, and he could not stop. Galla shook with laugher too, and enjoyed the plummet. She met a dust storm immediately, just as she had with Dagovaby.

"Aha," said Paul, "now I get it."

"Do you hear them? The voices?" Galla asked.

"Yes," he said, and he made no further comment as they worked through the turbulent air and finally landed. Galla recognized the place; even after decades, its strange markings leading to the Device still stood. She could see Paul's small stone glowing through his suit.

"We're close," she said in her helmet. And sure enough, they found themselves all too near the edge of another great pit.

Paul took hold of her and they held each other for several minutes.

"Please, please be safe," she said, her vision blurring from tears. "I'll be back for you."

"You'd better be," he said to her, and then he slipped over the edge onto the platform and slid down to what fate, he could not guess.

"Captain," called Jana, with an edge to her voice, "it's getting hot up here. Even for this bird."

Galla launched her bike upward and was met by stray stabs of fire from Valemog ships, which Aeriod and Jana worked to disable or destroy. *Why are there so many?* Galla wondered in dismay. She reached the atmosphere and readied the sky bike to enter the *Seltra*, when a brilliant blaze surrounded the planet. It was the reflection of hundreds of ships, the same fiery metal as hers, and of all different sizes. They faced the Valemog ships and unleashed an extraordinary assault of firepower.

She perched just under her own ship and watched in awe.

"You did it!" she whispered in her helmet. "Thank you, Oni-Odi!"

The Trozzhian fleet had arrived.

48

____

PROPAGANDA

The Trozzhian ships set up in an array around the entire planet, and Galla and her crew stared out of the *Seltra* stunned at the shimmering sight.

"Well done," Deming said to her proudly, and he exhaled. "I feel a lot better about Paul now."

"So do I," said Galla. "Now we have to hope that all the other ships have made it to the Device worlds, or will soon."

Aeriod called from his ship and said, "It's time we got you back to Quopeia and into position."

Galla tensed up for a moment, but then Deming put his arm around her, and she relaxed.

"*Seltra*, follow Aeriod's fleet again."

"I will," acknowledge the ship. "Please note there is an incoming transmission from a distant source, not in this system. It is a strong, clear signal."

"Hazkinaut?" Galla wondered.

"No," and the way the ship said the word gave Galla a deep chill.

"Show me," she said.

An image appeared inside the ship, holographic, and even though it was not actually inside with them, Galla stumbled back. It was a woman, pale and beautiful and dark-haired, with diamond eyes.

"No!" whispered Galla.

"Galla," called Aeriod urgently. "Are you seeing this?"

"Yes," said Galla hoarsely.

"I'm trying to locate the signal origin," he called back.

"It's Veronica!" she cried.

"Ah...is it, now?" Aeriod asked, his voice icy.

For then the image rotated, revealing another face on the back, staring out. A pale face, also with dark hair, but much longer, and the eyes were leaf-green yet also crystalline.

Galla cried out in horror. It was the face of Ariel Brant.

And both faces spoke: "You have no further power here. We are transmitting to all worlds in the galaxy: you are traitors, and you will be eliminated. No world shall accept your leadership. Paosh Tohon is the leader of this galaxy, and soon will link to all others."

Then the dual image spoke the words Galla had heard long ago, in the Device on Rikiloi: "You cannot stop us. If we cannot harm you, we will take everything from you. We will feed upon the pain of those you love."

These last words looped over and over. Galla covered her ears.

"Shut if off! Shut if off!"

The *Seltra* said, "It is difficult to avoid the transmission. I am learning to ignore it. I caution that this may not be possible for others receiving it."

"Jesus," Guru whispered. "Ariel!"

Deming stared at the image with haunted eyes, and his breath came quickly. Galla reached for his hand and held it in hers.

Gradually the image faded, as the *Seltra* began to ignore it. The ship sat silent, until Nalag let out a mournful, high howl that set everyone on edge.

Finally, Galla said, "I don't understand. Paosh Tohon hasn't made an appearance until now."

Aeriod's image shone in the round room. "It hasn't needed to," he said with a long sigh. "Valemog has been its tentacles for years, allowing it to gorge itself without leaving its stronghold."

"I'm cutting off the feeding supply," said Galla, cheeks flushed, hair wild. "I'm closing the Event. Then I'm going to find this thing and get Ariel back."

Aeriod shook his head. "Galla, you just saw what happened. There's nothing *left* to get back."

Deming glared at him. "How do you know that?"

Galla squeezed Deming's hand. "It's not just her, Aeriod. It's everyone who has suffered. It's the people taken from Stormworld. It's the parents of the children Hazkinaut took watch over. And now it's everyone who's listened to that message, who might fall under its sway. We have to take it on."

Aeriod sighed. "There's no coming back from it, Galla-Deia."

"There's no surrendering to it, Aeriod," she said firmly. "Now on to Quopeia."

A junction opened and the *Seltra* sprang through, followed by Aeriod and his raven-like fleet of ships.

49

EVE OF DUTY

The splendid blue-green-white arc of Quopeia only came into view upon close approach. Galla sighed, disturbed that Paosh Tohon and Valemog had already infiltrated this beautiful haven. Gindoo had done his best. A terrorist and possessed animals were massive breaches in the security of the last bastion, but Galla knew it could have been far worse. She worried about the old mage, but was glad that Dek at least could be with him and help.

Deming folded his arms around her and looked out at the only home he had ever known. He could see the scattering of now-derelict Valemog ships adrift in space. And the gleaming, enormous star-city Trozzhia perched in orbit between Quopeia and its moons. The north pole of the planet still danced with green auroras, no longer tethered to the city of androids. He took it all in and thought fondly of Gindoo, Paul, and his life of exploration and hard work. He did not miss the isolation he had experienced in Gindoo's home. He realized that now. Knowing and loving Galla meant a life of constant growth for him, but he also knew that it would be dangerous.

"Where do you need me to be?" he asked her.

She had been biting her lip in increasing anxiety, not knowing everyone's statuses at the Devices. She tried not to think of what horrors Ariel and Dagovaby had been put through, or even if they still were really alive.

"Deming, I really don't know," she said. She leaned back into his embrace, and her hair drifted to the back of his neck and curled there. She had never felt so secure in her love for anyone else, but she still missed Rob, and realized she probably always would. And her legacy with Aeriod was long, and would be undeniable even if she had not been carrying a hybrid child of his, hers, and Deming's. She did not want Deming to suffer the fate or Rob, or of Ariel and Dagovaby.

Jana cleared her throat. "Looks like we're getting a message from the surface."

Gindoo's gnarled forehead and long, braided goatee appeared; his eyes were resolute, but they twinkled.

"Yes, well!" he exclaimed. "Welcome back! I see you're ready?"

Galla widened her eyes. "Um. Not really? But I will do what needs to be done."

Gindoo nodded and his goatee bobbed. "Bring the ship down here then, and unload the crew. No living thing should be on Trozzhia when you position it for your Task."

A chill coursed through Galla.

Deming asked, "What does that mean? What about Galla herself? She's alive."

Gindoo shrugged. "Yes. Well. For now."

Jana, Guru, and Deming all stared in shocked silence.

Galla took a deep breath. "Then I have my answer. I need everyone else to be safe in Allurulla. We'll bring the *Seltra* down, and my crew will stay with you and Dek."

Gindoo clapped his hands together and then rubbed them back in forth. He grinned. "I'll put young Dek to work!" he said, and everyone could hear a note of glee in the old fellow's voice.

"Aeriod," called Galla, and the pale-haired mage stared at her with his platinum eyes on her screen. The image flickered ominously. "We're going down for now. Delivering precious cargo. Stay up here with the fleet, and encircle Trozzhia. Just in case."

"As you command, my lady," he responded, his lips curling at the corners. His image vanished.

Galla nodded to Jana, and said, "Think you know turbulence?" She looked back and forth between Jana and Guru. "You don't. Take us down."

Jana tilted her head and glanced over at Guru, who smirked. He said, "Can't be any weirder than anything else we've been through."

Galla and Deming laughed out loud.

"Good luck!" said Deming, and he followed Galla to sit in the round room with Prilanna, Nalag, and Beetle, who instinctively held tightly to the furniture and tucked its spectacular wings in as best it could.

"Will we be flying through a storm, Captain Deia?" Beetle asked.

"Something like that," she said, crossing her arms and leaning back in her chair.

The *Seltra* bounced and bucked and spun upon reentry. *Couldn't Gindoo have made this easier?* she thought furiously, fighting back against the urge to vomit.

The molten-hued ship burst out of the atmosphere and began its final descent. A jolt through the ship sent everyone reeling, and then it abruptly stopped, and leveled out.

"Uh, Galla," called Jana, "something is pulling the ship."

"Let it," replied Galla. "That's Gindoo. He'll guide us the rest of the way."

The *Seltra* landed with a tilt and a gentle bump, shielded from view, in the quiet cul-de-sac beneath the gleaming coral and turquoise spires of Allurulla's skyscrapers. With a hiss of steam, the bay ramp of the ship opened, and Galla walked out hand in hand with Deming. Following her, Jana, Guru, Prilanna, Beetle, and Nalag exited. Beetle extended its wings like an immense moth, catching the sunlight of Siloxxa, and shivered, its body sparkling. Its yellow eyes swiveled this way and that, and its antennae flicked back and forth.

"There are many plants here," noted Beetle.

Galla and Deming grinned at each other.

"I think you'll like Quopeia, Beetle," said Deming.

"There's a lot of room to fly," noted Guru, and he held his hands in fists, looking upward, strongly tempted.

"We *just* got here," said Jana, nudging him. "I'm not ready to bolt up into the blue yonder yet!"

Nalag pranced forward, happily sniffing, glad to be back on its home world. The deengyne ran up to the steps of the old round boardinghouse, and the great stone door opened with a creak.

Gindoo and Dek stepped out, blinking in the sunlight, and Galla could tell they had both been down in Gindoo's labs for quite some time. Dek, all long legs and too-large smile under his curly dark hair, swiftly walked over to his adoptive sister and gave her a hug.

"He's working me to *death*!" the boy groaned. "And I have so many assignments at school. Still...it's safe, and it's good."

"That's what I like to hear," said Galla, ruffling his hair.

"We really could use some cake," Dek said bluntly to Deming, who laughed.

"I can help with that," he said.

Galla introduced Jana, Guru, and Beetle, and Gindoo leaned on his cane, looking at the three of them.

"Yes, well," he said, and for a moment Galla thought he might make some kind of pronouncement, but he said nothing more, which surprised her.

Deming caught her eye and shrugged.

"Come on in," Dek beckoned to the guests. "Plenty of room for all."

He looked up at Beetle, tilted his head to one side, and said, "Well, there's one larger room..."

"Beetle will be looked after," Gindoo called. "We can make a shelter in the backyard. Plenty of nice vines and late-blooming flowers back there still."

Beetle lifted its wings and tested them out before entering the old house. Eddies of dried leaves spun from the wake of those wings, and floated up and away from them.

Inside, the floors echoed with the number of footsteps, and

Deming and Dek set to work preparing a feast for everyone. Gindoo lingered back by Galla.

"Can you help them?" she asked him quietly, looking at Jana and Guru.

"That I am unsure of, lass," said Gindoo. "This is a unique situation. I am not sure their transformation is complete."

Galla gasped.

"What do you mean? What could happen to them?"

Gindoo pulled on his long, braided goatee. "Hard to say. I would like to sample their tissue, if they will allow it. What has happened to them so far?"

Galla recounted their recovery, the side effects, and their new abilities.

"Aeriod seems to think of this as more of a gift than a curse," she said.

"He would say that," sniffed Gindoo. "I like to think of the whole person. How are they *really*? Yes, well, can't know that until I ask. But don't you worry about it. I'll deal with it. You have enough on the agenda! How are you feeling? What did he give you for the nausea?"

Galla showed him the silver spheres, and he snatched them from her and squashed them in his little fists until smoke arose between his fingers.

"Why did you do that?" she cried loudly, hair rising up.

"I make better medicine than Aeriod ever could," said the little wizard, lifting his chin. "Not to worry. I'll give you something better. Come, come. Cake first. Nothing before cake!"

And he took her hand gingerly in his wizened, clawlike fingers, patted it, and smiled up at her, and she sighed and smiled.

After dinner, Nalag begged for scraps as though it had not already been given a heaping bowl of food. Beetle squeezed out of the dining room and followed Gindoo down the hall past Galla and Dek's rooms, and out the back door. There, Gindoo had constructed a heated yurt, and inside, piles of leaves of all sorts lay in neat rows.

"There, there, Beetle," said Gindoo warmly. "I hope this will be more comfortable for you. A bit more room to stretch, yes?"

"Yes, this is quite adequate," said Beetle, flicking its antennae about approvingly. "I do wish I could spin better. My silk has changed since I changed. I want to make things for Galla and Deming's larva."

Gindoo considered the creature thoughtfully. "You can help them in other ways," he mused.

Back inside, Jana and Guru were settled into their respective rooms.

"Delicious food, great room, a nice bath, comfortable bed," sighed Jana. "And look at this!"

Galla peeked in her door.

"Emeralds!" exclaimed Jana, and indeed there were small dishes full of emerald earrings. She promptly put them in her ears.

She looked back at Galla.

"This is where you stayed so long?"

Galla's smile faded. "No. I wish."

Jana, shrewd as ever, nodded slowly. "Took you a while to heal, then."

"A long while," agreed Galla.

"Wonder if we will?" sighed Jana.

"Ask Gindoo," Galla advised. "He might be the best person to ask...well, anything!"

"Better than Aeriod?" Jana said with surprise.

"Definitely. There is much more to Gindoo than any of us knows. Aeriod included, I feel sure."

"Interesting," said Jana. "Look, I'm still me."

"I know you are!" said Galla, her smile returning. "And I'm so glad you're here."

"But Galla, you know I can't stay here," she said. "I need to know. What happened to Misun? When can we leave? I won't sit this out."

"I know that too," said Galla. "Let me get through what I need to do and—and if—well, Jana, if I don't make it?" Her lips trembled. She gripped her hands together tightly. "Will you please make sure *you* make it? Go do whatever makes you happy."

Jana nodded. "I'll do that and more. That boy? Your brother, Dek? I'll keep an eye on him. You can count on that."

Galla's eyes brimmed, and she dashed forward and embraced Jana, who hugged her back with strong arms.

"You have to come back," said Jana, "because we have to go flying together again!"

Jana's cheeks were wet.

Galla squeezed her hands and left to go to her room. Inside, she found a little vial next to her bed.

"Not Stroffy liqueur!" she moaned. But when she held it up, she found that its contents were a clear, jade green. Opening it, she could smell a hint of fruit and flowers, but it was subtle. An undercurrent of a warm spice rounded out the scent. She took a sip. It tasted like diluted honey and went down easily. She could feel her insides warming, and then she felt sleepy.

It was nighttime then, and Deming found her standing quietly in her room when he returned from cleaning the kitchen.

He watched her undress, noticing her small bulge, and he went to her and kissed her from her lips to her neck and down, relishing the moment and her.

"I am going up tomorrow," she said to him, feeling cold spikes of fear.

"Then we've got tonight at least," Deming said softly.

So they spent it well.

50

THE PRISM OF MINDS

Galla was up before dawn, watching Deming as he slept. She touched the little woven bracelet that he had made for her. She tried to push it off her hand, but it was just snug enough that she could not remove it. Reluctantly, she took hold of her diamethyst, cool to the touch and dark, and snicked the bracelet in half. She set it on her little desk and scribbled a note.

"I had to take this off," she wrote, her throat tight from stifled sobs, "because I think it might burn off. I don't know. I don't know what's going to happen. If I die, I hope it's not in vain. If I live, stitch me back together again, like you always do. I love you more than anything."

A teardrop fell onto the note, smearing it a bit, and then it evaporated, leaving tiny purple crystals. She hastily dressed and fled the room before Deming could awaken.

She slid quietly down the hall and toward the front door. Gindoo stood waiting for her. Her stone began to glow, and so did the little one she had given him.

"Hurry," he urged her. "They will all start glowing now."

"It's that close?" she asked, holding her stone, which began to heat up.

"Do you want to miss it again?" Gindoo snapped. Then he held out his hands, and she put hers in his.

"Lass," he said, his voice quavering, "you won't be alone up there. But it's your Task to do. Focus, Galla-Deia. Focus. Everyone else will know to do the same. And—and try not to fly apart, will you?"

Galla stumbled out onto the stone steps, blinded by her tears, because she knew what Gindoo could not say to her.

She marched to her ship without looking back, entered it, let it close, and sat in silence. Her shoulders shook.

"Oni-Odi," she said softly, "I don't want the same fate as you. But I'm going to use your gift as well as I can." Then she wiped her eyes with her fists.

"*Seltra*," she commanded, "take me to Trozzhia."

And up she shot in her firebird ship, piercing Quopeia's atmosphere, which it reluctantly allowed her to do before resealing to all traffic. She looked down, which made her dizzy, for the planet and its moons had vanished. Trozzhia loomed into view, and surrounding it, Aeriod's stealthy fleet hovered.

A deep voice startled her.

"Are you ready, Galla-Deia?" it said.

I know that voice!

"Coniuratus?" she asked.

"The one and only," he responded. "Our stones are heating. Is yours?"

Our stones? She wondered about that.

"Yes," she answered. "Where are you?"

"All around Trozzhia, waiting for entry," said Coniuratus.

"I—I don't understand," said Galla.

"I think it will make more sense in a bit. You'll need to allow twelve of us entry."

"Twelve!" cried Galla. "Who are they all?"

"Representatives," said Coniuratus, "and we're ready to help you focus on the terminus of the Event."

Dawn crashed through Galla's spirit, pushing her sadness down.

"More of us!" she exclaimed.

"More of us," he said, and his voice bore a higher note of good cheer.

"I will let Trozzhia give you entry," she said, and she commanded her copper star-city.

Then she shifted to her comms. "Aeriod," she called.

"I'm here," he answered quickly.

"Did you know about them?"

"Of course," he answered smoothly. "They are not all here. But that, my dear, is a tale for another time. Now, if you'll excuse me, the enemy is pushing through the junctions, and I have work to do to distract them. Galla."

"Yes?"

"I know you know it," he began.

"You don't have to say it," she responded, pushing her rebellious hair furiously out of her eyes. "In fact, if you must say it...can it wait until this is over?"

"If that is what you want."

"It is."

"In that case, ad astra, Galla-Deia."

"Ad astra, Aeriod," she replied. She bit back any temptation to say more, and was grateful that he did too.

Trozzhia opened for her and her unseen cohort, but by and by she could distinguish them dropping through the city's barrier in little pods, much like Demetraan's older ships. She hovered the *Seltra* over the bowl-like basin of Trozzhia's upper surface and it opened up for her, so she lowered the ship down inside. From her pants pocket, she withdrew the little vial of green medicine Gindoo had given her and dropped some of it under her tongue. This warmed her and calmed her a bit. She took off her diamethyst, suited up, and placed it around her helmeted neck once more. Her hands sweated and she could feel her hair rebelling against the inside of her helmet.

I'm not sure what to do next.

But she closed her eyes and faced an old, quashed memory from her horrific years on Bitikk, when their "training" of her resembled torture much of the time. She had learned to discharge from her own body a bolt of energy. After she had faced recordings of this with her friends on the *Fithich*, she had practiced it again, but with her stone for the first time, to far greater effect. This time, she knew, she would need a more sustained blast. For how long, she could not guess.

I am afraid. She placed her gloved hands over her abdomen. *For both of us.*

"Galla-Deia," crackled the deep voice of Coniuratus in her ear. "We are in position. And Galla, you won't enjoy what we have to do. I don't know what it will do to you or to us, but we have to combine our stones' power on *you*. And you discharge the final bolt."

"Oh," said Galla in a small voice. *Don't throw up. Don't throw up.* "Oakay."

"Are you ready?" he asked, and his voice was kind. She remembered their meeting fondly, at the vice worlds of Yaddifor's Delight, and how his green stone had flashed in concert with her own diamethyst. She had felt even then that she could trust him. So she nodded to herself.

"Yes," she said simply.

She looked up at the ceiling above her and said, "Trozzhia, take me onto the surface."

The floor bulged beneath her feet, and she steadied herself as it rose, and the ceiling opened just enough for her to exit. The opening blended back into the city's surface, and she stood on the still expanse of shimmering copper, reflecting both Siloxxa and Quopeia. She walked down toward her command tower.

She grew uneasy. Then she commanded, "*Seltra*, return to Gindoo's boardinghouse. If something happens to me, I want them to have you, at least." The surface beneath her feet opened, and her ship rose upward and pierced the thin veil above her. She watched the fire of it grow to a tiny spot of light, and then it was gone. She sighed and bit her lip.

"Trozzhia, I need the tower adjusted. Please lower it so I can stand on it. Shrink it a bit; it only needs to hold me in position. Then lift it high, higher than the outer edges of the city, above the other Representatives."

The city responded by lowering the tower and folding it inward on itself. She felt amazed, for even though she knew the city's capabilities, it continually surprised her to see it in action. She walked over to the lowered and narrowed tower and stood in its center.

"Now carry me up," she said, and she swallowed, looking below her and outward. Small figures spaced apart around the city's edge flashed with varied colors of stones. She felt then something tremendous.

I belong, she thought. She could not help but wave at them, and their stones sparkled even from that distance. Her own stone had grown hotter, the higher she went. Then the tower stopped.

"It's time," she said hoarsely into her helmet.

She began breathing quickly, as she could see the other stones beginning to brighten until they were unbearable pierces of light. Her stone glowed in turn, and her suit began to smolder.

Oh no, she thought, and then she was pummeled by one, two, three beams of light, then more, and her entire body began to glow.

She gasped. Aeriod's voice began to speak to her in broken bursts of static.

"Galla—breathe—focus—love—" and then the speakers in her helmet fried.

She took hold of her diamethyst, so bright white-violet now that the air around it distorted.

"Trozzhia," she croaked, "open the shield."

The protective atmospheric dome vanished, and her gloves began to burn as she held the stone. How hot it had become, she could not guess. She looked over her shoulder to hidden Quopeia.

You gave me my trial by fire, she thought. *So here I go.*

As if yanked, the stone thrust upward, high above her head, as she held onto it. The beams from the other stones all focused on her, and she could feel her entire body reverberate and enflame, and a blinding column of light burst from her stone into space. The city moved in its position slightly, and she realized then that Trozzhia's bowl form was amplifying her burst and correcting her position to aim at the Event terminus, in what manner, she knew not.

Thank you, Oni-Odi, she thought, and then she screamed.

Everything around her went white, and her voice vanished, and her arms bucked from the stone's power. Her gloves burnt off, and then her outfit, bit by bit, and then her helmet cracked and disintegrated. She floated just above her tower position, now, and from long ago, she remembered on Bitikk someone telling her, *Make your bubble.* She focused on controlling her sustained burst, but also imagined a bubble around her. Her skin began to burn as well, and she would have given anything to scream. A pivot toward panic sat just at the edge of her thoughts, like a perilous slope into an abyss. *It is killing me.*

"Shit!" Kein cried. "Go time, I guess?" His little purple stone burned hot on his chest, and he jumped up from where he had been dozing on the metal floor inside the Device on Rikiloi. The other stone, which had been resting on the floor since Galla left it there decades prior, had risen and now hovered in the air. Somehow this was not the strangest thing to him, for the visions he had experienced upon entering the Device haunted him: the face of Rez, Perpetua being attacked by black, forking lightning, Galla's face in pain.

"What do I do?" Kein asked no one. "Okay. Okay. Don't freak out. Shit! Breathe, dumbass, breathe," and he approached the levitating stone. His own stone began lifting off his chest, so he pulled it over his neck. It flew out of his hands and joined the other floating stone.

"Uhhh…" Kein said. Then he approached them. He reached out to touch them, but he met resistance, as if a small bubble had formed around them that he could not see. He held his hands around it, and they glowed brighter.

Then he heard a deep, scraping, horrific sound, and the floors began to vibrate, and the dim lights in the hallway of the Device level he stood on flickered. He looked out to the door he had entered, and lights began to spin. He turned back to the stones, and with his hands cupped outward, he pushed against the resistant bubble and found that it worked. So he moved the coupled stones forward, trying not to look at their piercing light. He advanced toward the door.

"No idea what the *fuck* I am doing," he whispered. At the door, he stood above the platform that had taken him down, and the lights spinning inside the Device made him nauseated.

"Shit, no," he moaned, for a migraine aura had entered the outskirts of his vision, and his head began to pound. "The lights!"

But he was stubborn, like his ancestors Forster and Auna before him. He held his hands over those stones, which now hung above the endless pit beneath him, glowing.

"Do what you need to do!" he said, feeling silly, but in awe just the same, and when he gave the stones a push with his hands, they drifted out over the abyss. The spinning lights and the deafening sounds of the Device made him realize *he* was spinning; everything was; the Device itself spun. The stones then flashed so brightly he cried out. A coil of purple-white light rose out of them, spinning along with the Device, and shot skyward. If he could see above the surface, he would have beheld a spiral charging out of the Device at unthinkable speed, up and out of the atmosphere and into space. He stood mesmerized by the stones. Not once did he realize that he was the one keeping them in place.

PAUL HAD JUST USED what served as a latrine in one of the catacombs of the Device that spread out from the door. *Better than shitting my pants,* he thought, for he had endured much in his days inside this strange structure. He had learned not to pay too much attention to the whispers and cries and screams that echoed and swirled around him on Stormworld. The visions that had met him upon arrival puzzled him more than frightened him. He could see a set of blocks being built, like a child's toy, over and over, and he wanted to know what lay underneath them. He tried to seek that in his mind, but found he could not.

Something is trapped in my mind.

It served to keep him more focused. And his military training kept him in tune with himself as well. As he zipped up, and cleaned himself with his own sanitizer, he wondered how much longer this would take. His supply of rations was getting low. Then a horrible shaking sent him scrambling on the floor. His stone began to glow. He touched it, wincing as it burned his fingers. He ran back out into the hall and found the partner diamethyst floating at eye level. He took hold of his own stone and, as Kein had done, approached it, and the two stones snapped together and began to rotate.

"I think I understand now," he said out loud, and he focused only on the stones. He did not cover them with his hands. He willed them forward and walked behind them as the structure around him screeched and spun. He approached the open door, where the spinning of lights made him dizzy. But Paul focused still.

He willed the stones out into the pit, where they emitted a brilliant coil of light up and out of sight.

For my mother and father, he thought.

THE PRINCE THOUGHT he was ready. He attempted one more message to Silderay.

"Silderay!" he called. But he received no answer; nor had he in the days prior. He hoped against hope that his young apprentice could figure out what to do, and how to cope with who knew what lay ahead.

For his part, Hazkinaut was exhausted. Days ago, his drone ships had entered the system where dark 947 Tauliope spun, seemingly unguarded. He had kept his own ship hidden from view and sent the drone scouts ahead. As soon as those scouts approached the grey world, lancets of light burst forth, picking off each one in balls of flame.

Hazkinaut clucked his tongue. "Nuisance, these barbarians," he muttered. "I supposed I can't be too elegant this time, can I?"

So he had swept through in his flagship, resplendent in gold and pearl, much like his attire, and rained blast after blast in all directions as he careened down into the planet's atmosphere. He knew a few tricks and sent more drones forth, each a bomb. They hovered as decoy ships at first, but once struck by the Valemog anti-aircraft, they activated, and hurtled down to the weapon source, crushing the base with huge explosions. The Prince lowered his great eyes in satisfaction and took his turban off.

"Now for a little fun," he said silkily. "No one deserves it more!"

With his mind, he had sent his ship's weapons straight to any panicked thought he could detect, vaporizing the Valemog minions on contact. A few ships began to launch in retreat, and Hazkinaut yawned and sent his weapons forth anyway.

What the Prince did not realize was that, knowing they were doomed, and their experiments at risk, the Valemog beings had set their base to detonate. It sat right at the edge of the very Device the Prince needed to enter. As he aimed for each escaping Valemog craft, he thought it had gone rather well. He detected no more thought patterns anywhere. And then their base blew.

The massive explosion struck his ship and set it spinning skyward. He tried his best to ride it out, but the ship's shield buckled and its engines lost power. "Well, that's unfortunate," he muttered, and as the ship fell, he managed to steer it manually straight into the Device pit. Burrowing down past the lingering smoke and flames, the Prince helmeted up and dashed to an escape pod, which jettisoned. The ship fell down below him, he knew not how far; he never saw a blast or anything from it.

Now he sat in repose, worrying over Silderay and how it might be going on *his* Device world. Then Hazkinaut's stone began to burn.

"Good," he said. As Kein and Paul had done, he moved the soon-adjoined stones with his mind out over the activated Device. "Let's get this over with. I'm tired of wearing the same old outfit."

And so the coil of light and power launched from the Device to join the twenty others far away, and they all met at the bottom surface of Trozzhia, just as Galla felt herself come undone.

51

COMPELLED

The yells of Deming brought everyone in Gindoo's boardinghouse to their knees.

Prilanna got to him first, desperate to help him, for he was in a state of excruciation, feeling everything that Galla felt, even at a distance. This, coupled with his own fear for her life and horror at her suffering, sent him to the brink of madness.

The girl tried to reach Deming's face, but he bucked without even realizing it, holding his temples, his veins bulging through his face and neck and forearms. Guru ran into the room with Jana and held him. Gindoo and Dek ran down into the laboratory and back up, winded, carrying vials.

Deming was stronger than anyone had realized, and in the moment of holding him, Jana and Guru looked at each other.

"We're the only two who can," he said to her.

"Thanks for that much, Beetle," Jana muttered, holding Deming down.

Prilanna whisked her little lavender fingers across Deming's temple and along his neck, and he began to gasp, and then drool, and finally he relaxed just enough that Gindoo could drop something liquid between his lips. Nalag slinked in and wriggled next to Deming, trying to help, but Deming flailed, so the deengyne backed off with a plaintive howl. But Deming did calm, either through Prilanna's efforts or Gindoo's, or some combination of both.

No one liked what he had to say then.

"I can't feel her," he whispered. His eyes closed and he lay still. Guru and Jana carried him to Galla's room and laid him on her bed. He then opened his eyes. Still motionless, he stared at the ceiling. The brilliant gold rings around his pupils had dulled. Next to him, on the little table beside his bed, lay Galla's cut bracelet in an S-shape.

Jana turned away swiftly, holding her mouth, and in the hallway, she bent over and sobbed.

"Is she dead, then?" she croaked, when Guru closed the door behind him.

"No!" shouted Dek. He had been hovering close by. "No! She's not dead! She can't die!"

Prilanna appeared behind him, and dared to touch his elbow.

"We should let him rest," she said gently, and she motioned for everyone in the hall to leave. Nalag sat outside the door, curled up, wet snout on its paws.

Beetle then scraped on the back door at the end of the hall. Jana sighed.

"I'll talk to Beetle," she said.

Everyone else left the hall, somber and quiet.

Jana opened the back door.

"What is happening?" Beetle asked, its clicks frenetic. "Deming is distraught! His thoughts are most dire! Tell me, is Galla-Deia hurt?"

Jana took a deep breath and nodded slowly.

"I think so. I don't know anything else. He's connected to her, emotionally."

Beetle bent its head and its great, iridescent new wings flicked up and down. "I am sad."

"I am too, Beetle."

Beetle then jerked upward.

"He is leaving!"

"What?" said Jana, whipping her head around. She could see down the hall a tall shadow leaving, and she heard the click of claws as Nalag scrambled to follow.

"Now where the hell is he going?" Jana wondered aloud.

"Jana," said Beetle, a tone of urgency in its voice, "Deming is going after her."

Jana turned to stare at him. "No. No!"

"I will fly to the ship," said Beetle. "Come with me."

"I don't know if I can control my own flight right now," said Jana worriedly.

"Then climb on," Beetle urged, lowering its body.

Jana wasted no time. She climbed on the back of the great insect, slipped a bit, and then held on tightly as Beetle spread its wings fully and pulsed up into the air.

They surged up over the stone house to where the *Seltra* began spinning its engines to launch.

"Stop him, Beetle!" yelled Jana.

Beetle took her and soared over the *Seltra*, beating its wings just over the larger ship. Nalag was outside the ship, barking and jumping, begging to be let on board. Dek, Prilanna, Guru, and Gindoo tumbled out of the front door of the house, Gindoo raising his cane up at the ship.

Deming's voice broadcast outside the ship: "Beetle, stand down. Gindoo, I'm going. If she's hurt, I need to be there. You understand, right? And if—if she's—I'm going. Get out of my way."

Gindoo looked as if he had aged another two hundred years, standing there. He lowered his cane.

"Beetle and Jana, come back down, my friends. Let Deming go be with his love."

Jana stroked Beetle's neck, and they landed on the front lawn of the house.

Dek yelled out, "Tell her I love her! No matter what!" and rubbed the backs of his hands across his dark brown eyes. Prilanna leaned against him and squeezed his hand.

"I will," Deming's voice rang out.

He launched the *Seltra* skyward, soaring through the atmosphere, undeterred by what resistance he might meet beyond.

"I'm coming for you, Galla," he said, swallowing his fear and charging forward.

52

CRITICALITY

A distorted ripple appeared before Deming's eyes the moment he broke free of Quopeia's atmosphere. It was Aeriod.

"What are you doing?" he demanded, eyes like lightning.

"I'm rescuing her," Deming answered simply.

"You need to stay away," urged the governor. "The other Representatives are attending to her."

Deming gritted his teeth. "Is she alive or not, Aeriod?"

Aeriod blinked. "I do not know."

"Incredible," said Deming, jaws clenched. "You claim to love Galla, but you don't even go see if she's alive?"

"As I said—"

"I fucking *heard* what you said, you dick!" Deming roared. "Get the fuck off my screen. You're useless!"

Aeriod lowered his eyelids. "I will meet you there," he said simply, and his image vanished.

Deming shook his head, enraged, and wishing more than anything that he could feel some thread of Galla through space. Trozzhia loomed into view, dazzled on one side from the rays of Siloxxa. A tower of white light still burst forth from its center, and its outer edges were lavender. As he flew the *Seltra* closer to the star-city the light began to narrow, from meters across down to a thread, still piercing to see. And then it vanished. The thin arc of Trozzhia's shield could be seen then, covering the top of the city.

"Galla," he whispered, closing his eyes, reaching out; he was not even sure how. He began to pick up on several things at once, and then he realized he was feeling the other Representatives. But he could not feel her.

"*Seltra*," he said softly, "please fly carefully around the tower, and tilt so I can see."

"Approaching," said the ship simply.

The ship did as he asked, smoothly curving its descent. It entered the city's shield without any turbulence.

A group of several beings, who looked human in size and shape, converged on the small top of the tower. Deming saw one of them bend, his green stone swaying, and he began to lift something. Then he lifted that something higher, and it was an oblong form of what looked like purple and white light. Deming shook.

The *Seltra* landed on the sleek copper surface. Deming ran out as soon as the ramp opened, and called out, "Trozzhia! Lower the tower!"

At first the city did not respond, and Deming wondered if his permissions had been tenuous. This disturbed him. But as he watched in this windless bowl, the tower began to shrink, and the people upon it held onto its edges at first. By and by, though, they began to leap down to the surface of the city. They all looked human to Deming, except for unusual features in their hair or eyes, and they wore a large jewel of a different color upon their chests. They stood at a respectful distance from Deming, heads bowed.

At last the tower melted into the surface, with one man standing, with very dark skin and patterns in his twisted, short hair. His great green gem shone brightly and reflected in his dark, reddish-brown eyes. He stared at Deming. But Deming had eyes only for what the man carried.

It was in the shape of a woman, only made of sparkling violet and white light. A slow pulse of that light radiated from her midsection, and it grew slower and slower as Deming watched.

The man approached Deming, and Deming could feel heat coming off that figure of light.

"I am Coniuratus," he said to Deming.

"Deming," answered the young man.

"Yes." Coniuratus nodded. "She performed her Task."

Deming tried to pick up the man's emotions, but he must have been skilled at hiding them, for what initially had seemed like anxiety and sadness then disappeared. The man looked utterly calm.

"Is she—" Deming began, and he reached out.

"You will burn to death," warned Coniuratus.

Deming stepped forward anyway. "Then let me. If she's dying, I'll die with her."

"No," said Coniuratus. "The truth is, I am not sure what is happening to her. She is not returning to her normal form, but something is keeping her from fading away."

Deming's tears ran hot down his cheeks, as he watched that slowing pulse of light.

"It's our child," he said, choking.

Coniuratus then lay the light-form onto the surface of Trozzhia, and the city sparked and sizzled and indented underneath it. But even with the heat, the city continually repaired itself.

A great, reverberating voice boomed all around them.

"You are home, daughter," it said.

Deming knelt before the blazing form. "Oni-Odi," he whispered. "Can you save her?"

"I cannot," his voice crackled. "I do not know whether she will live or die."

Deming moved as close as he could, feeling heat on his face and hands, as if he sat before a blazing fire. A shape moved behind him, and he saw a long, dark shadow stretch over him.

"I'm here," said Aeriod. "I will look at her." He pushed forward, ignoring the protests of Coniuratus, and bent down to try to pick the form off the ground. A spectacular arc of power threw him several meters into the air, and he swiveled his body to land on one knee.

Deming watched, stunned, as the light pulse began to speed up.

Before anyone could stop him, he crawled on hands and knees toward the scalding form and threw himself onto it.

"Fool!" cried Aeriod, but Deming refused to scream at the anguish he felt.

For indeed he was burning. But as he held onto the form, it began to cool rapidly and darken. Then the light extinguished. And there lay Galla-Deia, motionless, pale, eyes closed, nude, hair limp and damp. Her skin was covered in tiny purple crystals. And at her breast, her diamethyst sat, dark purple, still, and cool.

Wincing from his burns, Deming carefully brushed the crystals from Galla's face and kissed her cold lips. She lay still, so he reached underneath her and lifted her carefully in his arms. Aeriod swept forward, removed his cape, and draped it around her. He stood cradling her head while Deming held the rest of her. They looked at each other.

"She is alive," Aeriod said. And in his face, Deming could see lines of anguish begin to soften. "But barely."

Coniuratus and the other Representatives approached them.

"Is there anything we can do?" Coniuratus asked kindly.

Aeriod said, "Check on the status of the Event. Has the sealing begun? I want to know if it worked. I don't want her to have—we need to know."

A popping sound startled everyone, and the voice of Jana said, "We're detecting multiple junctions opening. Gindoo can't stop them all. Looks like an invasion."

Aeriod's shoulders lifted as he inhaled, and then he slowly exhaled.

"So, it worked," he said, a look of both satisfaction and sadness flickering over his sharp face.

Coniuratus said, "Paosh Tohon, then."

"Ah, and no doubt the filth Valemog," said Aeriod with a down-turned mouth, as if he tasted something bitter.

Deming said, "So they're pissed."

"Quite," agreed Aeriod.

"Good," said Deming, and he kissed Galla again, this time on her forehead.

"I'll attend to my fleet," said Aeriod. "Tell me the moment anything changes. And the city is yours to command, in her stead. I suggest you start."

He caressed Galla's still head once more, then turned about, marching back to his great, raven-like ship.

Deming nodded, and began walking back toward the *Seltra*.

"Trozzhia," said Deming, "give each Representative a ship, just like the *Seltra*."

"But we have our own ships," Coniuratus protested.

"Not like these," said Deming with a twist of the corner of his mouth. He continued commanding: "And for each ship, make dozens more," and his skin flushed from rage. "Attack the invaders. Fire at will."

"Do you need me on board with you?" asked Coniuratus. He watched in awe as amorphous, copper blobs rose from the city's surface and began shifting into ships.

"No, thank you," said Deming. "I'm glad you were there for her," he added.

Coniuratus bowed his head and offered what smile he could muster. "It was an honor," he said. "I pray she recovers. For all our sakes." He looked up at the field of stars beyond Quopeia. "One part of the Task is done. But the final one might be the end of us all. We need all the help we can get."

Deming felt protective of his lover, and thought, *I am never letting her risk herself again.* But then he felt ashamed.

"It's my turn to save *her*, somehow," Deming said. "If I can, then she decides what to do. Not me."

Coniuratus nodded. "Then we part for now. I will not be far away, should you need me." He began walking toward one of the new ships, and his companions did as well.

"I do have a question," Deming said. Coniuratus turned back around and tilted his head.

"Have you ever seen this before? Has this happened to—to one of you before?"

Coniuratus shook his head. "No," he answered. "And for alien Representatives, I doubt it as well. I think only she could have done what she did. And I'm not just talking about her Task. None of us has ever reproduced. Galla-Deia is unlike anyone else."

Deming closed his eyes, nodded, opened them, and smiled down at Galla's head.

"One of many reasons I love her," he said. "Be safe out there."

"And you as well," replied Coniuratus.

Deming entered the *Seltra* and commanded, "Take us back down, and be ready to leave after everyone's on board. I don't know how we'll do this, but we have to finish the fight. She'd want it that way."

The *Seltra* replied smoothly, "Indeed she would. I will carry you wherever you need."

53

DISSENT AND ASSENT

"Take this," urged Dek. "You were exposed to a huge amount of radiation."

The boy thrust a vial at Deming, who, bleary-eyed and with wild hair and beard, downed it and winced. It burned his esophagus, and he coughed and gagged. Then he took a breath and patted Dek on the back.

"You're getting good at this," he said, managing a smirk.

"Thanks," said Dek, with a confident smile.

Prilanna hovered close by in the hall of the boardinghouse.

"Deming," she called, "Gindoo and I have stabilized Galla. I cleaned her, and saved the crystals, as Gindoo asked."

"Good," said Deming, and his shoulders slumped from exhaustion. "Wait...the crystals?"

"Yes," said Prilanna, "the ones covering her body. Gindoo said we should save them. He didn't say why."

Deming shook his head. "I...don't know what Gindoo's going on about, but...I suppose that's also good. Can I see her?"

"Not yet," said Prilanna, and she positioned herself in the hallway to block him. She folded her arms and stood with her feet apart, as if bracing.

Jana appeared behind her. "Excuse me," she said, and Prilanna let her through.

Jana pulled Deming aside.

"I just got a message *through my earrings*," she whispered, tweaking those very same emerald earrings. "Don't ask. But it was the *Seltra*, alerting me that all Trozzhian ships have left the Device worlds. The ship said that 'all obstacles were removed,' whatever the hell that means."

Deming nodded. "It means those ships punched a hole in whatever offense Valemog threw at them. Any word from Paul?"

"Not yet," said Jana. "Do you want me to ask?"

"No, thank you, Jana," said Deming, and he gave her a relieved look.

"Deming, you look like shit," she said frankly, "and Galla would want you to rest. So, go do that."

Deming sighed, "I couldn't sleep if I wanted to."

"Mate, you've got to," said Guru, walking into the hall behind Deming. He held a rack of tiny vials in one hand and a bag full of paper packets in the other. "Coming through," he said with a determined grin.

"Wait. You can go through, but I can't?" Deming asked, frowning.

"Ah, easy does it, friend," said Guru kindly. "I've been working with the wizard on some distillates. I'm going to see if any of them might get her back up to speed. Leaning on that botany and mixology background never hurts. Look, Deming, get some rest. There's nothing you can do right now except that. Fuck it, take this," and he handed Deming one of the packets.

Deming looked at its label and rolled his eyes, and laughed in spite of himself.

"This would knock out three of me," he said.

"Then take a third," suggested Guru, and he pressed on, and quietly opened the door to Galla's room, closing it behind him. Deming watched him, looked back at Jana's waiting face and Prilanna looking most bossy, and shrugged.

"So be it," he said, and he returned to his old room, poured a bit of the powder in his packet into a mug of water, and then lay down.

"I'm really glad nobody else but me can read the dreams you're broadcasting," a voice boomed. Deming shot up in his bed, soaked in sweat.

Paul stood beside him, and then sat down on his bed and roared with laughter.

Deming fell back onto his pillow and groaned.

"Would you stop with that? Those are private dreams," he muttered.

"Then maybe stop dreaming about Galla and you together," Paul laughed. "It's pretty steamy. Day after day of it."

Deming threw his pillow at his brother.

"Hey, is this the thanks I get for my hard work out on the front lines?" Paul complained, grinning.

"Oh, fuck off," yawned Deming. Then he sat up sharply again.

"How is she?" he asked, and he moved to get up, but the room began to spin, so he sat back down quickly. Paul handed him water.

"She's sleeping. Truly sleeping. It's a deep sleep, according to Prilanna. You know, she's really a perfect nurse."

"She should be a doctor, one day," mused Deming, rubbing the sleep from his eyes.

"Agreed," said Paul. "Determined girl. And territorial. She chased me right out of that hall!"

Deming smiled. "What about Nalag?"

As if in answer, a wet snout shoved into Deming's right hand, and Nalag jumped up onto the bed. It flapped its tail on Deming's legs and nuzzled into his armpit.

"Hey, buddy," said Deming affectionately.

"Nalag was sleeping alongside Galla for a long time, and would growl if anyone but Prilanna came around," Paul told him. "Guru was at his wits' end, trying to get medicine in!"

Deming laughed and patted the animal's head. "My favorite deengyne," he said. Nalag snorted.

"Nalag is definitely yours and Galla's, or maybe the other way around." Paul stroked Nalag's amber fur, and the deengyne lifted its great purple eyes to him. "Yep, I know!" Paul answered the animal's thoughts aloud. "I don't think our friend here would have left Galla until it felt safe to do so. And so here we are. I think that's good news."

Deming noticed a purple lump hanging from Paul's chest. He held up his own diamethyst.

"What's that?" he asked.

Paul lifted his necklace and his forehead pinched together. "It was pretty crazy. The stone in the Device joined with the stone I brought with me. They hovered together over the center of the Device and I just kind of...drifted, focused only on those stones. I don't remember very well what happened after that, except that when the Device shut down, it happened suddenly, and sent a shock wave, and that threw me on my back. And when I came to, this was beside me. The stones are joined together, and I can't break them apart."

"Weird," said Deming.

"Right?" said Paul, holding the larger amalgamate stone in his palm.

Deming leaned back against the wall behind his head and drank more water.

"So is it over?"

"Is what over?" Paul asked, green eyes half lowered.

"The war. With the Event sealed. Is Paosh Tohon done?"

"Are you fucking kidding me?" said Paul. "No. After we finished up, it began broadcasting more propaganda in every system it could reach. Thankfully, Aeriod said it can't make it to some of his protected worlds. Prince Hazkinaut was trying to scramble the signal. Now that the Event is closed, transmissions are improving. But it took a while to unravel, and it'll take a while to fix. As for Paosh Tohon, do you think I'd forgotten about our mom and dad?"

Deming shook his head. "How can they still be alive? After all this time?"

"Look," Paul said, his teeth gritted, "I'm not giving up on them. If you are, fine. Stay here. I'm going out there. And as soon as she's well enough, so is Galla. She's the only person who can stop that thing."

"Galla nearly died, Paul," said Deming, with a flush consuming his face. "How can we ask her to go out there and face this thing?"

"Because we don't have a choice. It's merciless, and it's angry. An entire galaxy of Valemog forces will come looking for her, and for us. That's our mother's face it's broadcasting."

"Yeah, meaning she's compromised and beyond our help," protested Deming.

"I know you don't remember them as well as I do," spat Paul, "but they're still our parents. I'm going. Galla's going. Go hang out in Gindoo's basement for the rest of your life if you want; it might not be a long one either way, once this thing figures out how to get to us. Gindoo is already fighting to defend this planet. Trozzhia is too."

Deming threw off his covers and stood.

"Don't put words in my mouth and be an asshole," he said, standing up to Paul. "I'm telling you. If we go face that thing in its lair, or whatever the hell it's in? We're as good as dead. Galla can't defend us all *and* fight that thing."

"Maybe not," agreed Paul, "but we've got a helluva fleet now. And we might have Bitikk's help too."

Deming made a disgusted sound. "Bitikk? The planet that tortured Galla? Like I'd trust them."

"They've been in a siege with Paosh Tohon for over twenty years, and they're one of the only worlds that hasn't truly fallen. It's been a stalemate."

Deming shrugged. "Let them collapse, for all I care. If they can't break through that, they're of no use to us anyway."

"Okay, well, we also have Prince Hazkinaut and the other telepaths. Kein's on his way now," said Paul.

"Which is exactly what Paosh Tohon would like more of: telepaths," said Deming grimly.

"Exactly," said Paul, his green eyes glowing. "So we'll give it what it wants."

"Wait, hold on," Deming protested. "Isn't that what our mother tried to do?"

"She didn't have Galla," Paul said, eyes shining.

"We'd better make sure we actually do, then," Deming said. "This sounds like a really goddamned terrible idea."

Paul crossed his arms. "So are you in or not?"

"Of fucking course," said Deming.

54

DIRECTIVE

Kein shivered in his fiery-colored ship. The cabin was warm enough, but he could not stop obsessing over what had happened in the Device. After the Device halted its spinning and its power surge, a great clap rang through the hollow depths, and Kein found himself flung head over heels back into the metal courtyard where he had spent days waiting. He groaned, stiff and sore, and crawled on hands and knees in the dim light. He could see something glittering on the floor, and he reached out and picked it up.

It was his diamethyst, fused with the other one he had found in the hall. Their work done, they sat cold and dark. Kein put the chain around his neck and looked out the hall to the dark doorway. He heard the telltale scraping of the platform. He stood and began walking toward it.

"Kein! Kein! Kein!" a voice echoed through the hallway, as if coming from the Device itself.

Kein had frozen where he stood; the hairs on his neck all shot up.

"Who—who's there?" he called, his voice hoarse. He felt a strong urge to urinate.

"Kein! Kein! Kein!"

"Look, motherfucker, show yourself!" yelled Kein. "I've had enough crazy shit!"

And at the door of the Device a shape shimmered and crackled, like a broken transmission. Kein stopped and stared. He could see a man standing there.

It's me, he thought, stunned.

But he rubbed his eyes and looked again at the man shifting in and out of focus before him. It wasn't his own image, he realized. Yet he had seen this man before.

"Kein," the man had said more clearly, "the Innervation is strained. I'm afraid it won't hold. You can't let Paosh Tohon get into it. If it does, it can take everyone. Everyone! Hurry. Tell Galla-Deia. Tell Aeriod. We've run out of time!"

Kein had run up to the image, realizing who it was.

"Wait!" he had cried, for the image vanished.

Kein sat remembering all this, and shivering.

To the ship, he said absently, "I kept running from that voice my whole life. I finally followed it, and it took me to the lake on Perpetua. Then I took off in a ship and landed on a planet I didn't know, and I went insane. Now what? Now fucking *what*? I'm getting old. I can't keep following dear old great-grandad around...to what?"

And he curled up in his chair, reverting to his years as Caxxius Caxx, removed from anyone or anything that mattered. He could feel himself start to slide into that mindset again, of shutting down, returning to the cave of his mind.

"Kein," a calm voice now said aloud, and he jumped in his seat.

It was the ship. "We are approaching the planet Quopeia. Do you wish to land, or would you like to return with the fleet to Trozzhia?"

Tell Galla-Deia. Tell Aeriod.

Kein shook his head and swore. "Take me to Galla, wherever she is. If she's even still around."

"Galla-Deia is recuperating in the city of Allurulla."

"Oh good!" snarked Kein. "Crazy old wizard time! Well, hell.

Guess that's what I am too, now. Birds of a feather. Take me there, then. Please," he added, and then winced over being polite toward a ship.

55

HEAD TO WIND

Sunlight flickered in the curtains, and they looked for a moment like golden robes, from which a kind face stared out, some moments with short hair and dark eyes, at other moments with long, grey hair and green eyes. Always a smile shone in the face, and gentle words whispered from it. Two human women, matronly, spoke through a veil, and another woman, not human, desperately tried to hear them. She reached toward the fickle sun-dappled movement just behind her, and she tried to cry out.

Please come back. Please come back. I can't hear you. She opened her mouth and pushed with all her might, so that her breath might ring out as a shout, but no sound came. And although she felt as if she could see these women shifting behind her, her eyes were closed.

CRACK!

She thrashed and moaned, and then she sat up. She shivered, and looked behind her, but only saw the curtains drifting. Her shoulders shook, and her hair hung limply in long coils of gold, copper, purple, and every warm shade in between. Her skin glittered from dried, lavender sweat. She wept silently. And at first she did not see what had caused the sound that had awakened her.

"Galla," a man's voice said, and she turned to her right and found

Deming standing there, hands stretched out, eyes dark but brilliant, with the golden circles around their pupils.

She looked behind her again. "Meredith! Loreena!" she said quietly, sadly.

Deming watched her, aching for her, and murmured, "There's no one here but us."

Galla stiffened, and gritted her teeth, and her hair began to rise from its stagnant cables, drifting toward Deming. He smiled. Then he took hold of her hands and placed something in them.

"Would you like this back?" he asked.

She looked down and saw her little woven bracelet. Deming had repaired it while she had slept. She trembled again.

"Yes," she said, "although what I really want is you. Just you."

She pulled him down to her, and for a time the bracelet was pushed and pulled among the bedsheets and forgotten. Afterward, she stroked his bearded face, which nestled between her breasts, and ran her fingers through his dark hair, and he caressed her and kissed her. He slid his hand along her belly, which had grown just a bit, and he rested it there. Galla felt a tiny tap-tap sensation, and she gasped.

"What was that!" she cried. "Did you feel that?"

"No," said Deming, pushing up on his elbow and watching her vivid face, with its wide, amber eyes and wry little smirk. "What was it?"

"I...I think I felt the baby kick!" she said, and she exhaled, and felt for a moment a long, delicious bliss, as she also watched Deming's face erupt in wonder. She cupped his chin in her hands and kissed him.

"I was dreaming about Meredith and Loreena," she said.

"You felt glad and sad at the same time," he said. "I could feel you, and I knew that you were better. Dek wanted to come in first, but I thought I should."

"And you were right," she said to him. "Now tie that bracelet back on me. I need to get up."

"I'm not sure you should, yet," cautioned Deming, carefully knotting the little bracelet on her left wrist. He reached over to her nightstand and retrieved her oblong hexagonal purple stone. The diamethyst felt cool in his hands, and the only light within it was reflected from the morning sunlight, which danced in its violet depths. He placed the copper chain and the long gem over her head, and she adjusted it.

She threw off her covers.

"I'm not waiting a minute more. Well, maybe a bath first. Want to help me with that?" she suggested, and she grinned at him with lilted eyes.

"Only too willing to help my best friend," he laughed.

After that, she quickly dressed, and smoothed her outfit, and pulled on boots.

"You look really ready for something," he noted.

"I'm ready to go. Is everyone else?"

"Um…maybe? I'm just not sure you're—"

"Yes, you've shared that with me," Galla said with an impish grin. "But I'm going."

Deming nodded. "It's not like I could stop you. And I guess I'm ready too. So is everyone else."

"What?" Galla asked, opening the door to the hallway. "Who else?"

"Everyone. Else," said Deming, looking down at her. "They've been waiting for you. Kein was the last to arrive."

Galla felt a deep tremor of excitement build in her, and nervousness. "I want to see them all."

They walked down the hall, and doors began opening along them, with Guru, Jana, Prilanna, and Dek all rushing at her. Galla felt their ferocious hugs and her eyes streamed with tears. Nalag bolted from nowhere and jumped up to lick her face. She pushed gently through the crowd and out into the boardinghouse lobby, where Paul, Gindoo, and Kein stood. She ran toward them, and Paul picked her up and swung her around in his arms.

"She's mine for the moment, bro," he teased Deming.

"She's nobody's," a voice said, cutting through the moment, and they all turned to see Aeriod like a great shadow in the door. And alongside him, Prince Hazkinaut stood, much shorter in stature, but vivacious in every other way.

"Quite right, Aeriod," said Galla, "nobody belongs to anybody, really. But I do belong to the galaxy, and I'm ready to rescue it. But first," and she turned to Deming, "before we go, I have one request."

Hazkinaut stepped forward.

"Not without better clothing, Lady Deia," he said tartly.

"Oh, Hazkinaut," she laughed, "I don't have any—"

And an opalescent light flashed, and Galla looked down in dismay to find herself in an elaborate gown with shifting, pale colors, bare shoulders and long sleeves, a full and sparkling opal-hued skirt, and planets and stars embroidered along the hem.

"Which one of you—" she began, looking at Aeriod and Hazkinaut sternly.

Aeriod lowered his eyelids and gazed at Hazkinaut.

"I confess it was a team effort," he drawled.

"You two need to stop dressing me!" she cried. But she admired the dress just the same, and blushed, as she noted all the details. "Are there twenty-one worlds?"

"Twenty-three," Aeriod corrected her. "The twenty-one Device worlds, Quopeia, and Earth. And all their moons."

Galla turned to Deming, and with another flash, he stood in a tuxedo, with a small winged creature pin on his lapel. He touched it, and wondered.

"It's called a brant," Aeriod told him. "Your mother's last name," he explained, looking from Deming to Paul, "and her mother and father's. A brant, as I understand it, is a small type of animal called a goose, from Earth. And so, Meredith called Ariel her 'little goose.'"

Galla covered her mouth, and her eyes filled with tears.

"Gindoo," said Aeriod pointedly.

Galla seized Deming's hand. "We're doing this?"

He laughed. "We're doing this."

Gindoo hobbled before them and cleared this throat. "Yes, well, let's get you married then."

And the little fellow spoke simple words, which became more

shaken with each breath, and by the end, he was snuffling and sorting and swabbing his eyes with his tattered, draped sleeves. Galla kissed Deming, and it was his turn to sweep her up in his arms, with a saucy nod at Paul, who laughed.

"Tell me there's cake!" cried Galla, flushed and happy.

"Hey, you married *me*," said Deming. "There's *always* going to be cake."

Beetle shoved its head in the front door just then. "May I also have some of those special leaves from the backyard? They make me feel celebratory."

The little house rang with laughter such as it had never heard in all its centuries.

GALLA STOOD in her traveling suit alongside her Questri: Jana, Kein, Paul, Guru, Hazkinaut, Prilanna, Nalag, Beetle, and her husband, Deming. Aeriod stood off to one side, his black cape closely wrapped around him. Galla gave Dek a breezy hug and kiss, and kissed Gindoo on his forehead.

"Another set of goodbyes," she noted. "It seems we are always saying hellos and goodbyes."

"Yes, well," Gindoo said, avoiding her gaze, "such is the way of life." She squeezed his hand.

Then she walked over to Aeriod and took hold of his hands. A waft of spicy, smoky incense wrapped around her, and she knew that if she wanted him to, Aeriod would have taken her inside his cape then, and held her forever. She touched his sharp face and looked into his unreadable silver eyes. She could see, though, because she knew him so well, a deep sadness.

"You do not belong over here, alone," she whispered to him. "You belong with *all* of us. You are one of the Questri, too."

And he looked up. All eyes were on them. Deming inclined his head just a bit, and motioned with his arm. So Aeriod took Galla's hand and led her back to the family they had all made.

"Seltra," she said loudly, "we are ready."

"Not yet," Gindoo said. "Beetle?"

Galla stared, and Beetle walked forward on one set of its limbs, with something shimmering held in its four other limbs. It was gossamer-thin, but Galla could see it was a great volume of something woven. Tiny, purple sparkles shone among its folds.

"What is that?" she asked.

"I saved your crystals, from when you discharged the power to close the Event," Gindoo said. "Beetle has woven them carefully into a strong material that will stretch across several acres."

"Um...*oakay*," said Galla. "What's it for?"

Gindoo's eyes twinkled. "Consider it a protective cover."

Galla looked at Gindoo as if he had grown four new heads.

"What does that mean?" she asked, and she looked at her friends, and they all looked quite puzzled, except for Aeriod, who stared back as inscrutably as ever.

"You'll need to make a stop along your trip," Gindoo said. "A homecoming, if you will," and he looked at Jana importantly. She scrunched up her face, and then softened, and her eyes opened wide. He winked at Guru as well. "They'll need to evacuate, of course."

"Gindoo, you're not making sense," said Galla impatiently.

"Yes, well, lass," he snapped, "you'll have to make another stop along the way. To visit the Neuronids."

"The *what*?" Galla asked, growing irritated, her hair lashing around.

"The lake beings, lady!" cried Gindoo. "Didn't you learn what they were?"

"I—well, no," admitted Galla.

"Shit, wizard," Kein bellowed, "one took me under and I didn't have a *chance* to ask!"

Paul interrupted. "So...we're stopping at two worlds first, and then we're on to Paosh Tohon?"

Galla looked back at Gindoo.

"Yes?" she said, questioning the little mage with her eyes. He nodded. "So...any advice for all this?"

Gindoo leaned on his cane. "Go as far as you can go. There is a place you will feel before you ever see it, and that's if the junctions can even get you there. I think they will, though, because it will want you there more than you want to go."

Galla shivered, and by the looks on the others' faces, they had all felt a chill as well.

"Is it a planet?" she asked.

"There were planets, once," mused Gindoo, looking up at the turquoise sky above. "And there was a sun, too, but it used that up. Made its own strange system, of broken worlds and broken people. Everything that goes there is made to suffer forever, at the will of Paosh Tohon. It is a place to lose everything that you love. That is where you must go. It is called Oshtonen."

56

AQUEOUS

Galla stood with her arms crossed in the cockpit of the *Seltra*, looking out at a pale, rosy smudge of nebula. To her left, Jana sat at the helm, and to her right, Guru focused on a projected field of junction space. Deming stood beside her. Prince Hazkinaut's ship and its accompanying drone fleet hung beside the *Seltra*.

She licked her lips, feeling nervous, and called out, "Aeriod."

Aeriod's image wavered into view on the console screen. Galla nodded to him, and he tilted his head down in response.

"Yes, Galla-Deia?"

She bit her lip. "I need to know what you've planned with Gindoo. Are we separating? Or are you coming with me?"

Aeriod tossed his starlight-pale, long, straight hair over his shoulder and interlinked his long fingers under his chin. His eyes gleamed like new platinum.

"I think it would be best if we discussed this in person," he said smoothly.

Galla shrugged. "Very well. Come aboard."

"No," he answered. "I think you should come here."

The back of Galla's neck prickled, and she squinted at him. But Aeriod remained perfectly calm and still.

"I see," she said. *But really, I don't. What's he doing?*

Jana looked up from her chair. "Want me to dock?"

"Please do," said Galla, absently chewing her lip again. Deming touched her elbow.

"It's all right," he said. "We can handle things from here."

Galla shook her bright head. "It's not that. It's...I don't know."

"It's nerves," said Deming. "You're as wound up as a guitar string. Just go."

Galla nodded, kissed him lightly, and turned to leave. Nalag snaked between her legs, nearly tripping her.

The deengyne looked up at her with its vivid, dark purple eyes and sniffed.

"I'm sorry, but you can't go with me," Galla said, patting Nalag. The animal's ears sagged down. "I'll be back soon. He wants no one else to go along. I'm afraid I don't know why."

Galla stopped by the kitchen, drank some water, and twisted her hands together. She walked down toward the bay of the *Seltra*. Aeriod did not let her ship inside his larger one, but had made a connector between the two. So she crossed between the vessels and into the elaborate, vaulted space of his ship. He stood waiting there, hands behind his back. Only when the *Seltra* had disengaged and his ship's bay shut did he speak.

"We need to talk without any telepaths...or *empaths*...around," he said, looking down at her over his sharp nose.

"Why?" Galla asked, hair rising in impatience and anxiety.

"Because we are going to face Paosh Tohon," he said, "and anything that can be heard or picked up in conversation, or seen on faces, or felt," and he dared to sweep the curls away from her cheeks, "someone can retain. And Paosh Tohon can use that against them, and against us."

"But Deming—" she began.

"This ship is shielded, so he can't feel you," said Aeriod. "Come with me."

Galla swallowed and walked alongside Aeriod through his cavernous ship. It was larger than she remembered. The passageways were far larger than any humanoid could ever need. And they gleamed with the same iridescent black and silver as the exterior of the rest of his fleet.

"This thing is huge," she noted.

His mouth twisted a bit in amusement. "I've made some adjustments. For a specific task."

They finally entered his cockpit, which was far too beautiful to make any functional sense. It had etchings in silver of scenes Galla did not understand, and worlds she had never seen before. *Hazkinaut would love this*, she thought.

Two splendid chairs sat in that cockpit, and Aeriod waved his hand at them so that they turned toward him and Galla.

"Sit," he said, and Galla gave him a fierce look.

"You can't command me anymore," she snapped.

"Apparently I can, or you wouldn't be here," he said, lifting an eyebrow.

"Aeriod! What are you—"

He interrupted her and said loudly, "Jana, we're going on a brief mission. Alert all the ships to meet at the rendezvous point just outside the junction to Ika Nui. We will see you there."

"Hey, wait!" cried Galla, and she gasped as his ship powered up and burst into the nearest junction before she could brace herself. But he held onto her, and took her to her seat.

"What are you doing!" she cried, as the seat strapped itself around her.

The nether-space of the junction swirled around the ship, and she looked out in dismay.

"You—you stole me away!" she gasped.

Aeriod laughed loudly. "Oh, stop being so *dramatic*, Galla. I did tell you I wanted no psionic abilities around. You wanted to know what Gindoo wanted us to do. Now you're going to find out. So you may as well get comfortable."

"But Deming will worry!" Galla said, flustered, and feeling a curdling of nausea in her midsection.

Aeriod lowered his eyes to slits. "If he can't be away from you for this long, then the entire galaxy is doomed."

He sounded serious, and Galla stared at him. Their stones flashed at each other.

"Mages," she spat. "You hide *everything*."

"It's a good thing we do," said Aeriod, and he leaned back and watched the love of his life indulgently while her favorite foods began to appear around her, floating in the air.

"WHAT THE *FUCK*!" yelled Deming. "Where'd they go?"

"No idea," said Jana, wincing, looking up at him.

Paul and Kein raced into the cockpit. Deming's fists balled, and the veins in his neck popped.

Oh fuck, Paul thought.

Aeriod really screwed up this time, Kein agreed.

Guru scowled at them all. "You know what, mates, you need to back down from this one, I think." Deming shot him a look that would have quelled most people. But Guru did not flinch. "Let me just say that I've known Aeriod—in one form or another—a lot longer than the rest of you. There is nothing he does without having thought it through to the last detail. He's got a plan, and he didn't want anyone here to know about it. That's got to be for a reason."

Kein glanced at Paul, who nodded.

The *Seltra* said in an elegant voice, cutting through the humans' tension, "Prince Hazkinaut has sounded an alarm. Valemog ships approaching."

Soon after, the Prince's visage flickered into view.

"Are you done arguing?" he hissed, resplendent in his pearl and gold attire, head tilted in a regal fashion. "I can hear your thoughts like little poison-tipped arrows flying through space. Best to quiet it down. We have company."

And as soon as his image vanished, the *Seltra* rocked from an explosion just off its bow.

"So much for our stealthy cover," muttered Jana, and everyone ran to secure themselves from the assault.

"Wake up, dear heart," said Aeriod softly, sitting on the edge of the little bed he had made for Galla in an alcove of his cockpit. "We've arrived."

Galla yawned and stretched, then jerked upright in alarm. "I slept! Why! Where are we, what's happening? Any word from the others?"

"Galla," said Aeriod with considerable restraint, "trust them to figure things out. We have our own job to do. And for this, I need you, and only you."

Galla blinked, and picked up her stone from where she had placed it next to her. It was hot to the touch. Aeriod's glowed as well. He pulled her to her feet, and she gagged, so he leaned out of the way, and she vomited. He waved his hands and the mess cleared. He pulled a cloth from his sleeve and cleaned her face. She fumbled with her pocket and brought out Gindoo's tincture. He rolled his eyes.

"Mine are better," he said.

"Not for me, they weren't," said Galla. "And Guru helped perfect this one." She made a face after swallowing a few droppers of the bitter liquid. "Look, I don't know what we're about to do. But we need to have a conversation. I already don't trust you."

"Why?" asked Aeriod, genuinely surprised.

"You mean, why, other than your stealing me away in your ship?" she hissed.

"Fair enough, but you know why I did that," he responded.

"It's about Rob," she said.

He blinked at her.

She stared coldly at him. "Tell me the truth. When Rob died, a silver diamond fell off his arm. Did you put it there?"

Aeriod closed his eyes. "Yes," he admitted.

"Why?" Her voice was hard.

Aeriod opened his eyes and held out his arms, but she crossed hers defiantly.

"I knew you would cut our communications," he told her. "You had done it before, and I knew after Meredith's death I might not see you again for some time. He didn't know. I shook his hand and put it on his arm. I knew he would never leave you. I wanted a way to track you so I could find you if there was trouble. It was the only option left.

"But then he died," sighed Aeriod, "and I would have prevented that if I could have. I want you to know that. I did not like the man, and he did not like me, but we had one thing in common: we loved you. So, for that, I could overlook his other failings."

Galla scoffed at him.

"Yet you didn't find us when we needed you most," she hissed.

"Another great failure of mine," Aeriod agreed. He stood towering over her, but her eyes were embers burning him. "The greatest failure. The diamond was lost in the explosion, and I could only trace it so far. And then I had other distractions...and duty called. I had my own worlds to protect. I had to believe you were alive, somewhere, or I would have frozen.

"I did look, but Quopeia...there is much I don't understand about that world. It seemed to know, almost, that it held you, and it didn't want anyone finding you. I don't know if that was the planet's doing, or Gindoo's, or Oni-Odi's, or all of them together. But I'm glad it worked."

Galla lowered her eyes and considered his words. "Gindoo said once that it bottled me," she murmured. "It healed me, too, I think."

Aeriod smiled. "I think you're wrong, Galla-Deia. Humans healed you."

Galla looked up at him, and felt flooded with emotion.

"Yes," she said. "I may represent them, but I could not have survived without them. Now I have to return the favor. But I have one thing to ask of you."

Aeriod raised his eyebrows in surprise.

"It's about Deming," she said. "He's...mortal. Is there any way...I have to know," and her eyes filled with tears.

Aeriod sighed, and he took her hands in his. "He helped you the most," he said quietly. "For that I owe him gratitude. But I cannot extend his life. That is not a power I have, for humans. I am sorry, Galla."

She closed her eyes and let her tears fall. Aeriod wiped them with his cape.

"You do love him," he said, and she nodded. "How strange it all is. The Summoners never once saw him in any of their visions, and yet impossibly, you've found each other. And maybe that's the answer, somehow. I don't know what I can do for you when it comes to Deming. Ariel's son, and Meredith's grandson. How could I not want to help him? I can protect him or help him for you to an extent, but beyond that...I wish I could do more. For you both."

Galla felt stunned. "After everything, you would do this?"

Aeriod smirked. "I wouldn't hesitate. It's you, after all."

She flew at him then, and he lifted her up and took a deep breath, taking in the scent of her, her hair, her neck. She held him tightly but did not kiss him, and finally he lowered her, and they looked at each other for a long moment.

The ship chimed then.

"We've arrived," said Aeriod, and they both inhaled deeply and exhaled. "I have a suit for you."

Puzzled, Galla watched as he retrieved a suit and helmet from a panel in his cockpit.

"Where am I going with *that*?" she wondered aloud, and he gestured toward the window of his ship. She looked out and straightened up.

"I know this world," she murmured. "This is where the lake is! With the—the Neuronids!"

"They've been waiting for you," Aeriod said, watching her. She pulled the suit on over her outfit.

"What do they want?" she asked, staring out at the curve of the planet below. Her stone shimmered on her chest. She tucked it in and felt its warmth.

"You," said Aeriod. "I'll fly us down. And you need to ask them for what you want. They've already told you of the nature of Paosh Tohon—how it is a chimera of one of them and another being. And of course that being is a Raexian, like me."

His mouth went in a taut line, and Galla frowned at him.

What is he not telling me? she wondered.

"What I want?" she echoed. "I'm not sure what to ask."

"Do you need help in this fight or not?" said Aeriod impatiently.

"Of course!"

"Then go ask for it!"

Galla held her helmet in the crook of her arm and watched as the ship lowered through the atmosphere, and the view went white before long from a cloud deck. Aeriod then piloted it himself, skimming between ranges toward low hills, and ultimately to the long silver thread that Galla had seen years before: the lake. He landed the great ship by its shore, and it hissed and steamed, and sank a bit into the ground.

"Are you going too?" Galla asked, putting her helmet on.

"No," he said. "This is your Task, not mine. I'm just the pilot."

Galla huffed out an irritated breath and turned from him, then descended through the belly of his ship. She walked out and felt a sense of strange déjà vu. The sky was dark and starlit, and the lake lay still, silver from the reflection of the stars, with no wind to ripple it. She tried not to think of her last visit here. She walked to the lip of the lake, and little wavelets met her toes. She watched the surface of the lake change, and the reflection of the stars above broke into little arcs as waves formed. She could see something glowing now, deep in that lake. She began taking shorter breaths, until she felt sick, and then she tried to calm herself. The beings in the lake, the Neuronids, approached. And by the glow of the lake, there were more than a few. In fact, there were dozens. The lake shone and reflected in the hills around it. A phosphorescent tendril rose from the water and snaked toward Galla's feet. She braced herself, and it wrapped all around her body, lifted her up, and plunged her into the cold depths of the lake.

Before she could react much, a bubble grew around her. She sat on her bottom inside the bubble and took her helmet off. All around her, the beings drifted, twirled, and danced. They looked much as their colloquial name descried: like enormous neurons.

You have returned. We know, then, that it is time. We will assist you. We submit to your orders.

Baffled, Galla said, "I—I'm not sure what I'm supposed to say, or do. One of your kind was—taken, yes? By Paosh Tohon? And merged with it?"

Yes. The greatest obscenity. It has tried to access the Innervation that way, and has not succeeded. Yet. But we know the Innervation is weakened, after the sealing of the Event. There is an instability. Paosh Tohon will take advantage to gain access, and by doing so, all sentient beings in the galaxy will fall. And those in other galaxies would be at risk as well. What are your orders, Galla-Deia?

Galla crossed her legs inside her bubble, underwater, lit by the glowing Neuronids all around her. *I would never ask anything or anyone to go into harm's way*, she thought to herself. *But now I must. Such is the burden of command.*

"I need your help," she answered. "I'm not sure how you can help, but I need you. If you're related to the chimera, then maybe you can fight it."

We will help you. Governor Aeriod has readied his ship.

Galla stood, wobbled, then fell on her bottom in the bubble. "What?" she cried. "What do you mean?"

We are coming with you.

Galla's mouth fell open, and she leaned back on her hands.

"Now I understand," she said. "I'm not sure what happens next. But know that I am forever grateful."

We await the fight. Take us with you.

The creatures shoved Galla's bubble back to the surface, at the edge of the pebbled shore, and it burst. She stepped out and looked back. A group of Neuronids clustered near the lake's surface. She began walking back to Aeriod's ship, and it opened for her. She looked all around her at the size of the interior of the vessel, and she shook her head.

"I've seen many crazy things in my life," she said to Aeriod back in the cockpit. "But never anything like this."

He threw his head back and roared with laughter. "You're so young still! Just you wait."

And then he coasted his ship forward to hover over the water, opened its bays wide, and began siphoning water from the lake directly into the ship. Once it had reached a certain capacity, several Neuronids swam into the conduits of the ship. He sealed it up. Galla held her hands out to the window of the ship and looked down at the lake. Some of the creatures still glowed near the surface, but they began their descent, and the lake stilled and went dark. Only the starlight remained.

She looked over her shoulder at Aeriod and smiled.

"Now where, Space Mage?" she asked, teasing with part of Rob's old insult. Aeriod blinked in response.

"Mandira," he said.

INTRUSIONS

The *Seltra* bucked and dodged and fired at Jana's command into as many Valemog ships as it could, but they kept coming. Prince Hazkinaut's drones surrounded a few smaller ships before they could respond, disabling them with bursts of energy. The rest of the fleet, with *Seltra*'s clone ships and drones, combined with Hazkinaut's ships, could not match the continual arrival of Valemog.

"Why here? Why now?" Jana yelled.

Hazkinaut responded, "I suspect they can't get through to Ika Nui. So they're trying to prevent us from getting there too."

"And where the hell is Aeriod?" Jana cried, exasperated. She enlisted Deming to help Guru target as many ships as possible to disarm or destroy them.

Deming said, "I don't know where they're at, but we could sure use them now."

At that moment, several of Aeriod's other ships appeared and surrounded the *Seltra* and Hazkinaut's fleet in a sphere, sending pulses of firepower in all directions.

"Great," said Guru, "but where's his main ship?"

The larger Valemog ships were disparate, hideous vehicles from all across the galaxy. Their one unifying feature was the blood-streak symbol on their livery. Aeriod's raven-like fleet shielded the smaller Questri ships, but Valemog was nothing if not crafty.

A broadcast appeared inside the *Seltra*.

The ship said, "Unauthorized transmission. I am working to disrupt it."

But it came through long enough to send shivers down the spines of the crew. For there stood Ariel, looking as young as she had when she disappeared over twenty years prior, and her green eyes were faceted like diamonds.

"There is nothing you can do," her voice said, dead and toneless. "Surrender is your only option to survive."

Paul and Deming moved close together.

"Is she here?" Deming asked.

"No," said Paul, his eyes red. "It's a broadcast and nothing more."

Wild, high laughter then rang through the speakers, and the image of Ariel shifted into someone with shorter hair, red lips, and diamond eyes: the face of Veronica. In contrast to Ariel's image, Veronica's was vivacious, even coquettish, and her voice was undulating and lush.

"We're going to make it better!" she sang. "We will take good care of you. We know who you're protecting, Galla-Deia. It's all in the family. We will take back what is ours now."

Paul thought to Kein, *Still your thoughts. Think of nothing except surface thoughts. Bury everything else.* Kein nodded, and his hazel eyes glazed over. He rubbed his grey mustache absently. Paul's arms went limp, and his face went still. Deming watched them both. He patted his diamethyst to check that it was there, and sweated in relief that it was. He knew those stones were the only things protecting the living beings in the fleet.

"Come with us willingly!" Veronica went on. "We will make you better! We will—"

And the broadcast cut off.

"Successful disconnect," said the *Seltra*, and Deming fancied a hint of disgust in the tone of its voice.

The break in the broadcast sent Valemog into a frenzy, and they began aiming their own ships at the fleet. Slamming into Aeriod's ships, they met fiery ends; the raven ships, meanwhile, began to shimmer, and the great sphere they made around the Questri ships began to warp the space around them all. And they disappeared, to Valemog at least.

On all the Valemog ships remaining, a shrill scream blasted thought their speakers, bringing each malevolent, brainwashed creature across any edge of sanity that remained. "You let them escape! You will break before Paosh Tohon. We will feed!"

Long moments of silence met each Valemog ship as they tried to communicate with anyone in the sector, and failed. The dawning realization that they had been betrayed was shoved down amidst sheer panic. No one could rescue the Valemog crews from the excruciating eruption on board. Paosh Tohon sent tendrils of itself forking through space and into each ship, curling each being into extraordinary pain.

THE BALL of ships that Aeriod's fleet had encircled approached the junction that would take them to Ika Nui.

Jana's hands sweated as she watched the great spindle form before them. Kein winced at the piercing light and turned away.

"Shield us!" he begged. Jana obliged him.

"Next stop, Mandira," Guru announced.

"But where is Galla?" Deming wondered, echoing everyone's question aloud.

"I don't know," said Jana, "but right now we've got bigger problems. We're not alone out here."

Several strange ships of varying shapes and sizes appeared within the junction space, all around the Questri fleet. A huge ship hovered alongside the *Seltra.*

"Uh-oh," said Jana.

"What?" asked Kein. "Who the hell is that?"

"I know that kind of ship," she said. "It's an Associate ship. We've not seen any; I didn't know any were left. It's the kind that Galla, Ariel, and I—um—slipped in and out of. I stole some data. Hope they're not here to collect!"

Hazkinaut appeared on their screen.

"I don't know who this is," he cautioned, his freed head appendages billowing about. "It looks like some of the Associates, but I know many of them were taken prisoner, if not killed outright. I don't trust them. I didn't even trust them *then*."

"Rightfully so," said Jana.

"They request contact," said *Seltra* in a musical voice.

Jana shook her head. She glanced at Guru, who nodded uncertainly.

"Shit," she said under her breath. "*Seltra*, let them through."

They were met by a shimmering image of several individuals in robes, obscuring any faces or appendages the beings might have.

"Oh," Jana grumbled. "*Them*."

"We are the Summoners," they announced in unison. "We have come to aid the Questri. We seek an audience with Galla-Deia and Aeriod."

Jana twisted an earring and then brought her hands together under her chin.

"They're not available right now," she said. "But I am. You can talk to me. Remember me, folks?"

A moment passed, in which silence met everyone's ears.

Finally the voices said together, "You are Jana Okoro, of Earth origin, a member of the crew of Mandira Research Station. You compromised our data stream. Under the Associates' authority, we seek your extradition."

Jana burst out laughing. "You have no authority! Good luck with that! Now, are you gonna help us, or not? Oh, and by the way, your security sucks. I already have your entire database at my fingertips."

She winked at Guru. Then she jumped, for a hologram appeared behind her, next to Deming. Startled, he stepped back too. It was Hazkinaut.

"Summoners," his hologram said, "stand down and assist. We

need entrance to the Ika Nui junction. If you want to help us, you can guard the way. But I suspect you're not wanting to help in that regard. You're wanting *our* help. Yes?"

The shadowy group paused, and their voices then began to rise and fall, as if in argument. Finally they said, "We foresee mutual benefits."

"I'm sure that you do," said the Prince. "You can wait for an audience with the leader of the Questri. For now, stand guard on this side of the junction and let no one through. In return, we will provide support."

The Summoners muttered, then said, "We find this acceptable."

Hazkinaut tutted.

Jana said, "*Seltra*, cut the stream," and the Summoners vanished from view. She turned to the hologram of the Prince.

"So what do we do?"

The Prince said, "I'll leave a few drones ships with them."

Jana laughed. "That's not much."

"No," agreed Hazkinaut. "They don't deserve much. And anyway, I'm not staying in junction space. I never liked it."

"That makes two of us," quipped Kein.

Hazkinaut's image vanished. Jana breathed a sigh of relief. A tapping of claws met everyone's ears, and Nalag pushed forward and laid its head on Jana's lap. She stroked its fine amber fur, and it yawned.

"If this space fox could talk," said Jana, "I think it would ask, 'Are we there yet?'"

Paul laughed. "That's exactly what it's asking."

"Hmm," said Jana, rubbing its head. Its tongue lolled and it looked at her with lowered lids. She could swear it looked amused.

The *Seltra* announced, "Approaching final junction."

Jana straightened, and sighed. "I'm ready to go home."

The junction opened, and Aeriod's fleet shot through both in front of and behind the *Seltra*, the other Trozzhian ships, and Hazkinaut's Mehelkian fleet. And there spun blue-green Ika Nui, with a bright, coral, conch shell–shaped orbiter: Mandira Research Station.

Jana raised the light-blocking shields so they could all see better. Just as they approached the station, another spindle from a distant junction shone, and soon they found themselves looking at Aeriod's large ship.

"Did...did that thing *grow*?" Jana asked, marveling at the massive birdlike vessel, glittering in all hues from black to blue to violet to green, and etched with silver designs.

"It not only grew," said Paul, looking sternly out at the ship, "it gained...something along the way." He shot a look at Kein.

"Shit!" said Kein. "Not those guys again!"

Nalag's ears shot straight up as it looked out at the ship. It yipped and jumped on all fours.

"You're picking them up too, Nalag?" asked Paul.

"Picking up what?" Deming asked. But he quickly forgot everything else, for he felt warmth and vibrancy and love pulsating out from the great ship. "Galla!"

Jana's shoulders relaxed. "Thank God," she said. "I'm ready to pass on command for a bit. I want to see if my girlfriend is still around. Someone else take the wheel, please!"

58

DECOMMISSIONED

A small craft rose from Ika Nui and sped up through its high clouds and into space, aimed for Mandira Research Station, which turned silently in orbit above the splendid world below. The ship docked in Bottom Deck, in one of several bays that had been in active use in the station's heyday, but which had fallen dormant of late. Most of the original crew had relocated to the world below to begin a new life. Some of them had gone on other adventures, Jana and Guru among them.

When Galla caught sight of the station, she tensed up, made breathless by a white-hot spike of grief: for Rob, who had first kissed her there, and for Meredith, who had passed away there. She wanted to go inside, and so did the crew of the *Seltra*.

"I'm not docking on Bottom Deck," Aeriod told her, "but there is a bay in Top Deck, so we can park there. I'll check on our—ah—passengers before I join you."

Galla impatiently unbuckled and ran through a door Aeriod had opened off the cockpit. She found herself wandering through a narrow and quite rudimentary bay, until she reached the hallways of Top Deck. There, she was met with a dark, descending space, but as she stepped onto its floors, lights began to flicker on. The floors were the same spongy, soft material she had recalled from her former visit. She found it unnerving. But she descended, wandering around, until she reached Mid Deck and its great observation area, which was nicknamed the Dome Car.

She looked out at the planet below, remembering how it felt down there on the white sand with the strong sunlight. She walked out of the Dome Car and made her way along the old hallway where Aeriod and Meredith had lived, and where Forster had first been contacted by Ariel, decades ago. She found memorial plaques for Meredith, Forster, Dunstan Gibbons, and even Officer Derry. She scowled at that one, and took hold of the edges of it and pulled it off the wall. Then she smashed it under the heels of her boots.

"That'll show that plaque!" a voice behind her said, amused, and she wheeled around to find Deming there, with Paul and Kein close behind. She ran to Deming, who folded her in his arms in a tight embrace, and they kissed.

Kein whistled, taking a closer look at his ancestor's plaque, with its picture of Forster. "So this is where it all began," he mused. He lifted his feet up and down, watching his shoes sink a bit. "Man, I hate these floors."

Guru laughed, walking up behind him. "That's what Forster used to say! Thinking Man, I called him. Come, let's see if there's anything left in the bar."

Dim lights flickered on inside the bar, where once workers had gathered to eat and drink and feel some sense of normalcy out at the edge of Earth's solar system, years before. Guru ran his hands along the bar and wiped the thick dust on his pants.

"The air filtration isn't as good as it was," he said softly. The soft lights of the bar shimmered on the new, iridescent patterns on his skin. He sighed.

Galla watched him. "I remember you gave me a very delicious thing called a sundae, right at this very spot."

Guru grinned. "I did indeed. No more ingredients left for that anymore, I'm afraid. So what can I get you, Captain Deia?"

"Is there any chocolate left?" Galla asked, pining a bit.

"Afraid not, Captain," Guru answered. "To get that, you'd have to go to Earth or one of the outer colonies. We never grew cacao plants on Mandira, sad to say."

"Well, now I *have* to go to Earth," said Galla firmly. Guru laughed.

He handed out cocktails with what limited stocks he had left. There were some aged liquors and freeze-dried fruits, but otherwise much of his formerly well-stocked bar was a thing of memory only. He gave Galla water, but he placed a little dried fruit in the bottom of it, and she watched it bloom like a flower. She took a sip and smiled at him.

Aeriod swept in then, and for a moment, he did a double take, seeing Guru and Kein at the bar. Kein still looked so much like Forster, even at his older age, that the effect startled Aeriod. Paul turned to look at the mage, with green eyes like Ariel's and Meredith's, and Deming glanced with eyes like his father Dagovaby's.

"How strange you are, you humans," Aeriod mused, taking a drink gladly from Guru. "And what an odd bit of poetry to be here again, for the last time."

"The last time?" said Guru. "Mate, we're not done quite yet."

"I'm afraid he's right," said a woman's voice. They all turned to see a silver-haired Black lady, an older Korean man, and Jana and another woman.

"Ella!" exclaimed Aeriod. He rushed forward to greet the lady, who, while older, still stood ramrod straight and held an aura of confidence and command.

"Aeriod," said Ella in return. He introduced her and her husband, Darren, to Kein, Deming, and Paul. Darren looked a tad disheveled, as if he had been out in the sun a bit too long. "My friend, you look exhausted," Ella said. "You're doing great work, keeping us safe. The perimeter is secure. Miraculous!"

Aeriod nodded graciously. Galla noted with alarm that he did look suddenly quite aged, and quite fatigued.

"Misun!" cried Galla, darting to Jana, who stood arm-in-arm with a woman with glasses, round cheeks, and straight black hair shot through with grey. One of Galla's diamethysts shone from where it hung from Misun's neck, winking in unison with Jana's.

"Thank you for bringing Jana back to me," said Misun, gratefully taking Galla's outstretched hands. "I'm afraid I'm a bit older to her now," she said sheepishly.

Jana stroked Misun's cheek. "I'm afraid I'm a bit...buggier now," she said, a tad ruefully.

"Maybe not forever," suggested Galla.

"Gindoo didn't know one way or the other," said Jana, looking into Misun's dark eyes.

Misun said, "As long as you're with me, that's what matters."

Galla swallowed. "You can stay as long as you wish, Jana," she said.

Jana shook her head. "I'm in for the final flight."

Galla squeezed Misun's hands. "I'll do my best to protect her."

And as she moved away from the women, Galla hoped against hope that she could fulfill that promise.

Jana said, "No, it's really fine. I can do some...interesting things now."

Misun stared at her. "I didn't say anything."

Jana scrunched up her face. "Yes, you did. I heard you. You said, 'I hope you're okay.'"

Misun's mouth opened a bit. Then she closed it and said, "I *thought* it. I didn't say it out loud."

Jana stared back at her. "Oh. Oh!" She rolled her eyes and rubbed her temples. "I see Beetle gave me another gift. Well, this'll keep us on our toes, won't it?"

Back at the bar, Ella said, "I got your message, Aeriod, and I've spoken with Dr. Singh," explaining to the others, "she is Director Emeritus of Mandira Research Station, basically in retirement on Ika Nui. Since I'm in charge now, I make the final call. So yes, I am prepared to decommission Mandira."

"What?" cried Guru. "Why?"

"It's time," said Aeriod, mercurial as ever. "It will make more sense soon. In fact, quite soon. So I suggest you say your goodbyes, take anything you deem important, and then we'll head back to our ships."

"What about the plants in the conservatory?" asked Guru.

Ella said, "We already transferred the last viable specimens to the greenhouses on Ika Nui. The only things left on this station are memories...and maybe some bots."

Galla stood quickly.

"I have to go," she said.

Aeriod scowled. "Don't be long. It's time we emptied the place."

"Ugh, fine," said Galla. She seized Deming's hand. "Come with me."

They walked swiftly on the squishy floors to a lift. It trembled open, showing its age and lack of use. "Bottom Deck," she said to it. The lift began descending to the bottommost portion of the station, which narrowed to a point. Here were most of the bays and docks, the antennae, and the steerage. When the lift stopped, Galla sprang out, hand in hand with Deming, and they met full darkness. A low, humming din from the station's operation met their ears.

Gradually little lights began blinking on, not just above, but all along the floor. A few little hooting beeps rang out, and several objects began whirring. Soon Galla found herself surrounded by several bots, all in an arc before her, hooting and squeaking and flashing.

"Hello, friends!" she cried excitedly. "I'm back! And I have news. Do you remember the star-city I told you of?" Affirmative robotic sounds answered her. "Well, it's changed, but it's mine now. And I would like for you to come and live there, with all the other bots, if you would like."

Deming stood back in amused awe and watched the excited assortment of bots cluster around Galla. He felt stirred by something comforting, watching them. *She will never be alone*, he thought, and then a spike of awareness struck him. He had been dancing around whatever it was, but now he felt it intruding into his thoughts. He let out a soft sigh, and readied himself for whatever it meant.

Arm in arm, they walked back to the lift, with their bot entourage in tow.

"Did you think you'd ever have a wife like me?" Galla asked, nudging him with her elbow and grinning.

"Not in my wildest dreams," he said with a laugh. "I have a pretty good imagination, but not *this* good. And I'm glad the real thing is better than any dream."

AERIOD STOOD in the Dome Car, alone at first, staring out at the black stretch of space, the brilliant yellow-white star, the gleaming world Guru had named Ika Nui, and the cluster of ships in the Questri fleet. Galla found him there. She walked over and stood beside him, following his gaze.

"A lot of beginnings happened here," she said, her voice low and soft. She brushed her fingers across her lips, thinking fondly of the secret little space Rob had led her to on the station, where he had first kissed her.

"And a lot of endings," Aeriod answered. "It is time to say goodbye to it. But I find it strange, now that the day has come. I've not often been reluctant to leave a place. But then it's not often I've felt so at home."

"Meredith would be proud of you," said Galla, stepping closer and holding his hand.

"She would be proud of you, as well," he said, his silver eyes reflecting Ika Nui in their depths. "And she would be so happy for you. But so sad for Ariel." His face looked pained, and again, quite old.

Galla pulled gently on his arm.

"Then let's go get her," she said.

59

OSHTONEN

Aeriod's image appeared in the *Seltra*. "Everything is ready. Paul and Kein, I hope you got a good look at the station."

"Confirmed, sir," said Paul crisply, slipping back into his military role.

"Uh, sure," agreed Kein, glancing sidelong at Paul.

No, Paul answered in his mind, *I still don't know what he's up to.*

Kein whistled. *I'm almost afraid to find out.*

"Suit check," called Galla to her fleet, jarring the two men to attention. "Make sure your thrusters work. Helmets, sealed. Diamethysts, secured. We'll begin junction jumps on my mark."

The fleet of Aeriod's shining black ships, Galla's fiery Trozzhian crafts, and Prince Hazkinaut's gold and pearl vessels arrayed before the junction to leave. Galla took one last glance at Mandira, gone dark except for some faint splashes of light that no one else seemed to notice. But she did, for she knew what they were: the Neuronids Aeriod had brought to the station. He had sealed off Top Deck, and released the contents of his massive flagship into it, so that they swam unimpeded around the upper deck.

The light of the system's star sparkled on the crown of Top Deck.

Galla knew why it sparkled as well, for there Aeriod had stretched Beetle's gossamer webbing with the help of his ship, and the tiny diamethysts woven into that net were barely perceptible. She swallowed the gnawing sense of guilt that festered inside her, thinking of the inhabitants of that station, and what they were asked to do.

Deming pressed his hand into hers, and she let it linger there, feeling as though time had stopped, and she remembered again when she had first felt that hand. *Before you were born*, she thought again. *But how?* She felt comforted and assured now, as she had then.

She took a breath, stood tall, and said, "Go."

And one by one, the ships entered the junction, brilliant and familiar yet new as well. For they were going far beyond anything Galla had seen before. Jump after jump would take them closer to Paosh Tohon, and what fate, she could not guess, and in fact did not want to think about.

She slid her hands around her diamethyst and held it tightly.

"You'll feel it before you see it," Aeriod cautioned them. "Do not take off your stones, not for one second. They're the only things between you and your mind's immediate destruction."

They were not given easy passage for long. As they ventured through more junctions, Valemog ships waited, trolling them, attempting any possible capture. Aeriod was ready to destroy them, and Galla's Trozzhian ships immobilized anything in sight. But as before, the *Seltra* encountered ever more ships, all with the carnelian, scablike marking of Valemog.

Coniuratus hailed the *Seltra*. "Commander Deia," he said, "permission to break away with the other Representatives."

"Why?" she asked sternly. "We need you."

"I know. And we'll be back. Let's just say I've got a favor to call in, and the next junction is the time to do it," he answered, his face confident but his eyes betraying a sense of mystery, and if Galla was reading them right, even mischief. "Trust me."

Galla sighed, "Officially, I don't like it. But I do trust your instincts. Good luck. Ad astra."

"Ad astra," answered Coniuratus. His signal disconnected, and his group broke away.

"Why did you agree to that?" Guru wanted to know.

"Hmm," said Galla, "he's a smart man. If he's got a resource we don't, then more power to him."

"I hope you're right," Jana said, and she and Guru shook their heads.

Aeriod's voice broke through and he said, "We're getting close."

They passed through the next junction unimpeded, and the next. Galla began pacing.

"No one is here," she murmured.

Paul looked out at the junction space and shivered. "They don't need anyone now. They know we're coming. Paosh Tohon has called off Valemog, I'd bet money. It doesn't need or want them now. But I have a feeling they won't like that arrangement for long. It's the kind of shit I saw with the President back home. Zealots. They have their own thing going on. They don't need the figurehead so much anymore; they've been given carte blanche to maim and torture. And they like it. Not for the enemy, but for themselves."

"I really, really don't like the sound of that," said Kein.

Prilanna joined them then, and said, "I've outfitted the medical bay as best I can. I'm ready for whatever we need."

Galla turned to her. "Good. We're approaching...it. Stay here with Nalag at all costs. I still wish you could have stayed behind, but I know better than to argue with you. And you're the best medic in the fleet, I'm sure of that."

Prilanna beamed, her large brown eyes bright, and turned to leave the cockpit.

Galla said quickly, "Where's your stone?"

"Oh, it's in the med bay," the girl replied.

"No," said Galla, so firmly that Prilanna winced. "Go get it, and keep it on, always."

"I just thought, with your geode on board—"

"No," Galla said again, feeling cold, remembering the attack on the *Fithich*. The geode had not saved them then. "Put it on. Please. And keep it on. That goes for all of you," she added to the rest of her crew. "Nalag too; check that collar."

She eyed her crewmates, and then walked up to Kein. She picked up his own amulet and looked at it confusedly.

"It's bigger," she said.

"Yeah," said Kein. "The stone you left behind fused with it."

Galla stared at him. "I hadn't even noticed!" She turned to Paul. "Yours too?"

"Yes," said Paul.

She put her hands on her hips. "I knew I could break them apart," she said slowly, "but I never thought of fusing them back together."

"They did it on their own," said Paul with a shrug. "Strange material."

Kein snorted.

"I'll be back," Galla told them, and she quickly walked through the hall of her ship to the room where she kept her geode. She walked up to the tear in the stone, and felt the spikes and knobs of all the diamethysts within it. She pulled off two knobs with a quick snap. She held the pale purple crystals apart, and then she slammed them together. They fused, emitting a burst of purple light.

What can I do with this? she wondered. She began snapping off more of the stones and fusing them together. She added a few more, and then she held a sort of small club. *Now what?* And she looked at the large crystal around her neck. She had smoothed it with her own hands over time, and it was polished and sharp. She knew that no one else could have done this but her. So she took her hexagonal stone and knocked it against the club. Shards of crystals fell off, and she pressed them back on. She had been working at this for about an hour when the *Seltra* spoke.

"We are approaching a final junction, which is sending unstable energy readings. Should we proceed?"

"Yes," said Galla absently, whittling away with her stone. "I'll be up in a minute." She took the object and held it, and carved at it, and smoothed it. Then she set it down beside the geode.

"Beetle," she called on the comms, "come to me. I need for you to weave me something."

TURBULENCE STRUCK the ship in the final junction. She ran to the cockpit flushed, her hair wild, and Deming glanced at her with a curious expression. She grinned back at him. Across her back, a strap sat secured, with an object sheathed within it. Deming squinted at her, and she shrugged.

"What's the situation?"

"This," said Jana, pointing with a shaking hand.

A strange sight lay before them. The junction space was pulsating, as usual, but in between flashes, a deep blackness, a nothingness, flickered in and out of view.

"Galla," called Aeriod, through considerable static, "we've reached the final point of no return. I do not see Coniuratus. Should we wait or proceed?"

"We need to go ahead," said Galla. "No more waiting. It's not going to get any easier."

"I agree," said Aeriod, and his communication popped out.

"Captain Deia," Prince Hazkinaut chimed in. "My telepaths are sensing something strange. Are yours? Silderay is recoiling from something."

Galla turned to look at her crew. Kein looked unfazed, but Paul and Deming had moved close together, and stared out in unison at that final spindle, black and red and spinning and flashing, like spokes of a menacing wheel.

"Something," agreed Galla. "But not all of them. I think—I think it's history. Family. Yes?"

She asked Paul, and he stared at her briefly, as if she were a stranger. She felt herself go cold.

Kein touched her shoulder.

"He's shutting down," he whispered.

Galla looked at Deming in alarm. "Deming," she asked, "are you feeling something?"

He looked at her, and the gold rings around his pupils had gone dull.

"Yes," he said. "There's something on the other side of that."

"What does it feel like?"

"Malice," he answered, and he shuddered.

Galla closed her eyes and heard Kein hiss, "Shit fuck."

Please be ready. Please be ready. Galla thought the words over and over, but she was not sure if she was wishing it for herself or for everyone else.

"We have to go through," she said. "Jana, take us in."

Jana sat up in her seat, rubbed her hands together, and piloted the *Seltra* toward the spinning nightmare opening. The ship entered, and immediately the lights on the ship flickered and the controls warped and sparked.

"*Seltra!*" cried Galla. "Are you all right?"

"I—am—learning," the ship responded, its voice garbled. With a long, scraping shudder, the ship suddenly shot forth into normal space. But nothing about what lay before them looked normal.

The crew began to clench their jaws and hold their stomachs. Kein fell to his knees. Deming's fists flew to his temples. Paul still stared ahead, but he had lost some of his color, while his bright green eyes radiated into the flickering cockpit.

Galla could not feel what they were feeling; she heard the clicks and pops and high-pitched shrieks of Beetle, the howling of Nalag, and Prilanna crying out. Guru retched on the floor. Galla could feel none of this, but she could see what they could not: long, black tendrils, like black lighting, whipping forth, some of them in little stalks, sent in all directions from a central core. And this core was made of a destroyed star and its remnant worlds, all encircling what looked like a black and red sphere of flickering flames. A rusty haze of dust and debris hung in rings around this core, and among that hung wrecked ships, floating bodies, immense skeletons of animals, and strange spheres everywhere that contained objects within them that she could not discern. Against this backdrop, an enormous image appeared, as vast as a planet itself, and it was of a two-faced woman. One side was of Veronica, the other was of Ariel.

A lustrous voice rang throughout every speaker of every ship in the Questri fleet.

"Welcome to Oshtonen, Galla-Deia. We have been waiting for you to bring us more food!"

60

POTENTIALITY

"It's all right! You're going to be *oakay*!" Galla cried, pressing her hand on her stone. Her crew settled and relaxed.

Then an electrical surge burst from the core of Oshtonen and buffeted the *Seltra*. The ship's lights flickered momentarily, and then restored. A chiming alarm began to sound.

"Captain Deia," said the ship, "we have been separated from the rest of the Questri fleet by an energy field."

"What?" Galla asked, and she leaned forward onto the console. "Show me."

The *Seltra* switched its camera view to reveal a wall of plasma-like charge behind the ship, extending over the core and planetary remnants. Beyond that, the Questri fleet hovered, including Aeriod and Prince Hazkinaut's ships. Galla cried out. Spindle after spindle opened in space all around those ships, and out spilled thousands of Valemog crafts. A barrage of firepower launched from both sides.

"Aeriod!" she shouted. He did not respond.

"Communications with the fleet are not possible at this time," said the *Seltra*.

"Make it possible!" Galla yelled.

"I am learning," the ship responded.

Galla pressed her palms onto the console. "Learn faster!"

"They've got us," Paul said, his voice grim. But his eyes remained emotionless. Deming watched his brother closely.

"What's the plan, Captain?" Jana asked.

Galla shook her head. "We keep going," she said. "Yes, we brought it what it wants. But we'll give it a fight it didn't ask for. *Seltra*, full speed ahead. Get us inside that core."

Laughter from the Veronica-Ariel broadcast echoed over and over throughout the ship.

"Can't you turn that off?" hissed Galla. "And don't tell me you're learning."

"It is not possible to block this signal," the *Seltra* responded. Galla thought that she heard a tinge of regret in its voice.

Galla groaned, and the others closed their eyes.

"Fine! Play some music. Something really loud," she ordered.

Guru grinned up at her. "*Seltra*, play something metal."

The ship hesitated a long moment before saying, "I do not understand the request."

Guru rolled his eyes. Jana snorted. "Right," said Guru, "bring up Earth music. Whatever you've got. I'll pick something."

Mystified, Galla shook off the moment and focused on what lay ahead of them. She jumped as the sounds of electric guitar and drums pulsed through the speakers of the *Seltra*. A great fluttering and clicking followed as Beetle shoved its winged form awkwardly into the hallway.

"What is happening? Are we being attacked inside the ship?" Beetle exclaimed, its antennae swiveling.

"No!" shouted Kein over the din. "It's music! Supposedly!"

Beetle shivered. "Captain Deia, if you perhaps need a volunteer to leave the ship first, I would be happy to oblige."

"No, Beetle, I'm sorry," said Galla loudly, "but I want you and Prilanna and Nalag to guard the ship and stay put."

"Hey Beetle!" cried Jana. "Cover your hear holes!"

Guru looked at her and burst out laughing.

Beetle swung its great yellow eyes from Jana to Guru. "I will cover my ear holes."

And Beetle retreated.

Paul spoke up then. "It's letting us go right in. I'm hearing whispers."

"Even with all this noise?" asked Galla.

"The whispers are in my mind, Galla," Paul answered, locking eyes with her.

Kein nodded. "I'm hearing them too."

Guru gave them a strange look. "So am I."

"And so am I," said Jana.

"I thought this was only the telepaths," said Galla, confused.

Jana and Guru looked at each other.

"Um," said Jana, for she did not know what else to say.

"Yeah," Guru said in response.

"I don't hear anything," Galla said, exasperated. "Do *you*?" she asked Deming.

He shook his head. "No, but I'm feeling more than malice now, Galla. I'm feeling pain and fear. You're still outshining them, but they're there, and they're getting stronger."

Over the loud music and the continual broadcast of Veronica's voice, Galla could hear one other thing: Nalag howling.

"This is all going to drive us insane before we ever get there," she said.

"I kind of like it," Guru yelled. Galla rolled her eyes.

Deming pulled her aside, and said, "Look, I have no idea how to block what I'm feeling. I've never been able to block you, after all. I've learned to cope. But what I'm feeling is growing. And each time we pass by one of those floating spheres, I feel something terrible."

Galla looked out the window.

"*Seltra*, magnify one of those spheres," she commanded.

The ship obliged, and Galla stared in dawning horror. The spheres looked very similar to the bubbles made by Neuronids, as they orbited around the core of Oshtonen. And within them, Galla could see faces: faces of beings trapped in screams, or contorted in agony, but immobile.

"Their whispers are quite clear now," Paul said with a sigh. "They're saying, 'Kill me.' All of them."

"Jesus," said Jana. She trembled. "I hear them too."

"They're everywhere!" cried Kein, his eyes stinging from the thoughts entering his mind freely.

"Kein, block them," advised Paul.

"I'm not very good—"

"Do it!" Paul said, heated.

Jana and Guru glanced up at him. "Okay, but how do *we* do that?" she asked.

"I—what?" Paul asked. Then his eyes went wide. "You're psionic now!"

Guru shook his head. "Another side effect from Beetle's...rescue."

"Hold on," said Galla. "That means there are only two of us on board with no psionic ability: myself and Prilanna. This...isn't good. It's going to take advantage of this. Whatever you can do to block them, do it."

"Towers," said Paul. They all turned to him. "Build towers in your mind. Like blocks you played with as a kid. Imagine that. Put everything personal to you at the center of your mind and build the towers around it."

"I don't think that works for empaths," said Deming grimly.

"Let me try it with you, then," said Paul, and he took his younger brother's face in his hands and leaned forehead to forehead against him. He stood back suddenly, sweating. "I can't. You're different. And you—you're experiencing something unbearable. I can't even enter your thoughts anymore, brother."

Deming went pale. "It's not—it's not that bad, honest, Paul."

Paul shook his head. "How are you not completely unhinged right now? You're feeling everything!"

"No, I'm not, I'm mostly feeling her," Deming started, but he stopped. He began breathing quickly. Galla placed her hand on his cheek.

"You're diligent, and you're disciplined," she said softly to him. "If

I can outshine them all, then let me do that. I love you, and I believe in you."

Deming's gold eye-rings burst forth in brilliant light then, and he kissed his wife, and stood straight and determined.

The *Seltra* announced, "We are approaching the inner core. It is made of a substance I cannot analyze. I do not know if the ship can withstand the material. What do you command?"

The inner core, a sphere of black and red with forked black lightning only Galla could see, most closely resembled basalt over lava, churning, with flames licking out. It was the size of a large moon, much like Lume from Quopeia. Stalks of black lightning shot out from it in all directions, reached the plasma field, and disappeared through it into space. Galla could see explosions and lancets of light beyond that energy field.

Please hold the line, Aeriod, she thought desperately.

"Something is leaving that core," said Galla, "and I think that's how Paosh Tohon is spreading through the galaxy. If I had to guess, it's focusing on the fleet right now. If something can leave it, we can enter it. Fly through."

Jana wheeled around and looked at Galla with dead serious eyes.

"That thing could burn us to a crisp. I don't care what kind of tech this ship has. How's it going to make it?"

Galla chewed on her lower lip.

"We've got this far," she said. "We have to try. Go, *Seltra*. Go!"

"Confirmed. Entering the core," the ship responded.

The light and heat of the black and red fire became unbearable, and the *Seltra* shielded its crew from both as best it could. It entered the material, and shook violently, and steamed and groaned and whined. But it made it through, and what the cameras revealed made them all go cold. And then they all went weightless.

"*Seltra!*" cried Galla. "Turn the gravity back on!"

Paul, Kein, and Deming seized onto Jana and Guru's chairs. Galla let herself float.

"Captain Deia, regretfully, I cannot. We are now being pulled toward that structure."

For structure it was, after a fashion. In all directions, tubing and broken ships and millions upon millions of spheres full of tortured beings stretched out from a central, multifaceted sphere of sorts. The light inside this realm was dim and yellow-orange. Black, forked bursts erupted from that sphere. Galla's human crewmates bent over, clenching their abdomens, while Nalag curled up and howled and Beetle folded its wings in all around itself; both drifted in weightlessness. Prilanna wrapped her thin arms around her legs in the medical bay and bobbed back and forth. For they all felt punched by malevolence, by something so sick and twisted and cruel that it seemed called from each person's nightmares.

Galla alone withstood this horrible shock.

"Keep those stones on," she urged her crew, hovering. "Without them, you'll end up in one of those bubbles out there. That's what it wants."

She held her own stone, and it grew hot, and it burst forth with light all around her, shining throughout the ship. "Ignore that thing, and look to me," she told them.

The light stirred each of them, and they arose feeling stronger, their own stones glowing in concert with hers. The ship jerked a bit, but Galla touched her stone to its console as well.

"*Seltra*, let it pull us in. Don't fight it. We can't resist now. Save your energy."

The ship let out a strange sound, most similar to a resigned sigh.

The light outside grew dimmer as they approached this final inner sphere, and upon closer approach, it looked as though it were made of great sheets of rusted metal, welded roughly, to give it a faceted appearance from a distance. Several holes perforated this, large enough to allow ships to enter, and the *Seltra* was pulled into one of those holes.

Suddenly Galla felt herself go heavy. Gravity returned, and everyone came back to their feet, some with awkward grunts. She decided not to hover anymore, and let gravity bring her back down as well. With a nauseating lurch, the *Seltra* scraped and listed, then came to a halt.

"Captain Deia," it said, "I have landed as best I could."

Galla looked outside at darkness broken by long trains of dim orange lights, stretching along the inside of a ridged tunnel of some kind.

She turned to her crew.

"Jana, find any tech you can, and exploit it, break in, anything you can do. Don't call attention to yourself."

"On it," said Jana, and she placed her helmet over her head.

"Guru," Galla said next, "go with Jana. Look for any structural weakness. Once you're both done, get back to the ship. Give all the data to the *Seltra* and get it ready to leave. Weapons check?"

Everyone patted their suits, with fire blades on their wrists and pulse guns at their waists. The diamethysts all glowed from under the suits.

"This thing is going to try to turn you against yourself," Galla told them all. "Whatever mental block you can come up with, use. Towers. Songs. Um...metal music. Whatever works for you. Aeriod's stuck up there. We have to find Ariel and Dagovaby and get them out. If there's anything left of them to get out."

And she glanced ruefully at Deming and Paul, who nodded at the same time.

"Deming, Paul, and Kein, you're with me. We go to the beast."

"And then what?" Kein asked.

"We kill it," said Galla with a shrug.

"Oh, that easy?" he scoffed.

"No," agreed Galla, hands on her hips. "But if we don't, it'll kill us, or worse. Look at all those spheres out there. Do you want to be in one of them? If that thing gains access to the Innervation, we're all as good as dead. You've actually been *in* it, briefly. So, I'm hoping you can help. Or you could stay behind."

"Hell no!" cried Kein. "I'm going. Not sure what the hell I can do. I don't have much of an ability. But I'm going."

Galla closed her eyes. "The Summoners weren't completely wrong. They thought Forster and Ariel were the most important assets to them. Forster's gone, and Ariel is enslaved. But you three are what's left of their legacy. They were strong telepaths. Yes, they had Aeriod's help. But you're strong too. Maybe you don't need him. But I definitely need you. Help me find Ariel and Dagovaby, and free anyone else you can. The people of Stormworld too. Anyone. Everyone. No more suffering. Let's get them out!"

They all nodded, helmeted, and followed her down the hall toward the bay. Prilanna, Nalag, and Beetle met them.

"What can we do?" Prilanna asked.

"Stay put," said Galla firmly.

Prilanna glanced down at Nalag, whose nose twitched.

The great voice of Veronica stopped suddenly. The *Seltra* in turn shut off the music.

Galla shuddered, almost missing the noise. The bay opened, and she and her team stepped out. The ramp began to close, when a little shape jumped out and darted ahead and out of sight.

"Oh, shit," said Kein.

"Nalag!" cried Galla, but the deengyne had gone. She looked back quickly to the ship and was relieved to see Prilanna and Beetle had stayed aboard. The *Seltra* glowed in deep fiery colors where it sat in the great tunnel, and whistles of steam erupted from it occasionally.

Inside the tunnel, even through their helmets, the reek of its contents struck each of them. A piercing ammonia scent, interwoven with a sickly smell of decay and bitter mercaptans, made Galla so nauseated that she thought for a moment she might vomit inside her helmet. Her helmet light swiveled as she looked this way and that along the rough tunnel, so like the gullet of an immense beast. At first it was silent, but by and by they could all hear the echoes of screams and shouts and gurgling noises of torture. Then the floor beneath them throbbed slowly, and as it did, they could each hear a tapping, sighing, almost-laughter: "ah-ah-ah-ah" over and over.

"Fuck," Paul whispered. "Block it, people. Music, thoughts, anything."

But they could not completely hide that chattering, low, slow laugh. The tunnel itself seemed to contract and expand, with webs from some creature billowing about them, and long, curdled ropes of slime and droplets of liquid falling in the dim light. Dark shafts of other tunnels branched off, unlit like the one they were in. Galla dared not speculate what foul creatures lay in wait down those tunnels. Something slithered along beside them at one point. And something else hung from above, shifting slightly; in fact there were many of these. If they had eyes, the team could not see them. But they felt as if they were being watched hungrily.

Galla could see something the others could not. The dancing of little, black tendrils, snapping through the air and up through the ceiling of the tunnel, out of sight. Paosh Tohon sent more of its metastatic stalks, and more, and while her team could feel the madness and dread from these things, they could not detect them in any other way. She shivered, glad that they could not witness what she could. She also cursed her own poor night vision.

Presently something clicked rapidly in the tunnel ahead, and then jumped and struck Galla, who seized it and fell onto her back. It was Nalag, and its purple eyes were wide. She held the trembling animal and stood up.

"It's terrified," said Paul, stroking the creature with a gloved hand.

"And it's able to breathe," said Galla. "So I think you all can too, if you want to remove your helmets. Keep your comms open, either way. What's wrong, dear?" she asked the animal.

She looked up at Kein and Paul.

"It found something," said Kein.

"Some*one*," corrected Paul, his green eyes glowing yet bloodshot. He put a hand on Deming's shoulder. "I think it's our father."

Galla turned quickly to Jana and Guru. "Go. Find whatever you can to lower the defenses. Use your full potential and whatever it takes to get the job done. You both have your own special abilities. Use each and every one: new and old. Ad astra."

"Ad astra," they said to her, and they dropped back behind and out of sight.

Nalag pressed itself between Kein and Paul.

"It's saying there's a big chamber up ahead," Paul told Galla.

She knelt and took the creature's head in her hands.

"Dear friend, thank you for tracking. You do not need to be here. Go back to the ship where it's safe."

Kein shook his head, his helmet light swiveling.

"No," he said firmly. "There's something back the way we came. No way am I letting Nalag go alone. It comes with us until we're done."

As if in answer, something lashed out and seized Nalag where it stood, and the wedges of helmet lights cast quickly back and forth could only see long, spiked tendrils. The deengyne let out one yelp and went silent.

"No!" cried Galla, and she began to rise up, covered in violet light, to try to find the animal.

"Galla!" cried Deming. "It's gone. We have to keep going."

In tears and enraged, Galla drifted back down to her team. Kein shook constantly and swallowed his own anguish. Paul patted him on the back.

A broad sweep around with their lights revealed no other creature. But they all felt compelled to keep marching ahead, as if each of them was being dragged slowly by their spirits alone. At last, they made it to an opening, revealing a massive space.

"The chamber," whispered Galla.

They all stood still and gawked. More of the spheres of tortured beings coated the interior walls of the place, like clustered bubbles. Each bubble emitted light, so that its horrific contents could be seen by all. Some of these had been stacked on top of each other within towers wrought of foul metal, so that they looked like columns. Several of those columns led to an enormous anvil shape in the center of the chamber. And from that shape, black, branching tendrils emerged every few seconds; Galla knew that only she could see them. The "ah-ah-ah-ah" gibberish grew quite loud, and Galla's companions recoiled as if they had been struck.

The air itself seemed to spark and ignite, and wavered, and in front of the anvil, three humanoid shapes began to form. One of them was tall and pale, with short, dark hair, in a deep red dress. As

Galla walked forward, she could see the woman's eyes were no longer diamond, but their natural, deep violet color.

"Veronica," she said aloud.

The woman laughed in a purring, rich voice, sultry and inviting.

"Not just me, darling," she cooed.

Another figure solidified, and it had greasy, grey, chin-length hair. Something covered its lower jaw, a metal covering like a mask. Its eyes sparkled like diamonds.

"No!" cried Galla, tensing. She remembered a man with a great gun, shooting acid pellets that drilled into Rob, long ago. "You're dead!"

For it was Derry. He lifted his metallic jaw up and a muffled laugh erupted.

"Not dead," he said, and he patted a great weapon strapped to his leg. He unsheathed it and brought it forth. "I've had a lot of time to think about things. And how *stupid* Rob was for killing himself. It could have been better for him. We can make it better for *them*," and he aimed his gun at Deming, Kein, and Paul, who drew their guns as well. Galla bounded in front of them. But Derry simply laughed. He gestured with his free hand, and to his right, the third figure emerged.

There a small woman appeared, with long, dark hair and brilliant green eyes. She held out her arms wide, and cried, "My boys!"

It was Ariel.

61

NODES

Jana and Guru stalked back through the tunnels, trying their best to ignore the throbbing chatter that their helmets could not drown out. The "ah-ah-ah-ah" was impossible to ignore. Guru chose to try focusing on music, and Jana tried going through programming notes in her thoughts. Both were so exhausted they could barely move. But Jana patted her stone, where it lay warm on her chest, and it cheered her.

Guru felt tense, whipping around at the slightest movement. No stranger to odd creatures on the planet Ika Nui, he still felt unnerved by this dark place and its noisome reek. Every so often, something would make a whipping sound, and he would think he had seen dark movement out of the corner of his eye. He swept his helmet light about and saw nothing.

Almost wish I could see, even if I might not like what I saw, he thought.

Hey, shut up, will you? I'm trying to think! Jana thought back.

He shook his head. "I don't like this," he said aloud. Something ran in front of him, and he halted, gun drawn. Jana held hers at the ready also.

"How much farther? Do you see anything?" he asked her quietly, urgently.

"I'm following this light conduit," she said. "But we're not far from the ship now, so I'm going to see if there are any cables, or tubes, or whatever, off in some of these other tunnels."

"Good fucking luck with that!" Guru hissed. "Who knows what's down them?"

"Fuckery, I guarantee. Just like everywhere in this place."

"Great," Guru responded, his strong Kiwi accent rolling unabashed in his fatigue.

"Here," Jana said suddenly, looking up. They stood at the mouth of another branching tunnel with no lights, like a dark throat extending downward. She pointed above, and there were strange, thick cables, with gaps every few feet. "You know what those look like?"

Guru stood and stared upward. "Well, my biology lessons tell me those look like myelin sheaths. Like on a nerve."

"Yeah," murmured Jana. "Let's follow them."

Guru did another sweep behind them, and they descended into the dark tunnel. The throbbing sound continued, and the smell grew worse. They made it a few yards before something thumped softly beside them, and when Guru turned his helmet toward the sound, they saw something that made them both jump. It was a faceless creature, but with appendages that looked stuck onto it, as if it had been assembled from several different bodies. It twisted and bucked in front of them, and sent out what looked like forked tongues.

Instinctively, Jana and Guru leapt up, and this sent them flying to the ceiling of the tunnel, shining their lights on the creature below.

Jana found her head bumping along the cable above, and Guru began shooting the creature.

The bay that escaped it horrified them from their perch along the ceiling. But Guru did not stop, and the creature fell back, though not before sending out one of its tongues upward to snatch at Jana's leg, and it yanked her back to the ground with a crack. Guru gasped, and forced his body to lower to the ground, and he shot at the tongue wrapped around Jana as she struggled to get her own gun. Her hand reached it and she fired upward, for the beast's body rolled toward them, its limbs flailing. Dark liquid spewed from it in all directions, and then it burst, eviscerated, spilling a column of acidic and foul material all over the surface beneath it. Jana and Guru sprang up again, to avoid the liquid.

Clawing their way along the nerve-like cables on the ceiling, they could see below them better. They both panted. They could see that other creatures of different sorts slid and twisted below them, and some threw tentacles upward to try to grab them. So they leapt and bobbed and roughly coursed their way through the dark tunnel as it descended further, until a faint, red light shone in the distance. The cable above them crackled, with a long, slow-moving spark working its way along it.

"Let's head down to that light," Jana said.

Guru fired his gun five times next to her head. Jana gasped as a toothy creature fell from the ceiling where she had almost reached her hands.

Shaking, she said, "Thanks."

He shrugged, and they drifted along again, until they could see where the light came from. They blinked in the red light, and could see movement all throughout the cave-like space they found themselves in. At its center, a presence stirred. Dozens of cables such as the one they had followed could be seen extending from this central thing.

"It really does look like a nerve!" whispered Guru.

The creatures surrounding this form noticed them, and all sprang forward toward the ceiling. So Jana and Guru dropped to the floor and ran toward the nerve-like shape.

Guru fired shots to cover Jana as she approached the pulsing object, which sent charges through the conduits up and beyond their sight. She found an oblong, smooth surface, and recognizing it as a panel of some sort, set to work analyzing it. She unzipped a pocket on her suit and brought out a little cylinder. With her fire blade, she aimed at the smooth control panel, and it cracked, revealing wiring and circuitry. She held her little cylinder near it and it jumped forth, opening to reveal its own inner circuitry, then fused.

"Jana, to your left!" shouted Guru, firing above him and out. Another amorphous, limbed creature, like the one before, roiled up and arched at Jana. She held onto her cylinder with one hand and fired her gun with the other, over and over, until the creature fell forward. Jumping, she hovered above the mess it made on the floor.

Guru looked all about him and followed the cables down to the control panel. A long, pipe-like extension connected those cables to the panel.

"Do you need this?" he yelled, pointing at the pipe.

"One second," Jana said through gritted teeth, fiddling with her cylinder. "Come *on!*" she urged the device. She gasped with relief. "There. I think I found the shield controls. Deactivating...now!"

The dim red lights wavered, flickered, and then a sudden electrical burst surged forth through all of the nerve-cables.

She flew back up and fired blasts downward, this time to cover Guru. He seized hold of the pipe above the panel, yanked it out, and began bashing everything within reach with it.

"You're crazy!" she yelled at him.

"Never underestimate a man with a stick!" he called back, swinging, the pipe crunching into exoskeletons and skulls as more creatures flew at them, and he dodged Jana's blasts. "Some wizard told me that once! Now let's"—he thrust the pipe into the hollow eye sockets of a creature and pulled it back out—"get back to the ship, and let that wizard in!"

62

BLOCKADE

Coniuratus sat at the helm of his fiery-golden Trozzhian ship and gazed at the hazy, green world before him. He checked the positions of the others in his small fleet of Representatives. He looked at the scene: an ever-present stalemate, full of ships, surrounding the world. Occasionally explosions bloomed from the orbiting crafts. Nothing got in or out of that planet, however. Coniuratus gritted his teeth in disgust.

"Bitikk Traffic Control," he called out from his ship. "We've come to assist."

The response was swift and acidic. "We do not need your assistance," a layered, hissing voice responded. "Return to your origin or surrender to Bitikk."

"Mm, I don't think so," said Coniuratus. "I've come to parlay. We can help you finish off these Valemog goons, which are going to keep coming, otherwise. And as an extra favor, we'll make sure you don't get charged for war crimes when there's a new galactic order. What we need from you is firepower, at Oshtonen, now. Galla-Deia is taking on Paosh Tohon. Be on the right side, or collapse. Up to you."

In response, a brilliant green light flashed toward his ship. He held his stone, also vivid green, and grinned. The light struck his ship, but he sat straight and confident.

"Reps," he called out to his fleet, "go ahead and do them the favor. Take on Valemog. Whatever it takes: bring those dirty birds down. Bitikk will come around. Or they'll go down. Fire!"

63

AERO

Aeriod's silver eyes gleamed.

"Ah!" he said, watching the dissolution of the crackling plasma shield around Oshtonen's core. "Now to go help my family."

With a satisfied grin, he turned his ship around and fired in every direction at all of the Valemog ships he could see. One of them burst extravagantly, with silver spires erupting from it. Aeriod's mouth hung open as he watched another ship emerge from the wreckage. He held off from firing at it, as he realized what it was.

An icy voice filled his ears before he saw its origin, and it said, "And I'm here for my family as well."

Before him, in his cockpit, the tall form of T'Lexxa appeared, projected. Dressed as resplendently as ever, her head-spires sparkled even in holographic form. Her expression was cold and merciless. His face fell.

"T'Lexxa!" he cried. "No!"

She tilted her gorgeous head, and her sharp teeth sparkled as she parted her lips to say, "Oh, yes."

"Why?" he demanded.

She laughed, a chilling sound that sent shivers through him. "It's all about family, remember? Get out of my way."

Aeriod turned his ship and aimed straight for Oshtonen, not daring to waste a second.

"Find me the *Seltra*, dammit!" he urged his ship. It shot forward at great speed, while T'Lexxa's ship followed.

Aeriod's ship homed in on a shape and a faint signal, as the *Seltra* could not emit more than its baseline functions allowed. His ship's wings folded in, and the craft charged into the tunnel-like bay toward the Trozzhian ship. Even with the collapsing of his ship's form into a smaller configuration, it still scraped inside the tunnel, as Aeriod pushed it along nearly to its breaking point.

"Close enough," he gasped, and he pelted out of his ship and ran toward the *Seltra*. Looking behind him, he could not see T'Lexxa's ship. "Hopefully this way is shut, at any rate," he muttered, his cape flying behind him.

He ran up to the ship just as Jana and Guru approached from the opposite side.

"Aeriod!" yelled Jana, and he quickly joined them outside the ramp to the fiery ship.

Aeriod clasped her and Guru's arms, gratefully, but they saw the worry on his face.

"I have you to thank, don't I?" Aeriod asked, looking from Jana to Guru, and smirking at the pipe Guru still held. "Look, we have an unexpected kink. We need to get to Galla now!"

"It's a bit of a haul," cautioned Guru.

"No time!" cried Aeriod. "What else can we do? The *Seltra* won't fit in these tunnels."

"That ship is parked anyway. Not sure it's ever getting out of here," Jana said.

The ramp opened just then, and the three of them looked up to see Beetle. The great insect crawled down on all its legs, and once it reached the floor of the tunnel, it spread its wings.

"I sensed urgency," said Beetle. "I have wings, and I can fly, though it is dark. I may need more light. I think I can hold you all."

"Not sure we need it," Jana said, rising upward.

"You have not been flying as long as I have, Jana Okoro," said Beetle placidly, with a few interlaced pops from its mouth.

"Good point," she said. "You do it."

And so she, Guru, and Aeriod climbed on the back of the great, mothlike creature, and it fully extended its wings, grateful for the room, and pumped them until it rose into the air. Little Prilanna watched from the ramp, then let it close, walking back inside with a great sigh.

Beetle carried its passengers, and they in turn lit the way for it with their helmets, aiming their guns, as it was still not the only creature along that conduit. Aeriod then shone a brilliant light between his palms as he sat on the creature's back, and so they sped forward.

64

RUSE

"You are not Ariel," said Galla, her voice thunderous in the great chamber. She held her stone high, and a brilliant, white-violet light sprang from it in all directions, covering Deming, Kein, and Paul. They marched behind her.

The three figures did not move from where they stood. Derry shouldered his acidavyper gun and sprayed its pellets back and forth like a fire hose. Several of them ricocheted off the floor of the place and bounced toward Galla's crew, but her light shielded them. They burrowed into the floor and hissed. Derry looked uncertain, but brought his gun forth again.

Galla advanced, furious, nauseated, and setting her stone back on her chest, she yanked off her helmet. Her hair flew out, wild, whipping, gold-copper-violet, reflecting the ferocity of her mood. She could smell everything then, the foulest rotting smell she had ever encountered, but still she stepped forward, toward Derry.

He skidded a bit where he stood, and tried firing again. Next to him, Veronica and Ariel merely watched, but Veronica began to laugh.

"The gun's not working, darling," she said in a flirty voice. "Let the pros finish the job."

Galla walked up to the dais where they stood, and abruptly, Veronica and Ariel vanished, then reappeared several yards away, and to the side of Galla's crew. But she stood in front of Derry.

"You killed the man I loved," she said, choking back tears.

Derry laughed, his metal-covered jaw moving oddly as he did so.

"Yeah, well," said the smarmy man, "you left me wounded. I was defending myself. And *he* killed himself. I didn't do that. *He* did." His possessed, diamond eyes sparkled as he tilted his head back and forth, taunting her.

Galla felt rage boil up inside her.

"No," she hissed. "You shot him. Your bullets killed him. He only tried to take you out as a last resort, but he was dead already."

She could smell Derry's sweat, old and unbathed and mixed with preserving chemicals, and all this combined with the ammonia and other rank scents made her start to shake. She reached out to seize the man, but he laughed at her.

"What're you gonna do? Kill me? You can't. They kept me alive. There's nothing you can do."

Galla heaved and vomited on his face.

He screamed and scratched at his eyes, and Galla stepped back, and watched as the man dropped his gun and fell to his knees. His exterior began to burn, as if he had himself been exposed to acid. His diamond eyes began to collapse inside his skull, and an inhuman moan rose out of him. The man fell backward, and his metallic jaw fell off, and he became aged and stared up eyeless as something drifted off of him, a black, twisting, forked mass, which flew into the great anvil shape and disappeared. Derry lay motionless and colorless, dead at last.

Galla stepped back from the dead man, sweating, and heard Kein whoop in delight. As soon as he did, Veronica swept forward, the air crackling around her, and she raised her arms. Tendrils rose from the floor and entwined Kein.

"Good, we need you," she said with a high laugh. "You're the only one here who's been in the Innervation."

Galla aimed her stone at the tendrils around Kein, but they wove too tightly too quickly, and he was completely obscured, so she feared she would injure him. He strained and tried to yell. Veronica motioned with her arms, and the tendrils dragged Kein up the dais and straight into the anvil itself. He screamed. Paul leapt forward, but then Ariel disappeared and reappeared before her older son.

"Paul," she said softly, reaching out to touch his face. But he stumbled backward and bumped into Deming. She reached for her younger son then.

"Deming," she sighed.

"It's not her!" screamed Galla, and she aimed her stone at the figure that looked like Ariel, but it vanished.

"Where'd she go?" whined Paul, and he began weeping.

"Paul! Stop!" cried Deming.

"Mama!" cried Paul.

Deming shot Galla an alarmed look.

"He's regressing!" he yelled. She ran forward and took hold of him. She pressed her stone onto his forehead.

"You're all right, you're *oakay*," she whispered. "That wasn't your mother. That wasn't my friend. It's a mirage. Paul! Wake up!"

The man trembled, and shook his head from side to side, flinging tears out as he did so. Galla ached for him. She and Deming held onto him from either side.

"Paul," she said urgently. "We have to get Kein. If they remove that stone from him, he's done for. If they get access to the Innervation, we're all doomed. Help me!"

Paul staggered where he stood, and Galla despaired. Deming squeezed her shoulder and looked into her eyes. And Ariel appeared again, right in front of them, as if floating, her dark hair drifting.

"Galla," she said, as if from a long distance, "Kein will die soon. Surrender so that he won't have to."

Galla's eyes blurred from tears.

"No," she said.

What can I do? Universe, help me!

A high yip echoed through the chamber then. Galla swung her head.

"Nalag?" she called. And she looked until she saw two eyes staring at her, from atop the anvil. The deengyne stood up there, blood dripping from its mouth of some dark, unsavory color, and its own blood caking its ribs. In its mouth, Nalag held something. It spat the object down, and that rolled to Galla's feet. It was a hand, blackened and withered.

"Aroo!" Nalag called, and it tossed its amber head.

"It wants us to follow it inside," said Paul, numbly.

"Not yet!" yelled a voice from behind them.

Galla wheeled around to see Beetle flapping in at great speed, and on its back, Aeriod, Jana, and Guru. At the same time, another form appeared, drifting down, covered in thousands of crystalline blue-grey spikes, and the being within them pierced Galla with her cold, beautiful eyes. Aeriod leapt down from Beetle and ran to Galla, placing himself between her and T'Lexxa.

"T'Lexxa, do not do this, I beg you!" cried Aeriod.

The Raexian woman lifted her head back and laughed heartily, and when she did, the chamber shook, as if an earthquake had rumbled through the space. Galla looked for Ariel's image and could not find her.

"What is going on?" she cried.

"Ah!" T'Lexxa said, walking forward slowly, deliberately, elegantly, gorgeously, as if modeling the galaxy's highest couture in the most deadly fashion possible. The spikes on her head glinted in the dim light of the chamber. "So you are the famed Galla-Deia. You're so *tiny* and *disheveled*! Really, Aeriod? Was she worth it?"

Galla flushed, and looked sternly from T'Lexxa to Aeriod, and then noticed the other woman's pointed ears. She nodded to herself. But she had no time to dwell on things, for a cry behind her startled her.

Again, Veronica had sent tendrils out, and they now wrapped around Deming and Paul, hauling them in so quickly that Galla had no time to react. Guru tried firing at Veronica, but the pulses only bounced and fizzled.

"Stop!" yelled Galla. "We can't risk hurting them."

"They'll be far worse than hurt, and so will we. We need Paul and Kein!" Aeriod hissed. "T'Lexxa, stand down."

The woman raised her arms and said, coldly, "No," and she lifted herself into the air and sped toward the anvil structure. Galla rose too, and followed. Aeriod ran forward, as did Jana and Guru. Beetle flapped in the air behind them. And in the air above him, ships burst into view, without any shield to stop them: Trozzhian, Valemog, and the great, organic shapes of Bitikk's fleet. The three parties fought, and ships splintered everywhere. It quickly became apparent that Valemog's ships were the target, and Beetle dodged flaming shrapnel.

Galla made it inside the anvil just as T'Lexxa did, and she stumbled at the sight.

Something sat at its center. At first glance, it appeared tall, as tall as T'Lexxa, and humanoid, and blackened and burning, like the core of Oshtonen itself. But Galla could turn her eyes just so and see branches coming off of the being, very like the Neuronids. To its right stood three twitching pillars, wrapped in black tendrils: Paul, Deming, and Kein. To its left stood Veronica, as gorgeous as she had ever been in her true form. In her hand, she held a knife.

Galla looked behind her, expecting to see Aeriod and T'Lexxa, but she found herself alone.

"Make a move," Veronica dared her. "I'll cut their diamethysts off, and there will be nothing to stop the collapse of their minds. Just like Ariel and Dagovaby. Time to surrender."

Galla shook her head. Her eyes were drawn back to the seated form, however. She tried to find something resembling a face inside of it. Flames flickered where eyes might be.

"What were you?" she asked in a low whisper.

"You won't let me in your mind," it pouted. "I can get in through others' but not yours. Why won't you let me in?"

"I don't because I can't," said Galla. "And why would I want to?"

It spoke slowly with little slurping noises. "So I can shoooow you, girly. Shoooow you. And make everything better." Then she heard the clicking of teeth, and then their grinding.

She shuddered. She watched the being's arcing, snapping tendrils twirl all together, a vortex of absence, no light visible in it. Images formed in the fetid air above the whirlwind.

She fell to her knees.

She did not want to see anything this beast created, whether real or otherwise. But some part of her knew at least some of the images were true. For as with all terrible things, there is always an undercurrent of reality, no matter how unimaginable.

She kept her face up, but squeezed her arms around herself where she knelt. Veronica swept quickly forward with her knife and cut off the diamethysts from the necks of the captors. Galla tried to stop her but found she could not move, mesmerized as she was by the flame-eyes of Paosh Tohon.

She watched as Veronica flayed Deming's skin bit by bit, and his screams burrowed into her brain. Ariel appeared beside her, and her neck twisted around. Paul's limbs were torn off and flung aside. Kein's eyes were gouged with diamonds.

And it went further. It knew.

The moment of Rob's death, looping over and over and over until she forgot to breathe.

Choking, she watched as metal rained down on Rikiloi, and its skies were set ablaze, and Aeriod's asteroid castle was sent crashing into the homes of Indry-Kol below.

Cuz and Meeya, held over a pit of molten rock, and released.

Dek and Gindoo, caught in a fire in the study, all its bottles smashing and alighting, sending their shards into the two.

And then, Oni-Odi, his metal face torn off, his wetware yanked out, his cobalt eyes oozing down his front.

Galla stood and held her diamethyst high.

"Liar!" she screamed. Bolts of violet plasma arced from the stone, and from her as well, from her very eyes, and she rose to face the dark whirlwind.

"Step aside, Galla-Deia!" a woman's voice cried, and Galla, staggered completely, looked up to see T'Lexxa standing beside her. "You've been tricked by a powerful mage. Take your family and go before it's too late! He's opening the Innervation!"

65

RUINATION

Galla felt hands reaching under her armpits, lifting her up, and confused, she looked into the silver eyes of Aeriod.

"Come with me!" he shouted. "Nalag found something. Let's take everyone and go!"

T'Lexxa faced Paosh Tohon. Galla glanced back as Aeriod pulled her away. The Raexian woman's spikes blazed with light, scattering the forked branches the evil being sent even now.

"Hello, dear brother," she said, and she screamed as the shape rose to meet her, and a great energy blast shook the room.

Galla blinked, and saw that Kein, Deming, and Paul were still sheathed inside their tendrils, alive. She seized her diamethyst and sliced through those tendrils, and they hissed away. Aeriod grabbed hold of Kein and Paul.

"Come!" he yelled to Galla and Deming. "Get out of there!"

Yet even as they began to leave, a brilliant fissure erupted in the air between them and Paosh Tohon.

"No!" cried Kein. "I'm sorry! I'm sorry! I tried to stop it. It used me!"

"The Innervation!" Aeriod hissed. "Listen to me," he said to Paul and Kein. "Focus on your stones. And focus on Mandira. You can do this; your ancestors did. Now it's your turn. No, pay attention: focus on your stones. Hold them out."

Aeriod held his hands over the men's crystals, and they began to glow.

"Can you picture the station?"

"Yes," said Paul.

"Yep," said Kein.

"Now move it," Aeriod said. "Move it *here!*"

"Oh holy shit!" yelled Coniuratus. "Fall back! Fall back!" he screamed to his fleet, and he swerved his ship out of the way as a tremendous shape burst forth inside Oshtonen. "My God!" he cried. "It's Mandira!"

The station pummeled straight into the core, with the netted tip of Top Deck plunging forward into the black and red flaming sphere. The top section of the station shattered within, sending a sluice of water in all directions inside the innermost chamber, and the net with the tiny diamethysts waved about and attached to the ceiling, which shrieked as if alive. The Neuronids spilled forth upon the waves and lit the chamber with their glowing forms, but they all aimed with purpose at the anvil, which sent off great arcs of light from the battle within it.

Paul and Kein slid to the floor, exhausted. But Aeriod and Deming quickly picked them up.

Galla cried, "The Neuronids! You did it!"

Then something nudged her leg. She looked down to see Nalag, and knelt to touch her forehead to the beast. "I thought we'd lost you, friend." The beast readied a paw and pointed, and Galla could see three bubble-like spheres off in the shadows of the room behind

Paosh Tohon's throne. Then Nalag jumped, and found water coursing around its legs. It whined. Galla looked up quickly.

"Aeriod!" she cried. "Water!"

"We've got bigger problems," said Aeriod urgently. "I'm going back out there, to try and seal off the Innervation."

And he raced away, splashing through the water that Mandira had housed and spilled upon its crash. Nalag yelped and ran over to the spheres, which began to bob in the water. Galla motioned for Deming to follow, and Deming helped his brother and Kein to join them.

OUTSIDE THE ANVIL, Guru and Jana spluttered and swam and tried to stay afloat, in awe of the scene before them. A great company of Neuronids had surrounded the anvil, but the water had become a problem.

"What do we do?" cried Jana, and Guru had no answer, for this was not a situation that a pipe could help. She tried flying upward, but her suit, damaged from a tear, was waterlogged, and it held her down. She cried out, desperate, and tried floating on her back in the choppy water. Sinister creatures of all sorts swam around her, snapping and snaking, and some lunged for her. But then everything went silent, and she found herself inside a bubble.

One of the Neuronids shone a light into the bubble.

Thank you, Jana Okoro. We will take it from here.

She flailed about, but found herself quite secure, and she pressed her hands against the inside of the bubble. It bumped against another one, and she could see Guru grinning at her.

THE SPHERES behind Paosh Tohon's chamber were covered with a thick layer of slime. One of them was ruptured. Galla scraped the slime off of it and stared at the contents. The contents stared back up at her, with diamond eyes. She jumped back. It was a blackened husk of a thing, small, wrinkled, covered in white, matted hair, and it was missing a hand. She looked down at Nalag.

"You did this?" she asked. The deengyne jumped in the water and yipped in agreement.

"Who is this?" she wondered, but she could see a flickering shape begin to form above the thing. The visage of Veronica, beautiful and pure, shimmered there.

"It's going to be over for you soon enough," she said. "The Innervation will be open for us. I won't need this body anymore. I can become one with the Innervation and stretch my mind across galaxies."

Galla picked up her stone and held it over the blackened creature inside the sphere.

"No," a soft voice said. The image of Ariel hovered over another sphere. "Galla, it's not your fight. It's mine. Keep her alive. I'll handle her. Save my children, and save yours."

"Ariel!" Galla cried, and she rushed forward and split open the sphere under the apparition, which disappeared. Inside she found a human, curled up, smelling of preserving liquid, with long, grey hair, and for a moment, Galla thought it looked like Meredith, curled up asleep. Paul rushed over, followed by Deming, and they stood over this figure.

"Mama!" cried Paul, and he and Deming reached down in and touched the person. It stirred, and trembled, and opened its eyes, and they were green, as green as they had always been.

A tremendous blast shook the room, throwing everyone onto their backsides.

"What's going on out there?" Kein wondered.

Galla ignored him, and went for the third sphere, and cut it open. Inside, a man with brown skin and white, long, twisted hair lay curled up, as if asleep. Something sparkling shone in his forehead. Galla reached in and seized it, and pulled out a long, diamond-like needle, the one Derry had pushed inside his skull years ago.

"It's Dagovaby," she breathed. "We need to get them out of here, and back to the *Seltra*. Can you do that?" she asked Kein, Deming, and Paul, who nodded their agreement. "Good. I'm going to help Aeriod."

"Galla," Deming began, but he knew she had to go.

"Please," she begged. "Get them to the ship, get them to Prilanna. I fear they won't survive much longer. They've been kept alive and tortured for decades. Help them!"

"We've got them," said Kein. "What about Veronica?"

"Take her too," said Galla.

"No way," said Paul.

"Paul, it's your mother's request. I don't know what we can do for her, but we have to try." And Galla crossed her arms. Paul shook his head. He and Kein and Deming began pushing the three spheres out along the water sloshing in the room.

Galla ran forth and kissed Deming.

"You'd better come back to me," he whispered to her.

"Always," said Galla, and she turned to face the battle.

66

FOR LOVE

When she entered the chamber, she did not understand what was happening. Bolts of silver and of black, forked lightning flashed and streaked, and then a surge of brilliant, phosphorescent light shone, as bright shapes burst into the room, and water churned and hissed. The Neuronids leapt forth toward Paosh Tohon, but T'Lexxa stood between them, and Aeriod tried to defend the rupture of the Innervation.

"Can you seal it?" Galla yelled to him.

"I don't know!" he cried.

"Is she fighting him or helping him?" she called back, as the brilliant battle continued, tentacles whipping in every direction.

"I don't know that either!" he yelled.

Galla winced and adjusted the strap on her back, as her sheathed crystal weapon dug into her. Her fingers twitched to bring out the blade she had made, but she did not know how she could help, or who to stop first. The Neuronids had clustered all around Paosh Tohon, who rose in more of its tentacled form, while T'Lexxa dove at its humanoid side.

"I'm going to try and seal it with myself," Aeriod called suddenly.

"What?" cried Galla.

T'Lexxa hesitated, hearing Aeriod, and the mass of shapes around her swiveled. Paosh Tohon reached out with tendrils toward the rift, but the Neuronids fought back. Aeriod marched up to the scintillating rift and plunged himself into it. Seconds later, it threw him back out, onto his back, into the water that roiled all around the chamber.

"Ah," he said. "It's not letting me in!"

"How do we close it?" screamed Galla. "That thing's going to get in!"

Deming brushed up beside her.

"Galla," he said, and he looked deep into her copper eyes and held her face in his hands. "I'm going in. I love you."

Galla went ice cold, and before she could stop him, Deming advanced on the sparkling rift and entered it. It closed with a bright flash, leaving only a swirling, jagged, rainbow-hued circle in the air.

She screamed and ran at it, but it threw her back.

"No! No! NO!"

A horrific roar erupted behind her, and Aeriod seized her, as Paosh Tohon threw off its attackers and lunged at the circle. The Neuronids snapped at its heels and its tentacles, wrapping themselves around it.

T'Lexxa, panting, her spikes bent or snapped in the fray, pulled Galla away from Aeriod before he could stop her.

"Do you love him?" she asked, her eyes like grey marbles, shining, staring down into Galla's eyes.

Galla looked up through tears and said, "Of course."

T'Lexxa smirked at Aeriod. "Then that is more love than he has ever received in all the time I've known him. Take care of each other. Now, I will do what I can. Brother!" she called. "It's time we ended this." She turned again to Galla. "Help me," she whispered. "I'll do what I can, but in the end, it must be you." She looked back at Aeriod, and for a moment, regret flickered in her pointed face.

She leapt forward, and with her fingernails, dug into the eyes of what was once her brother, and it did the same with her. And they shrieked and spun, the Neuronids trailing around them in a watery cyclone.

Galla took out her sword, blinded by grief and rage. She ran toward the mass, with Aeriod yelling in protest, but he was thrown away from them all by another blast.

She rose and focused all her energy, and her hope and her dreams and her love toward everyone she had ever known, and pulled herself into the air, above the snapping coils of battle beneath her. And then she turned her body, and she dove straight down into that mass.

Paosh Tohon bit at her, it gnawed at the edge of her sanity, it crunched on her body with many-faceted teeth. She felt something burning; it had thrown acid onto her, and her flesh seared and boiled. Still she swam deeper into the storm of hate and fear. She stabbed and thrust with her sword in one hand and waved her stone with the other, weeping and screaming in agony.

"Gonna eat you up, girly!" its smooth, wicked voice said in her ears.

Help me, she thought desperately, for the jaws of the monster thrashed her, its poison burned her, its voice sickened her.

Focus.

A voice said it so quietly, she at first did not hear.

Focus, Galla. Focus!

It was clearer now, and she turned her head to look for it. She could see something, a shape forming beside her, from the light of the Innervation's closed window.

Put your thoughts aside. Focus. Focus on me.

"Who are you?" she yelled.

The swirling nightmare surrounding her bayed back, "I am your end!" and it squeezed her on all sides so that she could not take a breath, and she felt as though it would smash her into bits.

Put your thoughts aside and focus.

And she could just see a pale image growing in the darkness. A man! Was it Kein?

It wasn't Kein. She squinted, in her abject state, and looked more closely.

"Forster!" she screamed.

And there he was, fully visible. She threw her arms upward, and he grabbed them, and he pulled.

"But you...you're...you're..." Galla stammered, gasping, feeling his touch.

"I'm here. That's all you need," said Forster. "Use me to amplify your stone, and yourself. Kill it!"

Galla felt him pull her out of Paosh Tohon's grasp. It bellowed and shrieked in rage. She embraced Forster, and he held her tight.

"Focus!" he said in her ear.

She stared into the grey-black-brown storm as it nipped at her and chewed on her legs. She heard T'Lexxa's agonized wails as it burrowed into her as well. The Neuronids sparked and twitched, and she knew they must be dying as well. But Forster's arms felt strong and warm. She focused on him, and then she focused her mind, and so did he.

All around her, bright sparks of violet and magenta swept and swirled, shining into the darkness. She and Forster screamed in unison. She felt as though her mind were spilling out, piece by piece. Her tears were crystalline and they flung off of her and into the hellscape. And where each tear fled, a great moan erupted, so loud it blasted their ears.

"Now!" Forster yelled.

Galla held up her diamethyst sword, and Forster raised his eyes to it, and then he locked eyes with her. "End it," he said.

She shrieked at the swirling madness, her own stone's vibrant light spinning into it as well.

She screamed, "You mean nothing, you stand for nothing!"

And she felt herself awaken, as if for the first time, her geode opening, the kind eyes of Oni-Odi greeting her, lifting her up, sweeping the crystals off her body, carrying her to warmth and safety. A memory. A memory of love. And all her loves swam in her vision:

her friends, her family, Deming. She took in a great, shuddering breath, and exhaled.

Then she breathed again, as Loreena had taught her. And she remembered Forster's words.

"I put my thoughts aside. I take your power away!" she shouted.

And a blast of violet lancets burst from her stone, shards with points as tiny as atoms. She seized her crystal, fused it to the end of her sword, and plunged it into the beast.

She fell, and she looked up to see the dark maelstrom above inundated with bright purple light as the remnants of her stone enveloped it. A blinding flash erupted all around her, and she felt herself slam into the ground.

67

BEQUEATHED

Paul began shaking, and Kein reached over to calm him.

"What is it? What's happened?" said the older man kindly.

"I can't sense him," said Paul, trembling violently now. Prilanna moved from her patients over to Paul.

"Who?" she asked softly.

"Deming," he said, and he covered his face with his hands.

Prilanna gasped.

"Oh no," she said.

The *Seltra* spoke: "Jana and Guru approach. I will be opening the ship to let them in."

The ramp opened, and a clattering sound startled Prilanna. She ran into the hall and found Nalag bounding toward her. The beast leapt up, nearly knocking the girl down, and licked her face.

"Nalag!" she cried. "Come, dear friend, let's get you cleaned up and patched up." She looked up to see Jana and Guru, exhausted, their outfits gashed. They chucked their helmets off and let them fall.

"You would not believe the shit we just saw," said Jana, and with a groan, she rubbed her back. The iridescent patterns in her skin glowed in the shadows.

"Where's Galla? Deming? Aeriod?" asked Guru. He drew in a breath at the sight of Paul, hunched over the form of a woman in the medical bay.

"Is that—is that Ariel?" he asked. He stepped in carefully, but then withdrew.

Prilanna stood with feet apart and hands on her hips, staring up at him.

"Do you have a medical problem?" she demanded.

"I—what?" Guru answered. "No, I—I just—I knew her."

Prilanna pointed down the hall.

Guru nodded. "I can take a hint. Let me know what happens."

Prilanna stepped into the hall then, and the door shut behind her. She approached Guru.

"What's happening is she's dying," the girl said to him. "The man, Dagovaby, is barely clinging to life. And Deming has disappeared."

Guru rubbed his face with his hands and closed his eyes. He bowed his head.

"Let me know if I can help," he said, and he lurched toward the cockpit, deeply saddened.

Prilanna turned back to her charges. She was startled to see Ariel blinking on the bed. Most pale, she was very weak. Prilanna dashed over and administered water. The woman's muscles were so atrophied, she could barely sit up, even with the assistance of Paul. A haunted expression in her bright green eyes disturbed Prilanna.

"Where is Deming?" Ariel asked, and Paul looked at her solemnly. She could only shake, for she was too dehydrated to shed tears. She looked over at Dagovaby, who lay still, but quiet.

She said then, "I left something inside you both. I didn't know if it would ever help. Or if you would ever really need it. Just know it's there. And when I'm gone, it'll always be there. I love you so much."

Paul held his mother gently. She was frail and aged now, and had endured too much for too many years, enslaved by Paosh Tohon.

"Galla is carrying his child?" she asked, holding Paul's hand.

"Yes," he answered her.

She managed a smile. "Good. She always deserved a good person.

I just wish…they could've had longer. He's beyond my reach now. You be a good uncle to my grandbaby, Paul." She sighed and fell into a doze.

"ARIEL," his voice rang in her mind.

I know that voice. I've argued with that voice.

"Forster," she said back.

"I'm going to reach out to you. Hold onto Dagovaby, and I will hold onto you."

"Where are you taking us?"

I am afraid.

"Out of the darkness, just like when I woke you from that pod. Where you belong. No need to be afraid. Just *focus*."

"I can't see you," she said. She could only see Dagovaby, bent and broken next to her.

But she felt him: she felt his hands on her face, just as she had when he had saved her long ago. So she reached for those invisible hands, and they took her hand, and they pulled.

The branching whiteness grew even brighter, and radiated in front of her, and she could almost make out the shape of a man. Dagovaby grew alert and clear, and she felt warmth from him, and love, and hope.

I forgot what that felt like! But no, Forster. Leave him behind. Paul has no one now. He needs family.

"He's not alone," Forster reassured her. "But I will leave Dagovaby if you wish."

And through the radiance Forster pulled her, and by and by she could see more of him, his wry face and his eyes, no longer haunted, but resolute. She hesitated.

"Will they be okay? Do you know?"

Forster turned and smiled at her. "I never knew everything, and I never will. But I think they have a good start. Leave your regret behind, so you can go ahead."

I hope I see them again.

"Forster, I have to look for her, you understand that, right? It's my fault she turned. I abandoned her. I'll look for her forever."

"If you do, I'm not sure I can bring you back."

"I understand."

And he pulled her through a brilliant, rainbow-hued light.

68

HIRAETH

Galla knew nothing, only stillness, as she lay on the steps of the broken dais in the chamber of Oshtonen. Seconds seemed to her years. She did not know if she slept or dreamed. But by and by, a familiar face appeared.

"You again!" she said softly, and she rose from where she lay. She looked down at her body, and found herself dry and clean. She walked toward the face, which swam in the strange, spinning, iridescent portal that Deming had entered beyond her reach. The hazel-eyed man who stood there, looking so very like her friend Kein, shifted into and out of view, as if she were trying to focus on him.

"The first time I saw you, you were a hologram on Aeriod's ship," Forster said fondly. "I thought you looked human, but Aeriod said you weren't. That's when I knew things were even stranger out in the galaxy. But truly, they're stranger within."

Galla watched Forster's image flicker in and out and wished desperately he were solid. But she said, "And now I'm looking at a hologram of you, essentially."

Forster smiled, and she could see the crinkling of his hazel eyes, so like his descendant's. It was a wonder to her that Forster could retain so much of himself in this strange place.

Still, he held out his hands, and she held hers toward them. They were separated forever, in many ways, but no one else could be together in the way they were just then, either. Their hands met.

Galla shivered as an electrical sensation pulsed through her, and Forster did for a moment feel solid. So their fingers interlinked, and they smiled at each other. Iridescent chevrons of light arced around them, very like the aura Forster experienced in his migraines. Galla could only wonder at the sight, and Forster meanwhile watched Galla's diamethyst pulse in response.

"If it weren't for you, I could not be here," Forster said to her.

"Is that good or bad?" Galla asked, a bit worried about his answer.

"I am..." and Forster paused, thinking. *Thinking Man*, Guru had called him. Some things never changed. "I am," he continued, "able to continue here. I'm able to help, because of that. I can't do some of the things I could in normal life. But my possibilities are greater. It's hard to explain. But...yes, I would say it's good. Because of you, I can do more good."

Galla bowed her head. "Can you save him?"

"Deming?" Forster asked gently. Galla nodded.

"Truthfully, I do not know. I don't see how any living human could withstand the Innervation for any period of time. Sealing it shut, and keeping it that way? But he's not fully human, of course. He's the only true connection between this and the rest of existence. I don't know that I could save him. I don't know that he would want me to, if I could. He's persisting of his own free will, and he seems rather stubborn. Just like his mother."

Forster grinned to himself, as if remembering.

"Can you save *her*?" Galla asked, watching his face.

Forster's smile faded.

"I don't know what might be left to save," he said, "but I'm trying. I'm trying, and I won't stop trying. I know my fate, then," Forster said, and a look of relief and calm passed over his expression and settled there.

It suits him, Galla thought.

"I will always be looking for Ariel," he said. "And she will always be looking for Veronica. Maybe we find each other, one day. Maybe we don't. But it never stops."

He looked at peace, and determined.

Galla took a deep breath and slowly exhaled.

"When I leave this place, will I ever see you again?"

Forster looked at Galla affectionately. Once, he might have been intimidated by someone so ethereal and powerful, but he could see she was a loving person, and in many ways girl-like and still youthful. There was an innocence to her that he recognized as once having had in himself, long ago.

"I held a part of you against my heart as a living man," Forster said slowly. "I would have loved to have experienced that life as your friend. But I'm your friend now. And I don't know how all of this"— and he held his arms out and gave a shrug—"works, makes sense, or any of it. I learn constantly. And time doesn't seem to matter much here. So, who knows? Maybe we'll meet again."

"But Dagovaby," sighed Galla sadly.

Forster looked at her fondly. "Dagovaby has a family. He didn't for a long time. And like my own wife, Auna, he will learn to live without her, the person he loves the most. And in so doing, he will help his children, and their children, to remember Ariel, and to grow. They'll want their own lives now."

"His family is my family now, too," Galla murmured, brushing her hands across her growing belly. "And so is humanity."

He looked pointedly at her abdomen. "We might see each other again. I think it might be some time from now, though," he mused, "because you'll be busy for a while. But you are the person to do it. Protector, keeper, mother. They need you, and now you need them. We may be messy, but the effort to make even one of us better? It's worth that. Keep going forward.

"One more thing," Forster said, and in his face she could see that of her dear friend Kein. "Tell my own family, should you see them: tell them to be open, tell them to listen. If they see a light, a beacon in the dark when they need it most: tell them to follow it. Will you do that for me?"

"I will," said Galla, smiling through tears.

His image distorted a bit then, and he said quickly, "I can feel the pull back. I have to let you go."

Galla felt her eyes sting. She was not ready to release him, and he was not ready to recede from her. But Forster and Galla leaned forward, and touched their foreheads, as if giving each other a benediction. And Forster dissipated in little sparks and rays.

Galla was flung back and out. She caught herself for a blunt landing. She stood, smoothed her clothes, and looked at her hands, which had held Forster's just moments before. Or years? It felt like an epoch, and yet so very fleeting to her.

Aeriod found her, raving a bit, talking to someone who was not there. She let him lift her up, and he carried her in his arms. So he took her out of Oshtonen, thinking of many things, her spirits wavering between uplifted, downcast, and hopeful.

"I won't let your sacrifice be in vain, Forster," she murmured softly, against the folds of Aeriod's cape. She felt a deep sense of longing, but of purpose also. "And I certainly won't let Deming's either. So I'll work, and I'll hope, and I'll make all of you proud, and Meredith, and Oni-Odi too, wherever his spirit lives. I have work to do."

69

———

BEARING AWAY

Prince Hazkinaut, Coniuratus, and the telepaths and Representatives that made up the Questri gathered in the copper city of Trozzhia, where it floated above Quopeia, now tranquil and devoid of invaders. Valemog had fled as best it could, crawling back into the dark corners of the galaxy where vice and deception still ruled. It was an unspoken agreement that the Questri's work had only begun, for though wounded, the deranged former sycophants of Paosh Tohon held much malice in their souls still.

Galla spoke to them all from her tower and congratulated them on their victories. For Bitikk, who were not invited, she had delivered a message: cooperate and shut down their "training" or they would answer for their crimes with banishment from governance. And as for that governance, she leaned into Aeriod, who although greatly fatigued from guarding multiple worlds with his powers still remained the highest authority in the galaxy. With Ezeldae a husk of what it once was, Aeriod did not want to set up a new seat of government there. Nor did he wish for it to be on Rikiloi.

"It really ought to be you, you know," he told her.

"No," she answered. "If you don't want the job, ask Hazkinaut, or Coniuratus. The Prince says he will soon give up his title, and convert his world to democracy. Coniuratus is a free agent, but he is a cool and collected person. As for the Summoners, well, you know what I think of them."

Aeriod roared with laughter at that.

"Just...keep searching, Aeriod, for a way to bring him back," said Galla. She thought ever of her husband, Deming. And the mage knew it.

"I might know of some possibilities," he said. "Either way, when it is time," and he glanced at her growing abdomen, "I will take you to be near him."

"You'd better," Galla said, chin high, hair whipping about. "You do have the fastest ships, after all."

"WHAT WILL YOU DO?" she asked Dagovaby, over the table in Gindoo's boardinghouse. The man looked affectionately at the old wizard, who leaned on his cane and watched him intently. Galla nibbled on a slice of pie Dek had made. He sat to her left, happy to have her back, though he knew she would not be as frequent a visitor now.

"I'll be around as I can," said Dagovaby, the gold rings around his pupils gleaming. Paul sat next to him and pressed a hand on his shoulder. "But I've always been a wanderer. It's nice to have an anchor to come back to, though. I want to be part of Paul's life, and your and Deming's child's as well. Ariel would want that. I wish she could be here. I'll wish that forever. She gave me a family."

"She gave *us* a family," Galla said gently. She reached across, her diamethyst swinging above her chest, and touched the side of Dagovaby's face. His expression relaxed.

"Thank you for him," he said to her, nodding at her growing form. "I can't wait to meet him."

Galla started. "How do you know it's a boy?"

Dagovaby laughed. "My mother would have said it's the way you're carrying him. One of those silly, human legends."

"Hmm," said Galla doubtfully, but she looked down, and began to wonder what she should name the child.

.   .   .

SHE LEANED her head against the window and gazed at the blue-green-brown-white world the humans called Earth. She cradled her belly and said softly, "This is where your ancestors lived, long ago. Some of them, anyway. I wish your dad could be here to see it. Maybe one day."

And she kept thinking in terms of "one day," a day when Deming could be free, maybe.

Oh, Universe. Why do I look like them? Why did you choose this form for me? But if you hadn't, I would not be here now. And I would not have met Deming, maybe. I don't know how long he'll last. And I don't know how long I will last either. I suppose that's very human of us, after all.

"The Earth admiral is ready, Commander Deia. He reports directly to the President," said the voice on the comms.

I am ready too. For whatever comes. I'll keep them all close, as long as they need me. And when they don't anymore, I'll let go.

After a long and tense debate, Galla sat uncomfortably, and wished she were anywhere but there.

"Commander Deia," the admiral whined, "you have to understand: we don't know *any* of you. You could be from anywhere! We appreciate the gesture, with your expecting a child and all, but that alone won't gain much influence."

GALLA FELT rage boil up inside her. The admiral and the others at the table watched her hair twist around her like a living thing.

My husband is stranded in the Innervation, and I am here without him, in the home of his ancestors. And this is how they greet us.

"I'm not using my child as a prop!" she declared. "And I suggest you take a closer look at your defenses, Admiral."

"What do you mean?" he asked, sternly.

Galla nodded to Jana, who stepped forward with her hand outstretched. A silver diamond on her hand projected an image above the table.

"You may recognize," Galla said casually, gesturing to the image, "each of your bases throughout the solar system."

The images progressed rapidly through every single outpost and base from near the sun to the outer reaches of the heliopause. The table of people squinted up at them, and a few faces went pale.

"Yes, we know about the secret ones as well, buried in the asteroids, Admiral," she said with a wry smile as he gasped at one of the images. "We know about *all of them.*"

She folded her arms. "Now take a look at them."

The images reversed, or seemed to, for each base was shown yet again. And above it or near it, a fiery-copper ship shone hovering at every single one.

"What is this!" cried the admiral, standing up. "An invasion?"

Galla smiled. "It's your protection," she answered. "You can thank me later. Now that I have your full attention, let's move on to intelligence."

Later, Jana asked wearily, "Do you think they bought it?"

"I hope so. It was real," said Galla, with a wink.

"What!" exclaimed Jana. "You said they were holograms!"

"I'm sorry, Jana," Galla said, bowing her head. "It's the first time I've ever lied to you. I didn't want to take the chance that one of them was a telepath, and knew the whole thing was a ruse."

Jana tilted her head at Galla, then burst out laughing. "You're pretty good at this human stuff, you know?"

Galla beamed. "That's high praise!" And they slapped their hands together in a tight grip.

"I hope you can stick around," said Galla warmly.

"I just have some things to do," said Jana, and she looked pointedly at Galla's little bulge. "It's all about family. I want to visit those who are still here. It's been a long, long time. I want to introduce Misun to whoever is left."

Galla felt her eyes sting. "I understand. You've been so amazing. I'll miss you while you're gone."

"Same here," said Jana, and they hugged each other. "Goodbye for now, Commander. I can't wait to meet that baby one day!"

. . .

"CAN'T YOU GO ANY FASTER!" Galla shouted. She gasped and held her taut, swollen belly as contractions rollicked through her. Prilanna sang soothing words to her over and over, but kept darting her large eyes to Aeriod in panic.

"No!" barked Aeriod, his nerves worked to near insanity. He bent all his will and power, and at last made the final junction. They shot out of it, and there they beheld the remnants of Oshtonen, now cleared of all debris, and the former core now a solid, silver sphere. Aeriod gasped with relief. He flew his ship right through the core and found the old chamber, which the Summoners had taken on to clean, repair, and restore into a temple of sorts.

The ship hissed and crackled as it settled. The ramp opened, and Aeriod scooped Galla in his arms, with Prilanna in tow, laden with a backpack. They ran as fast yet as gently as they could. Aeriod hovered in front of the Innervation portal.

"Deming," he called into it. "It is time."

And there he beheld Deming, motionless, his eyes closed. But as soon as they approached the dais, his eyes shot open, looking straight ahead with brilliant gold rings.

"Aeriod," gasped Galla, and he set her down carefully in front of Deming.

"I have to be quick, Galla," said Aeriod crisply.

She clasped his cheeks. "Thank you. If it's too much—"

"It won't be." And Aeriod looked at her as she bent over again in pain, and he put his hands on her belly. She relaxed a bit and looked at him, relieved and grateful.

He quickly set forth detaching Deming from the portal, pulling him through as sparks burst all around them both, and the man fell in a heap onto the ground. "Deming!" cried Galla in a strained voice.

But Deming was determined. Aeriod quickly gave him a small vial.

"Drink, now," he ordered, and then he tossed off his cape and hurried into the portal himself.

Deming, weak and haggard and pale, stumbled over to Galla where she now lay on the floor on one side. They looked up to see Aeriod snatched into the swirling portal, and he let out a long, deep groan, and shook as if throttled by a great hand. And then his silver eyes went flat grey, and then they closed, and his head hung limp, as if he were trapped behind a mirror.

Oh Aeriod, Galla managed to think.

"Will he be all right?" Deming managed to say, but Galla could not answer. He swiveled to her, and Prilanna said, "Move her over here!"

Prilanna and Deming moved Galla to a lower area, and she panted. A ripple of shapes moved all around them, and in her pain she could only guess they were Summoners.

One of them said, "We did not foresee this."

Galla managed a rage-laugh.

"No shit!" she cried, and then winced in agony.

Prilanna stood, small but with a formidable look on her face, and faced them all.

"Get over here and help her, or go away!" she shrieked.

A few of them did approach, one bearing blankets, and another laden with things Galla could not make out. The pain was too much, and though she could take pain from others, she could not take it from herself. Deming, weakened from his months in the Innervation, fought through his own fatigue and the emotions of Galla, and let her grip his hands.

One Summoner moved forth and knelt behind Galla's head. Another approached, and positioned her, and she could only cope by watching the pulse in Deming's neck. Everything moved out of focus for her except for that jumping pulse.

Prilanna cried out, "Breathe, Galla! I see the baby's head. Breathe and *push*!"

It seemed to her hours, but within minutes, Galla felt the extraordinary pain suddenly wash away in a flood of release. She lay with her eyes closed, gasping.

"Galla, open your eyes!" said Deming, and she did: and there he was, a tiny, squalling baby, who Prilanna deftly separated from his umbilical cord. She handed him to Deming, who then laid him at Galla's breast. The warm little fellow looked up at her with dark eyes, like Deming's, and fine, tiny, pointed ears, like Aeriod's, and she smiled at him, and then he quickly latched onto her to nurse. She lay surrounded by her four helpers, and kissed Deming and stroked their little one's head.

"My sweet little Linden Forster Ambrono," Galla said, proud yet exhausted, flushed from emotion and her body's endorphins. "Welcome to the Universe."

THE END

EPILOGUE

Prilanna Optison set aside her class lessons and brought forth her special notebook, given her by Deming. Her little cadre of students gathered around. She opened up the view of the twilit sky for them to see.

"If you watch closely, you might see them," Prilanna said, pointing to the stars above. "Every year, Aeriod takes Galla and her family to see Deming, and Aeriod takes his place in the Innervation portal so Deming can be with them. There are two sons and a daughter, and they are growing fast, though more slowly than full humans. The eldest is Linden Forster, the younger son is Robert Kein, and the daughter is Mariel Brant, named for her grandmother and great-grandmother. She has her grandmother's dark hair and green eyes. Galla calls her 'Little Goose,' though nobody around here remembers what that means."

"And they are only with their father for a month each year?" one of the children asked.

"If they are lucky," she went on. "Sometimes it is only for days. Sometimes it is too much for Aeriod to take his place, for he is very old, after all. When they return with him to Rikiloi, he teaches the children while Galla works from Trozzhia for the humans of the solar system. Linden says he wants to take his father's place when he grows up. Galla gets very upset about that, but then again, she is known for her temper!"

"Don't they miss their father?"

"They do, but he loves them so, and when he sees them, he tells them wonderful things: all about the galaxy's hearts and minds, all about his ancestors. He senses them all. And their mother, she works to protect the humans, whom she represents. Go watch the night sky, and you might see Galla, a streak among the stars, going to her love Deming, every year. They hold the galaxy together. The Questri protect us, always."

"And what happened to Paul, and Kein, and Jana and Gindoo, and Coniuratus? And Beetle—tell me about Beetle!"

"As Aeriod would say, that is a tale for another time. Off to bed!"

Prilanna's assistant came to take the children to their sleeping quarters. As soon as they had left, she turned back to her notebook and wrote:

"Some say the Questrison Era began with the birth of Galla-Deia. Some say it began when Linden Deming Forster and Ariel Brant moved Mandira Research Station across the galaxy, with the help of Aeriod. But of course, they could not have done this without Galla's stone. Still others say it began when the Seltrason Era ended: but that is not true. When the Seltra left our galaxy, there was a long wilderness.

"What matters is that the Questri, made of the Representatives of spacefaring races and those who aided them, came together to heal the galaxy and fight its greatest threat, Paosh Tohon. Since Deming was a descendent of the Innervation from his father Dagovaby's parentage, he was the only person who could keep the galactic rift intact, with Forster's assistance through the Innervation.

"Only one member of the Representatives could reproduce, and that was Galla-Deia. She bore only three children, all with her husband, Deming Ambrono. A note on their parentage: Galla's unique physiology meant that she retained part of her partners' genetic material. As such, her children were chimera of separate fathers, respectively, with all still sharing Galla and Deming's genes: a son by Aeriod, a son by Rob Idin, and a daughter with only Deming as the father.

"I say these children are the true beginning of the Questrison Era. We do not know what abilities they may reveal, but I think it is likely they will draw upon their families' legacies: Meredith, Ariel, Dagovaby, Aeriod, Rob, Galla, and Deming. The galaxy is in good hands."

PRONUNCIATION GUIDE

Aeriod (AIR-ee-od)
ailfern (ail-fern)
Allurulla (a-LURE-a-la)
Auna (AWN-a)
Birannon (beer-AN-on)
Bitikk (bit-ik)
bulbenberries (BUL-ben berries)
Caxxius Caxx (CAX-ee-us CAX)
Cogniz (COG-niz)
Coniuratus (con-yur-AH-tus)
Dagovaby Ambrono (da-GOV-a-bee am-BRO-no)
deengyne (deen-gyn)
Demetraan (DEM-eh-tron)
Deorn (DAY-orn)
diamethyst (di-amethyst)
Eindynn (AY-in-den)
Ezeldae (ez-el-DIE)
Fael'Kar (fail car)
Fithich (fith-itch)
Fyaldant (fie-al-DAHNT)

Galla-Deia (GAL-a DAY-a)
geelybans (GEE-lee-bans)
Gindoo (gen-DOO)
Hazkinaut (HAZ-ken-ot)
Huntren (HUN-trun)
Ika Nui (IK-a NOO-ee)
Ildion (IL-dee-on)
Indry-Kol (in-dree coal)
Kayalhaas (ky-al-has)
Kein (cane, rhymes with skein)
Mandira (man-DEER-a)
Mehelkian (me-HEL-kee-an)
MindSynd (mind send)
Nalag (NAL-ag)
Neuronids (nyu-ON-ids)
Oni-Odi (oh-nee oh-dee)
Orboaanya (or-bo-AHN-ya)
Oshtonen (osh-TONE-en)
Paosh Tohon (pay-OSH to-HON)
phyron (FY-ron)
Pliip (plip)
Prilanna Optison (pree-LON-a OP-ti-son)
Quepahi (qwe-PA-hee)
Questri (QUEST-ree)
Quopeia (quo-PAY-a)
Rez (rez)
Rikiloi (RIK-i-loy)
Rynaati (ry-NOT-ee)
Seltra (SEL-tra)
Silderay (SIL-de-ray)
Siloxxa (sy-LOX-a)
Stroffy (stroff-ee)
Sumond (soo-MOND)
sylcaah (SEEL-ka)
Talonii (ta-LONE-ee)

Tananaat (TAN-an-ot)
Tartiph (tar-tiff)
Tauliope (TOW-lee-oap)
T'Lexxa (ta-LEX-a)
Trozzhia (TROZH-a)
Ushalda (oo-SHAL-da)
Valemog (vale-mog)
wakeroamer (wake-roamer)
Whoenaat (WOE-not)
Yaddifor (YAD-i-for)

ABOUT THE AUTHOR

Dianne dreamed up other worlds and their characters as a child in the 1980s. She formed her own neighborhood astronomy club before age ten, to educate her friends about the Universe. In addition to writing stories, she drew and painted her characters, gave them outrageous space fashions, and created travel guides and glossaries for the worlds she invented. As an adult, Dianne earned a Bachelor of Science in Ecology and Evolutionary Biology and spent several years working in research. She published *Heliopause: The Questrison Saga®: Book One* in 2018, *Ephemeris: The Questrison Saga®: Book Two* in 2019, and *Accretion: The Questrison Saga®: Book Three* in 2020. Dianne is writing anthology stories for some of the characters and settings in *The Questrison Saga®*. She is also a science and content writer, short story writer, and watercolorist. She lives with her family.

jdiannedotson.com

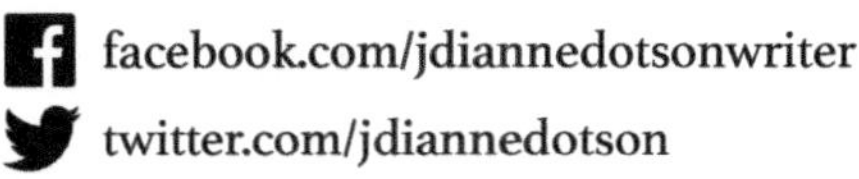

facebook.com/jdiannedotsonwriter

twitter.com/jdiannedotson

www.ingramcontent.com/pod-product-compliance
Lightning Source LLC
Chambersburg PA
CBHW072001110726
47910CB00005B/1615